THE
SECOND
CUT

Also by Louise Welsh

THE
SECOND
CUT

LOUISE
WELSH

CANONGATE

To Paul Sheehan and John Jenkins

This paperback edition published in Great Britain, the USA and Canada
in 2023 by Canongate Books

First published in Great Britain, the USA and Canada in 2022 by
Canongate Books Ltd,
14 High Street, Edinburgh EH1 1TE

Distributed in the USA by Publishers Group West and in Canada by
Publishers Group Canada

canongate.co.uk

1

British Library Cataloguing-in-Publication Data
A catalogue record for this book is available on
request from the British Library

ISBN 978 1 83885 089 0

Typeset in Perpetua Std by Palimpsest Book Production Ltd, Falkirk,
Stirlingshire

Printed and bound in Great Britain by Clays Ltd, Elcograf S.p.A

Nights like these, the dying see clearly,
reach down lightly into the growing hair
whose stalks out of their skulls' weakness
in those long hopeless days *sprout*
as if they want to remain
above death's surface.

From *The Book of Images* by Rainer Maria Rilke

But the beds of married love
are islands in a sea of desire.
Its waves break here, in this park,
splashing the flesh as it trembles
like driftwood through the dark.

From 'Glasgow Green' by
Edwin Morgan, *Collected Poems*

One

SOME THINGS CHANGE, some things never change. The grooms were about to cut the cake when I caught sight of Jojo lurching through the wedding guests, a bashed-up puppet on badly mended strings, head nodding, knees loose. I raised my third glass of fizz to my lips and kept my eyes on the grooms, hoping Jojo would take the hint and piss off, but there was no escaping Jojo. He waved a hand and made a beeline for me with an urgency that suggested the streets beyond the Glasgow Art Club were teeming with military insurgents or zombies on a spree. Jojo was out of breath and wheezing whisky by the time he got to my side. He put a hand on my shoulder.

'Christ, there should be a limit on how many tartans are allowed in one room.'

The two Bobbys had gone for a traditional theme. The Art Club looked like a boozy gathering of clan prodigals made good, an oversweet, whisky liqueur advert of plaid and heather, ghillie brogues and fluffed-up sporrans. Bobby McAndrew had gone full Bonny Prince Charlie with a lace jabot and cuffs. Bobby Burns had settled on a bow tie in the same tartan as his kilt. I was in no position to judge. The Bobbys had been good to me. I was showing my respect by wearing a Harris Tweed jacket and Black Watch trews.

I whispered, 'Glad to see you're doing your bit for sobriety.'

Jojo was a tartan-free zone. He was wearing a rumpled black suit over a white shirt. His funeral tie was loosely knotted around his neck. It might have been part of a *Reservoir Dogs*-style decision or the only tie he could find. Or maybe it was his own funeral Jojo was anticipating. His skin was grey, the bags under his eyes a blue-black cascade.

Jojo propped himself against the wall, sending an oil painting skew-whiff. The naked woman in the picture had been admiring herself in a hand-held silver mirror when someone, the painter presumably, had interrupted her. She was half turned to face the intruder, revealing the full stretch of her bare back. The painter had paid special attention to her spine, the ridge of vertebrae beneath her skin that led down to a hint of cleft. The painting invited you to imagine what happened next: fight or fuck? Jojo turned to see what he was leaning against and snorted. 'Bare-arsed and an expression like butter wouldn't melt.'

The Bobbys had already given speeches testifying their love for each other. Now they were fiddling with the two plastic grooms from the top of the cake, amusing their guests by casting aspersions on the white fondant icing. There were no parents of the grooms in attendance. Bobby McAndrew's wee mammy (as he always called her) had passed away six months before and Bobby Burns' relatives fell into the never-to-be-mentioned category. Bobby McAndrew gave me a stern look and I nodded, trying to convey that I would keep Jojo in order. Bobby Burns put an arm around his new husband and called the assembled guests his 'chosen family'.

Equal weddings, surrogates, gay community, queer allies, trans rights, drag queens spilling-the-T-on-prime-time-TV. The world changes, the world stays the same.

Jojo nudged me in the ribs. 'Families are meant to share. I wouldn't say no to some of their gelt.'

Some of the guests turned their heads in our direction. A Belle Époque panto dame in oyster satin and ostrich feathers raised a finger to her lips and *shushed*.

I put a hand on Jojo's shoulder. 'Fancy a drink?'

Jojo looked at me. 'Plenty of drink here.'

But he let me cup his elbow and guide him back through the crowd of guests, out of the Art Club and into the grey, afternoon drizzle. I had been hoping to decant Jojo into a cab, but he slung an arm around my back and we half walked, half waltzed along Bath Street.

'Here's a place.'

Jojo took out his phone as we descended the stairs towards a brightly lit basement café bar that was doing a brisk trade in lunches. He stumbled and almost lost his footing. I caught the back of his collar, steadying him.

'You started early.'

The energy that had propelled Jojo across the floor of the Art Club had vanished. The phrase dog-tired had been invented for him.

'Started early, started late. I've been going for days, Rilke.'

The café was a floral bunting, lacy doily place that served cocktails in mismatched china teacups. A mother-and-daughter couple vacated a table by the window as we entered. I steered

Jojo towards it, not bothering to wait for their plates and glasses to be cleared. Jojo sank into a seat and started to pick at the remnants of the women's discarded salads. He was thinner than I remembered. Gaunt and hollow-cheeked.

A waiter hovered, ready to clear the table. Jojo put a protective arm around the leftovers and asked for a rye and dry. I told the waiter to make it two. He looked doubtful, but he was young, and it was clear Jojo had potential to be a handful. Maybe I looked like I could be a handful too. He left Jojo to his salads and returned with our drinks and the bill.

Jojo barely noticed. He had his phone on the table and was scrolling through Grindr, commenting on profiles. He held the screen of his phone up for me to see.

'I had him last week.'

The man in the photograph was somewhere in his mid-twenties, blond and preppy with a come-hither innocence.

'Lucky you.'

Jojo shrugged. 'He was the good time that was had by all, if you know what I mean.'

'I hope you washed your hands afterwards.'

Jojo stuffed a tomato in his mouth and chewed. He had had the kind of baby-faced good looks that age badly. His chipmunk cheeks had sagged and the dimples that had been cute when he was younger looked vaguely sinister in his fifty-plus-year-old face.

'It's a whole new world from when we were kids, Rilke. Remember the bars? The looking over your shoulder all the time? Who'd've thought poofs would be allowed to marry? Who'd've thought they'd want to?'

I took a sip of my drink. Beyond the café window the rain grew heavier.

'Still no harm in being careful.'

Jojo blew a raspberry. Tomato seeds sprayed across the table. He wiped them with the cuff of his suit. 'Says the Night Crawler.'

'The Night Crawler was a serial killer. I've got my flaws but multiple murder's not one of them.'

Jojo's eyes were back on his screen. 'Aye, well, you're a serial shagger, so don't go judging me.'

'Wouldn't dream of it.'

Jojo barely made a living running collectables between auction houses and antique shops. There had been an older man he palled about with, a decade or so ago, who I had assumed was his boyfriend. I had not seen him for years – dead or moved on – and as far as I knew no one had taken his place.

Jojo held his phone up to me again, eyes bright with anticipation. 'What do you think?'

Another blond man in his late twenties, floppy fringe, blue V-neck, whitened teeth.

'Out of your league.'

Jojo grinned. His own teeth were dingy and wine-stained.

'That's the thing, Rilke. No one's out of anyone's league anymore.' He knocked his drink back, downing half of his whisky and ginger in two quick gulps. 'I'm on the party circuit.'

'Good for you, but even Noël Coward put his feet up now and again. You look knackered.'

Jojo scooped an ice cube from his drink, shoved it in his mouth and chewed.

'You got that wrong. I'm rerrrrrring to go. You should come with me. I'll get us an Uber. I promise you, it's a different world. Every porno fantasy you ever had come to life.'

He waved a hand at the café, its ironic floral décor and adverts for naughty gins, the mainly female clientele sprinkled with compliant husbands and boyfriends. The wholesomeness of the two Bobbys' nuptials, the excitement of their straight friends at witnessing old queers settling down had been starting to grate on me. For a moment I was tempted, but a glance at Jojo's face, his eager old-man-baby leer brought me back to my senses.

'I need to look back in on the two Bobbys. It's their wedding, remember?'

A glimmer of the old Jojo appeared. The keen-eyed dealer who could calculate untapped profit potential from the back row of the auction house.

'Oh aye. They're good customers of yours. Is it true they moved to a bigger house just so they'd have more walls to hang their paintings on?'

I nodded. 'They're nice guys.'

'A lawyer and a . . . what's the other one?'

'A lecturer at the uni.'

'A lawyer and a lecturer at the uni. They can afford to be nice.'

It was the second time he had mentioned money. I waited for the sting, but it did not come. Instead Jojo knocked back the last of his drink. He took another look at his phone and wiggled the screen in front of me crooning, 'I'm comin' up, so you better get this party started . . .'

There was no point in telling him it was only three in the afternoon. The kind of party he was going to had no regard for time. I slipped a couple of notes on the table to pay for our drinks, got to my feet and helped Jojo get to his.

'I'll tell the Bobbys you send them your love.'

'Do that. Christ, I almost forgot, I got them a wee pressie.'

Jojo reached into his pocket and shoved a small brown medicine bottle half full of liquid at me. I cupped it in my hand, concealing it from the view of the café's customers.

'What the hell's that?'

Jojo's eyes had an evangelical glint. 'Sexual energy. After thirty-plus years the-gether the Bobbys could probably do with some. There's a recommended dose on the label. Tell them not to go over it and not to have too many drams either. It can knock you dead if you don't take care.'

I slipped the bottle into my coat pocket, making a mental note to dump its contents down the nearest lav.

'I'll make sure to pass that on.'

'See that you do. And no snaffling it for yourself. You were invited to the party and turned it down, ungrateful sod that you are.'

I followed him out of the café. Some young guys were having a smoke in the basement courtyard. Jojo gave them an appreciative up-and-down stare that was too bold for safety. He made me think of a man who, after years of carefully crossing at traffic lights, had decided to fling himself across a three-lane motorway without bothering to look left or right.

I rolled a cigarette and offered it to him but Jojo's attention was back on his phone, following the progress of his approaching Uber. He batted the roll-up away.

'Those things'll kill you.'

I lit up. 'We've all got to die of something.'

Jojo glanced at his phone again. 'The cab's halfway along Sauchiehall Street, it'll be here soon.' He looked up, his face suddenly alive. 'I've got something else for you.' Jojo reached into his pocket again and took out a mess of business cards, receipts and scraps of paper. He fumbled through them until he found what he was looking for. 'I've got a tip for you. A big house in Galloway needing cleared in a big hurry.'

'You're a good man, Jojo. I'll make sure Rose sees you right.'

I reached for the note in his hand. He snatched it away.

'It's a top tip, Rilke. A mansion full of antiques. The old biddy that lives there is getting shifted out to a home. Her nephew wants the job done fast. I told him, there's no one faster than Bowery. It's worth something in advance.'

I reached into my wallet and pulled out a twenty-pound note. Jojo held the piece of paper between his thumb and forefinger, just beyond my reach.

'Fifty and it's yours.'

'What is this place? Sanssouci?'

'Got it in one. Houses like this don't turn up anymore.'

'You're a bullshitter, Jojo. Who told you about it? One of your party mates?'

'This isn't bullshit, Rilke. Believe me, you'll be sorry if you miss it.'

Jojo was drunk and on a downward slide. But there was a note of conviction in his voice. For all that he was a mess, Jojo knew antiques. I reached into my pocket and took out three brown bank notes. Jojo snatched them before I could change my mind and thrust the address at me.

'You're a scholar and a gentleman, Rilke. Remember that's just an advance. This is a good tip. It's worth five times that.'

'That's for Rose to decide.' I patted him on the shoulder, ready to go. 'Take care of yourself, Jojo.'

He looked up at me, skin the colour of ash, eyes over-bright.

'Don't you worry about me. I'm having the time of my life.'

The next time I saw Jojo he was dead.

Two

THERE ARE SOME objects that even men who would sell their own granny's kidneys do not want to handle. It was a cold Friday morning, a trudge through dark and damp to a dark, damp building. I had opened the saleroom's doors fifteen minutes ago but instead of warming up with a coffee and the fried egg roll I had bought on my walk to work, I was explaining Bowery Auctions' no-go policy on Nazi memorabilia to a determined woman in a blue fleece. The woman unfurled a red flag emblazoned with a swastika and draped it across the counter. A scent of camphor hung in the air. She plucked at the fabric.

'It's been well looked after. The moths haven't got at it.'

The flag looked strangely at home, as if Bowery was no stranger to fascist tablecloths.

'It doesn't matter what condition it's in, our policy is not to handle . . .'

The woman's face tightened with irritation. She reached

into her Farmfoods carrier bag and pulled out a Waffen SS officer's cap.

The cap was made of grey felt. Its black peak had lost some of its shine, its silver death's-head badge was dulled. I pushed it back towards her with my fingertip. 'This kind of memorabilia isn't as rare as you might think. There were entire armies wearing these things.'

The woman made no move to take the cap. She plunged her arm into her carrier bag again and drew out a small jewellery box. 'This is solid silver.'

Her fingers scrabbled for purchase inside the box before getting a grip on what they were looking for. She handed me a man's silver ring decorated with oak leaves. An eagle hovered above a swastika at its centrepiece. I placed it on the counter beside the SS cap, resisting an urge to examine the ring more closely.

'You'd be talking scrap weight, buttons.'

She stared at me. 'Look at the workmanship.'

'I've seen it. Who in their right mind would want to wear it?'

'I don't care if it goes to someone in their right mind or not. My father probably wasn't in his right mind when he collected this crap. I just need it out my house.'

Our new head porter, Frank, was directing the hanging of the last of the pictures for the next day's sale. I watched as his sidekick Abomi placed a print of a Hornel oil painting on the wall: smiling children playing amongst a background of fractured sunshine, dandelion seeds and cherry blossom. The catalogue dated the original oil as 1905. There were revolutions kicking off in Russia that year, massacres in the Congo, but Hornel looked to have been blissfully unaware of the chaos in the world. I envied him.

I wanted to tell the woman to take the lot down to the Clyde and fling it in the water, but her blue fleece was balding, her trainers down at heel. The Farmfoods bag-for-life looked like it might outlast her.

I tried again. 'I'm sorry, but no reputable auction houses handle this kind of stuff . . .'

The woman's expression tightened again, but she gave no other sign of having heard me. She drew out a small cloth bundle.

'My father used to call this the Koh-i-Noor of his collection.'

I knew before she unpeeled the wrapping that she was about to show me a knife. I took a step backwards.

'Like I said . . .'

The dagger was sheathed in a leather scabbard. She pointed with satisfaction at a small swastika in the centre of a red and white diamond on its hilt. 'That's the Hitler Youth symbol.'

I started to fold the Nazi flag away. 'Your best bet is online. Some American sites will be happy to do business with you. I'd advise caution though. Dealers in this kind of stuff aren't necessarily upstanding.'

She looked at me, her eyes a washed-out blue.

'Your job's to sell to the highest bidder, not judge people.'

It was the second time in two days that someone had accused me of being judgemental. I smoothed the final crease on the flag and realised I had folded the swastika top centre, ready for a Third Reich military funeral.

'I'm not judging you. Your father left you with these items. You want them out of your house. It's only natural you'd like to make some money from them if you can. Go online. It's your best bet.'

I placed the hat, ring and Hitler Youth dagger neatly on top of the flag and slid them across the counter towards her. 'It's a fascinating era. Good luck with their disposal.'

The woman stood firm, feet planted on the worn Axminster carpet, listed in the catalogue at £200–250.

'I took two buses to get here. You advertise a valuation service. All you've done is patronise me. I could have you up for false advertising.'

'I've given you a valuation. As far as Bowery Auctions is concerned, they're not worth anything.'

'That's not a valuation. It's a fuck-off. You're a bunch of charlatans.'

The more I dropped my voice the higher hers got. People were beginning to take notice. Jimmy James would have moved her on, but Jimmy James had retired six months ago and was waiting to see how large the cancer in his stomach would grow before it took him out. Abomi met my eye. I shook my head. His name was short for Abominable Andy. He was eighteen years old, oversized, and gentle as a neutered rabbit. I did not want to trust the frail women's exit to him.

I smiled at her. 'I'm sorry you had a wasted journey. Let me refund your bus fare.'

'Refund my bus fare? You condescending shit.' She gestured towards the long tables covered in neatly labelled lots. 'Look at this junk. *Antiques and Collectables*? I've seen better middens.'

Big Dave Ledger made his way across the saleroom floor towards us. Big Dave has been making bad investments at Bowery for more than two decades. He clapped my back and reverently lifted the Hitler Youth dagger from the table.

'That's a beauty. I didn't know you carried this kind of militaria, Rilke. Not many places do these days. Stupid, if you ask me. It's history, isn't it?' Dave gave the woman a kind smile. He had been a bouncer back in the dinner-jacket-and-bow-tie days but might have passed for a genial cleric who'd taken a few knocks on the rugby field in his youth. He slid the knife from its scabbard and ran a finger along the dull edge of the blade. Something was etched on the metal in a cursive script too small for me to decipher. Dave touched the legend with his fingertip and read, '*Blut und Ehre*. Blood and Honour. I wonder what happened to the boy who owned this. Poor wee bugger. There were thousands of them, you know.'

'I was just telling Mrs . . .?' I realised I did not know the seller's name and gave her a look. She was all smiles now.

'Mrs Henderson.'

'I was just telling Mrs Henderson these aren't as rare as people might assume. Sadly, they're not worth much.'

Dave turned the knife over in his hands. He had a vague, dreamy expression on his face. 'I don't know about that.' He looked at me. 'What sale will these be in then?'

'None that we're running.' Dave looked at me and I softened my tone. 'Company policy. No Nazi gear, no knock-offs and nothing sectarian. Can you imagine Rose's face if she came in and found a Nazi flag draped over the podium?'

Dave smiled. He liked Rose. 'She'd wrap it round your neck.' He turned to the woman. 'So how much do you want for all this?'

Mrs Henderson did not hesitate. 'A thousand pounds.'

Dave set the Hitler Youth dagger back on the counter. 'A bit rich for my taste.'

Mrs Henderson said, 'Make me an offer then.'

Dave looked thoughtful. He picked up the dagger again. I interrupted before he could make his bid.

'No unofficial dealing in the Auction Rooms. You'll have to take this elsewhere.'

Dave gave me a beseeching look. 'Come on, Rilke. It's freezing out there.'

Mrs Henderson gathered her belongings into the Farm-foods bag.

'He's got fascist tendencies. That's why he's scared of historical material. He doesn't know what it might bring out in him.'

Dave laughed. 'She's got you there, Rilke.'

I gave him a bright smile. 'I'll look into getting myself de-Nazified. In the meantime, I'm happy you found each other, but Rose is due any minute. She'll make a jump rope out of all our guts if she finds you doing deals on her auction floor.'

Mrs Henderson zipped up her fleece. 'My father always said your lot were untrustworthy.'

Dave winked at me to show there were no hard feelings and put an arm around the woman's shoulder. 'I'll give you a good price.'

I did not bother to ask Mrs Henderson what she meant by 'your lot'.

The saleroom door swung shut behind them. I headed to the kitchen to make a fresh cup of instant and dispose of my congealed egg roll. Frank reappeared carrying a tray of assorted paperweights estimated at £40–60.

I tried and failed to catch his eye. 'You should think about applying for *Strictly* with timing like that.'

Frank set the tray down without a word. I was a sad-fuck-of-a-ghost with nowhere better to haunt than my place of work.

Rose arrived ten minutes later, a flurry of perfumed wool and soft tweed. Her hair was folded into a leather flying helmet with sheepskin lining and ear flaps. The hat should not have gone with her Maria Callas red lips and smoky eyes, but it worked. She looked like a 1940s film star in search of a monster.

'I just caught Dave Ledger and Eva Braun holding their own private auction in the car park. Dave said you gave them permission.'

I stifled a yawn. 'If not expressly forbidding something counts as permission then he's right. I told them to take their side deals elsewhere. I didn't mention the car park.'

'I sent her back to her bunker.' Rose scanned the saleroom, taking in the exhibited lots, the porters and office staff, all suddenly more focused on their tasks. She glanced at me. 'You look like Death.'

I ignored her. Most days Rose told me I looked like Death. I used to think it was a compliment but recently Death had begun to feel too close for comedy.

Rose's smartphone pinged in her pocket. She read the message and pulled a face.

'Another one bites the dust. Wee Jojo passed away this morning. Remember when we used to get invited to the occasional wedding? Now it's all funerals.'

The strength seemed to drain from my legs. I sank into one of the dining chairs ranged along the wall.

'Are you sure? I just saw him yesterday.'

'Did you? Where?'

'At a wedding actually. The two Bobbys tied the knot.'

'They invited you and not me?' Rose's voice was indignant. 'They invited *Jojo* and not me?'

I shrugged and dipped my hand into the pocket of my coat. The bottle Jojo had given me was still there.

'He looked rough, but I wouldn't have said he was not long for this world. What did he die of?'

'I don't know. A heart attack? Stroke? Double-decker bus? I don't want to speak ill of the dead, but Jojo didn't exactly take good care of himself. You wouldn't have bet on him making old bones.'

I turned the medicine bottle over in my pocket, feeling the cap to make sure it was secure.

'Who told you?'

Over by the rostrum Hannah and Lucy were synchronising the display screen that would keep pace with bids during the sale. They flicked through the images, checking everything was in the right order. A series of gold chains appeared on screen, each with its own lot number, giving way to a succession of sovereign rings that surrendered in turn to ladies' diamond rings and job lots of costume jewellery.

Rose picked up a set of brass opium weights estimated at £15–20 in the catalogue and held them up to the light.

'These are surely obsolete.'

'Opium still needs to be weighed. Who told you about Jojo?'

Rose set the weights back on the table and turned her attention to me. 'Why are you so interested? You thought Jojo was a walking disaster. Now he's a dead disaster. Pretty soon he won't even be that.'

The miracle of death, here today, gone tomorrow, was on me. I said, 'I told you, I saw him yesterday.'

'I hope you were nice to him.'

'I bought him a drink. He was going to a party.'

Rose picked up one of the paperweights Frank had deposited on the table. She shook her head.

'Jojo had a better social life than I do.'

I took the paperweight from her and set it back on the table. 'You'd grudge a dead man a party?'

Rose shrugged. 'I can't believe the two Bobbys didn't invite me.'

Hannah and Lucy had moved on to musical instruments. A set of bongo drums, estimate £20–40, flashed up on the screen; an acoustic guitar, £10–20; a box of vinyl records, The Dickies, Deep Purple, Rolling Stones, Boney M . . . £20–30; another acoustic guitar, £20–40.

Rose muttered, 'Christ, this sale is a shit-show.'

A banjo complete with case estimated at £100–150 appeared onscreen. Someone hummed the theme from *Deliverance*. The girls at the desk were too young to get the joke, but a couple of punters joined in.

Rose said, 'Anderson sent me a text. They found an auction catalogue in Jojo's jacket pocket. Anderson wants to know if he's connected to us.'

Rose and Inspector Anderson had been on and off for about five years. I had got the impression that recently it was more off than on. Anderson and I had gone to the same comprehensive. He had helped me avoid a few skelps from the law and threatened me with a few too.

'You should text him back.'

'Jojo's dead. There's no rush.'

I thought of the Grindr profiles Jojo had shared with me, the bottle of 'sexual energy' he had wanted me to give to the two Bobbys. It felt strange, knowing he was dead.

'You're probably right.'

It was an ordinary viewing day. We moved like rickety clockwork through the routine tasks of sorting and labelling, cataloguing and describing, bantering with the customers, growling at each other. I was on my haunches, peering into the workings of a grandmother clock that had lost the will to tick when a chill fluttered through the already chilly saleroom. I looked towards the door and saw two of Strathclyde's finest, one male, one female, making their way across the floor.

Rose oozed from the office, beaming her best smile.

'Afternoon, officers, can we help you?'

The male officer scanned the goods laid out for auction like a well-trained dog confronted with a buffet, desperate to chow down but forced to rein in his instincts.

'We're looking for a Mr Rilke.'

Old habits die hard. I saw Rose hesitate. She had caught my eye as she came out of the office, but now she turned and looked in the opposite direction. I felt an urge to take the opportunity she was offering and slip away, down the side stairs, out into the car park and the streets beyond.

I got to my feet and walked towards them.

'What can I do for you?'

The police officers were bulked up by stab vests and tool belts. Rain glistened on their uniform caps. Neither of them returned my smile.

The female officer took a step towards me. 'We'd like you to come with us, please, sir.'

Three

EVEN WHEN DEATH is expected it comes as a surprise. I knew he was gone but it was a shock to see Jojo, who only the day before had been hearty, if not hale, now lying on a slab. The morgue assistant waited at a respectful distance as I viewed the body on a screen. Inspector Anderson stood at my shoulder, close enough for me to feel the chill radiating from his wax jacket.

'Can you confirm this is Joseph Nugent?'

Jojo's facial muscles had drooped, his features had lost all expression. I found myself wondering if the thing onscreen was the man I had seen the previous day. It might have helped if he had been wearing the same clothes, but the body was draped head to toe in white. Only its head was visible.

'I think that's him.'

Anderson let out a sigh and raised his voice to the person

operating the camera. 'Can you zoom into the face, please? Mr Rilke is unsure.'

The morgue assistant adjusted the camera lens. The corpse's face grew larger. Its skin was saggy, flesh and bone separating in preparation for the next stage of decay. I looked at the closed eyes, the bags beneath them, the span of its cheekbones, the thin hair brushed back from its forehead.

'He didn't wear his hair like that.'

Anderson sighed again. He was a man of long breaths and silences that day.

'Can someone adjust the hair, please?'

A hand appeared onscreen. It rearranged the corpse's hair while I gave instructions. It felt too intimate. When we finished, the face still did not look much like the Jojo I had shared a drink with, but I knew it was him.

Anderson adopted his formal voice. 'Is this man Joseph Nugent?'

I nodded. 'Yes, I think so.'

'"Think so" isn't an identification. Are you sure?'

I turned Jojo's medicine bottle over in my pocket. 'Sure as I can be.'

Anderson sighed again. 'I suppose that will have to do. I imagine Dr Merry has some forms for you to sign.'

The morgue assistant led me to a table. She set the forms down next to a box of Mansize tissues and a display stand stocked with leaflets on bereavement counselling and how to register a death. A sign on the wall warned that anyone found taking unauthorised photographs would be prosecuted. I signed the forms without reading them or making a crack about Dr Merry's name.

Anderson nodded to a young constable loitering by the door.

'Let's get Mr Rilke back to the station so he can give us a statement.'

I got to my feet, trying to look like a respectable citizen, but I am too tall, too thin, too cadaverous to look like anything other than a vampire on the make.

'Why do I need to make a statement?'

'You're the last person we know saw him alive.'

'How do you get that?'

'We found a wedding invitation in his pocket and managed to contact the groom, Mr Robert McAndrew. He said Mr Nugent briefly attended the reception but left early with you.'

'Jojo was a bit pissed when he arrived, so I took him for a drink next door.'

Anderson dragged his hands down his face and gave a yawn that threatened to swallow the room. He looked like an old man. Too old for Rose. Too old to have been at school with me.

'The logic of that escapes me.'

'It was a nice occasion and Jojo was in danger of making a nuisance of himself. I took him for a drink to get him out of the way. He was waiting for an Uber when I left him.'

Anderson placed a hand on my shoulder and steered me out of the morgue towards a waiting police car. 'Good to know, include it in your statement.'

'That is my statement. There's nothing else I can tell you.' People on the street quick-glanced at us and then looked away. 'Come on, Anders.' I used the inspector's schoolboy nickname. The grip on my shoulder tightened. 'You don't need to take me in. We can go for a coffee somewhere.' I glanced at my watch. It was four o'clock, early but not too early. 'Or a pint?'

'The last man who went for a drink with you ended up dead.'

The young constable waiting behind the wheel of the police car watched us through its windscreen, his bawface bland beneath his cap.

'It's a sale day tomorrow. I don't have time for fucking around polis stations.'

'But you do have time for a pint.'

'Not really, no. But you looked like you could do with one.'

'I could do with twenty but not when I'm on duty.'

A couple of likely lads turned the corner, laughing at something one of them had said. They saw us, wiped the smiles off their faces and crossed the road, shoulders hunched, hands in their pockets. Anderson watched them as if an antenna had pinged in his head. He let out another sigh.

'Fuck, what does it matter? The poor guy's not going to get any deader. Come by the shop after the sale tomorrow. I'll tell the desk to expect you around . . .?'

'Four-thirty – five o'clock.'

'Four-thirty – five o'clock. Don't forget. I don't want to have to put a warrant out for you.'

Anderson walked towards the police car. I called after him, 'Where was he found?'

I thought he wasn't going to answer me, then he stopped and turned.

'In a doorway in a lane off Ingram Street. The doc thought he'd been lying there for a while.'

The Merchant City was lined with trendy bars, all with dress codes and bouncers. It was not the kind of place I would have imagined Jojo hanging out. I closed the distance between us and lowered my voice.

'It's busy there. Someone must have seen him.'

'How many sleeping junkies do you walk by in a day? Do you check up on them?'

He had a point. Homelessness had worsened since Covid. It was hard to walk a block in the city centre without passing someone huddled in a sleeping bag. The *Evening Times* was keeping a tab on how many died over the winter. The tally made depressing reading.

Anderson said, 'It was a homeless man who raised the alert. He thought Mr Nugent had stolen his pitch. He went to move him on and found there was no moving him. He got a member of the public to call us.'

It was easy to imagine Jojo slumped in a doorway. It made me feel bad.

'What did he die of?'

'We won't know until the post-mortem.'

'Rose was fond of Jojo.'

Anderson made a face. He knew I was manipulating him but could not help responding.

'How is she?'

'Pretty cut up. Rose may not wear her heart on her sleeve but that doesn't mean she doesn't have one. It might help her to know what happened.'

Anderson humphed. 'Jojo made a lot of bad lifestyle choices. We won't know for sure until the PM, but the doc seems pretty sure it was drug-related.'

Bad lifestyle choice used to be code for homo. Maybe it still was. Now was the moment for me to hand over the bottle Jojo had given me, but the imp of the perverse that has ruled so much of my life intervened. I put my hand in my coat pocket and kept it there.

'He told me he was going to a party.'

It started to spot with rain. Anderson turned up the collar of his wax jacket.

'It was early when they found him. Somewhere around six o'clock.'

'It was an early party.'

Anderson turned away. 'Put it in your statement.'

I called after him. 'I'll tell Rose to call you.'

'Don't bother.'

He got into the police car and slammed the door. The young constable started the engine and pulled out without indicating. Traffic made way and they disappeared into the late afternoon rush hour, leaving me to find my own way back.

Four

THE ANTIQUES AND COLLECTABLES auction was not the shit-show Rose predicted. Death is not far behind sex in the sales league. Jojo's sudden passing had made the local papers, and the antiques crowd were out in force to turn over the gossip while they turned over our goods. I heard flashes of conversation from my place on the podium as we made our final preparations.

the poor soul . . . gone downhill . . . never the same since . . . saw him with a young lad . . . mind when . . . too young . . . I bought a . . . too young for him . . . nice piece of Meissen porcelain. . . too young for an old bugger like that . . . too young for comfort . . . back in '83 . . . save your pity . . . '84? . . . always left a turn in it . . . '83 or '84 . . . a sorry state . . . some state . . . a bit of Royal Doulton . . . state of him . . . whit a state . . . fuckof-astate . . . back then you could . . . a good eye . . . a young lad . . . decrepit . . . downhill . . . too young . . . dead in a doorway . . . spot a sleeper a mile off . . . ten mile off . . . let himself go . . .

*bufti boy . . . bum boy . . . poofter . . . half dead . . . the AIDS . . .
the HIV . . . arse bandit . . . a lovely wee gouache . . . a Georgian
tallboy . . . could've seen it coming . . .*

I straightened my back and cast my eyes around the auction
room like an executioner looking for business. The crowd
quietened. They took their seats or loitered on the edges,
catalogues and sales paddles poised, phones stilled. I smoothed
my lapels, raised the gavel high in the air and smashed it
down on the block.

'Ladies and gentlemen, welcome to today's sale of antiques
and collectables. Lot number one is a fine fifteen-carat pearl
and diamond brooch . . .' A photograph of the item dazzled
onscreen beside me. 'Who'll start me off at forty pounds?
Forty pounds to start, please! For this fine pearl and diamond
brooch . . .'

At the back of the room a hand was raised, and the bidding
began.

By 2 p.m. it was all over. Dealers queued at the cash desk,
settling their bills before collecting their lots. It was another
cold day, colder in the salerooms than outside where the sun
had started to show its face. We had turned up the Calor
Gas heaters, but Bowery Auctions cannot be warmed, and
breaths hung smoky in the air. Regular punters were bulked
up in layers of outdoor gear. There was enough fake (and
not so fake) fur, Harris Tweed and home knits amongst the
puffa jackets to make the scene reminiscent of a bad day in
the Klondike. I shook hands and slapped backs, smiling with
the smilers, commiserating with the disappointed. Some
customers collected their goods and bolted. Others loitered,
swapping gossip, delaying the return to their shops, stalls,
computer screens.

The removal boys, magpies of the auction rooms, were loading bulkier items into their Lutons with help from our small crew of porters. Frank directed the show, his hands in his pockets.

Rose sidled up beside me. She stared at our new head porter.

'Fuck's sake. What were we thinking?'

'When we hired Frank? That it'd be nice to have someone young for head porter after decades of Jimmy James.'

'Young and good-looking. We're idiots. Jimmy James gave his life to this place. Frank's the star of his own movie.'

'He's not that young and not that good-looking.'

Rose snorted. 'Oh, come on. Look at him.'

I did. Frank was in his mid-thirties. He hailed from some-where in the North of England and had the moody presence of an antihero in a kitchen-sink drama — black hair, slim waist, broad shoulders, square jaw and an air of suppressed violence. He said something to Abomi, who sprang into action, lifting an art deco easy chair onto his back and carrying it into the courtyard where the removal vans were lined up.

Rose leaned against a pillar. Today she was wearing a cream 1950s coat with large lapels over a black pencil skirt and tight polo neck. Her heels were vertiginous. 'He just stands there.'

'So do you.'

'I'm the boss. I've earned the right to stop and stare.'

Frank's hair was a short back and sides with enough left on top to flop becomingly over his brow. His dust coat was crisp, his work boots polished to a shine that would please a sergeant major. Everything about him suggested old-fashioned industry but he had turned out to be a lazy sod.

Rose sighed. 'You'll have to let him go.'

I pulled on my coat. 'Above my pay grade. You're the boss.'

'I'm your boss.'

I checked my pockets: keys, smokes, wallet, Jojo's medicine bottle. The thing had become a weird talisman, bottled guilt and possibility.

'I'm insubordinate and you don't pay me enough to hand folk their cards.'

Frank sensed we were talking about him. He looked in our direction, his face blank and handsome.

Rose whispered, 'Fuck him, then sack him.'

'Not very gentlemanly.'

She gave a lascivious smile. 'Not you, me.'

'You'll break Anderson's heart.'

Rose's smile vanished. 'Anderson has a logbook where his heart should be.' She straightened up, pulled the belt of her coat tight around her waist and raised her voice. 'Frank, maybe you could stop delegating and start shifting? We need this place cleared by next Tuesday.'

The head porter's expression darkened but he took one end of a couch and helped Abomi manoeuvre it through a cluster of departing dealers towards the door.

I used to have a soft spot for languid lads but in recent years I had found myself drawn towards men with energy. Frank pinged my Gaydar, but I was not in the market for moody layabouts.

I pulled on my hat and scarf. 'I'm off.'

Rose caught me by the sleeve. 'We should raise a glass to poor Jojo.'

'I'll save it for the wake.'

She made a face. 'Not like you to turn down a drink.'

'Things to do, people to see.'

'You mean you've had a better offer.'

I kissed Rose on the forehead. She smelt sweetly of face powder and L'Air du Temps.

'Not better, just different.'

She whispered, 'Be careful, remember what happened to Jojo.'

It sounded more like a curse than a warning. The aftermath of the sale was still going on around us. I watched a man examining a bisque figurine he had bought on impulse. His face creased with annoyance as he noticed the chip in its base. It was not for nothing our catalogues were marked *Buyer Beware*.

I said, 'Jojo was an idiot.'

Edinburgh Iain, a dealer in jewellery, wrapped his purchases in a silk handkerchief and slipped them into his pocket. He gave me a hungry look. 'I heard it was a heart attack. Was it something else? Something that could have been avoided?'

I shouldered my rucksack and headed for the stairs.

'You can always avoid high cholesterol, Iain.'

Frank passed me on the stairwell, hands in his pockets, which I guessed had been warmed by a tip from one of the buyers. I wished him a good weekend and he mumbled something that might have been 'You too' or 'Get to fuck'.

After my encounter with Jojo, blond-haired preppy types with floppy fringes were out. But then they had never really been my type. The profile of the man I connected with on Grindr showed a well-groomed thirty-something in a white T with good muscle definition and a scruff of beard. It was a studio portrait rather than a selfie. The sleekness of it almost made me hesitate, but then I noticed the tendrils of dark hair emerging from the neck of his T-shirt, his sharp eye teeth and wolfish look.

I walked the distance from the auction to his flat. The route took me past a park where I had had some adventures. It was early, not yet four o'clock, but the dark was coming in, mist clinging to dog walkers bundled up in winter clothes. Trees turned to murky silhouettes, a dog's collar flashed on and off. I felt the lure of chance, an urge to stroll through the gloaming and see what happened next. But I have had many a disappointing, cold trudge home and, whatever filters he might have used, the man in the photo was only a short walk away.

I sensed disappointment waiting when I saw his ground-floor flat, the carefully clipped front garden and neatly closed plantation shutters. The man who opened the door looked nervous. He was older than his profile suggested, with tired eyes and a small paunch he tried to suck in. The scruff of beard had grown to a full Edward VII. He looked me up and down. I detected dissatisfaction in what he saw too. I thought of walking away, taking a turn around the park and giving in to fate, but when he pushed the door wide, I entered, and when he invited me to hang my coat on the stand in his hallway, I did.

Five

I MADE IT TO the far end of Dumbarton Road and into Glasgow West End Police Station just before five-thirty. Anderson was nowhere in sight. A young policeman with problem skin led me into an over-lit interview room and took my statement.

I gave an edited version of my encounter with Jojo. It included Jojo's appearance at the wedding reception, his invite to join him at an afternoon party and the Uber he had ordered. I left out the bottle of sexual energy and our trawl through Grindr. It did not occur to me to include the tip Jojo had given me about the big house full of antiques. That was purely business.

The policeman looked up from the statement at the mention of a party.

'I take it this wasn't a tea party? Fairy cakes and the like?'

Something about the way he said 'fairy' raised my hackles.

'I didn't get the impression that cake was going to be on the menu.'

He shook his head. 'Some old guys don't know when to stop.'

The policeman did not ask any more questions. Men die on the street in the winter months. It was not yet the end of February. They probably still had a backlog of bodies from Christmas nights out waiting to be processed. He slid his pen into his pocket, picked up the statement and told me I could go.

A small, high window, designed to remind interviewees of what they would miss if they went to prison, revealed a glimpse of dark night and full moon. I got to my feet feeling melancholy, as if I had let someone down.

'Any news on the funeral?'

The policeman shrugged. 'The Procurator Fiscal will decide when the deceased can be released to the next of kin. They'll take it from there. It all looks routine. They don't hang onto bodies if they can help it, so I doubt it'll take long.'

Jojo had never mentioned any next of kin. Our conversations had been confined to buying and selling, with the occasional detour into men and drink. I wondered who would pay for the funeral and hoped I would not have to organise a whip-round.

The cold of Dumbarton Road was like the cold of my childhood. I pulled my cap low and walked towards Partick and the West End beyond, ignoring the taxi cabs sailing by, 'For Hire' lights glowing like winning tickets. A train rumbled the tracks as I passed beneath the railway bridge, disturbing a few pigeons from their roosts. I thought of the policeman describing Jojo's death as straightforward. I was forty-seven.

Most men die around the age of seventy in Glasgow. According to the stats I had about twenty years left. I wondered if my death would be routine. If it would be on time, or show up early like Jojo's.

A gang of youths in T-shirts sallied by, loud with drink and Saturday night possibilities, impervious to the cold. Smokers clustered outside Partick's bars. I thought about having a drink in Jojo's memory, but kept on walking, past the Chinese restaurants aglow with neon and the promise of hot pot, past the one-stop shops and off-licences, the beauty salons, closed for the night, all beauty done. There were absences in the street. Darkened fronts, shuttered pubs, shops and restaurants that had not survived lockdown. They reminded me of the gap sites of my youth, urban ruins untouched for decades. A hen night gusted towards me, the bride-to-be's lace-curtain veil catching in the wind and fanning around her head like ectoplasm. The girls hooted with laughter and one of them called out something as they passed. I waved a hand and kept walking. A living memento mori.

The weight of my phone dragged my left pocket. It would be easy to log on, find another encounter, another release. Acknowledgement, beyond the sound of my boots against the pavement, that I was alive. I turned it off. I had a feeling that I should not take any more chances that night. I kept on walking, homewards, to my own bed.

Six

I HATE THE COUNTRYSIDE. I hate hedges and twisty-windy roads and locals who know every bend. I hate freshly tilled fields and seas of shimmering corn. I hate the eco-set fox-hunters and second-homers, the let's-get-away-from-it-all tourists and rural arts-and-crafters with their potters' wheels and whimsy. I hate performative please-love-us countryside gays and rustic whiteness. I hate community shops and despotic pub landlords who can bar a man for prejudice or spite.

I prefer to stay where someone might hear me scream. Sheltered from the weather by city tenements, never more than twenty yards from a bar. The countryside is binoculars on windowsills, peering eyes and judgements. It makes me claustrophobic. But good stuff lurks in country houses and cottages guarded by high hedges and drystane dykes. So when the call comes, we answer.

Bowery Auctions' van felt too wide for the road we were on. I was driving, Frank sat hunched by the passenger window and Abomi was sandwiched between us. It should have been a day of rest, but the client had emphasised that speed was of the essence and we were on our way to see if Jojo's tip was good. There had been a small altercation earlier between Frank and I about our route. The only person who had spoken since then was the BDSM voice of the satnav. She had fallen silent a few miles back and I was worried I had missed our turn.

I drove into a tight bend that turned out to be tighter than I had anticipated. The van fought against the road's camber. Frank seized the grab rail above the passenger door. For a moment I thought we were going to lose traction and spin into a skid, but the road straightened, and I regained control. I was not the only one to find the turning tricky. A burnt-out Nissan Micra lay on its back in a field churned with the tyre tracks of whatever rescue vehicles had attended the accident. The fence that bounded the field was flattened. Strands of police tape fluttered in the wind.

Abomi sounded impressed. 'Wow. Some crash.'

Frank lowered the window, letting a rush of cold air into the van.

'Doubt anyone walked away from that.'

I thought I could smell burning on the wind, but it was probably an illusion. Abomi craned his head round, keeping the crash in sight for as long as possible.

'You think there are bodies in there?'

Frank snorted. 'Aye, wee shrivelled-up skeletons still wearing their baseball caps. The cops'll send a wagon round at the end of the week.'

I sensed the boy looking at me for a clue to whether Frank was mocking him or not. The satnav said, *Your destination is on the left*. A sign up ahead read Ballantyne House. I ignored Abomi and manoeuvred the van through the gate into an overgrown driveway at the end of which stood a neglected-looking Georgian house. I slowed our speed to walking pace and said, 'Welcome to Grey Gardens.'

'Look at the state of the place.' Frank sounded sullen. 'They're not going to have anything worth our while.'

Abomi shifted on the bench seat between us. 'Creepy as fuck.'

I bumped the van gently over the ruts in the drive. Three windows looked out from the top storey, two from the bottom. The middle window was balanced by the front door. I knew what Abomi meant. I am used to corrosion. But the façade of the house was chipped and water-stained, its stonework in need of repointing. The house's symmetry, the hint of a face formed by the blank windows and closed door, was unsettling.

I killed the engine and set the handbrake. 'Never prejudge. I've found good stuff in dumps worse than this.'

I glanced at Frank and saw him making a face. Rose was right. He was going to have to go.

The front door opened before we were out of the van. The man who stepped out to meet us was asymmetrical. His hair flat at one side, sticking up at the other, his grey cardigan misbuttoned. He raised a hand and crossed the drive to greet us. The front door remained open behind him and I caught a glimpse of the dark interior beyond.

'Mr Rilke? I'm John Forrest.' His accent was Scottish public school, almost indistinguishable from upper-class English, except for a faint Caledonian burr.

I shook Mr Forrest's hand, thanked him for inviting us and introduced Frank and Abomi. Forrest gave them a nod. He was a short man with powerful shoulders that lent him a bullish look, but his smile was cheerful, his walk verging on jaunty.

'Thank you for coming all this way. We're at the arse end of nowhere, but it'll be worth your while.'

Glasgow, the Dear Green Place, is surrounded by countryside. It had taken us less than two hours to reach Ballantyne House, but it was not an exaggeration to describe this corner of Galloway as the arse end of nowhere. It was on the way to nothing. The roads were poor and, as far as I could see, the attractions zero.

Forrest led us through a small porch into a spacious hallway. Nothing but time had touched the interior of this house for the past hundred years. The atmosphere was dry and dusty, beneath it a stronger stench. Decay. I saw Abomi about to exclaim on the pong and gave him a warning look.

Forrest noticed the exchange. 'I know, smells like a shithole. Something crawled in and died somewhere. My cousin and I have been searching high and low, but we've not found the culprit yet. We're hoping it didn't breathe its last under the floorboards.'

Frank said, 'How long has the place been unoccupied?'

Forrest gave a nervous laugh. 'Actually it's been more or less continuously inhabited since my great-great-grandfather built it back in 1840. Auntie Patricia is the most recent resident. She neglected the place somewhat after my uncle died. If I'm being honest, he neglected the place somewhat too, as did his father, my grandfather. It's all a bit of a waste. Auntie Pat's going to have to go into residential care and it seems we have to sell up in order to pay for it. The coffers are empty. That's the way it goes, I'm told. One generation makes the money, the next ones spend it, and at some point the family descends back to where they started.' His voice was untroubled, as if losing the ancestral pile was no big deal.

Forrest ushered us through to a gloomy drawing room.

He switched on the overhead light to reveal a clutter of Victorian furniture, oil paintings and ornaments. An elaborate chandelier hung dusty from the ceiling. The floor was covered in overlapping rugs, the room crammed with an accumulation of generations. Clearing the place would be an exercise in archaeology.

Frank walked to the centre of the room, taking it all in. I had told him and Abomi to wear their brown dust coats. Abomi's coat strained Hulk-like at the shoulders but Frank looked the part, professional and alert, unfazed by the riches on offer.

Forrest met my eyes. 'I'm not interested in someone creaming off the more interesting things and leaving the dross. I need the lot gone.'

I said, 'A strategic approach, sending pieces bit by bit to specialist sales, would allow them to realise their potential.'

Forrest sounded exasperated. 'Clearing the contents quickly is the priority. Your boss' – he paused, searching for the right name – 'Rebecca?'

'Rose.'

'Ah yes, the lovely Rose. She convinced me you would get enough interest in the sale to make it worth our while to go with your firm. She told me you could clear everything in less than a fortnight.'

Frank met my eyes, and for the first time I had an inkling of what he was thinking. If the other rooms in the house were as crammed as this one it was going to be a bigger task than Rose had assumed, but sales like this did not land on our laps often. This one could underwrite Bowery Auctions for the next six months, possibly longer.

I slid out my smoothest smile. 'We have a strong client base who will be enthusiastic about these kinds of items. The question is whether you want us to hold it all at our premises or whether you're happy hosting an auction here. Holding it in situ will make the process quicker.'

Forrest raised an eyebrow. 'And more lucrative?'

'Definitely. One-off, special sales always attract attention.'

Frank had taken a small black notebook of the kind favoured by policemen from his pocket. He picked up a porcelain ballerina, examined the base and made a few notes. He looked like a TV exec's vision of a young antiquarian. I half expected him to take a jeweller's loupe from his pocket and start peering.

Forrest said, 'Auntie Pat brought that back from Austria. She was especially fond of it.'

The hard edges and glottal stops of Frank's accent were subdued as he replied, 'It's a lovely piece, sir. You don't mind my taking a few preliminary notes?'

'Go ahead.' Forrest turned to me. 'Wouldn't holding the sale here just attract people who fancy a poke about the house?'

'No. We'll make entry by auction catalogue only and charge a larger than normal fee per catalogue. That usually deters timewasters.'

Forrest nodded. 'Let me think about it. I'm not sure how Auntie Pat would feel about lots of strangers roaming through the house.'

'I'm happy to answer any questions she might have.'

Forrest gave an upside-down smile. 'I'm afraid we're past that point. My aunt has succumbed to dementia, but that doesn't mean we can ride roughshod over her wishes.'

I made a sympathetic face and said, 'No, indeed,' like a waiter regretting a fly in the soup.

Forrest gave us a tour of the rest of the ground floor, through a dining room stacked with china, a library shelved with old leatherbound volumes and into a music room equipped with a Bösendorfer Baby Grand. Oil paintings and watercolours crowded the walls. There was quality stuff here. We would have to pull in our full panel of freelance experts to do it justice, the ex-Art School boys and girls, disgraced academics and museum rejects who nevertheless had the right knowledge and were happy to share it, for the right fee.

Forrest ran his hand over the piano's surface, revealing a shiny trail of dark, polished wood in the dust.

'My aunt was a concert pianist. She was well known in her day. Even after her mind began to wander, music had the power to draw her back. She played until dementia got the better of her . . . It's sad to see the piano sitting here untouched. It's gone from being a musical instrument to a bit of nicely carved wood. I'd like to think of it being brought to life again.'

Abomi was staring at Mr Forrest with fascination. I could see him working up to asking a question and interrupted.

'It's a beautiful piece. I've no doubt it will find a new home. You and your aunt were close?'

'Auntie Pat brought me up. My cousin Alec and I are more like brothers.'

I made a mental note to remind Abomi and Frank to treat Mr Forrest with extra care. His closeness to his aunt accounted for the thrum of nervousness I could detect beneath the surface of bonhomie.

Upstairs, the bedrooms were equally stuffed with furniture, art, textiles and ornaments. Forrest talked about the family history as we walked. The Forrest clan had been eager supporters of Empire. Their fortune had been accumulated in Malaysia via a rubber plantation and then branched into South African mining. They had been in India too, working with the East India Company, though Forrest was unsure of what that entailed. He picked up an ivory elephant that was leading a procession of smaller elephants along a bedroom mantelpiece and blew the dust from its surface.

'Cousin Alec and I come from a long line of enthusiastic looters and pillagers.'

I wondered what he did for a living but did not ask. The house was coming into focus. I was beginning to be able to discern between objects Auntie Pat had brought home from her concert tours and those that had been in the family for generations. The pianist had been inclined to quality-flash, hand-blown Murano and Venetian glass, Lladró figurines and Baccarat crystal. Previous generations had collected solid wood furniture, indigenous carvings, tamed landscapes, silver plate and still lives.

I set Frank and Abomi to making an inventory of the ground floor while Forrest gave me the rest of the tour. We were climbing the staircase towards what would have been the servants' quarters at the top of the house when I heard Abomi scream. His cry was high-pitched and terrified, the sound of a Hammer Horror virgin waking to a close-up of the vampire's fangs, but I knew it was him.

Forrest froze, his hand clutching the banister. 'What in the name of . . .'

I was already halfway down the staircase.

Frank was standing over Abomi, who was kneeling in front of a hand-carved camphorwood trunk. I stopped still in the doorway. My first thought was that he had found the body of a dead baby.

Frank had cupped a hand over his mouth and nose. He looked at me, his eyes wide. 'It's a dog. Christ knows how long it's been in there.'

Abomi reached out a hand to touch the dead thing.

Frank pulled him away. 'Don't touch it. For fuck's sake.'

Forrest was at my back. He took a deep intake of breath and looked into the chest.

'It's Schumann.'

Frank had guided Abomi away from the box. I stepped forward reluctantly and looked inside. It was a Jack Russell Terrier. The small black and tan body had been wrapped in plastic. Its mouth was open, its snout rigid.

Forrest stared at the dead beast. 'It was Auntie Pat's. She named it after the composer Clara Schumann. I asked her, why not just call the thing Clara? Everyone would assume it was named after her husband Robert, but she was insistent. That was what she was like, you could never be sure if she was joking or not.' Forrest wiped a trembling hand over his face. 'The thing went missing six months ago. Alec and I hunted high and low for it. In the end we gave up. Decided it had been supper for a fox or hit by a car and dumped in some ditch. I had no idea . . .' He looked at me. 'How the hell did it end up in there?'

Abomi was sucking on his inhaler. His frantic breaths reminded me of a car engine, trying and failing to catch. I snapped at Frank, 'Take Andy outside. Now.'

Forrest muttered, 'What the hell do I do with it?'

Frank put an arm around Abomi's shoulders and led him to the door. His voice was surprisingly gentle. 'Come on, mate. Let's get you some fresh air.'

I closed my eyes for a moment. The dog's fur was not completely still beneath the carelessly wrapped plastic. It shimmered like static, a mass of wriggling maggots. I took my handkerchief out of my pocket and placed it over my nose and mouth. My words came out muffled. 'Let's get it outside. I'll help you bury it.'

*

We dug the hole in the kitchen garden. Once we broke through the upper crust of earth the ground was softer than I expected, loamy and sweet-smelling. Forrest found some heavy-duty bin bags and we manoeuvred the dog's body into them with the help of our shovels before lowering it into the grave. It was cold outside. Our breaths fogged the air, but I felt a ribbon of sweat run down my spine. Forrest's expression was grim.

My first thought had been that the lid had slammed on the dog while it was investigating the interior of the trunk. No one had noticed and the poor thing had suffocated. But, once opened, the trunk's hinges were designed to hold the lid firmly in place, until someone released them with a nifty backwards-forwards action. I tested the lid myself. It was in perfect working order, and there were no scratches on the inside. The dog had been wrapped in plastic, but it was impossible to know if the creature had been dead or alive when it was placed inside. Either way, poor Schumann had been deliberately sealed in the trunk.

I waited until the last shovel of earth was heaped on the small grave before asking, 'What do you think happened?'

Forrest had taken off his cardigan. He wiped his forehead with the back of his shirtsleeve.

'My cousin runs the farm attached to the house. He had a dispute with a couple of his workers. It turned nasty and he sacked them. Perhaps they decided to take revenge.'

'Seems a bit hard on your aunt.'

'By the time Schumann disappeared Auntie Pat's mind was more or less gone. She didn't notice.'

My brogues were caked in mud. They had been handmade for someone else but were a good fit and I was usually careful of them. I wiped the sides of the shoes against the grass, one after the other, trying to clean off the worst of the dirt.

'Where's your aunt now? In a care home?'

Forrest jerked his head up towards the farmhouse at the top of the hill.

'She's living with my cousin and me in the farmhouse. I moved back after my wife and I divorced.' He shrugged his shoulders. 'We're coping, for now – better than leaving her to strangers – but it's not a long-term solution. That's the reason for the rush to sell up. I'm keen to get her settled before her condition deteriorates further.'

We walked back to the house together. Burying the dog seemed to have opened something up in Forrest. He took my shovel and dumped it beside his at the back door.

'I can't wait to get shot of this place. It was fine when we were kids. We were away at school and only here in the summer. Being here full-time, trapped for months on end during lockdown.' He shut his eyes, shook his head. 'There are other places: London, Paris, New York, Shanghai . . . Who in their right mind would choose to live in a backwater like this?'

The discovery of the dead little dog tarnished whatever shine the day had promised. We worked on, listing and logging objects, but no one was sorry when lunchtime arrived. I drove Abomi and Frank down to the nearby village of Ballantyne. The local pub was called the Black Bull. A plaque outside boasted that it had been in existence since 1782. It was possible to detect the bones of an old coach house behind an ugly, angular glass extension that stretched into a car park graced with a few outdoor tables. The interior of the pub had been modernised and re-aged. The place was another countryside sham, a Wetherspoon's rip-off, heavy on hunting scenes, horse brasses and copper warming pans.

Frank had ditched his dust coat in the van. Abomi had kept his on. He looked miserable and very young, despite his bulk. I bought them each a pint and got a ginger beer for myself. I set the beers in front of the two porters and told them they could order what they wanted from the menu. Abomi usually had an appetite to match his size but he shook his head. He looked like he might cry.

'Sorry, boss, I can't.'

Frank sipped the head from his pint. 'Me neither.'

My hands were still smarting from helping Forrest dig the dog's grave. I pressed my fingers against my glass, hoping the cold would calm the blisters threatening to form beneath the pads of my skin.

Frank looked at me over the top of his beer. 'You should have called the SSPCA.'

The head porter's tone annoyed me. 'The what?'

'The Scottish Society for the Prevention of Cruelty to Animals. Like the RSPCA but Scottish and without the Royal.'

I took a sip of my ginger beer. It was spicier than I expected. I coughed. 'It was dead.'

'That's not the point. We don't know how it died. Someone might have tortured it before they put it in that box.'

Abomi took a quick, deep sip of his pint. 'A boy in my class at school used to torture cats. We kicked the shite out of him.'

Frank nodded his approval. 'Only language scum like that understand.'

I set my drink on the table. 'There's no suggestion it was tortured.'

'Did you take the plastic off and have a look before you put it in the ground?'

'You saw the state of it. Why would I?'

'That's why you should have got the SSPCA in. They're used to dealing with things like that.'

Abomi said, 'I'm not going back there.'

I took the packet of crisps I had bought at the bar, split the plastic lengthways and placed it on the table between us.

'Sorry, son. I can't say it fills me with joy either, but we can't afford to turn this one down. We all have to work on it if we want to keep our jobs. I mean, Mr Forrest didn't kill the wee dog, did he?'

I sensed Frank was about to intervene with some objection and gave him a look that said I would sack him with pleasure. He got the message and stuffed a handful of crisps into his mouth. The pub was empty, except for a couple of old soaks loitering by the bar. The landlady started to wipe the surfaces of the empty tables, working her way towards us. She was somewhere in her mid-forties, handsome, with honey-coloured hair and well-covered bones. She saw me watching her and smiled.

'Clearing out the big house, are you?' Her accent was local.

'How did you guess?'

She nodded at Abomi and touched a space above her left breast, in the same place where *Bowery Auctions* was embroidered on his dust coat.

'Not many places around here that would warrant a firm of auctioneers. How's the old lady doing? I heard she was on her way out.'

Abomi opened his mouth to answer. I spoke first. 'We're dealing with Mr Forrest.'

'He'll be sad to see her go. Still, I suppose the money will be a help, unless it all goes to the other one.' She made a face to show what she thought of 'the other one'.

Not gossiping about clients is up there in the unwritten

rulebook alongside 'don't steal the silver' and 'don't shag the client's husband/son/wife/daughter/livestock', but it is not always easy to stick to the rules.

I took another sip of ginger beer. 'You mean Mr Forrest's cousin?'

The landlady set her cloth and cleaning spray to one side and rested her bottom on the next table. 'That's right. Young Alec. We call him "the other one".'

'Why?'

'Because that's what he is. The other one.' She looked at Abomi. 'Fancy a nice Sunday roast? With all the trimmings?'

Some of Abomi's colour had returned but he shook his head. 'No thanks. I'm not that hungry.'

Frank leaned forward. 'That was a bad crash we passed just before Ballantyne House.'

The woman lowered her voice in a way that seemed to emphasise her eagerness to chat.

'Bad as it gets. Two young lads who didn't know when to slow down. They're slowed down now, right enough.'

'Are they dead?' whispered Abomi.

'Rumour is one of them was alive but couldn't get out in time. The fire got him.' Her eyes shone with the horror of it. 'There were no witnesses, mind, so I don't see how anyone would know, but people like to talk, you know? Place was hoaching the night after it happened. Tragedies always bring the punters out. Bunch of ghouls.'

'Local lads?' asked Frank.

'No, thank Christ. City boys.'

'Bankers?'

The woman gave a grim smile. 'That's one word for them. No, I meant they were Glasgow lads. It's a shame for their families, but no one round here knew them, so . . .' She shrugged her shoulders as if to say it was hard to feel anything for non-locals. 'Lot of good antiques up there, I imagine. My granny used to work up at the big house and my mother after her, but the old lady gave up having people in after she took proper bad.' She picked up her cloth and spray. 'There was a time when the people in the big house were involved with the village. Now they don't trouble themselves. Mr Forrest shows his face in here once a month or so, pleasant enough, but you can't get anything out of him. The other one never bothers himself. If he does any drinking, he doesn't do it here.'

Abomi drained his pint. 'If I lived up there, I'd be in here all the time.'

'Like a drink, do you, love?' The landlady smiled to show she was joking. 'Don't you worry, we're busy enough. Anyway, Mr Forrest doesn't live in his auntie's house. He's up on Ballantyne Hill. The other one owns all the farmland that goes up there from the big house and down onto the other side of the glen.'

I finished my ginger beer. 'A working farm must be good for the local economy.'

'Might as well not exist for all the good it does folk round here. The Forrests don't employ locals. They bring in Glasgow lads. Ballantyne is too much of a one-horse town for those boys. Can't take advantage of a pretty girl without her father or brother clocking them.'

I said, 'So the boys who died in the crash?'

She smiled gently, as if I was a simpleton who had managed to unravel a basic equation.

'That's right. They were working for Alec Forrest, Mr Forrest's cousin – the other one.' Her voice was cool, unbothered. 'He's two workers down now though. Burnt to a crisp, I heard.'

Seven

IT WAS LATE by the time I got home. The sun had dipped below the tenements, taking its dreary tobacco-hued light with it. I hung up my coat, dumped my keys on the hallstand, went through to the kitchen and opened a beer, not bothering to turn on a lamp. My laptop blinked, asleep on the kitchen table. I woke it up and scrolled through the inventory of objects Frank and I had catalogued that afternoon. The list of words conjured images in my head of gold leaf and gleaming patinas, etched crystal and rough textured oils. I attached the itinerary to an email and fired it off to Rose without adding a message. The list told its own story.

The computer screen glowed, tempting, in the dark kitchen, a portal to wherever I wanted to travel. Vicarious and dangerous. I closed its lid. I was trying to teach myself self-restraint.

I rolled a cigarette and lit it. There was a tug of unease in my chest that predated burnt-out Nissans and entombed

Jack Russells. Jojo had been hell-bent on a party, but perhaps if I had not been so quick to speed him from the two Bobbys' wedding, he would still be around. The wedding guests contained a fair share of professionals. Some doctor might have sprung Jojo back from the brink. At the very worst, he would have died in an atmosphere of warmth and music, surrounded by people who, while they could not be said to love him, had a fair idea of what love was.

I took my phone from my pocket and called Anderson. The police inspector picked up on the third ring.

'What the fuck's up?'

'Sounds like you've been to community relations training again.'

Anderson sighed. 'It's almost midnight.'

'You're a night owl. Your midnight's the average man's nine o'clock.'

'What do you want, Rilke?'

I took a last drag on my cigarette, enjoying the glow of tobacco and sizzle of paper. But I remembered what Jojo had said – 'those things will kill you' – and stubbed it out in the ashtray. 'Any news on what happened to Jojo?'

'He died.'

'Any news on how?'

Anderson sounded weary. 'His body sat him down on a doorstep and gave up on life.'

'That's it?'

'There are worse ways to go.'

'No one did anything to him?'

'I'm not saying that. There were no stab wounds, no unexpected bruising, no sign of an OD, but he could have been overserved at that wedding you were both at.'

'They were serving champagne, not rocket fuel.'

There was a tell-tale whisky slur in Anderson's voice. 'Maybe the bubbles went up his nose.'

'So you're sure it was natural causes? Nothing anyone could do about it?'

An alert note entered the inspector's speech. 'You know something you're not telling me?'

'No, it's just that—'

'Just what?'

'Jojo looked rough as hell, but he was full of the joys.'

Anderson let out another sigh. The slur returned. 'People fall down dead, Rilke. Ask me, it beats a Covid coma. Three months in limbo, then swimming through brain fog for the rest of your days. Fucked liver, fucked kidneys, who knows what else fucked.'

'Plenty of people survived Covid.'

'All I'm saying is, suddenly isn't the worst way to go . . . Look, it's not unusual to experience a bit of guilt at being the last person to see someone alive. You had a drink with the man and then he dropped dead. It's uncomfortable being the Angel of Death, but unless it keeps happening my advice to you is, let it go. Life's too short to worry about what-ifs. Your mate Jojo proved that.'

I waited for Anderson to ask me how Rose was, but he hung up without a goodbye. I rolled another cigarette, lit up and turned my laptop to face the other way to avoid the temptation of its blinking light. Anderson was right. People dropped dead every day of the week, every second of every minute of every hour if you widened your radius far enough. Jojo's shuffling off was no big deal, but the bad feeling that connected my heart to my gut was still there.

I gave in and raised the lid of my laptop just as an email from Rose, garnished with exclamation marks, pinged into my inbox. Anderson's whisky slur was echoed in her rush of excited misspellings. I wondered if she and Anderson were together.

Someone had phoned Bowery that afternoon about a painting that might be worth something. Rose wanted me to man the auction rooms tomorrow so she could go to Ballantyne House and check out the treasure trove. I felt a stab of irritation. Jojo had given me the tip, but Rose was the boss. I would have to obey orders.

I shut down the laptop, finished my beer and went to bed, thinking how strange it was that even though I knew death, I wanted to shut my eyes and sleep.

Eight

I SPOTTED HIM for an Art School boy the moment he walked through the door of Bowery Auctions. He was somewhere in his early twenties, slight-shouldered, wearing a beige Crombie with a velvet collar, the type favoured by Arthur Daley back in the day. It was too big for him, the fabric scuffed in places, as if it had seen a few bar-room floors.

I was standing by the windows, working through a pile of sales catalogues, trying not to mind that I was missing the main show. It had been a long afternoon. The man who had phoned Rose about the painting had turned out to be a timewaster who did not know the difference between an oleograph and an oil.

The boy did not notice me amongst the clutter of the room. He picked up a brass Hindu goddess equipped with large breasts and more than her share of arms, the kind of item that served as a murder weapon in 1930s crime novels, and turned it around in his hands, feeling the weight of it.

I closed the catalogue. The movement startled the boy, and he almost dropped the brass ornament. He was a good-looking youth if you could see past the scrawny limbs and pale-as-root skin. Some other time I might have welcomed the interruption, but I was not in the mood for tourists or jobseekers.

'Can I help you, son?'

He raised the goddess in the air, showing her to me. 'How much is this?'

'Eighty-five to a hundred. Depends who's in the room.'

The boy replaced it on the table and crossed to where I stood. His trousers were too big for him. He had tried to make a virtue of it, fastening his belt tight and letting the legs bag. The effect was more Charlie Chaplin than David Bowie. His hair looked good though; bleached blond, razor cut at the back and sides, long on top. It added a touch of boot boy.

I put down my pencil. 'What can I do for you?'

'Are you Rilke? I'm Sands. I knew Jojo.'

I nodded, wondering where things were leading. 'A sad loss.' The boy smelt of cheap cigarettes and damp rooms. Jojo had preferred smooth preppy types, but Jojo was no catch. Despite his boasting I reckoned he would have taken what he could get. 'How did you know him?'

Sands caught my drift and made a face.

'Not like that. I rented a room in his flat. The polis want to release his body for burial. Turns out, far as they're concerned, I'm the nearest thing he had to family. They want me to arrange his funeral. Have you any idea what a funeral costs?'

I shrugged, wondering why I had had to identify Jojo's body when he had a surrogate family in the boy. 'A fair whack.'

'Just short of three grand for a pissy one. Sky's the limit for something decent.'

It was growing dark. The overhead lights were on, but shadows were creeping in, swallowing the images on the auction catalogues splayed across the desk. I turned on an Anglepoise. The pool of bright light made me think of a stage set, the boy and I spotlit in the darkness.

'The police are just trying to make it easy for themselves by lumbering you. Jojo never mentioned religion or next of kin. I don't imagine he'd care too much about a fancy funeral. He'd be happy to let the state bury him.'

I was lying. Jojo had thought of himself as something special. The idea of being the top storey of a communal grave or scattered on much scattered ground would have horrified him.

Sands made a face. He knew I was talking nonsense.

'I'm taking over the lease of the flat. Jojo left a lot of stuff in his room. I need it cleared so someone else can move in. I thought maybe I could sell it and use the money to bury the old guy.'

The previous night I had been touched by guilt that might have been grief. Now I felt resentful. Jojo had been a pain in the arse when he was alive. He was continuing to be a pain in the arse after death.

'I'm guessing you're at the Art School?'

'Fourth year Painting and Printmaking.'

'Concentrate on your studies. Leave Jojo's earthly remains to people who are paid to take care of these kind of things.'

My phone pinged. I glanced at the screen. More photographs of Ballantyne's treasures from Rose.

Sands stayed where he was, his feet planted on the rug.

'Jojo was your friend.'

'He was a regular client, but we can't sell stuff on behalf of the dead. We need to know who inherited it. Did Jojo leave a will?'

The boy looked exasperated. 'You knew Jojo. Paperwork wasn't high on his agenda.'

'If he'd left his effects to you in a will then we'd be able to act on your behalf; otherwise we can't touch it.'

'Even though it'll end up in a skip?'

I sorted the catalogues into a pile and straightened their edges, indicating that the conversation was over.

'Where things end up isn't our concern, it's where they come from that matters. We need to be sure of the provenance of what we sell.'

Sands rolled his eyes. His voice took on a singsong sarcastic lilt. 'Okay, now that you mention it, I think Jojo did write a will leaving everything to me. Do you need to see it?'

I sighed. 'Not really, but remember, you'd be giving me an assurance under law. Jojo wasn't always careful about provenance. If anything turned out to have changed hands illegally at some point, it'd land on your doorstep. Are you sure you want that responsibility?'

The boy muttered something that might have been 'wanker'.

My phone buzzed on the table. A text from Rose telling me that Forrest had agreed we could host the sale at Ballantyne House. It was good news. Holding the sale there would add prestige and save us the work of transporting the house's contents to Glasgow, but we would still need a small army and a tight battle plan to see it through.

Sands put a hand on the counter. 'When can you have a look at it?'

'I can't. We're at capacity.'

His voice gained an edge. 'Look. I've got to get rid of the stuff, you're an auctioneer and Jojo needs a funeral.'

An old Sunday School phrase crept into my head. I said it out loud. 'Let the dead bury the dead.'

'What does that even mean? It's just fucked-up biblical nonsense. Jojo talked about you like you were a great guy, and now you can't even be bothered helping to lay him to rest.'

'Jojo's dead. You can't get any more rested than that.'

The boy looked like he might punch me or start to cry.

'You're a fucking arsehole. You know that?'

He was right. I glanced at my watch. It was nearly five o'clock. I had been browsing Grindr profiles on and off throughout the afternoon and had decided, without deciding, to hook up once we shut shop. Jojo, who had been so keen on sexual energy, was fucking up my sex life. Sands turned to go. I caught him by the shoulder.

'What do you mean when you say he left a lot of stuff?'

The boy pulled free. He glanced at his coat where I had touched him, making sure I had not marked the fabric.

'I don't know. A lot of stuff.' He indicated the trestle tables. 'That kind of thing. If you're expecting a hundred for that brass ornament, we'll get three grand no bother for all the crap in Jojo's room.'

'Jojo wouldn't leave three grand's worth of stuff lying around.'

Sands glanced me up and down. He looked disappointed.

'Jojo told me you saved some girl from being murdered. He made it sound like you were something.'

'Jojo never let facts get in the way of a good story.'

I dragged my coat on. The prospect of working through his meagre effects was dispiriting. I called through to Hannah in the office, let her know that I was heading off and she should lock up at five.

'Okay, if we're going to do this let's do it now, before I lose heart and join our mutual friend on the slab. Then you'll be collecting for two funerals.'

Sands gave me a look that said I was kidding myself if I thought he would help bury me.

Dusk had slipped towards full dark. The wipers swiped across the van's windscreen, smearing away rain that kept on coming as we made faltering progress through rush-hour traffic. The van's heater was up at max, but the windscreen kept fogging and I was forced to lean over periodically and wipe it with the palm of my hand. Sands took a cigarette from a pack in his pocket and put it between his lips without bothering to light it. He rested his head against the passenger window and closed his eyes.

Outside, cyclists slipped through the traffic, neon-visible ninjas. As valiant nine-to-five workers, bundled in coats and hats, umbrellas bobbing, kept their heads down against the weather and trudged onwards, to whatever the night held in store.

Poor Jojo was dead. I felt bad about not feeling bad. Jojo had thought of me as a friend. I had thought of him as a punter. Perhaps Sands was mourning him. They had shared a flat and he was still young enough to be shocked by Jojo's sudden exit. I envied the boy's raw emotion. Maybe my helping him was an act of reparation for my own lack of emotion, or maybe I felt more than I thought I did. I remembered the morgue technician rearranging Jojo's hair as he lay on the slab. The mannequin stiffness of his corpse.

A cyclist appeared out of my blind spot and glided along

the side of the van, masked and helmeted, praying mantis-skinny. I glanced in my side mirror: rain, pavement, parked cars.

I wondered how Rose and the team were doing at Ballantyne House. I'd told her about the death of Schumann and she had said, 'I hope they weren't practising how to do away with Auntie Pat. Must be galling to know your inheritance is going to be swallowed up by care home fees.' I had laughed and told Rose to be careful about what boxes she opened. 'Watch out for anything the size of an old lady and make sure Abomi checks the wardrobes before you do.'

Jojo's flat was at the motorway end of West Princes Street, around the corner from a trio of brightly lit Chinese restaurants. A few diners were already settled at tables. Waitresses moved behind windows misted with steam. I realised I was hungry and made a private plan to eat at one of them on my way home.

Glasgow has its share of shiny Airbnbs but the old city clings on. Jojo's flat was two doors down from the tenement where Marion Gilchrist, an old lady with a cupboard full of good jewellery, had been beaten to death sometime in the early 1900s. Oscar Slater, a German Jew with a bad reputation, had spent nigh on twenty years in jail for the crime before it was agreed he was innocent of the killing. I had known an elderly gent who claimed to have crossed paths with Slater. He had called him a cut-price Dreyfus, a bookie and a pimp, too much of an outsider to be protected from the police. Slater was a lesson in the intersection of wrong face, wrong place, wrong time. But it was the kind of lesson that could only be learned retrospectively. I knew from experience that it was easy to end up cornered. The feeling of opening the door to trouble.

I parked the van and we got out. The concrete canyon of the M8 motorway was only a street away, cars and lorries pressing east and west, water fanning beneath arcs of artificial light. No rumble of it reached us. The street was dimly lit and silent as Mrs Gilchrist's grave.

A line of wheelie bins stood sentinel against railings, guarding a deep drop to the basement below. I followed Sands up a set of uneven steps. Multiple hand-written names were taped to the entry phone. Sands pushed the door open, no key required, and led the way into a darkened close. It was a cold night, but the smell of over-ripe refuse reached into the stairwell. I turned on my phone's torch and bounced the beam around the lobby. The stairs curved upwards in a leisurely curl, like the inside of a conch shell.

'We're on the top floor.'

I followed Sands up the stairs, making sure not to brush against the walls. Some Glasgow tenements have harboured generations of black beetles. I did not want any pioneers in search of new territories cadging a lift home with me.

Sands fished a set of keys from the pocket of his Crombie when we reached the top landing. He unlocked a pair of storm doors, and the front door within. It was colder inside the flat than it had been in the street. I turned the collar of my coat up and followed him down a long hallway. The keys were still in his hand. He unlocked another door and ushered me in to what would have been the drawing room. It smelt of unwashed clothes and fast food. I made out vague shapes in the dim light filtering in from the street outside.

Sands shoved the keys deep into his pocket. 'This was Jojo's space.'

I walked to the window. On the other side of the street, in a fluorescent room, a shirtless young man was fixing his hair in front of a mirror. He raised his hands in the air and did a loose-limbed dance.

Sands snatched the curtains shut. 'Arsehole.'

'Does he do that a lot?'

'It's a regular show.'

I peeled back the curtain for another look and then let it drop.

'Jojo must have loved that.'

Sands switched on the overhead light. 'Jojo thought it was all for his benefit. Better than TV he used to say.'

It was a nice room. The building was south-facing, its windows designed to let in maximum daylight. The ceiling was high and trimmed with intricate cornicing. A large marble mantelpiece framed a boarded-up fireplace. The room's pleasing proportions had not inspired Jojo to home décor. The place was basically a small warehouse, littered with cardboard boxes and discarded carrier bags. An unmade single bed was shoved into the far corner. I was sure I could still make out Jojo's shape indented on the mattress and pillow.

Sands had stowed his unlit cigarette in his top pocket. Now he took it out and sparked up without offering me one.

'I told you he had a lot of stuff.'

I made myself a roll-up and lit up to block out the smell of the room and the boy's cheap tobacco.

Music started up somewhere in the building, a bass beat whose rhythm was hard to catch. I crouched down and unfolded the tabs on one of the boxes. One of Bowery's auction tickets was still taped to it. A look inside confirmed my suspicions.

'This is the remains of a mixed lot.'

Sands looked bewildered. 'A what?'

I opened the box wider so he could see the jumble of bric-a-brac inside.

'When people clear houses they have to take the bulk of stuff they're not interested in, in order to secure the items they do want. Sometimes they make up mixed lots and put them into auction to move it on. Occasionally they miss something good amongst the dross. That's where runners like Jojo come in. They buy the lot, extract their prize and dump the rest. Only it looks like Jojo didn't get round to offloading the junk.'

Sands reached into the box and took out a small brass camel. 'How come this is worth nothing, but that brass piece in your auction might raise a hundred quid?'

'Taste, rarity, execution.' I took the camel from him and turned it over in my hands. 'This is souvenir-quality, a memento brought back by someone on a package holiday or a serviceman stationed in North Africa. It might have meant something to the original purchaser, but out of context it's just a geegaw. You quite fancied having a busty, multi-armed goddess on your shelf. How do you feel about that camel?'

The boy gave me a sullen look. 'Yeah, all right.'

'It doesn't make the heart sing though, does it? Not the way an exotic beauty with big bazoombas does. I reckon it'd raise three quid max at a car boot sale and you might wait a long time for that.' I dropped the camel back into the box. 'Sorry, son, you're not going to get the money for Jojo's send-off here. Let the authorities take over. There's no shame in it. I'll probably be in the same position when my time comes.'

Sands waved a hand at the boxes scattered around the room. 'You've not even looked.'

I pulled up the coverlet on Jojo's bed and sat down,

catching a faint whiff of sweat and stale sex. A half-drunk bottle of Famous Grouse stood on a World War Two Utility bedside table. I tipped the bottle to the boy, offering him a drink. He shook his head. I uncapped it, wiped the rim with the edge of my scarf and took a swig. I had the van. I would have to be careful, but the conversation was depressing me.

'Why are you so keen on burying Jojo? I could understand all this if you wanted the money for your studies.' I was censoring myself. I meant drink and drugs, a good time. 'You're a young bloke. Why are you so bothered about an old soak like Jojo? It's a shame he dropped off the way he did, but he had his time. It doesn't matter to him. RIP. Ashes to ashes, dust to dust. The rest of us keep going until our time comes around.'

Sands shoved a couple of boxes aside, making a clear space on the floor. He sat cross-legged, gathering his coat around him for warmth.

'Jojo and me spent a lot of time together during lockdown. He told me lots of stories about when he was young. He wasn't always the way he was.'

I took another sip of whisky. It burned on the way down. 'We're all someone's blue-eyed boy. Then we grow up and decide what to do with our lives.'

Sands was bringing out the bullshitter in me. I had never been anyone's blue-eyed boy and I was too aware of opportunities limited and hopes smothered to be a Tory or much of an existentialist.

Sands picked at a stain on the carpet. 'Jojo was at the Art School, like me, when he was younger. Things were different back in the day. You couldn't be gay – not openly. He fell in love with another student but Jojo wasn't Jojo back then – he was Joseph. Joseph was a wee Catholic Nancy boy who thought the only one entitled to a willy rub was the priest because he had been consecrated by God.' I could hear Jojo's voice in Sands' rendition, his choice of words. 'His boyfriend wanted to brash it out, go to London or New York, get involved in Gay Lib and stick two fingers up to Glasgow. But Jojo – Joseph – wasn't ready to come out of the closet.'

Jojo had been good with words when he was sober, even better in the early stages of a bender. I guessed the tale was a tall one designed to soften the boy up. I knew the trajectory of these stories.

'Let me guess: Jojo rejected his boyfriend and the poor guy killed himself?'

Sands looked at me with disgust. There was an empty wine glass on the bedside table. He stretched over and stubbed his cigarette out in it.

'His boyfriend went down to London and met someone else. Jojo always regretted not going with him. Jojo tried his hand at being an artist, but it didn't work out. He said he was a decent draughtsman but didn't have any ideas of his own. He met an older man, an antique dealer, and learned the trade. But the man took a heart attack and died. He hadn't made a will, so his family inherited the house and chucked Jojo out. That's how he ended up in this dump. He took on the lease, sublet it to students like me and took a commission on top.'

'What was the commission for?'

For the first time since I had met him, Sands grinned. 'Admin and maintenance.'

We both laughed. I took another sip of whisky and offered him the bottle again.

He shook his head. 'Jojo played the fool, but he could be interesting when he wasn't out of his head.'

'Sounds like you were a good friend to him.'

Sands looked serious. 'I got more than I gave.' He took out his phone, opened the camera function and scrolled through some images until he found the photograph he wanted and passed it to me. 'Jojo gave me my subject.'

The painting's colours were deep, its composition hectic. It was hard to make out its detail in the phone's small screen. I zoomed in and saw a crowd of grotesques. Sands had taken a God's-eye view. The people were looking up towards the viewer, their mouths raw and hungry, eyes piggy with desire. The scene owed something to George Grosz and Hieronymus Bosch. Perhaps that accounted for the sense of déja vu it prompted in me.

'Does it have a name?'

'The Auction.'

I looked again and saw a tall, skinny man with a skeletal face directing the sale – the conductor of an orchestra of the dead.

I pointed at the skinny figure. 'Is that meant to be me?'

Sands ignored my question. He nodded at the phone. 'There's more.'

I scrolled on. A tangle of naked male limbs and rictus grins, flabby flesh and exposed bones. A collage of cocks, mouths, hands, legs, beer bellies, tattoos, bulging muscles and bent-over arses. In their centre was a grinning loon with flushed cheeks and a manic smile.

Sands said, 'I called the series "Jojo's Progress", after Hogarth's "The Rake's Progress".'

I scrolled through three more paintings of Jojo's adventures from pub to saleroom to male-only orgy, each featuring the man himself, dancing through the action, the Lord of Misrule. Foggy faces smeared across a canvas, a drunken view of ambered revels. Sands had caught the intensity of a night on the lash, the camaraderie that could slip into love or fisticuffs. There was Jojo on his back smoking a glass crack pipe, on a piss-soaked pavement, curled into the shape of a womb-bound baby, boots driving into his body. Jojo bruised and alone in a café, a cup of tea and a full Scottish on the table before him, a queasy smile on his face.

I passed Sands his phone. 'You made a project out of his life?'

'Jojo loved it.'

'I bet he did. What did you do? Follow him around 24/7?'

I was not sure why the idea of the boy making Jojo's chaotic existence into an art project irritated me. Jojo would have liked the attention and there was no denying the paintings were good.

Sands wrinkled his nose. 'I got him to tell me stories. I'd take notes, pick a moment and paint it from imagination. You know Jojo. Part of what he told me would be made-up or exaggerated. I couldn't be sure what was real and what fantasy. But it didn't matter. The uncertainty adds something.'

'Is that the real reason you're so keen to give Jojo a decent send-off? It'll round off your art project?'

Sands took his packet of Mayfair from his pocket and turned them over in his hands.

'The funeral would make a good ending, but so would Jojo lying dead in a shop doorway or on a slab in the morgue. I composed the series from imagination. I can compose the final picture from imagination too.'

'You painted Jojo's stories. You don't have the experience to know what his death was like, and he's not here to tell you what happened.'

Maybe it was the whisky, but I could imagine Jojo's death.

A stagger along a neon-lit street, a zigzag reel down a darkened lane and an unsteady descent onto piss-stained steps. Jojo deciding to close his eyes, just for a moment, a doomed mountaineer overcome by hypothermia . . .

'Okay, I admit a funeral would enhance my art project, as you call it. It would help me pin down details for the painting. I could create a photographic archive, document some of the stuff Jojo left behind. I made some videos of Jojo telling me about his life and adventures. I could put it all together in an installation – a real portrait of the man that goes beyond my paintings. Two truths can exist at the same time, you know. I meant it when I said I owe him a decent send-off.'

I replaced the bottle of Famous Grouse on the bedside table. There was something actorly about the boy's speech that would normally have made me wary, but the whisky had mellowed me, or maybe I just knew how chuffed Jojo would have been to have his life and death immortalised on film and canvas. I glanced at my watch. It was six o'clock. I would have to sober up before I drove the van.

I got to my feet. 'Okay, you've convinced me. Let's see if the old git left enough to bury himself.'

Nine

WE WERE AN hour in when Sands discovered the bottles. I had set up a classification system – Crap, Keep, Charity Shop. The Crap pile was the largest. So far there was nothing worth auctioning, but I had called in a favour from Shug McDade who had agreed to give Sands a stall at the Barras rent-free for a couple of weekends. Sands saw value in things I knew were too ubiquitous to sell, but the boy's enthusiasm, combined with his cool, might shift stuff that would otherwise gather dust. It would not be enough to fund a funeral, but it was a way of turning some of Jojo's leavings into cash.

We were working in silence broken occasionally by random sounds from the street below when Sands said, 'I've found something.'

I glanced up from a bundle of board games that would be worth three figures, if their pieces were complete, and fuck-all if they weren't.

'What?'

'Have a look. I guess Jojo didn't tell me everything.'

The box that had once held a consignment of Jaffa Cakes was now filled with little bottles, brothers of the distilled sexual energy Jojo had wanted to gift the two Bobbys. I took a hanky from my pocket, wrapped it around a bottle and held it up to the light. 'Do you know what these are?'

Sands took one from the box and examined it. 'I'm guessing drugs.'

'GHB, aka G, club drug, date rape drug. It's Class B now. I'd be careful of getting my fingerprints on them.'

Sands wiped the bottle with the edge of his shirt. 'How do you know it's Class B?'

After Jojo had given me the bottle, I'd checked online, but I said, 'How do you not know?'

Sands counted the top layer of bottles, muttering the numbers under his breath, then gloved his hand in a plastic bag and gently rooted inside, investigating how many layers there were.

'I reckon there's a hundred in here.' He opened the lids of the other boxes, exclaiming out loud when he found five more stacked with bottles. 'Fuck's sake, that's six hundred of them.'

Sorting through the boxes had made me warm and I had discarded my coat. Now I pulled it on.

'I don't want to know.'

Sands said, 'What am I meant to do with this stuff?'

I tied my scarf around my neck, ready to go. 'Sorry, son, it's not my problem.'

He looked up at me, eyes shining. 'What am I meant to do with this stuff? Dump it? Pour it down the drain? Call the cops?'

'You're asking the wrong person. I'm an auctioneer. I deal

in antiques. This is beyond my skill set.' I waved a hand at the boxes. 'This has the potential to land us both in jail. A place I try to avoid.'

Sands' voice rose a notch. 'You can't leave me on my own to deal with this.'

'I don't see why not.' I wiped my face with my hands, wishing I had never set foot in the flat. I remembered Oscar Slater again: wrong face, place and time. Twenty years in the clink. I took a deep breath. 'Jojo was high as the Empire State last time I saw him, but this is too much for personal consumption. Was he dealing?'

Sands shrugged. 'Jojo didn't have a lot of folk coming and going, just me and a couple of lads who occasionally helped carry boxes up and down the stairs for him. They hadn't been round in a while. Jojo was getting more into "the party scene", as he called it. Maybe dealing was his new thing? I don't know. But he died before he got going.'

I sat down on the badly made bed. 'Maybe, or maybe Jojo was holding the stuff for someone.'

In the street below there was a smash of breaking glass and the sound of laughter.

Sands said, 'Why would someone get Jojo to hold drugs for them? He wasn't exactly discreet.'

'It's risky keeping quantities of drugs on the premises, especially if you've already chalked up a few cheeky convictions. Jojo would get a fee and cut-price drugs in return for looking after the stash. If that's the case, you could get into worse trouble than jail, if you hold onto them. But handing the lot to the police might not go down so well either.'

Sands looked queasy. 'So what do I do? Wait for some random drug dealer to turn up with a baseball bat?'

'Might be hard on your kneecaps.'

Sands snapped, 'Jojo was an inconsiderate bastard. He can fucking bury himself.'

His vehemence made me laugh. It was none of my business, but circumstance had landed us in the same room and trying to do a good thing had landed the boy out of his depth.

I got to my feet. 'First step, find out who they belonged to. Second step, give them back. Third step, collect a reward.'

Sands looked unconvinced. 'Easy as that?'

'Probably not, but we can give it a try.'

Ten

I CALLED LES from the van, Sands in the passenger seat beside me. The call went to voicemail three times and then Les was on the line shouting to make himself heard over a racket of chanting voices and blasting whistles. I raised my voice. 'Where are you? You sound like you're in the middle of a riot.'

'I'm in George Square in the middle of a fucking riot. Get yourself over here, Rilke. It's great.'

'Doesn't sound like my scene.'

'Sure it is. You love a bit of drama. This is a full song and dance number. Mounted polismen, salsa bands, lesbo drummers . . . the lot. What are you after?'

If it had been someone else, I might have asked why they assumed I was after something, but Les and I had a long relationship based on bartering and exchange.

'Am I on speakerphone?'

'What do you think this is? Radio Clyde?'

'Who deals in GHB?'

'You're way too old and way too skinny for that crap, Rilke.' There was a brief interruption as Les told someone to *fuck off if they didn't want their fucking face fucked up*. He came back on the line, his voice like sunshine in June. 'You know me, I can never say no to an old pal. How much do you want?'

'I'm not after any. I just want to know who deals in it.'

'Christ, you're an arsehole wrapped in a mystery inside an enigma. Probs best not to talk about it over the phone, eh? You in the van?'

'Yep, I'm crossing the Junction at St George's Cross.'

'Come and get me then. I'll be on the west side of the square, looking up Queen Victoria's skirts.'

There was a shriek of atmosphere, screams, drumming and high blasts of whistles then the call was cut, and I was left with the growl of the van's engine.

Sands' phone glowed in his hand. 'According to Twitter some TERF is due to speak at the City Chambers. It's kicking off outside.'

The last time they had met, Les had called Rose a TERF. Rose had told him that she had been called names by men since she was eleven years old and didn't have to put up with it from him, then she'd thrown a drink over him. Les had responded in kind. I had been caught in the crossfire, drenched in vodka, Red Bull and red wine. I knew it was an insult but had been too busy huckling them apart to grasp the nuance of it.

I glanced at Sands. 'Trans Exclusionary Radical Feminist, right?'

Sands looked serious. 'Yep, fascists. They deny trans women's right to be women.' He put his feet up on the dashboard. 'Who's Les?'

I reached over and batted his feet off the dash without taking my eyes from the road.

'An acquaintance of mine. He's full of shit. But he may be able to find out where Jojo's stash came from without compromising your kneecaps.'

I had known Rose long enough to know the bigger the freak the more she liked it. I had known Les long enough to know that he didn't give a toss about any trans debate. As far as he was concerned politics was for the straights. Rose and Les were natural rivals. Their real fight was competition for the limelight.

The sound of drumming and excited shouting reached us as we drew closer to George Square. A couple of police vans were slanted across North Hanover Street. A female police officer made a circling gesture with her hand, telling us to turn round and go back the way we had come. I lowered my window and the noise of protest reached inside the cab. The police officer made the circling gesture again.

'The square is closed.'

I stuck my head outside the window. 'I'm picking up a mate. If you let me park here for thirty seconds, I'll get him and be gone.'

The officer reached into her pocket. 'Push off or I'll book you.'

'It's a one-way street.'

'So back up.'

The van's window rolled electronically shut.

'Bet she got top marks at the Tulliallan charm school.' I steered the van into a three-point-turn and drove illegally up the bus lane. Sands pulled on a knitted hat. He slumped low in the passenger seat. I glanced at him. 'For fuck's sake. Can you stop looking so bloody guilty? You'll get us pulled over.'

'You're the one arguing with the police about parking spaces. Jojo always said it was a bad idea to bring yourself to the attention of the cops.'

I thought of the Partick Station policeman with bad skin who had dismissed Jojo's death as routine.

'Jojo was taken into permanent custody in the end.'

Sands gave me a look. 'You're not funny. Where do you think he is right now?'

'I'm not much of a one for the sweet hereafter. As far as I'm concerned, we get one shot. This is it.'

'I didn't mean spiritually. Where do you think his body is?'

I glanced at the boy, a slim silhouette in the darkness.

'In a freezer drawer in the morgue.'

He sounded unhappy. 'Jojo wouldn't like that. He wasn't a just-put-me-out-with-the-bins kind of guy.'

'If Jojo wanted a big send-off he should have made provision for it.'

'The stuff in his room's worth a lot of money.'

'It wasn't intended as a funeral fund though, was it? If there's a finder's fee you can spend it on a coach and plumed horses or a motorcycle cortege, whatever you want. I can probably put you in touch with some sad-faced fucks who can pretend to be mourners, if you like.'

Sands shook his head. 'You're a bigger arsehole than Jojo.'

'As long as you don't put me in any paintings.'

He snorted. 'Don't worry. You're not exactly inspiring.'

I parked in a loading bay round the back of Queen Street Station. We walked back down to George Square, past straggling commuters, and early evening drinkers, towards the sound of the demonstration. The carnival atmosphere grew more frantic as we approached the source of the noise. I texted Les, *Almost there*. My phone buzzed and I saw that he had sent me a photo of two pretty boys who might have been girls. *Got space in the van for two more?* I responded with an upside-down thumb and a smiling, coiled-turd emoji.

A few drinkers sat at tables inside the glassed-off bar of the Millennium Hotel, watching the action. I paused in the light thrown by the hotel's windows. There were around a hundred people in the square, fewer than the noise had suggested. Some trans men and women embrace gender conventions and slip into the social stream, barely rippling its surface. Others prefer to make a big splash. The protest had its share of broad-shouldered men in dresses and glitter beards, crop-headed youths with girly features, women with flat tops rocking rockabilly suits and ties. It reminded me of nightclubs I had frequented in what kids now called *back in the day*.

Sands and I crossed the road and entered the square. There was a stand-off, police dividing one group from another as they might separate supporters of opposing teams. The home-made placards came into focus.

NO TO HATE   SISTER NOT CIS-TER
TRANS RESISTANCE IS EXISTANCE
LESBIANS DON'T HAVE PENISES
TRANS WOMEN ARE WOMEN
WOMEN = NOUN = ADULT HUMAN FEMALE
GLASGOW = LOVE (I had my doubts about that one)
STOP GIVING KIDS SEX HORMONES
TRANS LIVES MATTER
HATE SPEECH DOES NOT EQUAL FREE SPEECH
LESBIANS NOT QUEER

NO TRANSPHOBIA IN OUR CITY
PARENTS HAVE RIGHTS
LOVE WILL WIN (I doubted that one too)

There was a lot of shouting, megaphones blasting from both ends of the square, but the two sides seemed content for the police to divide them. I turned my back on the City Chambers and we pushed our way towards the statue of a young Queen Victoria mounted on her horse. Victoria was riding away from the protest towards the Merchants House and the looted money that had once made the city great, a sword raised imperiously in her right hand.

'Rilke!!!'

Les was dressed down in a black bomber jacket, front pleated trousers and Cuban heels, a beaded black and silver evening scarf wound around his neck. There were times when Les had looked like a clown doll on a killing spree, but long years and YouTube tutorials had honed his skill with a make-up brush. His lips were bold red, his eyes smoky. Mysterious contouring emphasised his cheekbones and harmonised the proportions of his nose and face. A black beret sat at a jaunty angle on his head. He looked like Rudolf Nureyev might have, if he had survived HIV and given in to the occasional fish supper.

The young couple in the photo he had texted stood nearby. They looked like they shared the same wardrobe and bleach bottle. Their hair was short and choppy, the colour of winter mink, their clothes alt-leisure-'80s throwback. They were around the same age as Sands, but a different tribe. I gave them a nod. Sands did not acknowledge them, and they ignored him in return.

Les called, 'Hey, Midwich Cuckoos, our ride's arrived.'

He grinned at me. 'A while since you've been called a ride, eh, Nosferatu?'

The last time I had seen Les his teeth had been ground down. He had had new veneers installed since then and was taking the opportunity to show them off, grinning like a piano keyboard.

'I see you got the full Armitage Shanks.'

'The what?'

I indicated his teeth. 'The full porcelain.'

'Ah, fuck off, you're showing your age, Rilke. Nobody says Armitage Shanks anymore.'

Les had been in the same year at school as me and Anderson, but he was playing the boy in front of his new pals. I resisted the temptation to break his cover.

'What's this about?'

Les grinned. 'Fucking TERF coming to speak at some debate in the City Chambers. We're showing her Glasgow doesn't do hate speech.'

I pointed at a red on white sign that read STEP THE FUCK UP AND TAKE OUT THE TERF TRASH!!!!!!!!!

'That should convince them.'

Les patted me on the back. 'Debate never works. You've got to fuck them up to shut them up.'

'Who said that first? Cicero or Socrates?'

'You've always been a censorious smartarse, Rilke.'

That made it three people in a week who had accused me of being judgemental. I was beginning to take it personally.

'Call me squeamish but I'm not keen on violence against women.'

Les waved a hand at the crowd. 'Look around you. Most of this mob are chicks or chicks with dicks.' He winked.

'Girl-on-girl violence isn't wrong per se, Rilke. If it's the right girls, you can sell tickets.'

A roar came up from the crowd nearest to the station and people surged towards the City Chambers. A large woman shouldered me as she rushed by. Sands caught me by the arm, steadying me. His eyes were wide, his expression a mixture of excitement and alarm, a young soldier about to go over the top.

'She's arrived.'

'Who?'

'I can't remember her name, the TERF.'

Perhaps social media alerts had drawn more people from pubs and outlying streets. The crowd seemed to have grown. Our small group stood still, like boulders in a stream, as the protesters surged forward. The police moved too, hi-vis jackets shining like warnings.

I raised my voice. 'What's she done?'

Sands shrugged. 'Wrote some hate speech.'

Our side of the square was emptying, the protesters forming a mosh pit outside the chambers, the police attempting to kettle them. The crowd had started to chant 'No hate, no fear!', the words indistinct, like separate tables in the same restaurant singing 'Happy Birthday' to different people, names muddled in a jumble of voices. Then the chant came together again, shouting in unison, 'No hate, no fear . . . welcome here! No hate, no fear . . . welcome here! No hate, no fear . . . welcome here!'

I tapped at my phone. Google brought up just-that-minute-snapped photos of the protest, a Twitter deluge, a portrait shot of the nondescript woman who was due to give the talk, a long thread on Mumsnet and some newspaper opinion pieces. A weight of words and anger.

I closed it down and asked Sands, 'So, what did she say?'

Sands shrugged. 'I told you, hate speech.'

Les tied his scarf into a neat bow. 'She said it's impossible to change sex. Boys are boys and girls are girls. It's a binary world so stay in the box you were assigned. Stupid bitch.' He put an arm around me. 'Ach, I can't be bothered with this. It's too cold for standing around George Square waiting for them to send in the tanks. Where's the van?'

'Up by the station.'

Les's young friends looked like they might join the protest, but he said, 'Let's go,' and we started to walk in the direction of Queen Street. Les was right; it was too cold for standing around. I shoved my hands into my coat pocket. The bottle Jojo had given me was still there, less special now that we had discovered its brothers.

'Does this mean you're chopping off your cock and balls and becoming a woman?'

Les cuffed me. 'You don't get it, do you? Cocks and fannies have nothing to do with sex.'

'I must have been doing it wrong all these years.'

'You're a puerile cunt, Rilke. I'm being serious. This is a new world. Women, men, in-between, outside in, upside down. Mrs Bun the baker's wife can wear the butcher's trousers if she fancies it. We can be anything we want to be.'

'Except wrong?'

Les grinned. 'You got it. Don't be wrong. Not unless you want someone to put you right.' He nodded at Sands. 'Aren't you going to introduce me to your pal?'

Sands took off his hat, folded it into the pocket of his coat and held out a hand. 'I'm Sands.'

Les took it in his and they shook. 'What are you doing with this old poof?'

I interrupted. 'Business. You remember Jojo?'

Les nodded. 'Sold antiques? Looked a bit like Peter Lorre on acid? I heard he shuffled off.'

'He was this boy's uncle.'

'Ah, I wouldn't have mentioned Peter Lorre if I'd realised that.'

Sands said, 'It's okay. I don't know who Peter Lorre is.'

Les made a face. 'A black-and-white movie star, wee Hungarian Jew, best known for playing madmen and murderers. Talented, but ended up in a lot of shit films.'

It occurred to me that Peter Lorre would have been well cast in a screen version of the Oscar Slater story. I kept the thought to myself.

Les said, 'Sorry for your loss.'

Sands did not blink. 'Thanks.'

Les grinned at me. 'You're wanting some GHB to make Jojo's send-off go with a bang? Makes sense. I heard he was into it. Takes its toll. A good way to lose your dick, but fun while it lasts.'

A police minibus on its way to the square slowed level with us. The back was full of uniformed officers: white faces, stab vests, baseball caps, every brim turned towards us. I made a conscious effort not to up my pace. The minibus hovered for a moment and then moved on.

'Let's wait until we get to your place.' I jerked my head at Les's companions. 'What about them? Are they tagging along?'

'They're the new young team, Rilke. Why would you not want them to tag along? Cute wee femboys.'

One of the Cuckoos said, 'I have a vagina, actually.'

Les's grin was wolfish. 'Don't worry, we won't hold it against you. Won't hold it at all, actually.'

Sands and the Cuckoos looked nervous when I told them

they would have to go in the back of the van if they wanted a lift to Les's place.

Les showed his teeth. 'Don't panic. We're not going to take you up Mugdock Country Park, rape and murder yous. We only do that shit on Mondays.'

One of the Cuckoos said, 'Today's Monday.'

Les hooted.

I told him to shut up and the kids to bang on the wall of the cab if they felt sick. Sands could have squeezed into the cab beside us, but I wanted to speak with Les alone. The three of them climbed in and I slammed the door, leaving them in pitch darkness. Les and I hopped into the front. I started the engine and steered the van beyond Queen Street Station, in the direction of Les's place.

Les fiddled with the radio. 'Can they hear us back there?'

'Probably not, if you put the radio on and keep your voice down.'

Les found Radio 3 and the sound of *The Lark Ascending* flooded the cab. He leaned back in the passenger seat. 'I bloody love this.'

'I never pegged you for a classical music fan.'

'You know why that is, don't you? I'll say it again. You're a bloody judgemental bastard.' Les lowered the sun visor and checked his make-up in the mirror. He dabbed something from the corner of his eye with his pinkie and slammed the visor closed. 'Why shouldn't I like classical music?'

'No reason.'

'You think I'm an ignorant tranny. I'm a regular Classic FM listener.'

'I get it – you're practically Mary Beard.'

We sat in silence for a while, letting the sound of Vaughan Williams wash over us. I paused the van at red traffic lights beside the bus station and waited while an old couple drag-ging wheelie cases crossed the road and made for the entrance. It was dark and cold, and I found myself wondering if they had a long journey ahead.

Les straightened up, as if he had made his mind up about something. 'I didn't want to say anything in front of his nephew, but Jojo had it coming.'

'How do you mean?'

'He was an arsehole, right?'

The lights changed. I put the van in gear and drove on. 'That's hardly unique.'

'No, but Jojo was an arsehole who owed money left, right and centre. He was lucky to die peacefully. Sooner or later someone would have fucked him up.'

'You?'

Les shrugged. 'Probably not. He owed me four-fifty but I heard he owed others more. I would have left him to the big fish. No point in doing a nasty job if someone'll do it for you.' He looked at me. 'Death doesn't necessarily cancel debts. If I were you, I'd tell your wee pal not to let on he's related to Jojo. It's not my style, but there are others, maybe folk that were owed more . . .'

He let the sentence hang in the air. We passed the gates of Chinatown Restaurant and drove beneath the motorway bridges that crisscross Phoenix Road. I braked as a fox scur-ried from bushes at the side of the road. It crossed our path and disappeared into the overgrown embankment on the other side.

'Sands isn't Jojo's nephew.'

The lark ascended and the news came on. Les leaned forward and switched the radio to Heart FM. The Eagles told us to take it to the limit one more time.

'Why did you say he was?'

It was my turn to shrug. 'I don't know. He was Jojo's flatmate. He's got a thing about burying the old guy with dignity.'

Les snorted. 'Good luck getting anyone to contribute to that whip-round.'

I took the slip road onto Great Western Road. Deliveroo couriers were waiting outside fast-food shops. Smokers were chatting outside the Hug and Pint. A young boy sat on a scrap of cardboard on the street, watching them. Children played outside a sari shop, its window draped with sequin-studded fabrics. On the radio Lewis Capaldi told us he was getting used to being someone we loved. Les hummed along under his breath.

I said, 'I met Jojo at a wedding the day before he died. He was full of the joys and off to a party . . .'

Les snorted. 'No need to guess what type of party.'

I reached into my pocket and passed him the bottle of GHB. 'He gave me this, said it was sexual energy.'

Les cupped the bottle in his hand, concealing it from the street outside, and examined it.

'Why are you asking to score when you're already holding? Not like you to plan a big party.' He slapped his thigh. 'Ah, I get it. You're into wee Sandy–'

'Sands. And no, I'm not.'

I held out my hand. Les placed the bottle in my palm, folded my fingers around it and gave my fist a sarcastic squeeze.

'Excuse me, let me get his name right, as if it matters. And yes, you are. You've always liked arty types. You're into wee Sands and want to show him what a big man you are by helping him score.'

'We don't want to score. We want to get rid. Jojo's flat is full of boxes of the stuff.'

'No way.'

'Way. I'm guessing he was holding it for someone, maybe in lieu of debts.'

'Who?'

'That's what I was hoping you'd help us find out.'

'I don't think so.'

'There could be something in it for you.'

'A sair face? Two broken legs?'

'My gratitude and the gratitude of whoever it belongs to.'

'I can live without gratitude, but I'm fond of my face, and my legs.'

Les put his hands on his knees, as if the prospect of repercussions already hurt. I suspected he was playing me. The traffic lights up ahead turned red. A squad of students on their way to Wintersgills, the next stop in the Subway Pub Crawl, ambled across the road. They had chosen a Hawaiian theme: flip-flops, Hawaiian shirts, grass skirts, coconut bras, straw hats, sunglasses and leis. The students had drunk enough to be impervious to the cold, but some were more slaughtered than others. The merely wounded held their dying comrades up.

Les muttered, 'Look at those pricks. Probably medical students. Give it five years. They'll be licensed to slit you open and play with your guts.'

The students reeled on, a sicked-up-rainbow army.

I asked, 'Why would anyone fuck you up for trying to return drugs? You'd be doing them a favour.'

'The city's unstable. You can't be certain how people will take things. Maybe they'll be grateful. Maybe they'll kick your head in. Maybe they'll take you for a friendly walk along the Clydeside. Best not to take stupid chances.'

The lights turned green. I waited for the filter then turned the van into Napiershall Street. There was a space in front of Les's building but I drove past it and parked around the corner.

'Come on, Les. The stuff's sitting in boxes in the boy's flat. All he wants is to reunite it with its rightful owners before they come looking. Like you said, these guys are unpredictable. He's a young lad out of his depth. We both know what that's like.'

'It's a hard world, Rilke. No point in babying the youth. You do them a disservice.'

I turned to look at him. 'Remember that time Ronald Templeton stepped in? How old were you then? Twenty-three? Twenty-four? Older than this lad for sure. You learned your lesson just as well as you would have if Davie McGlone had taken that hammer to your hand.'

Les flexed his fingers. 'Ancient history.'

'You still remember what it felt like though, don't you? The boy's done nothing wrong.'

Les stared out of the van's window at the darkened street. 'I paid Templeton back plenty. He had me on a leash for twenty years.'

I shoved the van's keys in my pocket. 'I guess old age makes some folks timid, but I never thought you'd turn coward.'

Les closed his eyes. 'Fuck you and the fucking horse you rode in on.'

It was his way of saying yes. I clapped him on the shoulder. 'It'll be good karma.'

'Aye, the worse the fuck-up, the better the karma.'

I opened the van door and let Sands and the Cuckoos out. The drive in the dark seemed to have bonded them. They were all laughing as they hopped onto the road. The street-light in front of Les's building was dead. It was always dead.

He opened the close door and put his fingers on his lips. 'Keep the noise down. There's a new yuppie downstairs.'

One of the Cuckoos asked, 'What's a yuppie?'

We reached the top floor. Les unbolted the door.

'Lady Muck. Thinks this is going to be the next Finnieston if she can get scabs like me to move on. She's already complained to the Housing Association about my having too many visitors.'

Finnieston was a thirty-minute walk from Les's flat. Until recently it had been a post-industrial ghostland, nothing but abandoned warehouses, down-at-heel pubs and down-at-heel men. Now it was transformed by hipster bars and fancy restaurants that featured in Sunday supplements, where drug-dealing wolves in women's clothing were unwelcome.

Les clicked on the light and we followed him down a short hallway into his living room. He had rented the flat for twenty-odd years. The last time I visited, it had been so cluttered it had been hard to negotiate a route from the front door to the lounge and even harder to find a place to park your bum when you got there. Now it looked like the home of someone too hedonistic to be a Scandi aesthete but with pretensions in that direction.

Books were in the bookcase. The floor was clear, the couch and easy chairs free of clutter. The coffee table in the centre of the room, which had long been a mess of discarded cans, Rizla fragments, flyers and free papers, was empty. Les sank into an easy chair by the window. I took the other one and nodded to the tidy room.

'I see you've got a grip.'

'Aye, I Marie Kondo-ed the place during lockdown. Decluttered. It was about time. Fifty-two bin bags.'

The Cuckoos and Sands settled gingerly on the couch. I saw Sands looking at the portrait of Les, a clever illusion that dominated the room. Looked at one way, Les in a tasselled sombrero grinning a bandito smile and sucking a cigar. Looked at from another angle, a grinning skeleton with sombrero and cigar. Les flesh – no flesh – flesh again.

Les glanced at his watch. 'Okay, first things first. Midwich Cuckoos, what can I do you for?'

The one who told us that they had a vagina piped up, 'An eighth, please.'

Les left the room and returned with a small wrap of hash. 'Anything else?'

The other Cuckoo asked, 'Do you have any Rizlas?'

Les rolled his eyes. 'Do I look like a fucking Tesco Express?' He named his price and they paid in cash. Les folded the notes away. I was not sure why he bothered with such small fry, but Les was Mr Charm, a salesman on commission, full of smiles and bonhomie. 'Normally I'd extend an invitation to yous to stick around and make sure the merchandise is up to expectations, but as you can see, I've other business to take care of.' He got to his feet. 'Sorry, girls, it's time to hit the road.'

The Cuckoos got to their feet. The quieter of the two said, 'We're not girls.'

'For fuck's sake.' Les pointed at the other Cuckoo. 'You just told me you had a vagina.'

The quiet Cuckoo said, 'I don't.'

Les looked from one to the other. 'What does that make yous then? A nice, wee, queer-washed heterosexual couple?'

The Cuckoo who was equipped with a vagina looked outraged. 'Non-binary queers. We identify as gender-queer.'

Les rolled his eyes. 'Good for you. I identify as a tranny.'

The quiet Cuckoo gave him a sympathetic smile. 'You should have a better opinion of yourself.'

Les's tone was dangerously patient. 'My opinion of myself is just fine.'

The Cuckoo's voice was gentle. 'Seriously, I know it's hard for your generation to realise but you've nothing to be ashamed of. You need to learn to love yourself.'

Their companion said, 'If you can't love yourself, how the hell are you going to love someone else?'

Les snapped, 'I love myself fine.'

I did not mean to laugh, but I did. 'You said it yourself, Les. It's a rainbow world. Cocks and fannies are nothing to do with sex.'

Les gave me a poisonous glance. 'As far as I'm aware there's only two fannies in this room and I'm looking at one of them.' He returned his attention to the two youngsters. 'If you two don't watch out I'll take that eighth back — and I don't do refunds.'

The quiet Cuckoo said, 'That wouldn't be fair.'

'Life isn't fair, son.'

'You sound like my dad. I'm not *son*. And all I'm saying is, you don't need to hold on to self-hatred. Be brave. Be yourself.'

'For fuck's sake.' Les held out his hand. 'Give me that wrap back.'

I stood up. 'Leave them alone, Les. They're just kids.'

He turned on me. 'You can shut the fuck up too, unless you want me to throw you and your wee bum boy out with them.'

Sands said, 'I'm not—'

I silenced him with a look. Les grabbed the Cuckoo with one hand and snatched the wrap from their pocket with the other. Both of them protested, but they had enough smarts not to fight back. Les started to shove the kids along the hallway. I followed, in time to see him open the front door and eject them into the communal stair.

'Piss off and don't come back.'

The Cuckoo with a vagina raised their voice. 'Give us what we paid for or I'll kick your door and scream until your neighbour hears.'

'See this?' Les picked up the baseball bat that sat in a discreet corner by his front door. 'That's what I use on arse-holes who get on the wrong side of me.'

The quiet Cuckoo edged away, but their companion held their ground. 'You could get five years for threatening me with that. Thirty years to life if you killed me. All over an eighth of hash? I don't think so.'

On the landing below, a door opened. Someone was waiting, listening.

I said, 'Les . . .'

Les pulled the Cuckoos back into his hallway and closed the door. He reached into the pocket of his jeans and passed the wrap to Vagina Cuckoo.

'Fuck it. You win. But I love myself plenty. Now get to fuck and make sure you're quiet on the way out. If that cunt downstairs asks what you were doing, you were collecting for a charity of your choice.'

The quiet Cuckoo turned, ready to go, but the other one stood their ground. 'Make it an ounce.'

'Get to fuck.'

'Make it an ounce or we'll make a racket.'

Les lifted the baseball bat again.

I whispered, 'Les . . .'

Vagina Cuckoo said, 'Try it.'

There was the sound of ascending footsteps on the stairway outside.

Les reached into his pocket and passed something over. 'A quarter, and don't come back.'

The letterbox rattled. Les looked from me to the Cuckoos. He set the baseball bat back in its nook and flapped a hand at me, telling me to retreat to the sitting room. Les hissed something at the Cuckoos then opened the door.

Les was icily polite. 'Hello, Kirsty. How can I help you?'

The answering voice was younger than I had expected. 'Is everything okay?'

'Yes, no bother. I was just chatting to the youngsters here. They're collecting for charity.'

I could hear the smile in Vagina Cuckoo's voice. 'We're collecting for Fists Up. A charity that supports bullied children. Would you like to contribute?'

Kirsty from downstairs sounded unsure. 'I left my purse in the kitchen.'

'That's okay. Your neighbour's already been very generous.'

Les said pointedly, 'Aye, well, I know what it's like to be bullied. Good luck with Fists Up. It sounds like an excellent cause.'

'Thanks. Bye.' The Midwich Cuckoos giggled as they ran down the stairs.

Kirsty said, 'Did they show you any ID? I'm not sure they were legitimate charity collectors.'

'Don't worry about it.' Les closed the door without saying goodbye to his neighbour. He stepped into the sitting room, face flushed, sank into the chair by the window and began to roll a joint.

'Nosy cow. I've been here since 1999. That's longer than most of the legit businesses around here.'

I said, 'You should get a sign – *Purveyors of Fine Drugs Since 1999.*'

'Add *Artisanal* to that and she might become a customer.' Les got up and opened the door to the balcony. He sat back down, lit the joint, put it to his lips, inhaled and let the smoke dribble out. 'Cheeky wee fuckers.' He imitated the Cuckoo's voice. '*I have a vagina, actually.*'

Cold air gusted in, wafting the sweet resin smell through the room. A car drove by, a quick blast of grime, heavy on the bass. Somewhere a police siren sounded.

Les passed me the joint. I took a couple of tokes to be sociable and passed it to Sands, who raised it to his lips and inhaled. Les looked from me to Sands and back. I raised my eyebrows.

Les took the joint from Sands and took a long toke, his eyes on me. 'You're not going to let me off the hook, are you?'

'It needs done.'

His voice was dry and scratchy. 'Aye, but why is it me that needs to do it?

I shrugged. 'Your God's anointed?'

'Jesus Christ.' Les took out his phone and stepped into the next room, taking the joint with him.

Eleven

THE JAUNTY NOTES of my ringtone woke me next morning. The screen flashed ROSE. I was tempted to roll over and ignore it, but I knew she would call back or, worse, call in person if I did not answer.

'Where's the van?'

I could tell by her tone that Rose was in no mood for apologies, but I tried anyway.

'Ah, shit, Rose. I'm sorry. I meant to park up at the auction, but it was late by the time I got back. I'll bring it over.' My voice held the tell-tale creakiness of the just woken.

Rose pounced. 'Are you still in bed?'

'I'll be there, thirty minutes tops.'

'For fuck's sake. What is it with this place? Frank's not shown his face either.' Her voice darkened with suspicion. 'He's not with you, is he?'

'Don't be daft. Maybe he's taken the hint and moved on.'

'I didn't give him a hint. We need all hands on deck here. Did you give him a hint?'

I reached for the cigarette I had rolled the night before and lit up. 'No, but I may have subtly indicated that I thought he was a lazy bastard.'

'Says the man still lying in his wanking chariot at eight-thirty on a weekday morning. Frank's place is on your way. I'll text you the address. Drive past and scoop him up, then meet us at Ballantyne House.'

She hung up. I lay in bed staring at the ceiling, blew some smoke rings, then threw the covers off, got washed and dressed.

It had been a long night. Les had spent forty-five minutes on the phone then stuck his head round the door of the sitting room and beckoned to me, grim-faced. I had followed him into the kitchen, leaving Sands on the couch.

Les had Marie Kondo-ed his small kitchen too. The work surfaces were clear except for a kettle, toaster and a box of Crunchy Nut Cornflakes large enough for a family of three to set up home in.

He leant against one of the units. 'Okay, it's sorted. Someone will come round to Jojo's place tomorrow night. Be there for eight. They'll call you when they're on their way.'

I said, 'You gave them my number?'

Les's jaw bunched. 'Is that a problem?'

'It's Sands' business, not mine. I'm just helping him out.'

Les switched the kettle on. He took out the makings for coffee and one mug.

'So help him out. You don't want a softie like that anywhere near these cunts. Before you know it, they'll have him sitting on the side of the road begging or running drugs between here and fuck-knows-where.'

Les was right. Sands was easy prey. Even Jojo had spotted that.

'Fucking Jojo.' I took a deep breath. 'I told Sands there might be a finder's fee in it for him.'

Les spooned coffee and sugar into the mug and added a splash of milk.

'That's not happening. The reward is walking away with your balls intact. Make sure he's out the way by the time they get there and don't make any smartarse comments.'

The kettle came to the boil. He poured hot water into the mug, stirred and raised it to his lips.

I said, 'I'm not inclined to smartarse comments.'

He laughed and coffee spluttered. 'Just hand the stuff over and don't try to strike up any deals. This isn't a negotiating situation.'

'Okay.'

Something about the way I said it did not convince Les. He set his coffee on the worktop. 'I'm serious. You know what most drug-related murders are about?'

I shrugged. 'I don't know, someone getting in on someone else's territory?'

Les looked triumphant. 'Scotland isn't *The Wire*. Most of the aggro happens because someone didn't show enough respect. Don't piss these guys off, Rilke. They're insecure and have no sense of proportion. They'd rather fuck you up than lose face.'

'Understood.'

'Make sure it is.' Les picked up his coffee. 'Now piss off. It's been a long day and I've a boxset waiting to happen.'

*

Frank's place was in Partick. I called him on the hands-free from the van three times before he picked up. My voice had sounded rough; his was raw. I told him I would be there in ten. It was twenty minutes before Frank opened the passenger door and folded himself into the front seat. I nodded at the Greggs coffee and bacon roll waiting on the dashboard.

'I almost ate yours.'

Frank peeled the lid from the cardboard cup and took a sip. 'Thanks.'

'Heavy night?'

He slid the bacon roll from its paper bag and took a bite. 'Something like that.'

I should have given him a bollocking for being late; instead I put the radio on to numb the silence. We drove through traffic that shrank as we left the city behind us until we were the only vehicle on the road. A radio phone-in took calls about a top politician's guilty verdict in a sexual assault trial that had been making the headlines for weeks. Callers' opinions ranged from stitch-up to string him up. Frank finished his coffee and took steady sips from a bottle of water. The phone-in topic switched to the climbing toll of rough sleepers dying on the city's streets.

I should have been getting the lowdown on the previous day's work, but we were halfway to Ballantyne House before I asked, 'How did it go yesterday?'

'Okay. We sorted through the drawing room and made a start on a couple of bedrooms. Dr Barstow got stuck into cataloguing the pictures. He seems happy enough. Gail's valuing the china, and Hannah and Lucy have been photographing some of the standout items for the website.'

'How much do you reckon we've still to do?'

'It's a big job. We're not even a quarter of the way through.'

I sensed some unease in his voice and said, 'Weird, finding the dead dog.'

He looked at me. 'Someone locked it in that trunk, didn't they? Deliberately.'

I negotiated a series of bends in the road. 'Looks like it.'

Frank bit his lip. 'Abomi's spooked. He thinks the place is haunted.'

'I'll have a word. He has to get used to creepy houses if he wants to work in auctions.'

'I guess so.'

Frank took out his iPad and read out a list of items catalogued so far, stopping occasionally to answer questions or expand upon a description. He was a miserable git, but he was thorough.

He reached the end of his list and I asked, 'Did you meet, "the other one"?'

'Who?'

'Mr Forrest's cousin, Alec. That's what the pub landlady called him, remember? "The other one". I got the impression she had it in for him.'

'Never saw him. They seemed pretty busy up at the farmhouse. A lot of coming and going.'

We drove past muddy fields and trees bereft of leaves. The countryside had a dead feeling. As if winter was a permanent condition and spring would never come. I slowed down before the tricky bend that led to Ballantyne House. A rescue truck was winching the burnt-out Micra onto the back of its trailer as we rounded the corner.

'Thank Christ they're getting shot of that. It's not the first thing you want big spenders to see on their way to a sale.'

Frank nodded. 'The crash has freaked Abomi too. He said

we've found two graves since we've been here — the car and the dog's. He's convinced things come in threes.'

I repeated, 'I'll have a word with him.'

Rose was vaping, midway down the long garden. I stopped the van and slid the driver's door open. She looked at me through a haze of cherry-scented vapour.

'Nice of you to show up.'

I could tell she was not really angry. 'Where do you want us?'

Rose gestured towards the house with her e-cigarette. 'Take your pick.' She looked at Frank. 'You're not looking your usual bright-eyed, bushy-tailed self. Are you sure you're up to this?' The words were more threat than concern.

Frank tried to hold her gaze, but Rose outstared him, and he looked away. 'I'm fine.'

The house was freezing, but we left the front and back doors open to ease the flow of goods and people. It was a relief to lose myself in objects. I worked steadily through the morning, cataloguing and classifying, my mind focused on history, design, craftsmanship and provenance. It was almost lunchtime when I heard shouting. I set aside the Imari vase I had been examining and ran up the staircase.

Abomi was sitting on a divan in one of the smaller bed-rooms, chest heaving, his inhaler clamped to his mouth. Lucy had an arm around him. A peacock feather lay on the bed beside her. She looked up at me, her expression stricken. 'It was just a silly joke.'

Frank entered the room at my back. 'What's going on?'

Lucy looked like she might cry. She lifted the feather. Its fringed eye bobbed gently, winking at us. 'I sneaked up behind him and tickled the back of his neck with this. Is he going to be okay?'

Frank knelt beside the young porter. 'You're all right, mate. Take a good sook on that, then we'll go outside and get you a bit of fresh air.' He gave Lucy a murderous look. 'Have you photographed everything on the list?'

Lucy shook her head. She squeezed Abomi's shoulder, said 'Sorry, Absi,' and left the room.

Rose arrived just as Frank was ferrying Abomi from the room. Her hair was loose, her face flushed, as if she had come straight from a dance. She turned to me. 'What shitfuckery's happening now?'

I said, 'Lucy played a harmless gag on Abomi. He got a bigger fright than she expected and had an asthma attack.'

'It's like running a kindergarten. Think we should send him home?'

I was surprised by Rose's concern, then I remembered Abomi was the nephew of Ray Diamond aka Razzle, a well-known pawnbroker with a neck hold on parts of the city. A good customer and a dangerous man to be on the wrong side of.

'I'll take him down to the pub for a breather. I wanted a wee word with him anyway.'

Rose pushed her hair back from her face. 'Make sure it's a gentle word. Andy's not the sharpest banana in the bunch, but he's a good worker.' Her phone rang. She took it from her pocket, rolled her eyes and mouthed, 'Anderson.' Rose turned away, cupping the phone to her ear. 'No, I can't . . . No, not tonight, I'm busy . . . No, I told you . . .'

I left her to it and went to find the young porter.

The pub was quiet, the landlady absent. I bought Abomi a Coke and listened while he told me his granny had had second sight and that he suspected he might be gifted too.

'There's something wrong with that house. I don't like it.'

I masked my impatience with a smile and told him a few ghost stories of my own: the colony of squirrels that had sounded like dancers in an attic; the nightdress dangling from the tester of a four-poster bed that had looked like a spectre; the wet suit hanging to dry in a shower that, glimpsed through a smoked-glass window, had been mistaken for a suicide.

Abomi smiled at my stories, but his heart was not in it. 'My granny used to say some places draw bad things to them.'

I took a sip of alcohol-free lager. 'Ballantyne House is a couple of hundred years old. Sure, some sad things must have happened there – that's inevitable – but I bet lots of happy things happened too.'

The young porter looked unconvinced. 'Two guys died in that car crash . . .'

'Car crashes happen. Even more in the countryside than in the town. It's sad but–'

Abomi ignored me. 'And then I found the poor wee dug. Everyone knows things come in threes, Mr Rilke. I'm worried about what's going to happen next.'

'Things happen whether you worry about them or not, but I can tell you one thing for sure: ghosts don't exist, and places aren't cursed.'

Abomi drained the last of his Coke and sat up straight, gathering his dignity. 'My granny saw plenty of ghosts and she wasn't a liar.'

I knew better than to argue with anyone's dead granny. We walked together across the car park to the van, our feet crunching on the gravel. I pressed auto-unlock on the key and the van's lights flashed.

'You're a valuable member of the team, Andy, but we can't force you to work somewhere you're uncomfortable. Would you rather be kept off this one?'

Abomi looked startled. 'No way, boss. You need me here.'

I slapped him on the back. 'That's the spirit, son, but let me know if it gets too much.'

He straightened his shoulders. 'Don't worry about me. I won't let you down.'

The Scottish countryside is even whiter than its cities, but it should not have been a shock to see an Asian man on the road to Ballantyne House. He was running along the side of the verge, dressed in a singlet and cut-off leggings. For a moment I thought he was a jogger. Then I saw his lurching gait, the awkward way he held his shoulder as he ran. The sound of the van's engine startled the runner. He scrambled into the bushes as we drew close, but they were dense and thorny. He turned to look at us and I saw his face. He was younger than I had thought at first – gaunt and bruised, his expression stricken with terror.

Abomi murmured, 'I believe in God, the Father Almighty, Creator of Heaven and Earth, and in Jesus Christ, His only Son, our Lord, who was conceived by the Holy Spirit, born of the Virgin Mary . . .'

I stopped the van and got out, closing the door gently.

'Are you okay?' The man retreated against the bushes. Thorns scratched at his bare arms. I took a step backwards and held my hands in the air to show him I meant no harm. He said something I could not make out. I kept my voice low and soothing. 'Do you need help?' Now that I was closer, I could see that his arms and legs were bruised too. Some of the bruises were new and livid, others dark and discoloured.

I whispered, 'Who did this to you?' I heard the van door open and called, 'Stay in the van, Andy.'

Abomi ignored me and walked slowly to where I was standing. I heard his intake of breath as he registered the man's injuries and watched as he crossed the road. The Asian man was not short, but he was malnourished, and Abomi, with his height and bulk, towered over him like a bear. The young porter reached the opposite verge and squatted down. I could not see his face, but his voice was gentle.

'Hello, sir. My name's Andy and that gentleman over there is Mr Rilke. You're safe now. We'll look after you, but you need to come with us, or whoever did this to you might find you.'

The man was trembling. He said something in his own language. Abomi stood up slowly, unzipped his fleece and passed it to the man, who took it and hugged it to his chest.

Abomi repeated, 'You need to come with us, please, sir.' He edged closer and extended his hand. The man hesitated and then held out his own trembling hand. Abomi grasped it and embraced the man, who started to shake with sobs. Abomi carried him across the road and up into the cab of the van. He helped the man on with his fleece, fastened his seatbelt for him and kept an arm around him.

Abomi looked at me. 'I told you things come in threes, Rilke. This poor guy's our third thing.'

The nearest police station and hospital were both miles away. I drove back to Ballantyne House. The crew donated bits of their pack lunches, and the young man ate hungrily, still zipped up in Abomi's fleece, a blanket draped over his knees. The man's English was sparse. We learned his name was Fan. When I asked where he had come from and who had hurt him, he shook his head, eyes wide and frightened.

Rose and Lucy settled Fan in a bed in one of the untouched bedrooms. Abomi sat outside his door, half bodyguard, half nurse.

'Uncle Razzle knows some men that could sort out the folk that did this. Do you want me to give him a ring, boss?'

I did not want to spoil his illusions by telling him it was a toss-up whether his uncle's associates would be on Fan's side or on the side of his assailants.

'Not right now, son. Rose is on the case. I'll let you know if we need any help.'

Abomi nodded, satisfied he had been heard. 'No worries, Mr Rilke.'

Rose called Anderson from the kitchen. I leaned against the table, listening as she set out the situation.

'Fan needs to go to hospital, Anders, not to some godforsaken detention centre. And you'll need a translator if you're going to have any chance of finding out who did this to him.' She smiled, putting all her warmth and a dollop of sex appeal into her voice. 'I know I should have called 101, but that would put him straight into the system and on a fast track to Dungavel. This way, I know you'll have an eye out for him.' Anderson said something and Rose replied, 'What's the point in having friends in high places if you never ask for a favour? It'll be one I owe you and you know I always pay up.' She laughed at something he said, then added, 'I don't know what nationality the poor guy is. Definitely Asian but I don't think he's Chinese or Japanese. If he was a bit of porcelain, I'd be able to pin it down, but I'm not so hot on real, live men.' It was an invitation to be suggestive. Judging from Rose's laugh, Anderson took her up on it. 'Good. I'll see you soon? Watch the bend before the house — it's a bad one.' Anderson may have told her that he loved her because Rose smiled and said, 'You too,' before she hung up.

She turned to me. 'He'll be here in a couple of hours. Poor Fan's probably going to end up in detention whatever we do, but at least this way Anders can look out for him.'

I stood up. 'Someone's given him a bad time. Maybe he'll get asylum.'

Rose made a face that said she doubted it. 'Maybe. Who knows?' She smoothed her hair away from her face. 'Tell the crew not to breathe a word to anyone. He was in no condition to run far. Wherever he was being held, it was nearby, and whoever held him gave the poor guy a serious going-over. I don't want anyone knowing where he is or who helped him.'

Twelve

IT WAS A STRUGGLE to get back to the city for eight o'clock and my appointment with Les's associate. The atmosphere in the van was grim. Abomi had been reluctant to hand Fan over to Anderson's keeping and Frank was his usual morose self. My phone rang just as I accelerated the van down a slip road and onto the M8. There was no prospect of going hands-free while Frank and Abomi were in the cab. I lifted it to my ear, hoping no CCTV cameras would capture the transgression, and promised an anonymous voice I would be there in fifteen minutes. I hung up, phoned Sands and told him not to answer the door to anyone but me.

Frank gave me a suspicious look but kept his own counsel.

Abomi's expression was hopeful. 'Was it about Fan?'

'No, something else.'

I got out at the end of Sands' street, tossed Frank the van keys and told him to drop off Abomi.

Families were congregated around tables in the Chinese restaurants at the end of West Princes Street: children absorbed in their tablets, grown-ups eating and chatting. I felt outside myself, a dark shape slipping by brightly lit windows. I thought about Fan, the fear etched into his face, like the symptom of a long-term condition. We had done the right thing, but the situation made me uneasy. Someone would be looking for him and, as Rose had already said, wherever Fan had come from was a sick man's run from Ballantyne House.

Sands refused to leave the flat. We were in the hallway arguing in low whispers when someone rapped at the door. I hissed at Sands to bugger off. He told me to keep my wig on and slipped into his own room, closing the door behind him. I waited for the snib to click home as Sands locked himself in.

The man on the doorstep would not stand out in a crowd. He wore a dark suit beneath a black Crombie. He did not tell me his name and we did not shake hands. I led him through to Jojo's room and turned on the overhead light. Jojo had economised with a forty-watt bulb. The space was murky, cast in shadows.

The man's eyes flicked around the room, taking in the mess. 'What did he die of?'

'Jojo was found in the street after a party. I assumed it was some kind of OD, but it was a cold night. It could have been hypothermia, heart failure . . . something else.'

'No police interest?'

'They seem to think dropping dead in the street is par for the course.'

'Old guy like that, out of shape and partying like its 1999?

Risky behaviour.' The man reached into his pocket, took out a pair of latex gloves and pulled them on. His eyes met mine. 'Can't be too careful.'

Once upon a time I would have thought his caution extreme, but I had met a few people who had not been able to shake off the anxiety of Covid, hand washers and mask wearers, careful of their personal space.

Sands and I had separated the boxes containing the bottles from the rest of Jojo's mess. The man looked inside them and then walked to the window, pulled off his gloves and took out his mobile phone. Streetlights glowed beyond the drawn curtains, throwing soft shadows onto his face. He was street-handsome: thin and hard-featured, economical with his movements in a way that suggested pent-up energy. Whoever he was calling picked up straight away. The man rocked slightly on the balls of his feet.

'We're ready for you. Message me when you get here. Top floor. Don't worry about the door to the close. There's no lock.'

He killed the call. My heart started to beat louder in my chest. Maybe the man heard it. He caught my eye and winked, his expression card sharp straight.

'A couple of lads are going to come up and get this out of your hair.' He put his phone away. 'So how did you end up with these? Jojo snuffed it and . . .?'

'I knew Jojo through work. The police asked me to identify his body and then somehow it fell to me to try and organise his funeral.'

'Big responsibility for a work colleague. You're an auctioneer, right? Bowery Auctions?'

Privacy is a dwindling currency, but it did not feel good to be told that he knew who I was and where to find me.

'Jojo was a client for over twenty years. I thought he deserved a dignified send-off.'

'High standard of aftercare.'

I shrugged. 'No one else was going to do it. I thought there might be enough in his personal effects to pay for something simple.'

The man gave one of the boxes of bric-a-brac a gentle kick. 'I get it. You thought there might be a valuable or two lying around and there was no point in letting them go to waste.'

I felt my colour rise. 'Jojo was a client.'

The man took a bottle of hand gel from his pocket, squeezed some onto his palms and rubbed his hands together. A sharp smell of alcohol and peppermint perfumed the room. 'You're not married, are you? No kids, no pets, no significant other.'

'What's that got to do with anything?'

'Nothing much. Friendships are more important when you're single. You're good pals with your boss. What's her name again?' He closed his eyes as if trying to remember. 'Rose Bowery. Good-looking woman.'

I was taller than him, but I knew better than to meet his am-dram threats with a punch to the guts. 'All I want is to unite this stuff with its rightful owner, so I can forget all about it.'

'Good attitude. You weren't tempted to dip into it? Take a few bottles for yourself as a bit of a reward?'

The bottle Jojo had gifted the two Bobbys was still in my pocket.

I shook my head. 'Not my scene, but I did wonder if there might be a finder's fee – not for myself, just enough to put Jojo in the ground.'

The man's phone chimed with an incoming message. He stabbed out a brief reply. 'What is it with burying Jojo? Was he religious or something?'

It was the same question I had asked Sands. I did not have a good answer. 'It seems like the right thing to do.'

To my surprise, the man nodded. 'I get you. The Golden Rule. No one wants to be left dead in a ditch. Let me see what I can do.' He stabbed at his phone again, then paused and met my eyes. A brief, hard stare. 'A bit of privacy would help.'

I stepped into the lobby just as a knock sounded at the front door. I opened it, and two teenagers, around fourteen years old, walked into the flat. They cast nervous looks at me, not quite meeting my eyes.

A wave of shame washed over me. I nodded towards Jojo's room. 'In there.'

They muttered, 'Thanks, mister,' and went through.

The overhead light in the hallway was dead. I loitered there in the dark, checking my phone in an attempt not to look like a spare prick. I texted Anderson: *Any news on Fan?* I did not expect a reply, but it was a night of surprises. My phone pinged.

PHAN VIETNAMESE SCARED KEEPING SCHTUM. CAN'T HELP HIM IF HE WON'T HELP HIMSELF & TALK TO US. IN Q.LIZ FOR NOW. NEXT STEP DNGVL POOR WEE FUCK. WE'LL KEEP WORKING ON IT.

I had seen Phan's terror for myself and knew it would take gentle coaxing and trust if he were to have any chance of telling his story. I was not sure that Anderson, a man who only texted in capitals, was suited to the job.

The boys filed past, each of them carrying a box of Jojo's sexual energy. They were narrow-shouldered and skinny, but

I wanted as little as possible to do with the deal and did not offer to help. It took the boys three journeys. As they left their spokesman said, 'He wants you in there.'

The man was standing in the space previously taken up by the boxes.

'It's sorted. Jojo will be cremated the day after tomorrow at Maryhill Crematorium. You can do what you like with the ashes.'

'That's fast.'

He shrugged. 'Not like you've got a big guest list to sort out.'

'Will you be attending?'

His top lip peeled back in a sneer. 'You asking me on a date?'

I was not sure if it was an invitation to sex or a beating. I said, 'A funeral isn't much of a date.'

The man took a step towards me. 'No, but I didn't reckon you for a dinner-dance kind of guy.'

'I can dance.'

He held my gaze. 'I bet you can.' The moment passed. The man cast his eyes around the room. 'The way some people live. No wonder Jojo checked out early.'

It was not poor hygiene that had killed Jojo, but I nodded. 'Cheers for arranging the funeral.'

'It's one you owe me.'

'I've never owed anyone a funeral before.'

His expression darkened. 'Leslie said you were a smartarse.'

'Leslie says more than his prayers.'

'Just remember you owe me.'

It was the usual gangster cryptic. I saw him to the door then turned off the light in Jojo's room and opened the curtains. The man crossed the street and walked swiftly in the direction of St George's Road. He looked insignificant. A middle-aged office worker, heading home through the dark.

Sands joined me at the window just as the man stepped round the corner and out of sight. 'Is it all okay?'

I answered without looking at him. 'It's all okay.'

'What did they pay?'

'A funeral. Time to get yourself a black tie. Jojo's going to be cremated the day after tomorrow.'

Sands said, 'I'm going to miss him.'

'Jojo made a mess of his life. Look on this as a cautionary tale. Put the old soak in the ground and forget about him.'

'What about you?'

'Maybe I'm a cautionary tale too.' I fastened my coat, ready to leave. 'Be careful of the company you keep.'

It was more hypocritical bullshit. It was a waste of time telling young men to be careful and I had never cared too much for caution anyway.

I loitered in the doorway of Sands' building, scrolling through Grindr. A nearby man connected. We briefly messaged back and forth. His banter was standard, his spelling good. He messaged me an address somewhere in Hyndland and I summoned an Uber.

The address turned out to be a large villa that had been converted into apartments. He had propped the main entrance door ajar as he had promised to. I slipped into a hallway lit by a crystal chandelier, climbed the stairs to the second floor and rang his doorbell.

The man who answered was freshly shaved and showered. His dark curls were cut short, his white vest emphasised smooth olive skin and well toned muscles. He gave me a long look, up and down. A scent of basil and sandalwood reached into the hallway.

'No, I don't think so.' He shook his head as he closed the door in my face.

I stood there for a moment, breathing in and out, regaining my composure, then loped down the stairs and back into the night. The door to my childhood swung ajar, like the door to the villa I had just left. I focused on the rain hitting my face. A car slowed and someone shouted, 'Poof'. I ran towards them, ready to stave their car door in, but they sped on. I wondered how they knew and why I could not just leave things alone. My phone buzzed in my pocket, another alert. I ignored it and kept on walking.

Thirteen

ROSE HAD JUST FINISHED the team briefing when the cousins arrived unannounced in the kitchen of Ballantyne House. The room was overcrowded, and the team were forced to file past the two men as they departed for their various duties. John Forrest gave them a thin smile that switched on and quickly off again, like a wrecker's light. He waited until there was only the four of us left and then turned to Rose.

'Sorry if we're interrupting. You mentioned you had some forms for us to sign, and I thought it was time you met my cousin Alec.'

The pub landlady's description of Alec Forrest had conjured an image of someone dangerous and Byronic. The man John Forrest introduced as his cousin was scruffily bearded, half a stone overweight, and dressed like a backwoods prepper in rumpled jeans, scuffed work boots and an oversized brown hoodie. He did not bother to smile. 'Any thoughts on how much we're going to rake in?'

John made a face. 'You can always trust Alec to get straight to the point.'

Alec turned his drowsy gaze on his cousin. He had the same public-school Scottish accent, diluted by a touch of Glaswegian. 'Nothing wrong with getting to the point, Johnny.'

Rose caught my eye and glanced away. 'We've not completed our valuations, but I can take you through the running total so far if you'd like.'

A flicker of frustration crossed Alec's face. 'Sure. I'd like to go through some of the practicalities while we're about it. How long it's going to take for payment to hit my mum's bank account and so forth.'

John put an arm around his cousin and squeezed. 'We want to get her settled as soon as possible.'

He made his aunt sound like an account waiting to be squared.

I left Rose to look after the Forrests and got to work examining a 60-piece table service in the dining room. My phone rang just as I had discovered a hairline crack in a serving platter that reduced its estimate price by thirty per cent.

Inspector Anderson was in a large space filled with echoes. 'Tell Rose your friend Phan's being kept in hospital another night.'

'Why can't you tell her?'

'She isn't answering her phone.'

'How's he doing?'

'They're keeping him in so I'm guessing not that well. He's certainly not telling us anything.'

'Maybe he's frightened.'

Anderson's voice took on a sarcastic edge. 'You don't say.'

I went to the window and stared out at the overgrown garden beyond. 'Don't take this the wrong way, Anders, but you're maybe not the right person to coax out the guy's story. Like you say, he's frightened.'

'For fuck's sake, Rilke. I'm not a bloody psycho. I do know how to talk to folk. Anyway, I'm not the only officer in Police Scotland. We've got a unit for trafficking cases. I'm just taking a special interest so I can keep Rose informed.'

'So you think he was trafficked?'

'Wee Vietnamese guy who can't speak English running along a main road in his scanties in the middle of winter? I'd say it's pretty bloody obvious, wouldn't you?'

'I don't like to jump to conclusions.'

Anderson sighed. 'Neither do we, but he shows all the signs. My colleagues strongly suspect he's been enslaved somewhere near to where you found him.'

Frank stepped into the back courtyard. He lit up a cigarette and leaned against the wall, smoking, unaware of my gaze on him. I asked Anderson, 'Are you going to start door-to-door questioning or anything?'

'Why? You got a suggestion for particular doors we should be rapping on?'

'No. It's just we've got this sale happening soon.'

'And you don't want anything interfering with the wheels of commerce. Christ, scratch an antique dealer and you find a hard-arsed capitalist. You're worse than that Branson cunt.'

'I only asked if you were going to do anything that might be detrimental to the atmosphere of genteel country living we're trying to set up here.'

'Course we will. You should have left him by the side of the road if you didn't want us to investigate.'

I said, 'I didn't mean that.' But I half did. However respectable they are, antique shops and auction houses carry a stigma. The nine-to-five mob are eager to accuse us of cheating little old ladies or resetting stolen goods. Even if it had nothing to do with us, a police presence might put the punters off.

Anderson sounded weary. 'Just make sure you tell Rose what I told you. And tell her to call me back.'

I said, 'I will.' But Anderson had hung up.

I was re-examining the crack in the serving platter when the door to the dining room opened and Abomi stuck his head round the door. I was about to tell him about Phan but the expression on his face stopped me. 'What shitfuckery's happening now?'

Abomi edged into the room. 'There's a woman here wants to speak to you, boss.'

'What about?'

'I don't know.' He lowered his voice. 'She's a bit stressed.'

Abomi looked as if the stress was getting to him too. If he had possessed a cap, he would have been wringing it between his hands.

'For fuck's sake.' I placed the serving platter back on the table. 'Okay, send her in.'

'She won't come into the house. Says she's got a problem with Mr Forrest. Says she won't cross his doorstep.'

'Which one?'

Abomi looked confused.

I said, 'There are two Mr Forrests. Which one does she have a problem with?'

'I don't know.'

'Either way, it's none of our business. If she's got a problem with the Forrests she can discuss it with them.'

'Will you speak to her, please, boss? She won't take it from me.'

'Find Frank and get him to tell her.'

'Frank's busy.'

'I'm not exactly sitting on my hands.'

'Please, boss.'

I tried again. 'The last time I saw Frank he was out the back, having a smoke.' The young porter remained, stubborn, in the doorway. I should have sent him packing, but I remembered the panic attack he had had the day before and the way he had crouched down before Phan and offered him his fleece while I stood uncertain at the side of the road. I hauled on my jacket and went to the door.

It seemed that these days no one was how I imagined them. I had visualised an older matron, red-faced and strident. The woman waiting by the kitchen door was in her early thirties, slim with blonde highlights and an anxious expression. She smiled nervously, and I wondered why Abomi could not have dealt with her.

'Hello.' I held out my hand. 'I'm Mr Rilke, head auctioneer at Bowery Auctions. What can I do for you?'

The woman ignored my hand. 'It's not right what you're doing, breaking up Ballantyne House. It belongs to Mrs Forrest. The boys have no business selling her home from under her.'

I cursed my own stupidity in going to the door. 'John Forrest has power of attorney, and from what he's told me he has his aunt's best interests in mind—'

The woman interrupted. 'Have you seen her?'

I had been about to close the door, but the question was unexpected, and I stumbled over my words. 'She's a very frail old lady. There's no reason why we would see her.'

'No one from round here's seen Mrs Forrest for six months.'

I realised why Abomi had been reluctant to confront the

woman. There was metal beneath her slight exterior. 'If you're worried, I suggest you take it up with her son and nephew. Failing that, go to the police.'

A window opened in one of the rooms above. I looked up and saw Hannah and Lucy watching the show. I flapped a hand in their direction. The girls retreated inside and closed the window.

The woman looked at me. 'The Forrest boys were always able to twist Mrs Forrest around their little fingers. She'd tell the police she was fine if John and Alec told her to. Anyone who knows her knows she wouldn't want this place sold. Mrs Forrest loves the old house. It's the only home she's known.'

I started to close the door. 'Whatever dispute you have with Mr Forrest has nothing to do with us.'

The woman caught me by the arm. 'The Forrest boys are stealing from her. There was nothing wrong with Mrs Forrest's mind when I looked after her. She was sharp as a tack until John took over.'

'If you believe something criminal is going on, you should go to the police.'

She put her face close to mine. 'I told you, the police won't listen to me. But the truth will come out. When it does, I'll make sure everyone knows I warned you. You'll end up in court beside that pair of thieves.'

I stepped into the courtyard. 'These are serious accusations. We're a well-established, respectable firm. We take our business seriously.'

The woman paused, eyes gleaming. 'Are you threatening me?'

'I'm making you a promise. If you do anything to compromise this sale, it'll be me who calls the police and, rest assured, they will pay attention.'

'Everyone round here knows the Forrest boys are bad news. Always were, always will–'

'Hey!'

We both turned in the direction of the shout. John was striding towards us, his cousin following close behind. He crossed the courtyard quicker than I would have thought him capable and caught the woman by the arm.

'I've told you before, Rilla. You're not welcome here. Now sling your hook.'

Rose turned the corner of the building and hurried towards us. 'What on earth . . .'

John's face was heart-attack purple. 'This article sponged off my aunt for years, and now she's got the nerve to spread vile rumours.'

Alec grabbed hold of his cousin. 'Careful, John. She'll have you up for assault.' He turned to Rilla. His voice was calm, but I detected a thrum of nervous tension that made me think that if he were to let go, things might get out of hand. 'Mum isn't the woman she was. We're selling up so we can get her the help she needs. It'd be best for you if you accepted that.'

Rilla rubbed her arm where John had grabbed her. She looked at Alec. 'I took good care of your mum and you know it. I'd still be taking care of her now if you'd let me.'

John looked ready to explode. 'You took good care of her money too, didn't you? You abused my aunt's trust and made a fool out of Alec. If you're not off this property in thirty seconds, I'll change my mind and set the law on you. Auntie Pat won't stop me this time.'

Alec took out an e-cigarette. 'Leave her alone, Johnny. We've more important things to worry about.' He walked away towards the overgrown lawn, trailing clouds of apple-scented vapour.

Rilla turned to Rose. 'Don't be fooled by their posh accents. They're thugs. Thieves stealing from an old woman who can't protect herself.'

Rose was dressed like a sexy secretary today: tight pencil skirt, white blouse with pussy-bow tie, tortoiseshell spectacles and hair in a tight bun. She looked sternly from Rilla to John and back. 'I've just gone over the paperwork with Mr Forrest. As far as we are concerned, everything is in order.'

She turned her back on the woman and entered the house. I followed her.

Rilla shouted, 'Mrs Forrest would never sell her home . . .'

I could hear John blustering on about calling the police as I tailed Rose to the kitchen, shut the door on the noise of their argument and leant my back against it, so no one could surprise us.

Rose put her hands on her hips and turned on me. 'Fuck, shit and piss. Why did you let that woman go off on one like that?'

'I couldn't stop her.'

'Then do what I just did – walk away. Don't engage with her. Jesus fuck. Why isn't anything ever straightforward?'

'You heard him. She's a disgruntled ex-employee with an axe to grind. The legal stuff's in order. We've nothing to worry about.'

'Except we've just been told straight that she thinks an old lady is being cheated.' There was a cutlery drawer on the side of the kitchen table. Rose opened and slammed it shut. 'This sale was meant to put us right.'

I touched her arm. 'It will. Don't get this out of proportion.'

Rose looked up at me. There were fine lines around her eyes that had not been there when we first met, twenty-odd years ago. 'I'm worried that we're so desperate to have a good sale we've missed something. Does it smell bad to you?'

'Not as bad as poor Schumann.'

Rose pressed her fingers against her temples. 'Jesus. I'd forgotten about the dog. I was thinking about that poor Vietnamese man.'

'Phan? Anderson phoned to tell you he's still in hospital. He's hanging on in there, thanks to Abomi.' I pushed down a feeling of unease. 'Whatever happened to him, it's nothing to do with Ballantyne House.'

A tell-tale worry line creased Rose's forehead. 'Of course not. Christ, if I thought that, I'd forget the sale and phone Anderson. It's just . . .'

'Just what?'

'Don't they strike you as odd? John and his scruffball cousin.'

'No odder than a lot of the folk we deal with.'

'I just spent thirty minutes in the dining room with them, going over the paperwork for the sale. It looks in order but . . .'

'But what?'

'I don't know. Nothing I could put my finger on . . . just a feeling. They both seem nervous about something.'

'Selling the ancestral pile's a big deal.'

'But what if Rilla's telling the truth and they are robbing Mrs Forrest?'

Rose's instincts could be sound, but they could also misfire. I said, 'Public schoolboys are awkward around women. The sale's three days away. We get through it, then we're gone.'

Rose shook her head. 'I don't like playing with half a deck. It makes me edgy.'

I knew what she wanted me to do.

'We're both taking a couple of hours off tomorrow morning for Jojo's funeral. I don't have time to sniff around asking questions. Anyway, do you really want to know?'

Rose leaned against one of the kitchen units. She slipped off her shoe, massaged the arch of her foot and then slid it back on. 'Thanks to you, half the squad probably heard that women's accusations. We don't have the luxury of ignorance.'

'We don't have the luxury of time either.'

Rose looked up at me from beneath her eyelashes. 'I wouldn't ask if I didn't think it was important.'

I shook my head. 'Impersonating Princess Diana isn't going to persuade me.'

Rose gave me a punch on the arm. 'I was going for Betty Boop.' She turned serious. 'Come on, Rilke. We're putting money into this sale. I need to know if something dodgy's going on. We can't afford to screw up here.'

I let out a sigh. 'Jesus Christ. Okay, I'll take a lunchbreak, see if I can find anything out.'

Rose gave me one of her half-wattage smiles. It was still bright enough to dazzle.

'Thanks. I'll ask Anderson if the Forrests are on his radar. I seem to be asking for a lot of favours from him at the moment.'

'Be careful. He might call them in and ask you to marry him.'

Rose smiled again, her lips pillarbox red. 'Anders isn't the masochist he makes himself out to be. He wasn't made for real suffering.'

Fourteen

THE BLACK BULL was empty. The previous day's paper sat on the bar, its headline announcing yet another rough sleeper found dead on a street in Glasgow's city centre. Photographs of the recent street dead filled the centrefold. I scanned them as I waited for someone to appear.

The dead were all men. The photographs showed them in happier times, before their lives had shot the tracks. Blinking into the sun, wearing a football strip; a haircut that dated the shutter-click to a decade before; cropped from a wedding portrait, a carnation peeping from their buttonhole; toasting the photographer with a raised beer; standing proudly next to a motorbike, helmet cradled beneath an arm; a graduation shot, triumphant scroll and academic gown . . . It crossed my mind that the faces in the photographs probably bore little resemblance to how the men looked at the time of their deaths. Then I spotted Jojo's smile, near the centre of the page.

The photo showed Jojo somewhere in his early thirties, standing in a cosy living room that was busy with bric-a-brac. Someone else had been cropped from the shot, a man whose arm was slung across Jojo's shoulder. Jojo was laughing, his head thrown back in a way I remembered. His eyes were clear, his skin taut. There was none of the febrile craziness that had characterised him in later years. The text below the photograph read: *Joseph Nugent 1963–2022, artist and antique dealer.*

The journalist had got it wrong. Jojo was on the long spiral downwards, but he had been one last step from homelessness. The landlady bustled through from the back of the bar, drying her hands on a cloth. Her hair was bright against the dark wood of the pub interior, her pink blouse and pale blue jeans cheerful in the gloom.

'You back, are you?'

'Couldn't stay away.'

I ordered a bowl of split pea soup, a pint of IPA, and whatever she wanted for herself. The landlady slid my pint across the counter then free-poured herself a glass of red wine.

'How are things up at the big house?'

I took the head off my pint. 'Getting there.'

She ladled soup into a bowl from the crockpot on the counter and placed it in front of me. 'Driven you to drink, has it?'

'It may come to that.'

I started on my soup. Information and alcohol were the landlady's currency. She would fill any silence I left. The fridges behind the counter hummed. A car passed by on the road outside. The landlady stroked the stem of her glass, delaying gratification, and then tipped the wine to her lips. Her lipstick was the same bright pink as her blouse. It left a mark on the rim of the glass, X-ray lips.

'Quite a buzz going around about your sale. There's folks who haven't seen the inside of Ballantyne House for a long time – some of the younger ones, never.' I explained the part about having to purchase a catalogue to gain entry. She reacted as if I had suggested letting the pub go dry. 'Ten pounds?'

I gave her my what-a-world smile. 'I don't make the rules.'

'Ten pounds just to walk through the door of Ballantyne House? They can stick it.' She took half an inch off the level of her wine. 'Heard you had a bit of bother earlier.'

I stirred some pepper into my soup. Black particles disappeared into the yellow viscous liquid. 'Word gets around quickly.'

The landlady gestured to the empty bar. Her fingernails were decorated with tiny rhinestones. 'Social hub of the village.'

The altercation had been witnessed by our crew, the Forrest cousins and Rilla. The crew were too busy to pop down to the pub and the Forrests would want to keep the incident to themselves. Rilla had talked to someone.

I lifted my IPA to my mouth. It was good, hoppy and bitter. 'A disgruntled employee trying to make trouble.'

The landlady gave me a warning look. 'An ex-fiancée with good reason for being pissed off.'

'Alec Forrest and Rilla were engaged?'

'She was hardly going to marry old John, was she? It didn't last long. She came to her senses.'

One by one, my burdens were lifting. Jojo's funeral was in hand, his stash of drugs relocated. Now I could tell Rose that Rilla had a motive for slandering the Forrests. I finished my soup and tilted my pint to my lips, ready to down it and get back to work.

The landlady tapped her index finger against the wine glass in a way that made me suspect she was a smoker. 'Rilla never liked the way John treated his auntie.'

I bit back a curse and set my pint on the counter. 'He seems devoted to her now. Both of them do.'

The landlady started to polish a row of wine glasses. 'Devoted to her money. Poor Mrs Forrest financed scheme after scheme for those boys. Their land was a working farm back in the day, but farming's hard work.' She abandoned a half-polished glass on the counter and counted the Forrests' failed projects on her fingers. 'They tried to make it into a bird reserve. Then it was artists' residencies. They got some hippie to build what they called hobbit pods – looked like oversized privies. The poor artists used to come down here to try and warm up.' She shook her head, remembering the mess the Forrests had made of the enterprise. 'Then it was woodland burials. People want a picturesque woodland, not an overgrown windbreak where lads drink carry-outs and take acid. Now they're into soft fruits. You'll have seen the polytunnels.'

'You couldn't miss them. Must be all hands on deck come the harvest?'

'I told you last time, love. They don't hire anyone from around here. Not that they didn't try when Covid hit and they couldn't get foreign pickers. John went from house to house offering cash in hand. No one would open the door to him. Treat people bad in the good times and they'll let you sink when things go tits up.'

'I'm guessing there aren't too many local jobs about.'

She shrugged. 'There used to be the creameries. Anyone

who didn't work on a farm worked there. They closed thirty years ago and nothing took their place. The MOD had a base down here too. That went in 2000. I think that's when John had the idea for the bird sanctuary. The military requisitioned the land back in 1943 so the farm got first option to buy a few years ago. Mrs Forrest bought up the shooting range and the old base. I guess John thought birds would be attracted because the land had been left to its own devices. But as usual he hadn't done his homework.'

'The birds didn't fancy it?'

'Plenty of birds, but none rare enough for people to travel to see them. Shame, really.' The landlady looked out over the empty bar, the unoccupied seats and abandoned pool table. 'I've heard twitchers like a good drink.'

'You must miss the military.'

She raised her eyebrows and tipped her head saucily. 'What are you implying?'

I laughed. 'Soldiers like a drink too. The base must have been good for business.'

'Course it was. There's still a lot of love for the forces here. A lot of local lads join up, the ones that want more than a dole cheque and a baby mama. The boys that make a go of it mostly don't come back. Those that come home . . .' She shrugged her shoulders. 'They're like Alec, lost without someone to tell them what to do.'

'He was in the forces?'

'Highland Fusiliers. Wouldn't know it to look at him, would you?'

Alec had been scruffy and out of shape, but he had shown more restraint than his cousin. Perhaps some residual discipline lurked beneath the unkempt exterior.

'So who tells Alec what to do these days?'

She smiled. 'It used to be his mum. If you ask me, that's why Alec joined up. She had that boy under her thumb. They rubbed along all right when he came out the army, but Rilla reckons he changed when John moved back. It's Johnny who calls the shots these days. He and Rilla never got on. She reckons it was John that split her and Alec up. I reckon she had a lucky escape.'

I remembered what John had said about Rilla stealing from his aunt but kept my own counsel. 'John told me he came back to Ballantyne after he got divorced. He seems keen to get away again.'

'You're a nosy one, aren't you?'

'I like to know who I'm dealing with.'

The landlady weighed me with her eyes. I thought I had lost her, but the bar was as dead as a robbed grave and her appetite for gossip won. 'The army cured Alec's itchy feet. He barely leaves the farm. John's a different matter. You wouldn't guess it to see him now in his tweed suits and checked shirts, but Johnny Forrest was the last of the hippies. A long-haired, airy-fairy pot smoker.' She laughed. 'More airy than fairy. He liked the girls right enough. After they closed the artists' residencies he went on the hippie trail, travelled around India and God knows where. No one saw him for years, then suddenly, three years ago, he was back, divorced from a wife no one's ever seen and playing the laird. Johnny leads and the other one follows.'

'Sounds like the opposite of what you'd expect.'

'How do you mean?'

'The hippie leads and the soldier follows?'

She snorted. 'My mum said, never trust a hippie. They're all peace and love and slit-your-throat. Look at the Manson murders. Don't let the absent-minded act fool you. Johnny's sharp as a butcher's blade. He can be very persuasive when he wants to be.'

She winked, and I got the impression he had successfully tried his persuasion on her.

'So, John and Alec sponged off Mrs Forrest. It happens in the best of families. But there's no suggestion they stole from her. They seem to be doing the best they can for her now.'

The landlady shrugged. 'My sister doesn't seem to think so.' I must have looked puzzled. She laughed. 'Rilla. You've met.'

The resemblance came into focus. It was a shared style rather than form or features: the same blonde highlights and pastel wardrobe as Rilla, but on a more buxom frame.

'In that case, I'm guessing you have mixed feelings about the Forrests?'

The landlady finished her wine. 'Because my sister was engaged to one of them? Rilla's a good-looking woman. If I barred every man she'd been with, I'd have an empty pub.' She laughed. 'Not that I'm saying my sister's a slut.'

It was camp and bitchy, and I laughed too. 'Life's short. There's worse crimes than falling in love easily.'

'Rilla's got a big heart. She worries about the old lady. The Forrest boys would save themselves a bit of bother if they let Rilla visit. It'd put her mind at rest.'

I thought again about John's accusation that Rilla had stolen from her employer. 'According to John, his aunt's too confused for visitors.'

The landlady guessed what I was thinking. Her face hardened. 'My sister's not a thief. She worked way beyond the hours she was paid for. Mrs Forrest appreciated it. She used to give Rilla things. Nice things. She wasn't confused then. They were hers to give and she took pleasure in giving them to Rilla. Alec wasn't bothered, but when John found out he lost the plot. If you ask me, it was an excuse. Sacking Rilla was a convenient way to get rid of her without paying what she was due.'

The good feeling of a moment before had vanished. A van drew into the car park and a couple of men in jeans and waxed jackets got out.

'Looks like it's cocktail hour.'

The landlady made a face. 'Two lagers and a packet of dry roasted.' She took a couple of pint glasses from behind the bar and set them on the counter. 'You didn't just pop in for a pint and a bowl of soup. Why don't you tell me what you want?'

Rose would eviscerate me if she knew I had spilled our worries to the village gossip, but sometimes the only way to get information is to share some of your own.

'I want to be certain this sale is on the level.'

'A bit late in the day for that.'

I shrugged. 'There was no reason to think it wasn't straight-forward, until your sister turned up.'

'You want me to tell you she's talking crap.'

'Not exactly how I would put it . . .'

'. . . but yes?'

The new customers arrived at the bar and ordered their round. The landlady served them, and they settled at a table by the window with their drinks. She looked at me, waiting for an answer to her question.

I smiled. 'It'd be a weight off my mind.'

'I bet, but there's only one way you'll find out.'

'How?'

'By looking in on the old lady yourself. Rilla's angry with Alec. She hates John. Maybe she got carried away. Maybe not. You won't know until you check it out, and even then you might not know for sure. Abusers are crafty. They hide in plain sight.' Something about her tone made me look at my feet. I looked up and she met my eyes and nodded. 'I know what I'm talking about. Everyone thought he was a lovely man — including my sister, by the way. Maybe that's another reason Rilla won't let this drop. She bought all those excuses about cupboard doors and missed steps. It's good to be suspicious, love. You can't believe everything people tell you.'

Fifteen

ROSE AND DR BARSTOW were cooing over a painting of a young Victorian woman when I got back to Ballantyne House. Dr Barstow's thinning hair was standing on end, Van de Graaff generator-style, a sign that he had been running his hands through it with excitement.

'The painter was depicting a Shakespearean theme. My guess would be Juliet dreaming about Romeo. Look at the way her hand is resting on the book on the table in front of her . . .'

He was about to launch into a lecture when Rose caught sight of me and excused herself. Abomi was having his tea break in the kitchen. A look from Rose sent him back to work. She closed the door behind him. 'Well?'

I had decided to tell Rose there was nothing to worry about, but lying is a skill best practised on people who do not know you, guts and all. She saw my face and said, 'Oh shit.'

There was a teapot on the table. I touched its side, felt it was still warm and poured myself a cup of tarry PG Tips. There was no milk, so I drank it straight, tannin-bitter and furry against my teeth.

'Don't worry. It's nothing conclusive.'

Hannah and Lucy came giggling into the kitchen, ready for their break. Rose snapped, 'We're busy in here,' and they scuttled off. She lowered her voice. 'Why don't we take a trip up to the farmhouse and pay John and Alec a visit?'

'Both of us?'

'Why not?'

'Because it'd be obvious we're checking up on them.'

'Not necessarily. We'll make an excuse.' Rose pulled a kirby grip from her hair, smoothed back a loose strand and secured it again. 'Anyway, they want this sale to go ahead as much as we do. I got John to pay up front for the press ads and catalogues. They're in too deep to pull out now.'

It was after seven in the evening, long past dark, when Rose drove us to the farmhouse in her recently acquired orange Saab Sonett. I saw the polytunnels shining ghostly in the gloom and thought I could make out the shapes of plants inside, tall and spindly like triffids waiting to pull up their roots and start killing.

I said, 'I wonder what they grow.'

'John told me. Soft fruit: strawberries, raspberries, tomatoes, that kind of stuff.'

I thought of what the landlady had said, about the difficulty the Forrests had sourcing pickers from overseas, and about Phan, running for his life, half-naked, along a country road. I wondered if I should alert Anderson to the gap in cheap labour at the Forrests' farm and their proximity to where we had found Phan. But one did not follow the other. The police had a unit dedicated to trafficking and the district was chock-a-block with other farms.

Rose slowed down. The farmhouse gates were closed. A chain was looped around the gatepost, an open padlock dangling from it. I got out of the car and opened the gate. Rose steered the Saab into the farmyard. Its headlights swept across mud indented with the comings and goings of other vehicles, then bent across the farmhouse walls. The building was less impressive than Ballantyne House, but in better shape. Its stone was solid and sure, probably cut centuries ago from a local quarry, and its windows looked secure.

Rose killed the engine and got out of the car, smoothing her skirt down like a well-trained graduate of the Lucie Clayton Charm Academy. She said, 'I'll be glad when this job's over.'

'You and me both.'

I expected the sound of the Saab's engine to have alerted the cousins to our approach. But apart from the lights shining in the downstairs windows, and in one of the rooms above, there was no sign of life.

Rose rang the doorbell. A peal sounded inside the farmhouse. There was no response. She pressed the bell again. 'Maybe they've gone to the pub.'

'I doubt it. The landlady said John rarely drops by, Alec never.'

'John definitely said they're looking after his aunt here?'

'He made a point of it.'

Rose tried the door handle.

I hissed, 'Rose, for fuck's sake.'

The door was locked. Rose walked to the nearest lit window and peered inside. 'They can't have gone far.'

I followed her around the side of the house to the back door. The rear of the property looked out over the hill where the polytunnels were ranged on man-made terraces that sat like steps on the hillside. Ballantyne House shone below. The auction team were inside, making final preparations for the sale. I wished we were with them. Rose walked to the edge of the lawn, her high heels awkward on the damp grass, and looked out over the darkening view. The stars were beginning to prick the sky. She took a deep breath.

'The air's so clean. Can you imagine living somewhere like this? It could add years on to your life.'

I thought about Glasgow, the brutal scar of motorway that runs through the centre of the city, the petrol fumes and wind-blown litter tossed by rain. 'It'd kill me.'

'Me too.' Rose turned and retraced her steps. The farm-house had been modernised sometime in the late 1980s by the look of the French windows that had replaced the original door. Lamps were lit inside, illuminating a kitchen-cum-living room. Rose rapped on the glass then put her face to it and peered inside. 'No one home. You'd think someone would stick around to take care of the old lady.'

I knew what she was going to do. 'Rose . . .'

Rose turned the door handle. This time, the door opened. She gave me a mischievous look. 'It's true what they say after all – no one locks their doors in the countryside.'

I caught her arm. 'That's because they trust people not to break in.'

'Au contraire. It's because they don't want visitors standing outside in the pissing rain.'

'It's not raining.'

Rose shook free of me and stepped into the farmhouse. 'We're in Scotland. It's only a matter of time.'

I cursed and followed her. It was warm inside after the night-time chill of the hilltop. There was a smell of fried food, male sweat and stale air, as if the windows had not been opened for a long time. An unwashed frying pan sat on the cooker. Dirty dishes slumped beneath greasy water in the sink.

Rose whispered, 'Straight out of *Withnail*.'

A noise, the kind of snuffling sound I could imagine pigs making in their troughs, broke the silence. We froze, as if stillness might make us invisible. It sounded again. An exhalation. A loud and fruity, phlegm-rich snore. Rose hissed, 'Shhh,' although I had not said a word.

I followed the sound to a wingback armchair in a corner of the lounge. John Forrest was deep in sleep, his head thrown back, mouth open. Rose touched my arm and we edged away. She pointed at herself and then pointed upstairs.

I shook my head.

She pulled me close and whispered, 'If he wakes up, say I was caught short and went to use the toilet.'

I shook my head again. 'It's not worth it.'

Rose slipped off her shoes and started towards the door.

I caught her arm. 'Fuck it. You stay here. If he wakes up, turn on the charm.'

Rose squeezed my arm, and I knew that had been her plan all along.

The farmhouse stairs were original, each one housed with creaks and groans. I climbed them swiftly, light on my toes. The hall was decorated with faux Regency wallpaper, the stairs carpeted in floral sprigs that had been someone's idea of country-cottage chic. Four doors on the landing, like a riddle waiting for Bluebeard's wife. I crossed the floor and pushed open the furthest door. Froufrou furnishings that dated from several decades before. An unmade bed, clothes tossed carelessly on a chair. I recognised John's tweed jacket and closed the door softly. A black hoodie lying neatly on the bed in the next room identified it as Alec's. The third door led to a chilly bathroom, kitted out with a pink suite. I approached the final room on the balls of my feet. I could hear my heart in my chest, the floorboards creaking beneath my weight and the distant rumble of John's snores. I forced a smile, hoping not to frighten the old lady.

I do not know what I expected. An emaciated figure strapped to a hospital bed or a paper-thin woman bound by tubes and monitors? Blood on the ceiling? The room was empty, musty, as if no one had used it for a while. A tray of medicine bottles and prescription pills sat by the bed. I picked one up and checked the date on its label. It had been prescribed eighteen months before.

The wardrobe door was ajar. I pushed it wide and saw a rail hung with women's clothes. They were expensive. A mixture of tweeds and brightly coloured florals, the kind of things the Queen might wear beneath her coat. There was no sign that Mrs Forrest had been badly treated. But there was no sign of Mrs Forrest.

I closed the door behind me and slipped downstairs to the living room where Rose was waiting. I had barely caught my breath before Alec stepped through the French windows, a plastic bucket in one hand.

He looked from Rose to me and back. 'What are you doing here?'

Rose slipped a piece of paper from the pocket of her coat and went into full charm mode. 'Sorry to disturb you at home, Mr Forrest. There's a final piece of paperwork I'd like to file before tomorrow.'

Alec crossed the room and set the bucket on the floor of the kitchen area. He straightened up and I saw that he was battling to control his temper.

'Do you make a habit of walking uninvited into people's homes?'

Rose had faced off outraged gangsters, amorous bikers, fraudulent businessmen, conspiring politicos and furious relatives of the dead. She slid on a smile that was patience, steel and no apology. 'Perhaps I misunderstood the countryside code. The door was open. I took it as an invitation.'

Their voices should have woken John but he stayed slumped in his chair, immobile except for the rise and fall of his chest. His snores seemed to come from the well of his body. Long, deep inhalations that guttered into liquid rattles. I squatted level with his face. It was squashed against the wing of the chair, older in sleep; the skin was pale as faded linen, eyelids grape-dark. I resisted an impulse to check his pulse.

'Is he okay?'

Alec looked like he wanted to reach down my throat, pull out my guts and strangle me with them. 'My cousin has trouble sleeping. The doctor prescribes pills. Sometimes they knock him out.'

'I'd have a word with that doctor if I were you. He doesn't look so good.'

'He's fine, but if you need both of our signatures, you'll have to leave the forms here. There'll be no waking him tonight.'

Rose slipped the paper back into her pocket. 'It can wait until tomorrow.' She glanced around the room. 'This is a lovely space. I imagine it's a comfort for your aunt to be able to take in that view.'

If he had been awake, John might have riffed on country-side views and Auntie Pat's passion for them, but Alec was made of different stuff. He lifted the kettle to the sink, filled it with water and clicked it on. A stack of instant noodle packets sat on the countertop. He took one and emptied its contents into a pot sitting on top of the cooker.

'It's been a long day.'

It was our cue to go.

Rose said, 'Dried ramen aren't going to keep your strength up. I was going to order in some fish and chips for the crew. Why don't you pop down and join us? John, too, if he wakes up in time.'

The kettle came to the boil. Alec poured water over the noodles and lit the gas. 'Farmers don't knock off at dinner-time. I've a lot still to do.'

Rose fastened her coat. 'I'm forgetting you have your aunt to see to, as well. You have my respect. I looked after my dad in his final years. It wasn't easy.'

Old Joe Bowery had been killed instantly by a hit-and-run driver in Dublin, just after closing time, twenty-odd years ago. Witnesses said he had been dancing in the middle of the road outside the pub he had just left. Everyone agreed it was how he would have wanted to go.

Alec drained the water from the noodles. He lifted the pot by its handle and started to fork its contents into his mouth. He chewed with his mouth open, letting noodles drip into his beard, deliberately sloppy. 'Was there something else?'

It was intended as a fuck-you, but Rose did not look away. Alec gave me a hardman stare. 'You'd better get down the road if you want your fish and chips.' He made dinner sound like a weakness.

Rose bid Alec a cheery goodnight, which he answered with a grunt. I was glad to leave the farmhouse behind. Rose slid into the driver's seat of the Saab and slammed the door. I secured the gate behind us, then folded myself awkwardly into the passenger seat. We glided away from the farmyard, into the darkness of the road and the corkscrew of turns that led down to Ballantyne House.

Rose gripped the steering wheel. 'Don't keep me in suspense. How was the old lady? Did you talk to her? I wouldn't want to be relying on Alec and John for sustenance.'

'Mrs Forrest wasn't there. I got the feeling she hadn't been there for a while.'

Rose was silent for a moment, then she said, 'I suppose it fits with what that woman . . . what was her name . . .?'

'Rilla.'

'. . . It fits with what Rilla said. The Forrest cousins tried to make themselves sympathetic by pretending to be carers but it's a lot of trouble looking after old folk.'

'You would know, after all those years of nursing your aged dad.'

Rose made an exasperated face. 'I was just trying to establish a bit of empathy. A waste of time as it turns out. My guess is they weren't able to give the old lady the care she needed and did the right thing by settling her somewhere she'd be better looked after.'

The idea of Alec doing the right thing did not sit easily, but I could believe it of his cousin. I asked, 'Happy to go ahead with the sale?'

Rose glanced at me. Her earrings glinted in the faint light thrown by the dashboard. 'Fucking over the moon.'

'You do realise that just because we didn't find anything bad it doesn't mean—'

She interrupted me. 'Shut it, Rilke. I love you, but sometimes you push things too far.'

Rose bit her lip and drove on, shifting down a gear on the tight bends and turns. All we had found was an absence. We had both worked with enough collectors of elusive objects to know that absences did not mean there was nothing there. Sometimes you had to put feelers out, hunt in less obvious places to find what you were looking for.

I said, 'Is that it then?'

Rose's voice was brittle. 'Yes, that's it. We've done more than required. More than most people we know would do.'

I shut my eyes and let the throb of the car engine wash over me. I did not bother to remind Rose that these were hard times for our trade and most of the people we knew were after a quick buck. The knowledge was there in the silence between us, the set of her jaw, my closed eyes and the faint jerk in the Saab's engine that made me think the car had been an expensive mistake.

Sixteen

IT WAS ELEVEN O'CLOCK at night, post-fish and chips and heavy lifting, when Rose pulled into Argyle Street. She dropped me off at an empty bus stop and gave a grim smile. 'I could do without the funeral tomorrow morning. Jojo always was an inconsiderate bastard.'

I had managed to put it out of my mind. I wondered how far Sands would go with the formalities, whether he expected me to be a pallbearer. The thought of Jojo's weight on my shoulder was not a pleasant one.

I said, 'At least he got one last party in before he went. There's a chance he died happy.'

I'd kept Jojo's gift of GHB to myself, but had told Rose what kind of a party it was.

Rose's eye make-up was smudged. She had tied her hair back in a tight knot she called a Partick facelift. 'I've never been invited to an actual orgy. Were you not tempted?'

I made a face. 'Not my scene.'

'You never know until you try.'

'Some things you don't need to try.'

I hauled myself out of the Saab. Kelvingrove Museum was lit up like a palace in a child's book of fairy tales. I had been going there since I was a boy; I could walk the galleries blindfold. It had been the site of one of my first teenage pickups, a man who had seemed old at the time but was probably not yet out of his twenties. It had been quick and furtive, sordid and thrilling.

I had not told Rose the full truth about my reaction to Jojo's invitation. It was true that a G-fuelled orgy was not my scene. The prospect of a clamour of bodies, full-tilt out of control, the meatiness of too many men naked together, alarmed me. But I have always been drawn towards the brutal romance of brief encounters and sexual anonymity. Part of me had wanted to follow Jojo into his Uber and across town to whatever waited.

I turned into Kelvin Way and walked across the bridge beneath the statues dedicated to Peace and War. A car slowed beside me and drove on. The university shone gothic on the hill beyond – near and far away, the way the full moon sometimes is.

I turned off the road and slunk down a footpath beside the river. It had rained earlier, and the Kelvin was high. I could hear the water rushing down to join the Clyde. A man waited on a bench, a dark shape beneath the trees, the bright glow of a cigarette. I slowed my pace. He got to his feet. It was too dark to tell his age or what he looked like. A rush of fear and adrenaline fluttered in my chest, an urge to run away. An urge to walk towards the man, until I was close enough to touch him, close enough for him to touch me.

Sex and death are bound together, plaited like DNA. I did

not want a knife in the guts, the life-pulse of a final orgasm, but danger heightens desire. In that moment I was sure I was alive. I smelt his sweat, the smoke and alcohol on his breath. The stranger threw away his cigarette. The burning tip arced upwards, casting a quick galaxy of red ash, then fell into the grass. I remembered Jojo saying, 'These things will kill you,' and wondered again if he was right.

The man said, 'Quiet tonight. I was thinking about heading home.'

His voice was familiar. Glasgow is a small city. Too small for paths not to cross and crisscross. But I did not ask him if we had met before. He turned away and we walked together, down towards the river.

Seventeen

SANDS WAS STANDING outside the crematorium when Rose and I arrived. His funeral outfit was cobbled together: a pair of black jeans, dark bomber jacket with a white shirt and thin, black leather tie. I introduced him to Rose, who had embraced her inner Martini girl-cum-gangster's moll and was wearing a black Chanel-inspired suit, with a cinched-waist jacket and tight skirt. A pillbox hat equipped with a small veil topped the ensemble.

Sands said, 'I love your hat.'

Rose gave a sad smile. A stranger might have mistaken her for the dignified widow of the deceased. 'Jojo liked his glamour glam. You're looking good yourself. Very Gary Numan.'

Sands looked confused. 'Who?'

But Rose had spotted Anderson walking towards us from the car park and hurried off to greet him.

The crematorium was large and full of firepower, but it

could not shelter us from the snell wind sweeping across the Western Necropolis from Possil Marsh. I flipped up the collar of my coat and turned a shoulder to the wind.

'Gary Numan was a new wave singer, heavy on electronics and eyeliner.'

Sands did not answer. He was looking towards the crematorium's gates, where the hearse was due to appear.

Anderson kissed Rose on the lips and nodded at me. He was uneasy when the three of us were together, as if Rose's presence set the balance between us off-kilter.

I shook his hand. 'Any news on Phan?'

Anderson smelt of Paco Rabanne. His face was freshly shaved, his skin pink and vulnerable. 'Last I heard the cat still had his tongue.' Anderson gave Sands a look but did not bother to introduce himself. 'We're keeping an eye on him. Wouldn't be the first time some bastard's dragged a poor wee fucker out the hospital back to where they escaped from. All the same, your boy would make life easier for himself, and us, if he'd say where he was held and who hurt him.'

A black car appeared on the drive. Sands took a step forward, but it was a BMW, not the hearse. A trio of men emerged from it and walked towards the crematorium. I recognised the dark-haired man who had visited Jojo's flat and arranged for the drugs to be uplifted.

Anderson recognised him too. 'Aye, Aye.' His voice was low. 'How did Jojo know Jamie Mitchell?'

'Who's he?'

'A young man on the way up. The way a rollercoaster goes up before it comes crashing down.'

'Is that your prediction?'

'It's my fucking mission.'

If the sight of me talking to a police inspector, so soon

after our encounter, bothered him, Jamie Mitchell gave no sign. He nodded at both of us, as if we were professional acquaintances. Salesmen working for different firms, destined to be in competition for business, but no hard feelings.

Anderson said, 'So how do you know Lord Sugar's latest apprentice? Into antiques, is he?'

The arrival of the hearse saved me from having to reply. The funeral director ushered us inside. Sands slid into a seat midway down the hall. I sat beside him. The undertaker's men carried Jojo's coffin shoulder-high down the aisle and placed it gently on the small dais. They bowed to Jojo, or perhaps to Death – I had never been quite sure who was being honoured – and then backed away.

I glanced at Sands. I had wondered if he might be upset, but he was leaning forward in his seat like a boy at his first pantomime, enthralled.

The minister was a broad, red-faced man in a white dog collar and black surplice. He climbed into the pulpit, welcomed us with a warmth that could freeze a fizzing volcano and began his spiel.

'Man that is born of a woman is of few days, and full of trouble. He cometh forth like a flower, and he fleeth also as a shadow, and continueth not . . . '

Sands took a sketchpad and pencil from his pocket. His pencil strokes were quick and light, but he captured the austerity of the place, Rose's silly hat, the rash on Anderson's neck, the minister's corpulence.

'In the midst of life, we are in death . . .'

The crematorium door opened, letting in a blast of cold and damp that made me grateful we were not gathering around an open grave. I turned my head. Les had arrived. He was wearing a black suit that made me think of court appearances and sentence hearings. His companion was a heroin-skinny man with spiky peroxide hair who was sobbing. Fat tears were coursing down his hollow cheeks. Les slid into the pew beside me, his face like a clenched fist. His companion hiccupped as he slithered in beside him. Les punched him on the arm and hissed, 'Shut the fuck up, for fuck's sake. You're at a fucking funeral.'

The minister asked us to stand and join in the first hymn, 'The Old Rugged Cross'. A pre-recorded backing track juddered awake. We got to our feet but only Rose and the minister sang.

On a hill far away, stood an old rugged Cross,
An emblem of suffering and shame . . .

The minister's voice was flat, and Rose, who could usually be relied on to belt out a party turn, struggled to keep in tune. The hymn stuttered to a close with the vainglorious promise to '*cling to the old rugged Cross and exchange it some day for a crown*'. '*For a crown,*' the minister repeated, sonorous and off-key.

Les giggled, his friend started sobbing again and Sands' pencil scratched against the paper. The minister resumed his sermon on the inevitability of death and the need to keep on the right side of God.

Sands finished a sketch of Les and his skinny mate, and started to draw Jamie Mitchell. I touched his arm and shook my head. He gave me a quizzical look but got the message. Instead, the details of the crematorium started to take shape beneath his pencil. The wooden floors and arched windows. The austere pews, and stained glass depicting a sweeter death than Jojo's.

Thirty minutes later, we were outside, lighting up in the cold air. I felt the usual sense of relief at getting the death business over until the next time. Les and his friend walked on ahead, bickering. Rose and Anderson were billing and cooing by the Saab. I waited with Sands at the door to the crematorium, giving Rose and the inspector time to say their goodbyes before getting a lift to Ballantyne House.

Jamie Mitchell caught me by the elbow. 'So, you got your funeral.'

I felt like someone had walked over my grave. 'You mean Jojo got his funeral.'

'Aye, three grand's worth.'

It was my cue to thank him and I did. Mitchell nodded, accepting my gratitude like fealty. Les cast a look at us over his shoulder and kept on walking. Mitchell noticed Sands and raised an eyebrow. 'Who's this? Your boy?'

He might have meant my son or my lover.

Sands imitated Jamie Mitchell's gangster chill. 'I was a friend of Jojo's.'

Mitchell took a business card from his pocket and passed it to Sands. 'I guess that means you're a friend down. Get in touch if you need anything.'

Sands glanced at the card casually, as if dark men were forever slipping him their telephone numbers. He slid it inside his sketchbook, then broke the illusion of nonchalance by glancing shyly at the ground. 'Cheers.'

Mitchell grinned as if he had won a cheap prize on the slots. He turned to me, his face suddenly stern again. 'Heard you were clearing a house up in Ballantyne.'

Jamie Mitchell knew too much about my movements. I wondered who had told him.

'You heard right. We've got a big sale up there Saturday. Viewing's tomorrow.'

'Good stuff?'

'Good enough.'

'Owner died, did they?'

'Too elderly to manage the big house anymore.'

Mitchell nodded as if it was good news. 'Maybe I should take a look around.'

'What are you after?'

Mitchell shrugged. 'I've got a couple of pubs need kitted out. I fancy doing them traditional-style. Get the artsy West End crowd in.'

I wanted done with Jamie Mitchell, but money is money and you cannot stop a man from spending it. I took a copy of the catalogue from my bag and handed it to him. 'Have this on me. There are a few paintings in the sale that might appeal. It's a bit of a schlep to the house though. You might find it more convenient to make an online bid.'

Mitchell glanced at the cover of the catalogue and then tucked it under his arm. 'Cheers. Maybe I'll take a drive up tomorrow. I like to handle the goods before I commit.'

'Be careful on the bends. It's a bad road.'

Mitchell gave me one of his hard stares. 'So I heard.' He turned his back and walked towards the car park where the men he had come with were waiting beside the BMW. He raised a hand, acknowledging Anderson, but the inspector looked away.

I hoped Mitchell would forget about the sale. I remembered what Les had said about keeping Sands away from him and put a hand on the boy's shoulder. 'What did he give you?'

Sands passed me the business card. Black ink on medium-grade paper, Times New Roman font, *Mitchell Holdings* in bold text above a telephone number and email address. No business name. No hint of a profession.

Les tapped my right shoulder and leaned over my left. 'I see you made a new pal.'

I almost dropped the card. 'I thought you were away.'

'I wouldn't go without saying goodbye to my favourite auctioneer.'

I did not ask Les why he was avoiding Mitchell. There are things it is better not to know. I went to put the card in my pocket, but Sands plucked it from my fingers.

'I think that was intended for me, thanks.'

The skinny blond was at Les's side. His tears had left a legacy of smudged mascara. Close up, I could see he had not long tipped from handsome to scrawny. Les flung an arm around his shoulder. 'This is Anthony. Not Tony. *Anthony*.' Anthony laughed and gave Sands a look. Getting the funeral over with had made everyone skittish. Les exhaled a cloud of vapour large enough to emanate a full-size genie, pushed Anthony off him and turned to Sands.

'What are you again? A student at the Art School?'

Sands nodded. 'Fourth Year, Painting and Printmaking.'

'Slumming it before you graduate and get a teaching job?'

Sands' face flushed. 'No.'

'Going to be an artist, are you? You must have a rich mummy and daddy.'

I thought of intervening, but I had seen the way Sands' eyes shone when Jamie Mitchell gave him his card. It was better that Les frighten Sands off than the boy indulge his taste for exotic underworlds by making an art project out of Mitchell.

Les echoed my thoughts. 'Jamie Mitchell's not like Jojo. Jojo was a pussycat. Mitchell's the real deal. Sharper teeth. Bitey.'

Sands angled his head. 'Real deal sounds good to me.'

Les shrugged. 'Don't say I didn't warn you.'

Tears sprang to Anthony's eyes. 'Jojo was one of the best. He tried to look after folk. What happened to him was criminal. Soon there won't be enough folk left to have a decent party. Seems like everyone's dropping off.'

Les sneered, 'One old queen is hardly a massacre.'

Anthony's voice rose an octave. 'The paper made out like he was a jakie, but Jojo wasn't a jakie.'

'No.' Les snorted, enveloping us all in vanilla vapour. 'He was quite the man about town. No one gives a toss.' He nodded at me. 'He knows how it goes, don't you, Rilke? Remember HIV and AIDS? No one gave a fuck as long as it was just the poofs that were dying. No one cares that Jojo wasn't a jakie. Fuck, I knew him and I don't care. He's dead. Time to move on.'

The car park was filling up with mourners for the next funeral. Anderson got into his car and drove off. Rose waved impatiently at me, ready to go.

Les said, 'Dracula's daughter's calling you.'

I told him to behave and turned to Sands. 'Want a lift back?'

He shook his head. 'It's the first time I've been here. I'm going to have a look at the graveyard.'

Les muttered, 'For fuck's sake.'

Anthony perked up. 'I wouldn't mind a look around the graves. I used to spend a lot of time in places like this when I was a kid.'

Les gave him a shove. 'Me too, drinking Merrydown and smoking spliffs.'

I patted Sands on the back. 'You did a good thing. Jojo would have been pleased with his send-off.'

Rose beeped the Saab's horn.

Les said, 'I could do with a lift.'

I winked at him. 'Sorry, pal. Wrong direction, plus Dracula's daughter hasn't forgiven you for calling her rude names.'

'I'll remember that next time you want something.'

Putting Jojo to rest, disposing of the drugs and solving the uncertainties that had plagued the sale had made me a bit giddy. I punched Les playfully on the arm. 'I'll plank the next nice ball gown that comes into the saleroom for you.'

Les stalked off. He turned and gave me the V-sign. 'Ah, fuck off.'

The newly arrived mourners looked at us with disgust. An old man raised his voice. 'Show some respect.'

Rose beeped the horn again and started the engine.

I gave Sands a last smile. 'Look after yourself, son.' And went to join Rose. Paths cross and lives intersect. Glasgow is a small city, but Sands and I were on different tracks. I did not expect to see him again.

Eighteen

ROSE DUMPED HER daft hat on the back seat of the Saab. She threw me a smile as if she had cast off the memory of the funeral along with her veil. Laying Jòjo to rest had revitalised me too. The world looked brighter for the realisation that I was, for now, still in it. The route to the motorway took us through a housing estate. An old man stood in one of the neat front gardens tending to a rose bush. He looked up as we passed, perhaps admiring the car's smooth lines. I wondered if the regular funeral parades passing by his door sharpened his sense of mortality, or if hearses and mourners faded into the everyday.

Rose and I talked about the sale and the star lots we hoped would raise a good sum. It was a dreich morning, but it was warm inside the car and there was an atmosphere of optimism between us I had not felt for a while. Rose turned onto the inside lane of the motorway, frightening a lorry driver who was slow to give way. She put her foot on the accelerator and sang a verse of 'I'm The Hole In The Elephant's Bottom'.

. . . the eyes they are made of brown glass
Ventilation's completely forgotten
But you'd be surprised at the wind that can pass
Through the hole in the elephant's bottom.

It was the same verse she always sang. I reminded Rose of the points accumulating on her licence. She made a face and slowed down. 'I guess we don't want to end up like the poor bastards who crashed on the corner into Ballantyne.'

I leaned back in the seat, trying to adjust my body to the Saab's low centre of gravity. 'A fatal crash on the way back from a funeral . . .'

Rose pulled into the fast lane and put on a spurt as she overtook a white van. 'People would laugh.'

'And we'd miss the sale.'

We drove on in silence for a while then Rose said, 'Anderson checked up on the Forrest cousins.'

I had forgotten she had promised to sound the inspector out. I looked at her. 'And?'

'Pretty clean.'

Smoking was forbidden in the Saab. I rolled a cigarette and put it in my top pocket for later. 'What does that mean?'

Rose made a face. 'Clean-ish.'

'Clean-ish enough?'

'For our purposes.'

We sank back into silence. Rose glanced at me. 'I know you're dying to ask.'

'You're dying for me to ask.'

'If you don't want to know, it's fine.'

I did want to know. 'What's the stain on their character? Impersonating a police officer?'

Rose shook her head. 'No.'

'Impersonating a vicar?'

'Piss off, Rilke.'

'Impersonating a member of the royal family?'

'They didn't impersonate anyone. More to the point, they didn't rip off any old ladies either.'

'So what did they do?'

'Apparently Alec kicked around with one of the local biker gangs when he was younger. Got into a bit of trouble over drugs and got a rap on the knuckles. Then he joined the army and they made a man of him. No sign of trouble since.'

I sensed she was holding something back. 'And cousin John?'

Rose could not resist looking at me. 'Cousin John's a different matter. Your friendly landlady said he went travelling in the Far East, didn't she? She'd die if she knew where he actually was. John Forrest was given eight years for trying to smuggle heroin in on a flight from Istanbul. He was arrested in London and served his sentence down south.'

I whistled through my teeth. John Forrest's years in jail could explain the tension I had sensed beneath his bonhomie.

'And not a peep of it reached Ballantyne?'

Rose shrugged. 'Maybe it did, and the landlady didn't feel the need to share it with you.'

'She warned me not to believe everything people told me, but I got the impression she was being straight. Did Anderson have any details? Eight years is a long time.'

'Not really, but he did say not to assume Forrest was anything more than a dupe or a foot soldier. Heroin's Class A, so the sentence was always going to be hefty.'

I looked out of the car window at the passing traffic, the

motorway we would soon leave behind. 'Eight years would feel like a lifetime.'

Rose flicked the indicator switch. The indicator click-click-clicked and she took the exit off the motorway, onto roads that would grow smaller and smaller until we reached Ballantyne House.

'You wouldn't want to cross the law again.'

I nodded. 'Time's a killer.'

But I was not so sure. Prison has a habit of arresting development and encouraging hasty alliances. I had met men who had served long sentences and emerged so eager to win back lost years they had plunged into enterprises guaranteed to send them straight back behind bars.

I stretched my legs as far as the confines of the Saab would allow. 'I imagine John will be careful to stay out of jail after eight years inside.'

Rose brushed a strand of hair out of her eyes. 'After that length of time you'd run a mile from trouble.'

I glanced at Rose and knew from the set of her jaw that she had her doubts too.

Nineteen

IT WAS 6 A.M. on Friday morning – viewing day, the day before the big sale – when my phone chirped with a text. I was already up and dressed, drinking a large black coffee. I saw Sands' name on my screen and felt a stab of unease. There was no message, just a series of photographs of a party at its height. The photos ranged across rooms in what looked like a high-rise flat. The furniture was old-fashioned, the furnishings muted browns, reds and orange – a subdued background to the partygoers' ferocity.

I spotted Anthony, stripped to the waist, his arms in the air, ribs on display, a grin ripped across his face. He was caught mid-word, holding forth to someone beyond the camera's reach. I scrolled through the rest of the photos. The people in them were lost in the moment, caught in stages of nudity that increased as the photos progressed. I thought I recognised other men – a tattoo, a jawline, a scar, a length of back – amongst a jigsaw of naked bodies but could not be sure.

Sands had photographed an orgy. Wrinkled skin, sagging bellies, stubby cocks, distorted tattoos, sweat and rictus smiles that exposed bad teeth, but he had made it look worthy of high art. There were younger men amongst the melee too. Shaved chests and groins, tattooed sleeves. Their bodies tighter, muscles defined. Perhaps it was my mood, the aftermath of Jojo's funeral and once-cherished items tagged with lot numbers, awaiting sale at Ballantyne House, but the proximity of old and young flesh added a poignancy to the images. The past and the future together, the inevitable creep and slack of ageing.

I drank my coffee by the window that overlooked the lane at the back of my building. The pictures were too much for my stomach at that time in the morning, like a glass of cheap Rioja at breakfast. It was still dark outside. Most of the flats opposite were cast in black, but lights showed at a couple of windows, early risers readying themselves for the day ahead. I wondered why Sands had sent the photographs to me. I considered deleting them but didn't.

I pulled on my suit jacket, checked my pockets: wallet, tobacco, papers, flat keys, keys to the van, keys to Ballantyne House, keys to Bowery Auctions. I was an important man: I was a holder of keys. I slipped my phone into my pocket, locked the door behind me, went down the tenement stairs and out to where I had parked the van. It was the day before the big day, and I had promised to collect Frank and Abomi on the way.

A successful auction sale is a piece of theatre. If we had had a choice, we would have set the dissolution of Ballantyne House in the late autumn, when summer holidays are over and there is still a chance of sunny weather. I could imagine the lawn outside the old house neatly trimmed and set with a tea tent, the trees strung with bunting. As it was, the sky was grey with unshed rain, the house full-on horror movie gothic as I bumped the van down the rutted drive.

Frank looked as if he had had another hard night. He had slept, head bumping gently against the cab's window, for most of the journey, while Abomi had kept up a stream of chatter. It was Abomi's first country-house sale and he was excited. I let the boy's chat drift into the background, a babble of words that blended with the drone of the van's engine and the slip-slap of the windscreen wipers.

The Forrest cousins had given over the field at the side of the house to customer parking. Our crew had attached signs to the outside of the fence, announcing the auction. Deep wedges had been gouged in the earth where the Micra had ploughed its course, but it had rained almost constantly that week and new grass disguised the full force of the car's impact.

Abomi said, 'Uncle Razzle knew one of the boys that died in the crash. He said it was a shame, but Billy was never going to make old bones.'

I glanced at him. 'How come?'

'Uncle Razzle said Billy was a tearaway. He ran with the Young Team and kept on running when he should have grown out of it.'

Abomi's uncle had more than a glancing acquaintance with various Young Teams. They had supplied him with a small army of fodder and enforcers over the years. I kept the thought to myself.

'I heard the boys who died were working for John Forrest in the polytunnels,' I said.

The bumps in the drive had woken Frank. His face looked

bruised with sleep, his eyes hollow. The best-before-date on his good looks was approaching faster than I would have anticipated.

He rubbed his eyes. 'Wouldn't have thought there'd be much need for casual workers in the polytunnels this time of year.'

'Maybe I got it wrong.' It occurred to me I only had the landlady's word that the boys had been working at the farm. She had turned out not to be as well informed, or perhaps as trustworthy, as I had assumed.

Abomi sounded pleased with himself. 'Uncle Razzle said Billy should have screwed the nut and got himself a decent job like me, instead of joyriding around the countryside like a maniac.'

I parked the van at the side of the house. 'Your uncle talks a lot of sense.'

Abomi grinned. 'He likes you, Rilke, says you're the only poofter he has any time for.'

Frank burst out laughing and the boy flushed scarlet.

'Sorry . . . I . . .'

Frank hopped out of the van, onto the gravelled courtyard, still laughing.

I gave Abomi a playful shove to reassure him. 'Don't worry about it, son. Your uncle Razzle's a good guy. But don't use that word again in front of me.'

The boy repeated his apology as we crossed the courtyard and again as we entered the house. I set him to work with a reassurance and a stern look. I liked Abomi, but even if I had not, I would have resisted sacking him.

Uncle Razzle aka Ray Diamond was a junction in the criminal ley lines of the city. A quiet man who was interested in Eastern philosophy and making easy money. Diamond had learned, a long time ago, how to use violence. He once quoted Miyamoto Musashi to me over a post-auction pint: 'The way of the warrior is the resolute acceptance of death.' It had not meant much to me at the time. A lot of men who live on the edges see themselves as lone samurai, travelling through the world, guided by their own moral code. I am not immune to that kind of romanticism myself. But Ray Diamond had made his mark by facing off and – if rumours were to be believed – occasionally dispatching his rivals. I suspected the resolute acceptance he had spoken of was for the deaths of others.

Rose was already in the kitchen when we arrived. She clocked Frank's sickly pallor, his unshaven face and glazed eyes, and cornered me as soon as he left the room.

'What's wrong with him?'

'I'm guessing another hangover.' Rose was dressed in a formfitting black dress that was secured along one shoulder by knotted buttons known as frog fasteners. I said, 'You're looking very *Bride of Fu-Manchu*.'

Rose snapped, 'You sound like your wee clown pal. Do you think I don't know he calls me Dracula's Daughter? One day I'll tell him, it's better than being *Bride of Chucky*.'

Less than five minutes through the door and I was already on the back foot. I poured myself a cup of tea from the pot on the table and took a sip.

'It's a compliment. These old black-and-white female villains are stylish. Les loves them.'

Rose looked like she wanted to stab me. 'Try taking a look in the mirror – oh, I'm sorry, you don't have a reflection, do you?'

I rolled my eyes. 'Okay, I get the message.'

'Good. You can pass it on to your pal, or I will personally

ladder his stockings.' She smoothed her dress, collecting herself. 'Did you have a word with Frank?'

I put my cup back on the table. The tea was worse than usual. 'No point in alienating him the day before the big sale.'

Rose looked like she wanted to argue the point, but she knew I was right. 'His jacket's hanging from a shoogly peg.'

I poured my tea down the sink and rinsed the cup. 'I'll let him know.'

'And keep a note of his goings-on. I don't want a stupid employment tribunal when I sack him.'

The day was going to shit. I leaned against the kitchen table, my back to the door. 'Do your own dirty business, Rose. I'm not a Stasi spy.'

Rose lifted a catalogue from the table and started to flick through it, looking for something. 'Sometimes you forget I'm your boss. Every time I ask you to do something, you tell me to fuck off.'

'Next thing, you'll be telling me *my* jacket's on a shoogly peg. I run my arse off for you. Did I hesitate when you asked me to do a bit of breaking and entering?'

Rose looked up from the catalogue. Her expression suddenly switched from irritated to welcoming, but her eyes held a glint of panic. 'Hello, Mr Forrest . . .'

I turned to see John Forrest standing in the kitchen doorway. I had no idea how long he had been there and what he had heard. I forced a smile and added some warmth to my voice. 'Good morning, Mr Forrest. I was about to put the kettle on. Would you like a cup of tea?'

'A cup of cha might hit the spot.' John gave no sign of having overheard our conversation. He looked like death. There was an open packet of chocolate digestives on the table. He sank into a chair and helped himself to a biscuit.

I passed him a mug of tea. There was milk and sugar on the table. He helped himself, heavy on the sugar.

I kept my voice light. 'How are you feeling about the sale? It must be an emotional moment.'

Forrest slurped his tea and set it on the table, wiping biscuits crumbs from his jumper. 'I'm looking forward to it being over, if you want to know the truth. It'll be good to get the old lady settled.'

Rose leaned sympathetically across the table towards him. For a moment I thought she was going to take Forrest's hands in hers, but she settled for clasping her fingers together, black nail polish shiny as mourning jet.

'I remember looking after my dad towards the end of his life . . .' She avoided meeting my eye. 'It was hard work – rewarding of course, but relentless. How is your aunt?'

Forrest dunked another biscuit in his tea. 'As well as can be expected. She can't get down the farmhouse stairs anymore.' His face contracted with what looked like genuine concern. 'The sooner Auntie Pat's somewhere she can get the care she needs, the better. Alec and I do our best, but she needs more than we can give her.'

Rose nodded. 'Do you have a care home in mind?'

The soggy end of the digestive slid into Forrest's mug. He put the rest into his mouth and washed it down with the last of the tea. 'Actually, we have. Somewhere perfect. It's in Chiang Mai.'

Rose looked perplexed. 'Where?'

'Chiang Mai, in the north of Thailand. I spent some time there when I was younger. We looked at local care homes, but, to be frank, they didn't pass muster. In Chiang Mai she'll have four carers devoted to her needs. That means dedicated care twenty-four hours, seven days of the week. The care system in this country is broken. Remember Covid?' He shook his head. 'Old folk dropping like flies. I won't subject my aunt to that kind of risk.'

He spoke with such conviction I found myself picturing the geography of the upstairs floor of the farmhouse again. Was it possible I had missed a room? But there had only been four doors. One of them had led to an old lady's bedroom. It had been empty for months.

Frank put his head around the door. His hair was wet and slicked back. I guessed he had stuck his head under a cold tap. 'The troops need to know where you want them.'

I gave my apologies to John Forrest and followed Frank into the body of the house. The doors were opening at 10 a.m. The curtain was going up on viewing day.

The morning was deadly. The wind got up and rain streaked horizontal across the windows of Ballantyne House. I sent Frank for a disco nap in the bedroom where Phan had slept and told Abomi to wake him at the first sign of potential clients. The rest of the crew familiarised themselves with the catalogue and tweaked arrangements. They were skittish with anticipation and the house echoed with outbreaks of nervous laughter.

We'd cleared the drawing room and set up two screens against the far wall for Hannah to display photographs of each lot as it came up for sale. Abomi and Frank had placed a lectern from the library on a table in front of the screens and set my gavel on it. I stood behind the makeshift rostrum and practised my opening spiel, like an actor rehearsing to the wall. Every chair in the house was set out in rows before me, each tagged with a ticket bearing a lot number. In a day's time they would all be filled with people. If things went to plan, by the day after that, they would be sold and gone, dispersed like the rest of the house's contents.

Potential buyers ghosted through Ballantyne House pretending to be unimpressed, scribbling cryptic marks in their catalogues, sharing gossip, making side deals and trying to suss out the competition. The antique trade had been a buyers' market since Covid, but things were beginning to return to normal. If there was enough competition and if we generated the right excitement, prices could climb.

I patrolled the rooms, shaking hands, talking up prize lots, acquainting clients with items I knew they would be interested in. Hannah and Lucy tapped away at their iPads, uploading pictures to Instagram, tweeting and blogging. Rose toured the house too, charming clients, looking like a 1920s aristocrat in search of a strong cocktail.

Sleep appeared to have helped Frank's hangover. His stern exterior was restored, but I kept an eye on him, letting him know I was following his progress.

It was four o'clock, not yet dark but gloomy with impending dusk, when I nipped out for a fly fag break. It was still raining, a cold, sleeting spray that soaked me in seconds. I stood in the lee of the van, cupped my roll-up in my hand and attempted to light it. The wind was strong, but I was persistent and eventually the cigarette caught. I looked up the hill, past the lines of white polytunnels, towards the farmhouse. A black BMW was parked at its rear. Perhaps Mrs Forrest had been taken somewhere for respite care and was being returned home. That would explain the empty bedroom and John Forrest's deep sleep. I finished my cigarette and made a quick dash through the rain back to the shelter of the house.

*

Thirty busy minutes later, I went to check on Frank and found him deep in conversation with Jamie Mitchell. Jamie had a hand on Frank's shoulder, drawing him close, as if he was about to issue a threat or disclose a secret. I got the impression that Frank wanted to pull away but did not dare.

'Mr Rilke.' Mitchell saw me and let go of the head porter's shoulder. He reminded me of the auction-room cat, distracted in the middle of torturing a mouse. 'You said you had some good stuff to show me.'

I dismissed Frank with a look and measured my smile. 'An abundance, Mr Mitchell.'

'At good prices?'

'Price depends on bids in the room. What I can guarantee is, there are objects in this sale that will suit your pubs very nicely.'

It was busy on the ground floor. I led him upstairs to a small drawing room stuffed with paintings and brown furniture whose surfaces were crowded with china.

Mitchell stopped before a dreary still life of a dead pheasant draped over a pewter platter piled with gleaming fruit and vegetables. He stared at it. 'A bit of class. The kind of thing you'd expect to see in a museum.'

I nodded. 'It would add elegance without distracting anyone from their pints and it'll retain its resale value, so if you decide to change the décor, you can bung it into auction and get your money back.'

'How much?'

'Estimate price is four-fifty to five-twenty. You can leave a bid with me to save you attending the sale, or we can arrange a telephone or online bid.'

Mitchell gave an impatient nod of his head. 'What about the buy-now option?'

'Doesn't exist, I'm afraid.'

The man inhabited a world beyond HR, job titles, progress reviews and roadmaps to promotion. The ability to do what he wanted, regardless of rules, was more than simple gratification. It was confirmation of his worth.

He said, 'Even if you know the auctioneer?'

I brought out my warmest smile. 'Even if you know the First Minister. I reckon this will go in the region of four hundred max. It might go lower. Like I said, it depends on the interest in the room. If you place a presale bid of five hundred, you'll be in with a good chance.'

Mitchell stared at the oil painting. 'Like betting on the horses, but without the pay-off.'

'The painting is the pay-off.'

For a moment I thought he was going to bite, but then he shook his head. 'You're wasting my time. If I want to buy the painting now and I have the money, why can't I?' He reached into his inside pocket, pulled out his wallet and extracted a neatly folded bundle of fifty-pound notes. 'Here's four-fifty. Take it and I'll walk away with the painting. Christ, who's going to know the difference?'

I have never been keen on people shoving money in my face, as if the sight of it will make me lose my reason. I held up a hand. 'That's not the way it works.'

Mitchell's face was flushed. 'You're the guy in charge. It works how you say it works.'

I kept my tone friendly. 'It looks like I'm in charge because I'm the man on stage with a hammer in his hand, but that's an illusion. Auctions are highly regulated. I'm a slave to rules and regulations.'

Mitchell took a step towards me, so close I felt we were breathing the same air. I remembered the fastidious way he had applied hand gel and donned a pair of surgical gloves when I had shown him Jojo's boxes and wondered what had happened to make him change in a few short days.

He lowered his voice. 'Remember, you owe me a funeral.'

'My balance book's in order. I don't owe anybody anything.'

'Sure about that?'

'Certain.'

Mitchell nodded. 'I must be mistaken, then. It must be your young friend, what's his name? Sandy?'

I answered too quickly. 'He doesn't owe you anything either.'

Mitchell saw he had got to me. 'Someone owes me. If it's not you, it must be him.'

I took a deep breath, reached up and unhooked the painting from the wall. 'I'm the one who must be mistaken. I'll get Frank to wrap this for you and you can have it today for the estimate price of four hundred. As a gesture of goodwill Bowery will absorb the tax and commission.'

Mitchell looked at the painting. 'On second thoughts, I'd prefer something modern. Businessmen like me should support the community. I've always fancied becoming a patron of the arts. Maybe I'll back an up-and-coming young artist. An Art School student perhaps.'

I stood there, still holding the painting. 'There's no need to . . .'

He winked at me. 'I've always liked photography.'

Rose entered the room. 'Rilke, Tam from the National Trust is interested in talking to you about some kitchenalia . . .' She saw Mitchell and paused mid-sentence. 'Sorry, I didn't realise you were with someone.'

Mitchell's eyes glanced over Rose. He gave me a parting nod. 'Good to see you again, Mr Rilke. Let's hope the next time we meet it isn't at a funeral. I'm sick of funerals, to be honest.'

He glanced again at Rose with a ghost of a smile and left the room.

Rose turned and watched his exit. 'What happened there? He looked like you'd just offered him the fuzzy end of the lollipop.'

My phone started to buzz silently in my pocket. I propped the painting against the wall and took the mobile from my pocket. Sands' name flashed on the screen. I rejected the call.

Rose lowered her voice. 'I recognise him from Jojo's funeral.'

I wanted Jamie Mitchell continents away from Rose. I lifted the painting and hung it back on the wall. The pheasant's eyes were dulled by death. The pewter plate, heaped with fruit and vegetables, gleamed.

'He had something going on with Jojo. I don't want to know what.'

Rose shook her head. 'Fucking Jojo. He's more trouble dead than he was alive. What was his creepy friend doing here?'

'Looking for a painting for a pub he's opening. He liked the dead bird. Wanted to buy it off the wall.'

'And you told him to fuck off?'

I straightened the painting to avoid meeting her eyes. 'I told him we were bound by regulations.'

'You should have let him have it. That painting's a piece of shit. We'll be lucky to get two hundred for it.'

My phone buzzed in my pocket. Sands again. I turned it off.

'You're right. I should have.'

Twenty

IT WAS LATE by the time I returned Sands' call. I was in a cab, heading away from the Southside of the city and a hook-up who had suggested a cup of tea. When I made my excuses and pulled on my coat, he had offered me a whisky. Some other night I might have accepted, but it was late, and a whisky with a lonely man is never one whisky.

Sands picked up on the third ring. 'Anthony's dead.'

It took me a moment to place Anthony, and then I remembered. 'The skinny blond piece who was crying his heart out at Jojo's funeral?'

The mobile connection was hazy; some of Sands' words were lost in the bounce between satellite and phone. 'Someone found him . . . an alleyway . . . Just li . . . Jojo . . . I saw him . . . night . . . at a party . . . he was . . . it.'

'He was what?'

'Out of it . . . scarily out of it. Beyond . . . It got . . . lairy . . . I got going, but . . .'

The cab driver met my eyes in the rear-view mirror. He had been casting quick glances at me since I had got in. I thought it might be an invitation, but even if I had been in the mood, Sands' news would have killed the urge.

'Who told you?'

'It's in . . . *Evening Times*. I've . . . checking its website . . . since they did that . . . Jojo . . . could use it . . . my project . . . two people connected to . . .'

His words were lost in a fuzz of sound. I moved closer to the car window, as if it would help. 'What did you say?'

'I said . . . two people . . . dead . . .'

More static.

'What?'

We passed the City Chambers. The building was illuminated, the square outside empty except for the statues that punctuated its perimeter. It reminded me of the months of lockdown when I had taken my daily walk by night. This time the satellites aligned, and the boy's voice was clear and sharp in my ear.

'Someone else connected to Jojo was found dead in an alleyway. Do you think there's something going on?'

The cab left George Square and climbed Bath Street. Some of the bars on that stretch were still open. It would be an easy thing to invite the boy to meet and discuss the snakes and ladders of life, over a nightcap, but the next day's sale tugged at my conscience. A couple of drunks weaved across the road in front of us. The driver slowed the cab and muttered something under his breath.

I chose my words carefully, aware of his eyes on me. 'You wanted to get Jojo settled and his room cleared. I helped you. As far as I'm concerned that's the end of the story.'

Sands had sounded tired, now he sounded frustrated. 'If there's something wrong with those drugs, more people could die.'

'For fuck's sake.' I closed my eyes. I could feel the city scrolling past outside the cab's windows, the neon signs and traffic lights. I wished I had never seen the boy. Wished I had walked away at the first sight of Jojo's secret stash.

'I know Anthony looked like a fuck-up, but he was careful. He set alarms on his phone and only took G when they went off.'

We stopped at a set of traffic lights. The remnants of a stag party staggered across the road in front of us. The groom was dressed in a veil and tutu, his bare chest covered in lipstick markings. He had an arm flung round the shoulders of an older man who might have been his father. They propped each other up, weaving in shallow circles towards the beckoning bars on the pavement beyond.

Sands said, 'Don't you think it's a big coincidence?'

'Stop being melodramatic. This isn't a Tennessee Williams play.'

Sands' voice was fractured. 'This isn't a what? What are you talking about?'

I lowered my voice to a whisper. 'I didn't kill anyone and neither did you.'

'But we're part it. Maybe we should go to the police.'

My stomach clenched imagining Jamie Mitchell's reaction to a police visit. 'That's the last thing you should do – believe me. I'll make a couple of phone calls. There might be another way to get the genie back in the bottle.'

'Jojo and Anthony are both dead, Rilke. There's no bringing them back.'

I wondered when I had passed the point where every death

came as a shock. Even seeing Jojo on the slab had not felt like much of a surprise.

'You and me are both in good health. I'd like us to stay that way.' It was time to hang up, but I asked, 'Why did you send me those party photos?'

Sands' sigh reached down the line. 'I don't know. I thought you might like them, I suppose. Maybe I'm missing Jojo. I used to show him my stuff. He'd give me feedback.'

'I'm not Jojo.'

'No, Jojo had a kind heart.'

'Jojo was a fool. That's what killed him.'

The line went dead before I could remind Sands not to call the police.

The cab driver turned into my street. He parked beneath a dead streetlight and turned to look at me, eyes large and hollow in the shadows. I was not sure what to read in them – loneliness, desire or an urge to give me a beating.

'A row with the boyfriend?' He had a foreign accent I could not place, imbued with a Scottish lilt.

I met his gaze, my face blank as a brick wall. 'I don't have a boyfriend.'

'But you like boys, right?'

I hesitated too long for any denial to be convincing. 'What does what I like, or don't like, have to do with you?'

'I like boys too.'

When we were younger Les and I used to laugh about the cab drivers who turned their meters off, an invitation to pay the fare another way. But times had changed. Uber was a cash-free transaction, and I was getting too old for back-seat liaisons.

'Best find yourself a boy then.' I stepped out of the car and slammed the door behind me.

The cab driver lowered his window. His voice carried across the road, clear but not quite loud enough to wake my sleeping neighbours. 'You should be grateful, grandad. Pretty soon no one's going to want to fuck you.'

He drove away, headlights illuminating the empty road ahead. I turned and gave him the middle finger.

Twenty-One

MY FLAT WAS IN DARKNESS. I poured myself a glass of milk and drank it by the light of the refrigerator, staring out of the window at other windows beyond. Most were black, but one square of light showed that someone else was awake in the silent drift between one day and another.

My bedroom curtains were still closed. I clicked on the bedside lamp. It was after one in the morning, but I knew Les would be up. I took my phone from my pocket, threw my suit jacket over a chair and kicked off my shoes. It was cold in the room. I turned up the radiator and lay on top of the bed, not bothering to get undressed.

Les picked up straight away, his voice raw with smoke. 'What do you want?'

'I heard about Anthony.'

The whoosh and release of his inhale-exhale reached me down the line. 'Silly cow didn't know when to stop.'

'Sorry.'

Les snorted. 'What are you sorry for? You didn't kill the stupid bitch.'

'You don't think Anthony's death's a bit similar to Jojo's?'

Music was playing in the background wherever Les was. Something quiet and melodic that reminded me again that we were both getting older and soon no one would want to fuck either of us.

Les said, 'Not really.'

'Two sudden deaths, two friends . . .'

'Friends is an exaggeration.'

'Okay, two associates, found dead in alleyways, a stone's throw from each other.'

Les sucked on his joint. 'You're getting very Miss Marple. Do you think maybe what happened the other year is fucking your judgement?'

A few years back, I had got involved in a search for a dead man with a taste for snuff movies. It had got bloody, and I had got emotional. I had trained myself not to think about it. I plucked at the bedspread, let the fabric rise and fall, illusory hills, mirages on the counterpane.

'Maybe. I don't know. But two sudden deaths in a row. Doesn't it seem weird to you?'

'Not really,' Les said again. I heard the hiss of a sliding door opening and closing. The change in atmosphere that told me Les was outside on the balcony of his flat. 'They were users, Rilke. Maybe they died at a party and someone dragged them outside. Not nice, but no one wants to get involved with the polis if they can avoid it.' He talked as if it was the most reasonable thing in the world to dump a body in the gutter to evade the police. 'It's not the same as murdering someone. Let your little grey cells take a break. We're not talking serial killer.'

I smoothed the bedspread. 'If either of them was alive when they were dumped outside, it would count as manslaughter at the very least.'

'Big if.' There was not quite silence on the line. The dry whoosh of Les inhaling smoke. A car passing by on the street below. 'Can I get back to my well-earned rest?'

I ignored his question. 'Maybe there's something wrong with the drugs we found at Jojo's. Maybe they're what finished Jojo and Anthony.'

'For fuck's sake. When did I become your go-to guy on drugs?'

'Sometime around 1985.'

'Time you started to read the newspapers. Inform yourself.'

'I read a newspaper every day.'

'You dip into the broadsheets, the international news and all that, but the only bit of the local newspaper you read is the death notices. Fucking ambulance chaser.'

'That's not true.'

Another whoosh and crackle as he inhaled, exhaled. 'No? So you'll already know Scotland's top of the pops for drug deaths in Europe. Wee friendship groups wiped out because someone had the bright idea of mixing this with that. It's all poison, same as those fags you can't give up, same as alcohol and bareback riding.' Les sounded indifferent, as if I had asked him for directions to somewhere that was marked on every map. 'Two deaths is nothing. This city has hundreds – thousands – of dead junkies.'

I said, 'The stuff we found in Jojo's is still out there. If there's something wrong with it, more people could die.'

Les's voice hardened. '*We* didn't find it. You and that middle-class foetus you hooked up with found it.'

'What about checking in with Jamie Mitchell? He might appreciate a warning. This could bring the police to his door.'

Les inhaled again and the line filled with the sound of his breath. 'You want my advice, Rilke? Forget you ever saw that stash. Forget that fud Sandy, forget any thoughts of unexpected deaths, and top of the list? Forget about Jamie Mitchell. Oh, and while you're at it, forget this number.'

I said, 'Les,' but he had already hung up.

I lay back on my bed and lit a cigarette. He was right. The cab driver was right. But another thought persisted: Sands might be right. We were not responsible for Jojo or Anthony's deaths, but if they were connected, and if the drugs we had helped to move on were the cause, we might be held to account. I turned off the light and lay there, watching the trembling shadows thrown across the room by the tops of the trees outside, dancing in the moonlight.

Twenty-Two

THE TRACKS FORGED by the overturned Micra in the field next to Ballantyne House were now hidden beneath parked vehicles. I stood at the window of an attic bedroom watching as punters, dressed against the weather, heads lowered, made their way across the grass and up the drive. It looked like a funeral procession for a dead bohemian with a raggle-taggle band of ageing friends. Scarves were wound around faces, features hidden beneath hats and raised collars, but it was my job to know our clients. I recognised individual gaits, well-worn coats and flash styling, the slope of a shoulder, the jut of a hat. There was no sign of Jamie Mitchell's neat black Crombie and straight spine.

The procession became a queue as those at its head reached the front door and entered one by one, showing their catalogues to Frank. The big spenders we had hoped for were here. Our preparations were complete, everything in order.

There was nothing left to do except the job itself. I felt an urge for a quick tot of malt and was glad there was none there to tempt me.

Someone knocked at the attic door. I shouted, 'Yes?'

Rose entered the room. She was wearing another form-fitting dress, another variation in black, her hair pulled back in a torture bun, lips Communist red, eyes bright and smoky, like a flame within a fire.

I turned my back on the window. 'Not like you to knock.'

'Not like you to hide yourself away when there's a queue of wallets waiting downstairs. Everything okay?'

'Just getting into the zone.'

Rose nodded, unconvinced. 'Lift-off's in fifteen minutes. Hannah's checking the tech.'

'I'll be down in five.'

She hesitated in the doorway. The attic room was cramped and bare: a single bed we had not bothered to tag pressed against the wall, unvarnished floorboards and whitewashed walls. Rose looked out of place the lady of the house intruding on the servants' quarters. She leaned against the doorjamb. 'Anything I should know?'

The business with Sands had overtaken but not quite pushed Rilla's accusations about the Forrest cousins from my mind.

'Nothing.'

'Are you sure?'

I shrugged. 'My guess is Rilla's a bitter ex-fiancée. It's like you said: Auntie Pat's already in the home in Chiang Mai and, for whatever reason, John and Alec don't want the word out yet.' It was a feeble explanation. I added, 'Either way, the paperwork's in order. The Forrest boys have power of attorney. What they say goes.' I stuck my arm out, like a gallant father-of-the-bride preparing to conduct his daughter down the aisle. 'Ready to go?'

Rose grinned. Her pupils dilated, eyes black with excitement. She slipped an arm through mine. 'This is the sale we needed, Rilke. If I believed there was a god up there, I'd be thanking her right now.'

'The gods are known for their strange sense of humour. We're better off without them.'

The attic stairs were too narrow for us to descend arm in arm. I let Rose go first. The stairway became broader, the carpet thicker, the balustrade more ornamental as we left the servants' quarters behind. I leaned over the first-floor banister, surveying the punters below. I was surprised to spot Anderson loitering in the hallway.

'What's your boyfriend doing here? I wouldn't have thought this was his idea of a good time.'

Rose flushed. 'Don't call him my boyfriend.'

'Okay. Why is your lover, the police inspector, here? I hope he's not going to arrest anyone.'

'Don't be stupid. The Saab gave up the ghost last night. Anders gave me a lift. It's his day off. He's going to stick around. We've got a booth booked at the Anchor Line later.'

'Fancy.'

'I think he wanted to cheer me up. I liked that car.'

I squeezed Rose's arm. 'You can buy something better with the profit from this sale.'

She grinned. 'There's an Alfa Romeo Spider coming up at Central Car Auctions next Wednesday. Needs a bit of work but . . .'

'A broken-down spider, just your style.'

'Spiders regrow their legs.'

She spoke as if spiders' ability to regenerate their limbs was an example we could all learn from.

The noise from downstairs was building.

Rose's eyes met mine. 'Ready?'

'Ready.'

She upped her pace, high heels sure on the carpeted stairs. I matched her speed and followed, no thought of broken limbs, so close I could feel the heat of her body.

Every seat in the drawing room was taken. People were standing around the edges, propped against the walls like decommissioned waxworks. Rose and I walked to the temporary dais together. She gave a formal thank-you to the Forrest family, outlining their long history, the extensive nature of their travels, Patricia Forrest's distinguished career as a concert pianist and her love of fine things. It was all build-up. The kind of foreplay an old-time snake oil salesman would lay on a crowd gathered around his wagon. The punters sat straighter in their seats, clutching the auction paddles and catalogues, licking their lips, eager for the show to begin. John and Alec Forrest were in reserved seats at the front, dressed in suits that could grace a coffin. I saw the tension on their faces and hoped it was the auction that was making them nervous.

Rose finished her patter and I stepped up to the lectern, seeing the crowd's greedy eyes on me. Seeing myself too, a long-limbed spider in a three-piece suit, gavel in my right hand, ready to hammer out the bids.

'Ladies and gentlemen, it is my pleasure to welcome you to this special sale, hosted by Bowery Auctions. Lot number one is a very fine Gallé Cameo glass vase, dating from around 1900. Who will start me at two hundred? Two hundred for this beautiful Cameo vase made from frosted glass with an overlay of a dragonfly over foliage and water. Two hundred pounds, ladies and gentlemen. Who will start me at two hundred pounds?' A hand punched the air, and we were on our way.

There is nothing except this room: the caravan of objects. The hammer in my hand beats out time. What will you give me? What will you give me for . . .? Another ten? Another fifty? The hammer in my hand raps out the order of everything. The world is in my breath. Past and present, weighed and counted. Who will give me another ten? Another fifty? Here, the down-at-heel hold a king's ransom, the old and decrepit have the sharpest eye. In this place, courage may be folly or a leap towards a fortune. What will you give me? What will you give me for . . .? Ours is an ancient art, buying and selling. Profit and loss, turning a coin, chasing a hunch. We are caution and knowledge, steam and sixth sense. Here is the fist in the gut, the unwelcome touch, the soft caress. We are wealth and destitution. Fortune and death. Give me another fifty. Give me another ten. I am Magus of this house and my hunger is unbound. Another fifty. Another ten. Give me a hundred more. Give me your paper, your coins and your plastic. More, more, is there any more? Any more? The crowd breathes in. I raise my hammer, hold it high. The air is still. I let the hammer fly. Going, going, going, gone!

Twenty-Three

THE AFTERNOON SUN was close to setting, without ever having shown its face from behind a veil of grey cloud. The sale was over. Now came the dismantling of the house. The shifting of objects and furniture, some of which had sheltered within Ballantyne House's brick walls for over two centuries. I watched as Frank and Abomi ferried the camphorwood trunk that had held the remains of poor Schumann through the front door and slid it into the back of one of the furniture vans parked on the drive.

We had set up a temporary office in the dining room. The queue of punters waiting to pay and collect their goods stretched all the way down the hall. The process was slow, dealers getting fractious as the late afternoon darkened and the road home grew longer. The cousins had disappeared. I felt relieved by their absence.

We had hired our usual assembly of relatives of the crew, part-timers, out-of-work actors and students to help with portering. It was Frank's job to conduct their progress, mine to keep an eye on Frank. He looked in better shape today – skin brighter, eyes clearer – but there was something haunted about the head porter. I wanted to know what Jamie Mitchell had been whispering to him, but there was work to be done. Now was not the time to ask.

An hour later, I slipped out through the kitchen door for a fly smoke. The sky was gunmetal grey, the wind cutting, but the courtyard was as packed as a city beer garden on a sunny, post-lockdown Saturday. Inspector Anderson was hunched by the kitchen doorway, face slumped in the hangdog expression that is his sober, off-duty default setting. I lit up and drew smoke and nicotine into my lungs as Anderson stubbed out his Marlboro and pocketed the dout.

'How long do you think she'll be?'

'Rose?'

'No, the late Margaret Thatcher.'

'We close at five-thirty. There'll be a bit of flimflam and tidying up afterwards. Rose won't leave until everything's secure.'

Usually I would have been hailed by a dozen or so dealers, but the police inspector's company threw a force field around me. The only sign that my presence had been marked was a few discreet nods.

Anderson said, 'Can't you do the locking-up?'

'I could, but you know what she's like.' I threw my roll-up on the ground and squashed it with the heel of my shoe.

He made a harrumphing noise. 'Aye, and she knows what you're like.'

It was unfair, but I was too thick-skinned to take offence. I followed Anderson's gaze and saw Norris and Howe, a couple of dealers with a reputation for reset. I stepped in front of the inspector, blocking his view in case some other recalcitrant caught his eye. 'Sounds like you need a drink.'

Anderson took out his pack of Marlboros, tapped it against his palm, then decided against chain smoking and slipped them back into his pocket. 'I've got the car.'

'It's your day off. Let Rose drive.'

He shook his head and made the same rumpled face he used to make when something thwarted him as a boy. 'She can't afford any more points on her licence.'

'You're the law. Keep her under the speed limit.'

Anderson grumbled, 'It's like trying to keep Ayrton Senna in the thirty zone.'

But he followed me, through the kitchen to the butler's pantry. I unlocked it, ushered Anderson inside and locked the door behind us. It was a cosy room, a large cupboard equipped with a couple of worn easy chairs and lined with shelves that had once held household supplies too precious to be in general reach. I pulled out a chair for Anderson and poured two brandies from the bottle I had planked there that morning.

Anderson lifted his drink to his nose and sniffed. He took a sip. 'I'm guessing from the quality of this stuff that you had a good sale.'

I held my glass to my nose and inhaled: wood and sugar, whisky notes. I swallowed a mouthful. Fire hit my throat then my guts. 'It was all right.' The relief of the money – Bowery Auctions secure again – hit me. Maybe that was what Rose had meant about spiders regrowing their legs. Bowery would stagger on for a while yet. I tipped my brandy to my lips. 'How's Phan?'

'Your Vietnamese pal? Not bad, as it turns out. If he plays his cards right, he might be allowed to remain in the country.

Turns out he's younger than he looks. That is, he says he's younger than he looks, and his key workers have chosen to believe him. The social have placed him with a foster family. They don't speak any Vietnamese and his English is close to heehaw, but talking's overrated.'

I set my glass on a shelf. 'Is that your way of telling me to zip it?'

Anderson's voice was patient. 'It's my way of telling you to get on with it and tell me what you want. I've got a booth, a bottle of Veuve Clicquot and a dozen oysters with my name on them at the Anchor Line.'

I widened my eyes. 'What makes you think I want something?'

'You're a mercenary bastard. When you pour me a drink and ask how I am, I know you want a favour.'

'The police force has made you cynical, Jim.'

He touched his glass to his lips. 'I'm right though, aren't I?'

There was no point in continuing the dance. I leaned forward, though there was no one there to overhear us. 'You remember Jojo?'

Anderson nodded. 'Regular client of Bowery, found dead in a doorway in a lane off Ingram Street. You identified the body.'

There was no smoking allowed inside the house but suddenly I wanted something to do with my hands. I took out my tobacco and a packet of Rizlas and started to build a roll-up. 'That's the one.'

Anderson sipped his brandy, watching as I sprinkled tobacco inside the paper, rolled, smoothed and licked the papers, and inserted a filter. After a moment he said, 'I can't help you if you don't tell me what you want.'

I tucked the roll-up in my top pocket for later. My eyes met the inspector's. 'Another person, a friend . . . associate of Jojo's, died the same way.'

'Recently?'

I nodded. 'Anthony somebody, died a couple of days ago. He was found not far from where Jojo was discovered.'

A gust of laughter echoed in the courtyard outside. Anderson slipped a notebook and pencil from his inside pocket. He flipped open the book and scribbled something inside. Hailstones started to rattle at the window. Shouts of annoyance came from the courtyard where the dealers had gathered to smoke and gossip. Their retreating foot-steps sounded in the corridor beyond the butler's pantry.

Anderson leaned back in his seat and gave a small smile, as if the noise of people getting soaked had relaxed him. 'As I recall, Joseph Nugent was a party animal who should have hung up his dance frock and high heels a while back. His death looked straightforward. He was spotted in a doorway by a homeless man who thought he had nicked his spot. The toxicology report was off the scale, it was below freezing that night and Nugent wasn't a young man.'

I nodded. 'I get that. Jojo was out of control the last time I saw him. But two blokes, who knew each other, dead within a matter of weeks? Both found a stone's throw from each other. Doesn't that strike you as weird?'

Anderson swirled the brandy in his glass. 'If we were talking about some sleepy English hamlet, I'd agree with you and call in John Nettles. He'd have it wrapped up in a couple of hours' including ad breaks. But this is Glasgow. I'm guessing these guys had similar lifestyles?'

I nodded. 'I'd say it's a safe bet.'

Anderson tipped his drink to his lips and swallowed. 'There

you go. It's not pretty, but Nancy Reagan was right: drugs kill. I'm not sure why you're so exercised, unless there's something you're not telling me.'

I chose my words carefully. 'Do you think there could be something wrong with the particular drugs they took?'

Anderson looked at me, his attention piqued. 'Like what?'

I stroked the arm of the easy chair. 'I don't know. An impurity or something?'

'Street drugs are unregulated. Whether it's bootleg vodka or coke cut with rat poison, users are taking a risk.'

'People do that?'

He looked at me. 'What?'

'Cut coke with rat poison?'

Anderson shrugged. 'It was just an example. My point is, two dead junkies isn't the big deal you might think it deserves to be.'

It was the same thing Les had told me. I would have been reassured were it not that Jamie Mitchell was in the mix and Sands and I had helped get the bottles of G back into circulation.

Anderson stretched out his legs like an old duffer in a movie relaxing at his country club. All he needed was a Churchill cigar to complete the look. 'Why are you so interested?'

'Like you said, Jojo was a friend.'

'You told me Jojo was a pain in the arse. I had to send a couple of officers to collect you to identify his body.'

'Most of my friends are pains in the arse.'

Anderson did not crack a smile. 'I saw Jamie Mitchell at the funeral. Does he figure in your unease?'

It was as if he had read my mind. I stretched out my legs, mirroring Anderson's relaxed posture. 'The funeral was the first time I'd met him.'

'Really? You looked pretty matey to me.'

'He paid for Jojo's funeral. We talked on the phone the night before.'

'Interesting. I wonder why he would do that?' Anderson met my eyes, inviting me to speculate.

I shrugged. 'Guys like Jamie Mitchell tend to be keen on good causes and the arts. It adds an air of respectability.'

Anderson raised an eyebrow and repeated, 'Guys like Jamie Mitchell . . .' He did not bother to ask me what kind of a guy Mitchell was; we both knew what I meant. 'You think Jojo's funeral counts as a charitable donation?'

I topped up our glasses. 'Maybe. Who knows?'

'Or maybe you think paying for Nugent's send-off was an admission of guilt?' The brandy had ruddied Anderson's cheeks and sharpened his eyes. 'Our mutual friend Les was there too. Quite the convention.'

'Jamie Mitchell isn't the guilty kind. Anyway, you were there too.'

Anderson flashed me a brief smile. 'I was off duty, accompanying Rose.'

'Funerals are well-known hot dates.'

Anderson glanced at his watch. 'No. The hot date's tonight.' He set his empty glass on a shelf and got to his feet. 'Speaking of which, I should make a move. Rose might be looking for me.'

I doubted it, but the conversation was getting uncomfortable and I was not sorry to end it. I slid the brandy bottle into the corner of one of the shelves and took the pantry keys from my pocket.

'Good luck keeping Rose below seventy.'

Anderson shook his head. 'Maybe I should book her a shot on a racetrack for her birthday. Get it out her system.'

I unlocked the door. 'If I were you, I'd stick to something shiny and expensive from Blair and Sheridan.'

This time, he gave me a genuine smile. 'Aye, that would probably go down better. The roads around here are dicey though. That was some crash on the corner.'

Anderson's words were casual, but we had known each other since we were boys, and a glint in his eye made me wonder if he had been planning to seek me out all along.

'The wreck was still there when we started our evaluation for the sale. It was a nasty one. Two boys dead, I heard.'

'That all you heard?'

The pantry door was half open, but Anderson stayed where he was, waiting for my reply. It was quiet in the corridor beyond. The hubbub of the sale's aftermath had died away. Those who had not already removed their goods would be back the following day, but there might still be a few dealers haunting the premises.

I drew the door closed. 'What are you asking?'

He met my eyes, more policeman than friend. 'You've been here all week. Anyone say anything about the crash?'

Rain tapped against the window. Anderson's Paco Rabanne overpowered the room's faint scent of beeswax and rotting leather. A moment ago, the pantry had been cosy. Now it felt airless.

'Just that they were Glasgow lads working for the Forrests up at the polytunnels.'

'Nothing else?'

I hesitated. 'Abomi said his uncle Razzle told him one of the boys was a bit of a scally who ran with one of the Young Teams.'

Anderson nodded, indicating I was not telling him anything he did not know already. 'Who's Abomi?'

I cursed myself for mentioning names. 'One of our young porters, Andy Diamond. A good lad. Not the brightest, but eager to learn, a hard worker. Keeps his nose clean.'

'And he's the nephew of Ray Diamond? My, my. How the world ties up. You know some dodgy folk, Rilke.'

'I've known you for over thirty years.'

I put my hand on the door handle.

Anderson caught the pantry door before I could open it. His voice was low. 'I don't count. No mention of Jamie Mitchell in all this?'

'The car crash? Should there be?'

'Not necessarily. Daft lads drive too fast. Some of them crash and die, but I'd appreciate it if you'd tell me if you hear he's sniffing around anywhere close by.'

I shook my head. 'I'm not one of your snouts.'

Anderson laughed. 'Snout? You've been watching too much TV, Rilke. I'm asking as a pal, a long-time friend, man and boy. Mitchell's a nasty piece of work. Just let me know if you hear anything.'

He opened the door and stepped through it. The painting Jamie Mitchell had coveted sat unclaimed against a wall. I felt like putting my foot through its canvas. The sound of Rose's high heels clacked up ahead. She appeared in the hallway, glowing with the sheen of newly pocketed wealth. She raised her eyebrows at the sight of us.

'What were you two doing holed up together in there? Should I be jealous?'

I said, 'Bugger off, Rose.'

The inspector gave me a look then turned a warm smile on Rose. 'Only of the fine brandy Rilke's been plying me with.' Anderson reached into his pocket and passed Rose his car keys. 'Be gentle with me, please. I've not got the nerves for Brands Hatch.'

Rose weighed the keys in her hand. 'I don't know why everyone goes on about my driving. You'd have more points on your licence than me, if you weren't a policeman.'

Anderson put an arm around her waist. 'I'm allowed to break the speed limit when I'm chasing criminals.'

'And when you're late for a restaurant booking?'

He pulled her close. 'Less said about that incident, the better.'

Rose grinned. She looked at me. 'You happy to lock up and get Abomi and Frank back to Glasgow?'

'No problem. I'll let Frank drive.'

Rose gave me a wink. 'Don't worry if I'm running late on Monday. Just keep on top of the crew. We want to be clear of this place ASAP.'

'Sure thing.'

I touched the keys in my pocket, checking they were there. Ballantyne House had made us a lot of money, but I was eager to be shot of it – to drive away and never look back.

Twenty-Four

WE WERE HALFWAY towards Glasgow, windscreen wipers keeping up a steady to and fro. Frank was driving, his dark fringe flopping over his forehead, jaw set, morose as a funeral director steering a hearse loaded with miniature coffins. Abomi had regained his smile and was chatting about his uncle's Rottweiler, Rambo, and what kind of dog he would buy with the bonus Rose had promised him, if he could persuade his mum and Uncle Razzle to let him have one of his own.

'There was an Afghan hound that almost won Crufts, remember? It was a wee smasher, but Uncle Razzle says they're only good for advertising hairspray and Mum says they eat as much as Rambo. Westies are cute.' He held out his phone and showed me a photo of a white terrier, grinning at the camera. 'The SSPCA website says they're full of personality, but maybe they're a girl's dog. What do you think, Rilke? Are they a girl's dog?'

I was about to tell him that, with the exception of Chihuahuas, Toy Poodles, Pekingese and King Charles Spaniels, there was no such thing as a girl's dog, and that his bonus probably wouldn't stretch to the price of a pedigree when my phone buzzed. I took it out and saw Les's name flashing on the screen. I almost rejected the call, but it occurred to me that he might have information on the G-situation and I picked up.

Les clipped his words in a way that told me he wanted to hit me. 'What did you say to Jamie Mitchell?'

My stomach descended in the direction of my brogues. 'Nothing.'

Les was somewhere loud, full of swimming-pool echoes. He repeated 'nothing' as if it were a point for the prosecution. 'So why is he out for your blood?'

We overtook a lorry. An arc of spray engulfed the van. I whispered, 'Are you somewhere public? Maybe think about keeping your voice down?'

'My voice is fine. I asked you a question. Why is he out for your blood?'

'He's not out for my blood.'

'Here's Shereen Nanjiani with a newsflash: he bloody is. Think hard. What did you do that Mitchell might have taken offence to?'

I sighed. 'He wanted to buy a stupid painting off the wall before the sale. I told him he'd have to wait for the auction like everyone else.'

Les went ballistic in my ear. 'What the fuck did you do that for?'

Anger carried his voice into the cab. Frank glanced at me and then back at the road. Abomi turned to look at me, his mouth an O of surprise. I twisted round to face the window and lowered my voice, hoping Les would follow my example.

'Keep it down. I had to. It's the rules.'

Les's volume crept upwards. 'Since when did you care about fucking rules?'

I put a bit of steel into my voice. 'Bowery wouldn't last long if we didn't obey the law. Anyway, since when did you care about you know who?'

'Since he became the big man about town. Jamie Mitchell's hexed me because of you and now no one will sell me anything. Glasgow's swimming in gear and I'm suffering a lone fucking drought.'

The motorway blurred by. We passed a lorry loaded with sheep heading for their executions, their faces pressed to the gaps between the slats. Les had been arrested during lockdown. Caught in his key worker fluorescent jacket, he had been carrying a bag full of decoy ready meals he tried to claim he was delivering to his shielding (long dead) mother and a rucksack full of hash-filled baggies. The judge had decided the prisons were full enough and Les had got away with a large fine, but his card was marked, his bank balance fucked.

I hissed, 'Why would anything I do affect you?'

A Tannoy announcement crackled hazily in the background of wherever Les was.

'Ever heard of the fucking butterfly effect? I introduced yous. I warned you Mitchell was a touchy bastard and not to cross him when I gave you his number. He's withdrawn my line of credit, wants payment in full.'

A motorway sign told us it was forty miles to Glasgow.

'I didn't cross him.'

Les's voice rose an octave. 'He thinks you did, which means

you did. Now I'm out in the cold and you better watch your back.'

I laughed. 'Why, what are you going to do? Threaten me with your baseball bat? I'm not one of your Midwich Cuckoos.'

Les was shrill with outrage. 'Me? It's not me you have to look out for. I'm at the bus station waiting for a fucking Megabus to Aberdeen. There's a guy up there can maybe sort me out. I'm talking about Jamie Mitchell. He comes across as Mr Calm-and-in-Control but he's a mad fucking bastard. I hope that painting was worth shafting me and putting your own name on the wanted list for.'

I closed my eyes. 'It was ugly as fuck. A dead bird on a plate of fruit and veg. It didn't even sell.'

'Jesus Christ.' I could hear Les lighting up and inhaling, his breath sounded raw. 'If you'd had any sense, you'd have tied a bow on the bloody thing, made a present of it to him and thrown in a Picasso for good effect.'

I started to speak. 'It was a busy day and—'

'I don't give a monkey's crap. I've warned you. And I'd tell your pal Sandy to watch his arse too, if I were you. Mitchell knows you're soft on the wee tosser. If he can't find you, he might decide to take it out on him.'

I said, 'I'm not soft on . . .' but the line had gone dead.

Abomi continued to stare. Frank glanced at me and looked away.

I said, 'Is a man not allowed a private phone call?'

I dialled Sands' number. His phone went straight to voice-mail. I told him to call me and hung up.

Abomi whispered, 'Are you okay, Mr Rilke?'

I forced a smile. 'I'm fine, son. Don't you worry. My pal Les is a drama queen.'

Abomi grinned. 'I've seen drama queens on TV. They're a good laugh.'

I had no idea what he was talking about, but I said, 'Aye, bloody hysterical.'

I told Frank to drop Abomi off before me. He made no comment although it would mean doubling back to the West End afterwards. Abomi and his mother lived with Ray Diamond and his wife Mary on a peripheral housing estate, in two council houses that had been knocked into one. It was a smart arrangement that kept Diamond in relative luxury in the heart of the community on which he relied.

The street was empty. The curtains were drawn, lights on, in the Diamond house. I had texted Ray en route. He stepped from the front door into the garden as our van drew up. His dog Rambo followed lazily at his heels.

Abomi jumped from the cab. 'See you tomorrow, Frank. Bye, Mr Rilke.'

Frank spared the boy a smile. 'See you.'

Ray squeezed Abomi's shoulder and said something that made the boy laugh as he jogged up the path and into the house.

I took a deep breath and told Frank, 'I won't be long.'

The head porter nodded. He took out his phone and started tapping at the keys.

Ray waited, caught in the light thrown from the living-room window, watching as I pulled on my coat and got out of the van. It had stopped raining, but there was a chill on the wind that made me turn my collar up. Rambo wobbled over to greet me, tail weaving slowly from side to side. The dog was old and out of shape, with rheumy eyes and a tendency to slaver. But it was well known that

Ray doted on it. I rubbed the dog in the sensitive region between its ears. It sat down and rested its weight against my leg.

Ray said, 'He likes that.'

Despite his nickname, Razzle Diamond was one of the least flashy people I knew. No rings or chains glinted on his fingers or around his neck. He was dressed in shades of blue and browns. The kind of outfit no one would remember on the witness stand. His hair was thinning and cut in a not-too-short back and sides. His glasses were mid-range, current without being of the moment. I had known Ray for twenty years and had once stood next to him at a quiet bar without noticing he was there, until he said my name.

I straightened up. 'Hello, Ray. How's it going?'

His voice was soft, almost gentle. 'Oh, you know, Rilke. The usual. Navigating choppy waters. How's my nephew doing?'

'He's a good lad, puts his back into things. I don't know how we managed without him.'

Ray gave me a smile that showed his dentures. He was in good shape for his age. It was not sugar decay that had done for his teeth. 'Good to hear. First time you've come by the house. Normally your comrade drops Andy off.'

I did not bother to tell him that Frank was no comrade of mine. 'I thought I'd say hello. Been a while.' I took a small bundle of jewellery, bagged and wrapped in a soft cloth, from my pocket and passed it to him. 'Congratulations. You did well in the sale today. Got everything you went for at a decent price.'

Ray weighed the bundle in his hand but did not bother to unwrap it. 'I'm getting used to the internet bollocks. Not the same as being there, of course, but useful if you can't make it.' He nodded at the bundle. 'You didn't need to bother. Andy could have brought it home with him.'

It was unusual for Ray to miss a sale, but I did not ask what had got in the way. Ray was a man who told you what he wanted you to know.

Rambo sniffed the border of small conifers that edged an unseasonably green lawn. Ray saw me looking at it and smiled. 'The AstroTurf was Andy's idea. Vulgar, but Mary and his mum like it.'

'Practical.'

He shrugged. 'I guess so. Rambo doesn't like to piss on it, which is an advantage.'

He was waiting for me to tell him why I was there. The dog gave me a friendly look and lowered itself to the ground at his master's feet.

I said, 'I dropped by for a reason . . .' But I could not think of the right words.

Ray helped me out. 'You've been getting up the wrong noses. Not like you.'

'Like you say, choppy waters.'

He snorted. 'Big fucking waves. Shame we're not into surfing.' A wrought metal bench was tucked in the corner of the lawn, sheltered by a tall hedge. Ray nodded towards it. 'Fancy a seat? I'd ask you into the house, but you know what Andy's like. He'd be that chuffed to have you visit, we wouldn't get any peace.' The dog followed us to the bench and settled beneath it. Ray took a seat and set the bundle of jewellery by his thigh. He said, 'You've been good to young Andy. That goes a long way with me.'

'I didn't—'

He interrupted. 'I know you didn't do it to look for favours, but here you are, asking for a favour.'

'More like asking for some advice.'

'My advice is simple. Keep out of Jamie Mitchell's way.'

'Might be easier said than done. I'm a man of regular habits.' Ray threw me a look that said, never kid a kidder. 'I'm tied to the auction house. I get out and about, but I'm always there on sale days. It's not hard to track me down.'

He nodded. 'I get that. Normally I'd offer to have a word, but things are tricky right now. There's a delicate balance in the city I wouldn't like to upset. Do you have any annual leave due?'

'Do you think that's necessary?'

A gust of wind made me draw my coat closer. The pawn-broker seemed untouched by the cold. Somewhere inside the house a television was turned on. The sound of canned laughter leaked into the garden.

Ray shrugged. 'You asked for my advice.'

'We're snowed under with the big sale. I could take a couple of days at the start of next week.'

A couple of boys, around ten years old, started to kick a ball about beneath a streetlight, on the road beyond the garden. They were wiry, with buzz cuts and high-pitched voices. We watched them for a moment then Ray met my eyes. 'I was thinking more like a month or two's sabbatical. Why not go off to Italy or something? Visit some art galleries.'

'Are you serious?'

Ray leaned forward in his seat, playing with Rambo's ears. The dog huffed with pleasure. 'Jamie Mitchell doesn't have a refined sense of proportion. He's insecure. That tends to make people hot-blooded. He won't last. Deep down, he knows it. That's part of what makes him vicious. But for now, as far as you're concerned, he's a danger best avoided.'

'I don't have the money to go to Italy for a couple of months, even if I wanted to.'

Ray looked at me. For a moment I thought he was going to offer to lend me the funds, but he simply nodded, as if he had made up his mind about something. 'Andy's found a niche at Bowery. He'd be upset if something happened to you.'

I almost said that I would not be too happy either, but the silences left by quiet men like Ray Diamond invite too many confidences. I kept my mouth shut. The boys' football thudded on the road beyond and hit off the side of the van.

Ray straightened up and shouted, 'Hey, Lewis! Careful. That van belongs to a friend of mine.'

The boys started, and I realised we had been hidden in the darkness of the garden. They called, 'Sorry, Mr Diamond.' One of the boys picked up the ball. They moved further down the street and resumed their game.

Ray turned to me. 'You're a friend of Jim Anderson, aren't you?'

'More of an acquaintance.'

'An acquaintance.' Ray reached back down and patted the dog. 'I heard the inspector has it in for Jamie Mitchell.'

'I wouldn't know.'

'Of course not.'

Inside the house, the theme tune to some programme was playing. I felt the conversation about to end. I said, 'What I mean is, I thought I had my finger on the pulse, but I'd never heard of Jamie Mitchell until now. Turns out he's someone to be reckoned with.'

Ray sighed. 'Covid created a few openings. Jamie Mitchell would still be banging his head off the barbed-wire ceiling if it wasn't for that.'

Covid had taken a big bite from the criminal ranks. The virus had not been choosy, but it had had a special taste for those in their later years, with extra weight on their bones and fur on their lungs. Ray lifted the pouch of jewellery and got to his feet, indicating our chat about Jamie Mitchell was over. 'That was a funny business with the Chinese lad,' he said.

Phan was Vietnamese, but I did not bother to correct him. 'Andy did well there. I froze but your boy was quick off the mark. Put his fleece around the lad and helped him into the van before I'd even crossed the road.'

'Aye, he's a good kid. Thinks you walk on water, by the way.'

Ray strolled to the gate with me. The old dog heaved itself up and ambled behind him.

I had not intended to mention him, but I found myself asking, 'Did you hear about Jojo?'

'The poofter found dead in the Merchant City?' Ray's eyes met mine, suddenly dangerous. 'No offence meant.'

I watched my words. 'None taken. It's just that Jojo isn't the only gay man found dead in the street recently.'

Ray's voice was ice and glass. 'These guys play with fire. They shouldn't be surprised when they get burnt.'

I felt the hairs rise on the back of my neck, the way they sometimes did when I wandered through the park at night. It was a signal to walk away. Jamie Mitchell had me in his sights and Ray Diamond was not a man to cross, but I stood my ground. 'What do you mean?'

Ray looked to where the boys were continuing their kick-about, and then back to me. 'Do you need me to spell it out?'

'Maybe.'

'Okay I don't count you in this. I wouldn't let Andy work with you if I did. You're all right, Rilke, pretty straight for a bent guy. But most poofs aren't like you. They're unstable. They don't know when to keep it in their pants. That can lead to problems.'

It was nothing I had not heard before. 'Thanks for being frank with me.'

He did not smile. 'Like I said, Rilke, you're different. The exception that proves the rule.'

'How about Jamie Mitchell?'

'What do you mean?'

'Gay or straight?'

Ray paused, weighing up the odds. 'He deals with gays – everybody does. Money's money and gays like their drugs. I never heard anything about him being a bum boy though. You know something I don't?'

The last thing I wanted was for word to get back to Jamie Mitchell that I had labelled him homosexual. 'No. Nothing. I just wondered.'

Rambo leant against his master's leg, indicating it was time to go back into the warmth. Ray fondled the dog's ears.

'Yeah, well, if you were thinking of asking him on a date I'd think again.'

'Thanks for the advice.'

'You watch yourself, Rilke.'

'Don't worry. I'm like a cockroach – I'm a survivor.'

Ray looked down at the path. I followed his gaze and saw a small black beetle crawling slow and steady along the concrete. He raised his foot and squashed it under his heel. 'Surviving's not good enough. If you won't run, you're going to have to win.'

Twenty-Five

FRANK STARTED THE VAN and headed west. He did not bother
to ask me where I wanted dropped off and I did not apolo-
gise for keeping him late after a long day's work. The van's
engine sounded throaty and there was a faint tick-tick-tick
in its depths that might have been the timing chain or a loose
valve. I checked my phone. There was no missed call from
Sands. I texted: *Ring me when you get this.*

The scheme where Ray Diamond lived and ruled was a
grid of three-storey tenements and four-in-a-block villas,
built sometime in the early 1950s. The streets beyond Ray's
were a mismatch of well-tended gardens, overgrown hedges
and litter. We passed the occasional dog walker, hoods up,
shoulders hunched against the rain. An oversized high school
loomed, pale and pebble-dashed, fronted by a muddy playing
field. Frank weaved the van around speed bumps that felt
like a joyrider's obstacle course. It was dark and cold, but a
group of youths were huddled outside a fish and chip shop.

The shop's sign featured a smiling cod, leaping with joy towards a friendly bunch of chips. A bus coasted ahead of us, the top deck illuminated by the soft violet light that prevents veins from popping to attention. I had known places like this, where those who found the means escaped at the first opportunity.

My phone pinged. A photograph of a bottle of champagne and a dozen oysters on ice. Rose was having a good night. I angled the screen away from Frank and logged on to Grindr, but my conversation with Ray weighed on me and my heart was not in it. I logged out.

Frank steered us onto the motorway. His profile was silhouetted in the gleam thrown by the arc lights that stood a giant's pace apart, along the central reservation. It was difficult to believe that I had once found the head porter handsome. His good looks had receded beneath his personality. I shoved my phone into my pocket. 'What did Jamie Mitchell want with you at the viewing yesterday?'

Frank was staring at the road ahead. I thought he was not going to answer, then he said, 'He wanted to wind me up.'

'Why?'

'Because he's a cunt.'

The motorway widened into six lanes. Vehicles peeled off towards the Cathedral, City Centre, Dumbarton. I said, 'I won't argue with that. Why you?'

Frank overtook a pantechnicon then stayed steady in the centre lane. Overhead display boards flashed out a warning not to exceed fifty miles per hour. The van kept pace with the traffic, its speedometer fluttering a little over sixty.

'Nothing personal. Because I was there.' Frank moved out to overtake a lane of cars and glided into the fast lane towards the inexplicably placed right-hand exit to Charing Cross.

I waited until he slotted into the exit lane. 'How come you know Jamie Mitchell?'

Frank negotiated the slip road's tight turns and pulled to a halt at the traffic lights that bordered the junction. We were in the city now. A short walk from the Art School, a shorter walk from Sands' flat. A mixture of business types and students crossed the road in front of us. I wondered why the boy could not stick to his own kind, rather than seek out old reprobates and gangsters.

Frank glanced at me. 'I'm not working on the side for him if that's what you're worried about.'

'Mitchell's a tricky character. If he's putting pressure on you, it would be good to know. Bowery's got its quirks, but we're a legit organisation. We want to keep it that way.'

'It's not me you have to worry about.'

'What do you mean?'

The traffic lights changed to green. Frank put the van into gear and edged into the traffic. 'You're the one Mitchell's interested in.'

I could have told the head porter that it was none of his business, but I said, 'I seem to have got in his bad books.'

Frank kept his face blank, as if the reason why was of no interest to him. 'Easily done. What are you going to do? Get some protection?'

I shrugged. 'I don't know. Not really my style. Maybe.'

We sank into silence again. The traffic crept slowly forward. Frank negotiated the tricky junction that had been someone's idea of slick city planning sometime back in the 1970s.

'Mitchell's got a bar in Partick, near my flat, Lily Pinks. I took to having a drink there on my way home. That's how

I got to know him. Seemed like a nice enough bloke at first, but there's a side to him.'

Before lockdown Lily Pinks had been an unassuming old-man's pub called Flodden Field. Covid had finished it off, and some of the old men too. It had reopened as a decidedly hip bar, all post-industrial furnishings, exposed brickwork and unpolished metal. I had not been inside since it had been renovated and was surprised that Frank had picked it for his local.

'Plenty of bars to choose from in Partick. I'm guessing you found somewhere else to hang out.'

'Once you know Jamie Mitchell, he's hard to avoid. Easier to move to a different town.'

'Should we be looking for a new head porter?'

The rain had almost lifted. The wipers squeaked against the windscreen. Frank turned them off.

'I thought you already were.'

It felt like a long time since I had shared the brandy with Anderson in the butler's pantry. I wanted another drink. Somewhere busy where I could meet with some acquaintances and discuss the sale, then afterwards move on to an adventure that would make me forget about myself.

I said, 'You're still on probation. Rose is tired of you being surly and hungover. But there's time to pull things around – if you want to.'

Frank repeated, 'Surly and hungover,' as if the words amused him. 'That should be the slogan for this fucking city. I'll head home for an early bed and learn some show tunes, shall I?'

His reference to show tunes was a dig at me, as if all gays were flouncy *Oklahoma* fans. I whispered. 'Be careful.'

Frank drew into the kerb outside the pool hall on St

George's Road. A few men were congregated outside, smoking. It was nowhere we needed to be. He turned and looked at me. 'Or what?'

'Or you'll be signing on first thing tomorrow.'

Frank steadied his breathing. I calculated the reach from me to him, the power required to pack a punch in the confined space. One of the smokers loitering outside the pool hall made a joke and the men burst out laughing.

Frank hauled off his brown dust coat and bundled it at me. 'Fine by me.' He lifted his rucksack from the footwell. 'You don't deserve this warning, but Jamie Mitchell's a fucking psycho. He hates shitpackers like you. I'd tell you to watch your back, but you'd think I was being sarcastic. Find yourself a minder and stay out of his way.'

'Frank . . .'

But he had slammed the van door and was striding away through the drizzle.

I sat there for a moment trying to summon the will to cross over to the driver's side and head home. I had wanted rid of Frank, but now that he was gone, I felt guilty.

My phone buzzed. I took it from my pocket expecting another photo from Rose. Instead I saw a message from Sands: *PARTY – PARTY – PARTY 22 Hutcheson St, G1*. I swore under my breath and dialled his number. I expected it to ring out, but the boy answered, his voice all business. 'Up for it?'

It started to rain again. Raindrops coursed down the windscreen, individual beads stretching and connecting into tiny rivers. He was nothing to do with me, this boy. 'I told you already, I'm not Jojo.'

'No. Jojo's dead and we're alive.'

He was like an inverse Pied Piper, a youngster dancing old men to the grave. The Carnarvon Bar was a block ahead on the corner of Carnarvon and Ashley Street. A couple of women were outside, chatting. One of them waved a hand in the air to emphasise a point and half waltzed, half staggered across the pavement. Her companion caught her by the arm, steadying her. The women doubled over with laughter, then straightened up, taking almost simultaneous drags from their cigarettes.

I said, 'I'm just round the corner from your flat. Why don't we go for a drink?'

There was a new recklessness in the boy's voice. 'You want to talk me out of it.'

'You want to talk me into it. That makes us even.'

Sands' laugh was exasperated. 'I don't need to talk you into anything. There's plenty people want to party.'

I had known young men like Sands, had been one myself. Boys whose appetite for life was strong enough to be close to a death wish. I said, 'I thought you were an artist. Aren't you meant to stand on the edge looking in, recording the underworld for the chattering classes?'

Sands' words quickened, as if I had touched on the heart of things. 'You remember Jamie Mitchell? Paid for Jojo's funeral? He wants some photos for one of his clubs, the freakier the better, he said. He'll give me good money to take them and, in the meantime, I'll still be working towards my portfolio. It's perfect.'

I took a deep breath. 'You don't want to get too close to guys like Mitchell. He's a gangster.'

'Who cares? Jojo helped me, but you can only learn so much through stories or watching. Mitchell's offering me a chance to be in on the action. The way Caravaggio was in on the action. I'm going to call the project, *Looking in from the Inside.*'

'How far in are you planning to go?'

'As far as I can.'

I got out of the van and walked to the driver's side. A breath of fresh air and rain tainted by the tobacco smoke and sweet vape smells of the snooker players. I climbed into the cab and slammed the door. A feeling of sadness weighed on my chest. 'I get it. You enjoyed Jojo's funeral so much, you fancy one of your own.'

'Jojo was old. I'm twenty-two.'

I had thought myself invincible at twenty-two. It was a long time ago. A time of street beatings, bruised flesh and late nights that stretched into sleepy days. My friends and I had dressed as if we were always at a party, and when people took advantage of us, we had tamped down the shame and turned up the music. We were under the illusion that suffering brought us closer to our heroes. And most of our heroes had died young. Back then, death had been romantic, until people started to die for real. Les was the only friend who remained from that time. The others had straightened out, drifted away, left the country or left this world.

I remembered how it felt to have no future. It had been painful and glorious. Age had curbed my recklessness, but I still went walking by night – weighing up the odds, calculating risk.

I closed my eyes and pressed my fingertips to my eyelids, trying to diffuse the headache that was building there. I could guess the answer, but I asked, 'What happened?'

'This scene, Rilke. It's like landing in another universe.'

'Aye, realms of fucking gold, no doubt. You don't think that Jojo and Anthony felt the same way you do now?'

'They were older than me . . .'

'Doesn't matter. When they first took that stuff, they felt

the same way you do. Like stout Cortez and all his men cocks ahoy on a peak in Darien.'

'What are you talking about?'

I repeated, 'It doesn't matter. Point is, maybe you'll last longer than them, maybe not. Either way, you won't be painting pictures or making films or even dropping into lectures, playing computer games or going out clubbing with your mates. You don't dabble in this crap. It takes over your life.'

Sands sounded amused. 'All I did was ask you to a party. I'm not stupid enough to screw my life up for a few kicks.'

I leaned back in the driver's seat and closed my eyes again. 'No one thinks they're going to screw their life up until they do. You start off practising safe sex, then you slip up a few times, which you decide is okay because there's PrEP. But pretty soon that takes effort you no longer have. And you ask yourself, why fear the inevitable? Other guys are HIV positive and they do okay. Before you know it, you're pozzed up.'

'Okay. You're not in the mood for a party. I get it.'

'Yesterday you were worried that Jojo's drugs were tainted. Today you're Liza Minnelli and life is a fucking cabaret, old chum. Don't you think you should take things a bit slower?'

'I've found some good people, Rilke. They look after each other.'

'What about the Art School folk? Aren't they good people?'

Sands sounded exasperated. 'Even the gays are a bunch of straights. They don't get me the way these guys do.'

'Believe me, son – anything happens, these new pals of yours will leave your body in the gutter and never look back.' I wanted to tell him that Jamie Mitchell had offered him the commission to get at me, but I knew it would do more harm than good, so I said, 'Mitchell will be the first one to step over your dead body without a backward glance.'

The boy's voice took on a dignified tone, as if he had got to his feet and straightened his back. 'I'd rather take a few risks than end up like you. A sad fuck with no friends.'

I said, 'I have plenty of–' But the boy had hung up. That was how my phone calls ended these days, in abrupt silence that made me nostalgic for the dial tone.

Sands' flat was two blocks away. I could drive there in less time than it would take him to lock his front door and run down the stairs. But we had said all we were going to say to each other that evening.

Frank had left the keys in the ignition. I started the engine, executed a swift U-turn and drove towards town. Odds were, Jojo and Anthony had died of drug-related causes, but they had not found their way to the Merchant City's pavements by accident. Let Sands have his party, Les take the slow bus to Aberdeen and Anderson gulp down champagne and oysters. I would find out who had dragged Jojo into the gutter and left him there. And maybe in the process I would help Sands avoid his fate.

Twenty-Six

THE TRONGATE IS the old heart of Glasgow. A step from the cathedral, birthplace of the university, home to the city's gibbet. In the old days you could get educated, shriven and hanged within a short mile's radius. I had spent a lot of time around there when I was Sands' age, picking through Paddy's Market looking for things to resell at a profit. Paddy's is long gone, but second-hand shops cling on, tucked away in side streets and beneath railway arches: stamp collectors, radical books, comic shops, army surplus, brass instruments. Specialist premises nestle warm, and sometimes grubby, beside the plate-glass windows of the galleries, architects and designers who have colonised the district.

The quarter is an intersection between artists, artful business, people down on their luck and people who never had no luck at all. You can take in a play, grab some jazz, get pissed, order micro-Michelin or bag a kebab. You can get tattooed, fucked or fucked up, buy an air gun or maybe a real gun, hire a lawyer, get a trial – a fast track to jail or freedom.

In the 1980s, a time of unemployment and bleak prospects, a square mile in the shadow of the Trongate was rechristened the Merchant City. The new name was inspired by the Tobacco Lords, the Sugar and Cotton Kings who laid the foundations of Glasgow's wealth. It was an attempt at civic pride, but once you know the origins of the fine buildings that form the quarter, it is hard to walk its streets without smelling blood in their mortar.

The rechristening of the Merchant City relied on a collective forgetting. There had been no talk of blood, rape and murder, of fratricide and child exploitation. No mention of lynchings, beatings and families ripped asunder. But the district's history is re-emerging, as old crimes sometimes do. People have started to acknowledge that the Princes of the Pavements, who made the city 'great', wrenched their fortunes from Caribbean plantations, forcibly worked by enslaved Africans. I saw Phan in my mind's eye, half naked and beaten, running as if the Devil was on his tail. Whoever had exploited him would have fitted right in with the city's merchants.

I parked the van in a 24-hour NCP. It was a dreich night with an unholy chill in the air. The streets around the Merchant City were busy. Diners clustered in restaurants, and drinkers spilled, like slopped pints, from bars. There was a performance of *Carmina Burana* at the City Halls and a folk singer on at the Old Fruitmarket. Their audiences mingled, smart coats rubbing shoulders with leather jackets and kagoules, high heels and brogues stepping alongside trainers, DMs and hiking boots. There had been an Old Firm game that afternoon and supporters gusted eastwards towards bars that tolerated football colours.

I pulled on my cap and my raincoat. It was a deluge outside. Litter blocked the gutters, and here and there pavements had turned to shallow rivers. My feet were wet, the hems of my good suit trousers sodden. Perhaps it was the brandy still in my system or the sense of being alone after a day of kerfuffle and commotion. Or maybe it was an effect of walking the old district. The past was leaking through.

A drunk tipped against me and I touched my pocket, checking my wallet was still there. A giggle of girls in bum-skimming dresses flurried by on high heels, tenting their jackets over their heads to save their hair from the rain. I ducked into a doorway and tried to light the roll-up I had made earlier, but it was damp and the papers refused to burn. I tossed it into the gutter and watched it sweep away. A burly youth was sitting on the pavement opposite, his head in his hands, hair sopping, clothes sticking to his body like loosened flesh.

Even through the dark and the rain I could see that, sober, he would be strong enough to defend himself. But alcohol had dissolved his strength and his senses. He was a sitting target, the way Jojo had been a sitting target. I felt an urge to wake him up and send him home but stayed where I was. Straight men have a tendency to think every gay man is after their arse. I have known queers who count bagging a hetero as their highest achievement. I have never hated myself enough for that.

The drunk boy slumped forward. He was in danger of toppling into the watery drain. I crossed the road, keeping a wide berth between him and me. Two bouncers, one male, one female, were sheltering under an awning outside a shiny bar called Space Invaders. They watched my approach.

I pushed my cap back so they could see my face, my sober condition. 'That lad looks in a bad way.'

The bouncers were dressed in the same anonymous black trousers and waterproof jackets. I expected them to ask what business it was of mine, but the female bouncer nodded. 'Bit of rain won't do any harm. We're keeping an eye on him.'

The awning reached capacity and water streamed from it onto the street. I stepped out of the way just in time to avoid a soaking. A posse of young men jostled out of the bar and congregated around the hunched man. One of them said, 'Chris sakes, Davie, Jesusfuckman, Whatkindastateyouin?'

Another man shouted, 'He's fucking Corona-d,' and the rest of them laughed.

Their voices penetrated Davie's consciousness. He must have muttered something because one of his friends sang out, 'Aye, aye, aye,' in a way that was meant to soothe and shut up. Two men hooked him under the armpits and got him into a standing position.

'Early bath for Hanlon.'

'Taxi for Hanlon.'

They staggered off along the street, carrying their fallen comrade through the rain. Frantic, heart-pounding, brain-blasting beats pulsed from the bar-room beyond. The male bouncer eyed me, 'I'm not sure this is your kind of place.'

'I don't want to come in. A friend of mine died on a night out in the Merchant City a week back. Drank too much and passed out in the cold. I wanted to see where he died, pay my respects. When I spotted that boy sitting on the pavement . . . it's too late for my mate, but if someone had helped him, he might still be here.'

The bouncer was buff and clean shaven with the short-at-the-sides-gelled-on-top haircut favoured by young policemen. He gestured towards the end of the street. 'Aye, I remember.

I was on duty that night. Poor guy was found in a lane half a block away.'

The female bouncer was young with a blonde ponytail and a neat body nimble enough to wrong-foot clumsy drunks. 'Not much happening tonight, Billy. Take him round the corner and show him where his friend passed away. I'll phone if I need you.'

The man pulled up the hood of his jacket. 'Come on then.'

Neither of us talked as we walked to the end of the street. We turned a corner, and Billy the bouncer led me along a dreary cut-through punctuated by industrial-sized rubbish bins. Exit signs glowed dimly above forbidden back entrances to pubs and restaurants. The lane was a place of dark shapes and shadows. Billy pointed at a doorway half concealed by a rickety-looking fire-escape ladder that zigzagged up to the third floor.

'That's where it happened.'

A man and a woman were hunched beneath the fire escape, sleeping bags pulled up to their chests. I felt their eyes on us, assessing whether we were trouble or potential revenue. The doorway was not much of a place to die. The couple had chosen it because of a small overhang designed to keep the weather out, and the ladder, whose shadows offered some privacy.

The bouncer glanced at them, as if wondering whether to move them on. He decided against it and turned to face me. 'I saw your friend on my way back to work that night, after my break.'

'Before he died?'

He shook his head. 'Fraid not. He was gone by the time I saw him. I heard a commotion coming from down here and wondered what was happening. There was a bunch of rubber-neckers standing round the poor guy. Someone had their phone out taking photos. Can you believe it? Fucking ghoul. I told him to put it away or I'd shove it down his throat and let him shit it out. He moved off sharpish.'

I wiped rain from my eyes. 'Last time I saw him, Jojo wasn't looking so hot. I think he'd let things get on top of him.'

Neither of us speculated out loud on what might have got on top of Jojo.

'Someone had already called an ambulance. The paramedics showed up just as I was about to check him out. Whatever I did, it wouldn't have made any difference anyway. Like I said, your friend was gone.'

The homeless man in the doorway had been watching us. There was a rustling of paper and plastic as he leaned forward. 'It was me as called the ambulance. Your pal was in a bad way, but nobody would've noticed if it wasn't for us. They'd've thought he was street scum.'

The woman remained huddled in the doorway where Jojo had died. She had a woollen beanie hat pulled low over her face and was still wrapped in her sleeping bag. Her voice was strong and rasping. 'Don't listen to him. He talks a lot of shite. It was me saw him. I shouted *murder* and folk came running. A lassie called the polis. Nice wee thing she was. She saw I was upset and gave me a fiver.'

The man grumbled, 'What does it matter if it was you or me as called them? Thing is, we tried to get him help.' He started to sing in a surprisingly tuneful voice, '*When he needed a neighbour, we were there, we were there. When he needed a neighbour, we were there . . .*'

His friend threw a Starbucks coffee cup at him. It caught in the wind and tumbled into the darkness. She snapped, 'Shut up. He was beyond help, poor soul. Like you – you're beyond help.'

A crew of young men sprinted past the top of the lane, laughing. The couple cast wary looks in their direction. The youths kept on going.

The homeless man pulled his hat back, bright eyes in a weathered face. His teeth were a bomb site. 'I'm not deid yet. A tenner would help me.'

The woman rocked to and fro. 'You and me both.'

The wind was picking up. Litter rattled down the alleyway.

Billy the bouncer snapped, 'Piss off. We're trying to have a conversation here.' His phone chimed. He glanced at its screen. 'Best be getting back. Boss lady keeps me on a short leash.'

I shook his hand. 'Thanks for taking the time out. I heard Jojo wasn't the only guy to drop dead round here recently.'

He made a face. 'Like I said, it happens. The Merchant City had a good three years with no fatalities. Don't get me wrong — plenty of fisticuffs and broken bones but no actual deaths. You wait ages for a bus to turn up and then . . .' He let the sentence hang, perhaps realising it was in bad taste. 'Neither of them were drinking in our place, thank Christ.'

I said, 'Lucky.'

The bouncer glanced at his phone again. 'Sorry about your friend. I better go. Jacqui will be wanting her break.'

Chanting echoed from the street beyond. A gang of girls telling the world to 'blame it on the juice'. Billy stuck his hands in the pockets of his jacket and started to walk towards the top of the lane.

I walked with him. 'Nothing else you can tell me?' I was beginning to make a nuisance of myself.

'Like what?'

'I guess I'm asking if you suspect foul play.'

The bouncer stopped and turned to look at me. 'Don't beat yourself up. Sounds to me like you were a good friend to him.' He raised a hand in goodbye. 'Take care of yourself.'

I stood at the top of the alleyway and watched Billy disappear into the Merchant City's night-time crowd. I had not been much of a friend to Jojo in life and I was more concerned with the living than the dead. I turned around. The homeless man was standing in the dim light of the lane. He was thin and wiry with a straggly beard and unkempt hair. A large sheet of polythene was fastened over his head and shoulders, like a long transparent cape. It gave him a look of a sci-fi pilgrim. He met my eyes and nodded.

'Shame about your pal. Me and the missus could maybe give you some info, if you had a wee cash tip for us.' He beckoned back the way we had come. 'Not here though. It's not safe here. Too many drunks and bully-boys.'

In one direction lay lights and music, heat and chatter. In the other, dark and dampness: a doorway that had become a last resting place. I turned and followed the rough sleeper into the shadows. He had a bad limp that I guessed had been with him for a while, but the man was quick, and I had to up my pace to keep level with him. I sensed victory in his lurch. He had caught me, and I was money.

The man pointed at the doorway where his companion was still huddled. 'It was here your pal died.'

'I already know that.'

The woman looked up and called, 'He's a bullshitter. King of the shitters.' She pointed at him. 'King Shit. That's you.'

The man shouted, 'Ah, get to fuck . . .'

I straightened my back and put on my auction-room voice. 'If you've got something to tell me, get on with it. Otherwise I'm out of here.'

The man smoothed his plastic cape, gathering his dignity. 'No need to be like that.'

His wife patted the sleeping bag wrapped around her and rasped, in a voice that might have been meant to be seductive, 'You should talk to me.'

'Why?'

'I see things. I know things. What does Georgy Porgy the bouncer know? All he sees is trouble. Wants to be a polis but doesn't have the brains.' She giggled. 'Imagine not having the brains to be a polis.'

I stepped into the fire escape's shadows. Rain washed my face. I felt tired enough to coorie in the doorway beside her, but instead I gathered my raincoat out of reach of the alleyway's mud and squatted down, so our faces were level with each other. Her man settled down beside her. There was something pupae-like about his transparent plastic wrapping, but his face was sharp. He gave me a sly grin.

'I'll get Mary to gie you a gam if you want. She's not much to look at these days, but she used to be a beauty . . .'

The woman slapped him away. 'He's a bender. He widnae be interested in me. It's you he'd want the gam from.'

I spoke quickly before the man could make me an offer. 'If you know something, just tell me.'

Mary held out her hand. 'Money first.'

Plastic may be fantastic, but, in my world, cash is still king. I had three hundred pounds in my wallet. I opened it in the shadow of my coat, drew out a ten-pound note and held it out to her.

The man moved to snatch it, but she batted his hand away. 'It's worth more than that.'

The brown note dampened in the rain.

'I'm the only one buying.'

Mary wiped her face with her scarf. 'Maybe someone would pay me more to keep my mouth shut.'

'That's a dangerous game. How many episodes of *Columbo* start with a blackmailer being murdered?'

The man said, '*Columbo*'s a load of auld shite. Fucking dirty raincoat brigade . . .'

Mary threw an arm out and shoved him on the shoulder. 'Shut up.' She trained her eyes on me. Perhaps her man had been telling the truth when he said she was gorgeous, before street life took its toll. The woman had high cheekbones, well-spaced eyes and a broad mouth, but her nose had been knocked sideways and badly mended. Her skin was weathered, her expression wary. 'Thirty. You can afford it.'

The tendons in my knees were tightening like catgut. Jojo was dead but Sands was still alive, so I stayed where I was, hunkered down in the dirty alleyway. 'I'll give you twenty. Ten now, ten after.'

'Twenty-five.'

I nodded. 'Okay, it's a deal.' Mary held out a hand for the money. I ignored it. 'Tell me what you saw first.'

'Think I'm going to run away?' Mary pulled back the sleeping bag. She was wearing a skirt with no stockings. Her legs were puffy and pale, except for where they were livid with ulcers. A poisonous smell made me rock back on my heels. She said, 'I used to be able to give Mo Farah a run for his money. Not anymore.' She flapped the sleeping bag. 'Fresh air does them good. Trouble is, the air in Glasgow isn't very fresh.' She laughed at her own joke and let the sleeping bag drop. A police siren screamed in the distance. Mary muttered, 'Bastards,' and looked at me as if wondering why I was there.

I reached for my wallet, extracted another fifteen pounds, and kept the notes where she could see them. 'You were going to tell me about the night the man died on this doorstep. The night you phoned the police.'

Mary shook her head. 'I don't remember what night it was.'

Her man chipped in, 'It was whatever night he died.'

Mary's face tightened with concentration. 'That's right. Whatever night he died. Whatever night that was. Ronnie and me had had a wee falling-out.' She punched her man on the arm for emphasis. 'Because he's a selfish cunt.'

There was power behind the punch, but Ronnie moved with it, smiling as if it was an act of love.

Mary raised her arm like a biblical prophet and pointed down the lane. 'They came from down there. There was three of them. The dead man . . . I didn't know he was dead . . . maybe he wasn't dead then . . . maybe they didn't know he was dead . . . but they must have known he was sick . . . or OD'd . . . or whatever he was . . . they must have known he wasn't right . . . cause he was in a bad way . . . a really bad way . . . that man . . .'

Her arm was still outstretched, the finger she was pointing with shaking. I sensed her descending into a spiral and whispered, 'Take a deep breath.'

Mary opened her mouth and heaved in a deep breath that made her cough. She spat on the ground and nodded. 'That's better.'

I gentled my voice. 'Tell me about that night.'

'It was raining.'

Her man said, 'He's not interested in the fucking weather.'

Mary thumped him on the arm again. 'Ronnie was away for a piss. I was having a wee rest to myself. I heard them before I saw them. I thought they were laughing, then I thought maybe they were crying. It sounded like the Devil was coming for me. I don't believe in the Devil, but I was feart.' She looked towards the dark side of the lane, the refuse bins sheltering against the wall like cattle. 'Then I saw them. They looked like a monster. A big beast with three heads, limping along on six legs. I knew it was just men, two pissed guys carrying their pissed pal, but that's what it looked like. A great big three-headed monster. I thought they were taking a shortcut to the main street. Then I realised they were looking for somewhere to dump the drunk guy.' She corrected herself. 'The most drunk guy. They were all drunk or something. Maybe not drunk. Out of it. But he was the worst. He couldn't stand.'

Ronnie helped her out. 'He was deid.'

'I know he was deid now, but I didn't know that then. The gentleman wants to know what I saw and that's what I saw.'

I asked, 'Did you get a good look at the men?'

'When I saw they were going to dump him I sneaked up the stairs here. I thought maybe there'd be trouble if they saw me.' She pointed to the fire escape above. 'I'm feart of heights, but I knew they would choose this doorway. It's the best one. No one bothers us here, do they, Ronnie?'

He nodded proudly. 'It's our wee corner.'

The notes in my hand fluttered with the wind. Mary eyed them. 'It was the one with white hair that was making all the noise, bawling like a baby he was. The other one kept telling him to shut the fuck up. The dead man didn't say a word.'

I soothed my voice. 'The man with the white hair, was he old or had he dyed it?'

She touched her head, her beanie hat, trying to conjure the memory. 'It was all spiky on top. I didn't get a good look at his face. He was skinny – junkie skinny. Know what I mean?'

It could have been one of a hundred guys who like to frequent the Polo Lounge, but the description fitted Anthony. I nodded. 'I know what you mean. And the other man?'

Mary closed her eyes tight, summoning the night Jojo died. I saw her eyes flicker and waited for her to make something up, but her imagination failed.

'I didn't get a good look.' She leaned forward, suddenly motherly. 'Was he a good pal to you, son?'

'No. He was a bloody nightmare.'

'Nightmares make the best pals. You'll miss him, but he's in a better place than this.' She held out her hand for the money. 'Glasgow's a shitehole.' Her face suddenly brightened. 'One of them said something.'

'What did they say?'

'Put another ten on top of that one and I'll tell you.'

'You drive a hard bargain.'

Her voice was coaxing, all flattery and want. 'Aye, but you can afford it.'

I reached into my wallet, slid out another note and showed it to her.

Mary's right hand reached out to touch the notes. She caught her right wrist with her left hand and pulled it back onto her lap. As if each hand belonged to a separate entity. 'He said they'd done your pal a kindness.'

'A kindness?'

'A kindness. That's what he said, son. As if he'd bought him a bottle of vodka or something.'

'What happened next?'

'They dumped your poor pal here and went away, the way they came. I waited up there till Ronnie came back.' She shoved Ronnie's arm. 'He was gone for ages. You weren't happy someone had stolen our spot.'

Ronnie's eyes were bright in their nest of raindrops and plastic. 'I tried to wake the poor soul up.'

Mary snorted. 'You kicked him.'

'Aye, well, I didn't know he was deid. I wouldn't kick a deid man. It's not respectful.'

She accepted this as reasonable. 'Ronnie gave him a boot, but he didn't move.'

Ronnie toppled to one side, acting the part of dead Jojo. 'He fell over.' He pulled a ghastly face, tongue lolling out.

Mary gave him a half-hearted shove. 'Aye, he fell over. He didn't move, know what I mean? Just lay there. That's when we realised he was deid. I shouted blue murder and that wee lassie called an ambulance. She gave me a fiver.'

I wiped the rain from my face. 'Did you tell this to the police?'

Mary's eyes flitted away from me. 'Oh aye, son. Told them the full Bible, but you know the polis. Don't listen to a word they're told.'

Ronnie sat up. Water ran in rivulets down the plastic, but it could not wipe away the mud of the alleyway that clung to its surface. 'They don't like the paperwork.'

I said, 'You told me that you know what happens around here. My mate Jojo's not the only dead guy to turn up recently. What do you think's going on?'

Ronnie leaned back in on the step. He tilted his head upwards. 'Cheap thrills. Life's cheap. Piss it up against the wall.'

The rasp in Mary's voice softened. 'Maybe it was like the man said. Maybe he was doing them a favour, putting them out of their misery.' She nodded. 'I think maybe he's an angel come to help folk whose time has come. Maybe he'll come for us.'

Ronnie punched her on the arm. 'Don't be fucking daft.' But he looked as if he thought she might be on to something.

Twenty-Seven

SOMEONE WAS SINGING in a sweet, wavering voice that was only a little out of tune: '*Kilmeny, Kilmeny, where have you been? Lang hae we sought baith holt and den; By linn, by ford, and green-wood tree . . .*'

The singer sounded as if they were at my shoulder, but they were out of sight, somewhere in the gridwork of streets that crisscross the Merchant City. I took out my phone and checked the address Sands had sent me. I meant what I had said to the boy, about a frittered-away life that would become no life at all. But I understood the lure of the forbidden. Perhaps I had always been destined to follow him to the party.

The singer's voice fluttered and faded: '*. . . these roses, the fairest that ever were seen? Kilmeny, Kilmeny, where have you been?*'

Mountaineers leave a map of their route behind in case they have an accident and need rescued. I thought about sending the party's address to Rose, but the Anchor Line, where she and Anderson were having their swank night out, was a short stagger away. I did not want her to follow me on a drunken whim with a senior police officer in tow.

I walked away from the Merchant City. There were plenty of people I could talk antiques to, or meet for a drink or twenty, but Les was the only person with the right balance of indifference and investment in my life. I was in his bad books, but if something went wrong and my funeral was next on the calendar, Les would remember that I had sent him the address. Maybe he would do something about it. I texted him and turned my phone to silent.

The place turned out to be an anonymous sandstone office block that I had walked past countless times without noticing. A heavy wooden door waited at the top of three steps. A row of buzzers was set to the right of the door, each one accompanied by the name of a business. I scanned them, looking for a clue that might tell me who was hosting the party – a lawyer, a chiropractor, an accountancy firm, secretarial services . . . I reread Sands' message. He had ended it with a six-digit code, but there was no keypad to punch the code into. Instead, the door was equipped with a slot, designed for swiping entry key cards. A small hatch-like window in the door, too tiny for even a well-trained monkey to pass through, showed a reception hall whose walls and floor were faced in pale marble. I read the address again, looked at the door, the code, the buzzers for businesses closed for the night. I pressed the chiropractor's buzzer and waited. There was no response. I worked my way down the line with the same, silent result.

It was almost midnight. A diesel engine growled and faded into the distance. Someone in a nearby street shouted words I could not make out. Hundreds of blank windows stared from surrounding buildings. The hairs on the back of my neck rose like a mandrake towards the full moon. There was no point in hanging around. I had done my best. Sands would have to look after himself.

I loped down the stairs and stopped. A black key safe of the kind favoured by pensioners and Airbnb was fastened into a shadowy part of the doorway, low down on the wall. I pulled off its plastic cover and punched in the code Sands had sent me. The safe opened, revealing a key card. A label attached to it instructed me to leave the card for the next visitor after I had used it. It was all too *Alice in Wonderland* for my taste, but I did as I was told.

The entrance hall smelt of furniture polish and rain. It was larger than the door suggested, with high ceilings and a chandelier that harked back to the 1960s, Sputniks and atoms. A bank of three silver lifts stood to the right of the reception desk. I pressed the call button and waited as all three drifted down towards the lobby. The middle lift reached the ground first. It pinged its victory and its doors slid silently open, an invitation. The interior walls were mirrored. I was surrounded by myself, tall and dishevelled, hair straggly from the rain, coat and trouser hems edged with mud from the alleyway where Jojo had died. I felt nostalgic for my boyhood switch-blade. The other lifts rang to a halt on either side. I retreated into a corner, wondering if anyone had travelled down in them.

A gold star, of the kind good children are rewarded with, was stuck next to the fourth-floor button. I pressed it. My finger left a mark on the brushed steel surface. I thought about fingerprints and wiped it with my scarf, though I had not bothered to clean the buzzer, key card, lock safe, door handle, call button . . . How many surfaces had I touched?

The lift doors breathed shut, and I ascended, scraping my hands through my hair, slicking it to my head as I travelled.

The doors opened on the top floor. I stepped out into a beige corridor: a print of a pile of smooth pebbles on a grey-nothing background and a red fire extinguisher mounted on the wall. One male, one female toilet, white doors side by side, identical except for black-on-silver pictograms. The man's legs were spaced like an A, the woman's a mono-leg, beneath a triangular skirt.

I could hear music, a techno 120bpm, insistent and rutting. The noise was coming from behind a set of glass double doors labelled J. & J. Jennings, Chiropractor. Blinds had been lowered behind the doors' glass panels, concealing the view of the studio beyond.

Experience has taught me that it can pay to know where the emergency exit is. I walked along the landing and found the fire escape. It was unlocked, no alarms primed. I retraced my steps, gently pushed open one of the glass doors and stepped into a little portion of New York: polished wood floors and exposed red brickwork. Two faux Bauhaus couches faced each other. A black-and-white photograph of the Chrysler Tower hung above an oversized reception desk. The music was louder but there was no one in sight. I walked slowly towards another set of shaded glass doors. I could hear laughter now, and male grunting of the kind that denotes sex or hand-to-hand combat.

I stepped through the doors and into one of Sands' paintings, brought to life. The room was an exercise studio. A not completely dark space, crowded with bodies, some naked, others in various stages of undress. Some of the men were wearing medical masks, remnants of the pandemic. They flopped on naked chests or stretched tight around half-concealed faces, little squares of blue and white in the darkness. The place smelt pungent: of sex, sweat and aftershave. Its sprung floor moved queasily. I was the only person who was fully dressed.

I felt the appeal. The lure of no holds barred, no questions asked, no complications or recriminations, no judgement, no fucking straights, no liberal will-you-get-civilled, will-you-get-married, will-you-have-children, no are-you-dancing-are-you-asking, no asking, no being asked, just doing and forgetting. Alive in that moment and the next and the next until the lights go on and the action stops.

Some other time, some other place, I might have shed my clothes, stepped right in, and committed myself to the mayhem. But the mud of Jojo's death site was still on my clothes and, as I stood on the sidelines watching, I knew the scene was too frantic for my taste. The men were one body and I, with my mud-stained clothes and wild hair, was an intruder. It could have been a turn-on. But it made me think of butchery, the final scene of a zombie film where ranks of the possessed fix on some poor fucker, knock him to the ground and chow down on his flesh as the credits roll.

A bald man with a pot belly, hairy torso and stumpy cock tugged at my coat, eyes wild behind a druggy glaze. 'Bin bags and labels in the changing rooms. Dump your togs there and get stuck in.'

'Cheers, man.' I took off my raincoat and bundled it under my arm. 'I'm looking for a young guy . . .'

He gave me a slow grin. 'You've come to the right place. Plenty young guys here. Take your pick.'

The bald man faded into the crowd. I waited a moment, scanning the room for Sands, then followed him, pressing past sweat-slicked bodies. It was like stepping into a broth of steam.

A thin man in a leather harness and leather jeans dunted me on the shoulder. 'What you need? Tina? G?'

I shook my head and sidestepped him. Now that I was moving, I could see that the far wall of the exercise studio was a giant mirror. The space was smaller than I had first thought. The crowd, less than a hundred men.

The floor rocked. Someone was laughing. I pulled off my suit jacket and shoved it under my arm with my coat. My shirt shone whiter than the flesh around me. Here and there, tussles of men moved on the floor while others stood around them, shifting from foot to foot, tugging their cocks as they waited their turn. Shouts of encouragement and laughter filled the micropauses in the techno thump.

Someone grabbed me by the shoulder. 'Long time no see. How goes it?'

The man's eyes were lost in deep shadows. A winged heart was tattooed across his chest. The tattoo was familiar, but I could not place him.

I grinned. 'Goes good. Some scene, this.'

He plucked the sleeve of my shirt. 'Not like you to be shy.'

'I'm heading. Just need to grab my pal and take him home.'

The man was around my age, pale. A jogger's body. No meat. Sagging skin, tired and energised. A dancing corpse. 'Don't be a fucking killjoy.'

'He's had enough. Know what I mean?'

The stranger who knew me bounced on the balls of his feet. 'Too much is never enough.'

I gave his shoulder a friendly slap. 'Yeah, well, if I don't take him home it'll be murder on the dance floor. There's been enough of that around here.'

I had wanted to see if the word 'murder' prompted a

response, but the man was already gone, absorbed by the heave of bodies. His sweat still greased my palm.

I was tall enough to see above most of the men. I raised myself on my tiptoes and scanned the room for Sands. Someone landed a sly punch in my kidneys. I whirled around. Naked and half-naked men, shades of skin from deep bronze to fatty-white. Tattoos that moved too quickly to come into focus. Someone placed a misfired kick at my tendons. It scraped across my shin and almost toppled me. I spun around, one arm clutching my coat and jacket, my free fist clenched. It was impossible to tell who had aimed the kick. I pushed roughly past people towards the far side of the room.

A broad-shouldered man dragged his T-shirt over his head, revealing gym-sprung pecs. He leaned into the action. I felt an unwelcome stab of desire. Someone called my name. I turned to see who it was and almost tripped over a couple of men wound together on the floor. A man tugged at my shirt. Glossy beard in need of a trim. Northern Irish accent, butch and authoritative. 'Let's get this off you.'

I pulled free of him. Sweat was dripping down my body, my shirt stuck to my chest. I saw another familiar face I could not place, felt another hand on my back, another tug at my clothes. A man receiving a blowjob took his phone from his sock and opened Grindr, looking for his next hook-up. A glass bulb glowed and died, glowed and died. A man lay sleeping, naked on the floor, his face mask askew. Another man crouched and rolled him onto his side. He caught me watching and said, 'I don't mind sharing.' Someone touched me on the shoulder and pointed into the darkness. 'Biggest cock you ever seen over there. Split you in two if you're not careful.' A voice whispered, 'Want some G? Want some Tina?'

I stepped backwards and suddenly spotted Sands on the other side of the room. There were two of him, Sands and his reflection in the mirrored wall, both perched on top of some gym equipment. The boy had stripped down to his briefs. His body looked out of place – exposed ribs, concave stomach and skinny thighs – an underfed military service conscript waiting on his medical inspection. A casual observer might have thought he was advertising himself or that he was a voyeur trying to get a better view of the action, but I spotted the camera phone cradled in his palm.

I waved a hand and shouted his name. The music overwhelmed my voice. Perhaps Sands felt my stare, or maybe it was simply that I was one of the tallest men in the room. He turned in my direction, and our eyes met. He grinned and beckoned me over. I was too far away to tell if he had taken something or if it was just the joy of capturing the scene that stretched his smile.

I reached Sands' side.

He jumped down from his perch, still grinning. 'I thought you told me to get to fuck.'

His skin was paper-white, ribs like a xylophone. He looked too young to be in the middle of the sexual scrum, but he looked at home too. Les had accused me of fancying the boy, but I felt no desire for him. Felt no desire for anyone. I was a glutton confronted with a feast, suddenly disgusted by chewing mouths and slobbered chins.

I pointed back the way I had come. 'There's a guy over there, totally out of it. Some men were getting ready to take advantage.'

Sands scoffed, 'You sound like someone's old auntie. Maybe he wanted them to take advantage. Maybe that's why he's lying there naked with his arse in the air.'

'Yeah, his arse will be falling out his bum by the end of the night.'

Sands aimed his camera phone at me. No one seemed to notice the flash. 'That's not even possible.'

I had come to rescue Sands, but he was the most relaxed I had seen him. As if he had found his element, his calling. I said, 'I thought you were drinking the Kool-Aid?'

'What?'

'Taking GHB, crystal meth or whatever the fashion in killing yourself is.'

Sands focused his camera on a scrimmage of men, aimed and clicked. 'Work first, party after.'

I caught his shoulder and turned him to face me. 'Doesn't what happened to Jojo bother you?' Sands tried to pull away, but I held him there, his flesh warm beneath my hand. 'I went to the lane where Jojo died. Some street people saw two men dump him on that doorstep. They left him there to die. One of them sounded a dead spit for Anthony. Now he's gone too.'

Sands wriggled free. 'What if someone finds out you're asking questions? You could get us both into trouble. Let it go.'

'Jojo and Anthony didn't drag their dead bodies into an alleyway by themselves. I thought your generation were all #MeToo and consent?' I pointed in the direction of the comatose man, though he was out of sight. 'That guy back there's in no state to consent to anything.'

The skin around Sand's face was tight; he had lost weight he could not afford to lose. 'This isn't the kind of shonky party Jojo and his cronies got their kicks at. This is a professional set-up.' He leaned in close. I smelt the musk scent of his sweat. 'They've brought in a couple of porn actors, real donkey dongs. It's all about selling drugs. There's a lot of money involved. No one wants anything going wrong.'

A tall, dark-haired man in black jeans and a studded harness that emphasised his hairless chest put an arm around Sands' shoulder. 'How's tricks?'

Sands gave him an uneasy look. 'My friend's worried about me.'

The man met my eyes. 'Sweet, but there's no need. Deke and me go way back. He's in good hands. I won't let anything bad happen to him.'

I raised my eyebrows. 'Deke?'

Sands made a face. 'My party name.'

The tall man said, 'Suits him. Rhymes with peek.' He squeezed Sands' shoulder. 'You like to watch, don't you?'

Sand's said, 'I do more than that,' in a high voice that made me doubt it.

The man laughed and asked me, 'What do they call you?'

'You don't need to know.'

He nodded. 'Fair enough.'

I jerked a thumb in the direction of the door. 'There's a man back there in no fit state to give consent. He's about to get swarmed.'

The dark-haired man lifted his arm and lazily scratched his armpit. 'I'll take care of it.'

I said, 'Just to be clear, I'm talking about rape.'

'I told you, I'll take care of it.' He put his hand on my shoulder and squeezed, giving me a measure of his strength. 'This isn't your kind of place. Best you get going and forget you were here.'

I thought about arguing, but the man was right. Maybe there had been a time when I would have dived right in, committed myself to the mayhem, the way a diver commits himself to the water when he springs from his board, but it was not my type of place. I looked at Sands. 'Sure you're okay?'

The boy gave an impatient nod. 'I know what I'm doing.'

I could have told him these words had preceded many fatal endeavours, but it would have been a waste of breath. The tall man put his hand between my shoulders, on the sensitive spot where neck meets vertebrae, ready to propel me to the door.

I stepped sideways. 'I know the way out.'

Sands said, 'I'll call you.'

I turned my back on him. 'Don't bother.'

I expected the leather queen to follow me, but he stayed with Sands, watching as I negotiated my way back to the exit. This time I kept to the edge of the gym, away from the rise and fall of bodies. Les had called me a prude. Maybe he was right. I liked my sex anonymous. Why would I object to Sands, or anyone else, getting their kicks here? As long as everyone was into it and no one ended up dead.

I was almost at the door when I caught sight of a small scrum and realised that I knew the man in the middle. Frank was naked. His head lolled to one side. His arm and chest were muscled, but his face had lost its hard edges. Someone took Frank's cock in their mouth and tried to revive it. The porter did not stir. A flabby man with grey chest hair pushed the man attempting the blowjob aside and rolled Frank onto his stomach. Another man rubbed his hands in an excited here-we-go way.

I caught the older man by his elbow. 'Plenty of willing bodies here. This one's out of bounds.'

The man had a round face and bank manager glasses. His belly barrelled outwards, concealing his crotch. He scowled up at me. 'Says who?'

'He's so out of it, fucking him would practically be necrophilia.'

I expected the man to object but he laughed. 'Don't knock it till you've tried it, son – as long as the body's fresh.'

The other man put an arm round his friend. 'Don't wind the lad up, Stevo. You don't want him thinking you're a Jimmy Savile.'

The bank manager stuck out his stomach. 'I don't give a toss what he thinks.' But he moved on, leaving me with Frank.

I bent down and gave the head porter a shake. 'Okay, Frankie, time to hit the road.'

The porter's chest was rising and falling. He was breathing through his mouth. Spittle trailed down his chin. His eyes were half-closed slits, his pupils rolled back in his head.

'Jesus Christ himself couldn't resurrect that.' I looked up and saw the man with the tattooed heart watching me. My eye was level with his groin; his cock was soft and spent. 'This the pal you were looking for?'

I nodded. 'Aye. He's left the planet.'

The stranger-who-knew-me crouched down. 'Headed for outer space, right enough. Won't mind what you do to him.'

'What I'm going to do is get him to bed and up in time for his work in the morning.' I grasped Frank under the oxters and tried to pull him to his feet. There was no moving him. I shoved his arms into my raincoat and belted it round his nakedness. I looked up at the stranger. 'Help me get him on my back, will you?'

The man muttered, 'Right fucking pervert you are.'

But he helped lift the porter from the floor and sling him over my shoulder in a fireman's lift that threatened to topple me. I carried Frank through the doors, through the reception and out into the corridor. Somewhere was a bin bag containing his clothes. If he had any sense, he would have stashed his valuables before he arrived, but if he had any sense I wouldn't be dragging him dead to the world and all but naked out into a Glasgow winter. I got Frank down in the lift, propped him in a chair in the lobby, fastened my raincoat tighter around his body and called a cab.

Glasgow cabbies have seen every shade of inebriation and undress, but the driver refused to take Frank. 'No offence, pal. I know it's a payday weekend coming up, but if he's sick in the cab that's me off the road for an hour.'

I took thirty quid and shoved it at him. 'Stag do gone wrong. I promised his fiancée and his ma I'd look after him.'

The driver made a face. 'You did a good job of that.'

I shrugged, trying for a man-of-the-world attitude. 'His daft pals spiked his drink. I'll get short shrift if his wife-to-be hears about this.'

The cabby snorted. 'I got blootered at my stag do too.' He held out a hand. 'Make it fifty and I'll help you get him in the house.'

It was like manoeuvring a corpse, but Frank's snoring told us that he was still alive.

'He's going to have a head like a pneumatic drill in the morning,' the cab driver said, as he helped me manhandle Frank up to the top landing of my building, into the flat, along the hall and into the bedroom. We shoved him on my bed and laid him in the recovery position. I could see the driver taking in my home, reassessing me. I gave him the cash and the driver folded it into his pocket, but he looked troubled. As if he was wondering whether he had done the right thing.

Twenty-Eight

IT WAS A BIT before five in the morning when I heard a crash from the bedroom. Frank was sitting on the edge of my bed, a sheet draped loosely over his lap. Bruises had bloomed across his arms and chest, blue-black against his white skin. The glass of water I had left on the bedside table was smashed on the floorboards.

He looked up, too dazed to be surprised. 'What the fuck?'

I tightened the cord of my dressing gown. 'Don't worry. Your honour's intact − from me at least.' I jerked a thumb towards the other room. 'I slept on the couch.'

Frank put his head in his hands. His fringe flopped across his face. He looked as vulnerable as a new-born, cracked from some egg into misery. I had been angry the night before. Now I felt sorry for him. He rubbed his eyes and looked up, chin dark with stubble, cheeks flushed. 'Did you follow me?'

There was a towel on the radiator. I threw it over the

spilled water, the smashed glass and started to clear up the mess. 'Don't flatter yourself. I was there to see Sands . . .' I realised the boy and the porter had not met and added, 'A young guy I know . . . he shared a flat with my late friend Jojo. I was worried he was getting into bad company.'

Frank muttered, 'Part-time social worker, are you?'

A sliver of glass cut my finger. I swore under my breath. 'You're fucking lucky I've got a social conscience. I saw the vultures circling and took pity on you.'

I got to my feet and dumped the soiled towel on the windowsill. The street was dark, the trees opposite my building turned copper by the reflection of the streetlight. The wind was up; their branches danced. A few short hours and I would be out there, walking through the cold and the wet. I got a sudden spooky sense of what it would be like to stand on the street below looking up at myself: a thin man in an old tartan dressing gown, illuminated in the window. I drew the shutters closed.

'It's early. I'm going back to bed.'

Frank glanced around the room. There was a hint of panic in his eyes, but his face wore its usual carved-from-oak expression. 'Where are my clothes?'

I sucked the blood from my cut finger, feeling suddenly, illogically guilty. 'You were comatose. A queue of guys were oiling up their fists. I shoved my raincoat on you and got you out.'

Frank's voice cracked with disbelief. 'You left my stuff there?'

'I saved your arse.'

'My clothes. My bank cards, my cash bonus from the sale? My keys?' He glanced down at his bare feet. 'My fucking shoes?'

'I'll lend you shoes.'

'Why didn't you mind your own business and leave me alone?' Frank stood up and wrapped the sheet around his waist. 'I'm going back.' His balance was uncertain, and he sat down again.

'You're in no state to go back.'

The porter's usual belligerence reasserted itself. 'I will be. Soon as you lend me some clothes. And the cab fare.'

I had had less than four hours' sleep. A full day's work waited up ahead. I propped myself against the bedroom wall. 'Phone the bank and get your cards replaced. If you went to that place straight from work, the clothes you lost were no great shakes.'

Frank shook his head. 'I can't leave my ID lying around where anyone can find it.'

I shoved my hands into the pockets of my dressing gown.

'People lose their wallets all the time. Cancel your cards. Order a new driving licence. It's no big deal.'

'I'm locked out of my bloody flat.'

'Get a locksmith.'

'You've got all the answers, except the right one.' Frank looked at the damp patch on the floor where the water had spilled. 'I don't want anyone tying me to that place. Those parties.'

The chair in the corner was heaped with a pile of shirts waiting to be dropped off at the Iron Lady. I dumped them on the floor and sat down. 'You're a single man. It's the twenty-first century. No one cares that you went to a sex party.'

Frank kept his expression fixed. 'I don't give a stuff what people think.'

'So, forget about it.'

He snorted, 'Would you ditch your ID, your keys, your money?'

I glanced at the bedside alarm. 'You already have. Your gear will be long gone.'

'It'll be there. I stashed it good. Just lend me the cab money and I'll get out your hair.'

'For fuck's sake, Frank.' I opened the wardrobe door, found a T-shirt, a pair of sweatpants and a jumper. I tossed them on the bed beside him. I was bone-tired, but I was used to long days that shifted into long nights. A Venn diagram of the party and Jamie Mitchell would intersect on drugs, Frank, Jojo and Sands. It occurred to me that I was another, involuntary, intersection. I rummaged in the wardrobe for a fresh suit and shirt for myself. 'I'll drive you there.'

Frank drew the T-shirt awkwardly over his head, his bruised body. He pulled on the sweatpants, using the sheet to cover himself. I did not remind him that he had lain buck-naked with his arse in the air, in a room full of strangers, only a few hours ago.

He said, 'I don't need a babysitter or a social worker. I'm fine on my own.'

I pulled a clean shirt from the wardrobe. 'You'll be walking there in bare feet then.'

I thought Frank was going to argue, but he gave me a weary look. 'What is it with you? Why can't you butt out of other people's business?'

It was a good question. Maybe Frank made a habit of surrendering himself to the room. But he might also have kept a closer eye on his drug consumption the previous night if I had not lost my temper and threatened to sack him.

'I've got an overinflated ego.' I rooted in the wardrobe. 'What size shoe are you?'

'Eleven.'

I tossed him a pair of flip-flops I had bought for an ill-fated trip to Majorca with Rose. 'I'm a ten. These will have to do you.'

Frank picked up the flip-flops. They were red and yellow, their sole decorated with a stylised torro that had seemed amusing after half a jug of sangria. Frank gave them a look of disgust, but he slotted them on.

'The boy you went to see, what did you say his name was?'

'Sands.' I remembered his party name and corrected myself. 'Deke. Do you know him?'

Frank shrugged. 'It's not like anyone makes formal introductions.'

I remembered Sands posed semi-naked on top of the gym equipment, his camera phone discreetly focused on the action. I wondered if it had occurred to him that people might pay a lot of money to suppress his pictures and, if so, what he would do about it. The boy was slipping from observer into participant. It was a dangerous game, but Sands had made it clear that his business was none of my business. My ego only stretched so far.

The rain had eased to a soft drizzle. The Bowery Auctions van was still at the NCP car park where I had left it. It was a week since I had driven my own car. I walked in the wrong direction before remembering where I had parked it and doubled back. Frank hunched his shoulders and followed me along the ill-lit street, the Majorcan flip-flops slip-slapping against the wet pavement.

I had bought the Skoda Octavia a few months before. It had been a good deal, marred only by a faint smell of fish rot in the interior no Magic Tree could shift. Frank wrinkled his nose as he settled into the passenger seat. I turned up the heating and switched on the windscreen wipers. I glanced at Frank, ready to ask if he was sure he wanted to do this. His jaw was set. His mind made up. We drove off in silence.

I parked opposite the office block where the party had been held and told Frank to wait in the car. He ignored me, unfastened his seatbelt and stepped into the rain. I slammed the driver's door and followed him. It was still dark, the street deserted, but the tingle-on-the-back-of-the-neck feeling of being watched was with me again. Frank flip-flopped awkwardly across the rainy street. I reached the doorway before him and crouched down, ready to tap in the code, but the key safe was no longer there.

I straightened up. 'Sorry, Frank, the party's over.'

Frank pushed me out of the way and checked for himself. 'Fuck.' He kicked the wall and doubled over in silent pain.

I touched his shoulder. 'Are you okay?'

Frank shook me off. He hobbled back to the car, got in and slammed the door. Perhaps the porter had lost more than just his clothes, keys and bonus.

I followed him and folded myself into the driver's seat. 'Where did you stash your stuff?'

Frank scowled. 'It doesn't matter.'

I started the engine. 'I'll drop you at your flat. You can take it from there.'

Frank sighed. 'People were bagging their gear and leaving it in the locker room. The lockers ran out, so people were dumping their bags on the benches. It didn't look secure to me, so I waited until no one was there and hid my stuff in the jannie's cupboard.'

I looked at him. 'The jannie's cupboard? That's your perfect hiding place?'

He shrugged. 'No one notices a brick in a wall. A full bin bag would be invisible there.'

'Aye, until someone threw it out.' As if on cue, a Ford Fiesta parked two spaces away from us. A slim woman in a zip-up rain jacket and jeans got out and crossed to the building we had just left. 'Wait here.' I turned off the engine, jumped out of the car and jogged quickly across the road. She had already taken a key card from her bag and was swiping it. 'Excuse me.'

The woman turned around and gave a gasp that seemed to draw all her breath into her body. She scrabbled inside her bag and an electronic scream split the air.

I put my hands over my ears and moved backwards, off the steps. I raised my voice. 'I'm not going to hurt you. I just . . .' I pointed at the door.

My words seemed to panic the woman more. She tried to fumble her key card into the electronic slot, but it slipped from her hand and landed on the step. She took a tightly coiled umbrella from her bag and used it like a baton, lashing out at me. I could have easily taken the umbrella from her, but I moved beyond its reach, holding my hands above my head. 'I'm sorry.' Her rape alarm was still making its electronic wail. I looked around to check if a police officer or some Good Samaritan was coming to save her and saw Frank hobbling towards us.

Something about the sight of the porter, dressed in sweatpants that were too long for him, a Willie Nelson T-shirt and souvenir flip-flops, reassured the woman. She lowered her umbrella, turned off the rape alarm and looked from Frank to me and back.

'What do you want?' She had a foreign accent, Eastern European or perhaps Italian, cut through with Glaswegian.

I glanced at Frank, but embarrassment, or the after-effects of whatever he had taken, had struck him dumb.

I smiled at the woman. 'My friend left something behind in the building last night, an important piece of work he needs for a presentation today. We came over to collect it but turns out he forgot his entry card.'

She shrugged, almost, but not quite, reassured that we were idiots. 'So? He'll have to go home and fetch it.'

'If he does that, he won't make it back in time.' I slipped twenty pounds from my wallet and offered it to her. 'Maybe you could let him in?'

The woman looked incredulous. 'Twenty pounds is no use if I lose my job. Go away, please, or I'll call the police.'

'My friend's already had a warning. If he screws this up, he's out on his ear.'

'I'm sorry, but it's not my problem. I clean the offices, that's all.' She glanced at Frank and asked me, 'Why is he dressed that way?'

I took another twenty from my wallet. My cash bonus was shrinking fast. 'Eccentric genius.'

The woman shook her head. 'Everything's on CCTV. We'd be caught. Anyway, I don't believe you.'

I looked at the camera angled above us. The lens was capped.

Her eyes followed mine. She saw the deadened eye and her own eyes widened. 'What's going on?'

Before I could answer, a couple of dishevelled men appeared on the other side of the door. They struggled with the lock for a moment then found the release button and reeled into the street, looking like they had got dressed in the dark.

'All right, mate,' one of the men mumbled as he pushed past us.

I shoved the forty pounds into the woman's hand and caught the door before it could close.

'Please don't call the police. I promise you: we'll grab this eejit's stuff and be out before you know it.'

The woman caught the arm of my coat. 'Wait . . .'

I slipped free of her and slid into the foyer. Frank was close on my heels, feet slapping against the marble floor. The woman shouted something after us. I called back, 'Don't worry. We'll be in and out in no time,' and made for the stairs. Frank had had a hard night, but he possessed the recovery powers of youth. He passed me on the second floor. I saw that he had dispensed with the flip-flops and was running in his bare feet.

I said, 'Better be quick. She's going to call the police.'

My phone buzzed in my pocket. I saw Les's name on the screen and ignored it.

Frank was already in the service cupboard when I reached the top floor. I glanced inside and heard him hiss, 'Yes!' as he located his bag of clothes. I said, 'I'm going to check out the gym. Don't bugger off without me.'

He looked up, 'Why the fuck . . .?'

I let the door swing shut on his question.

The chiropractor's reception area, that little slice of New York that had been someone's design triumph, looked worse for wear. The pale suede couches were stained and grubby. Broken ampoules of G crunched beneath my feet. A used condom flopped opaque and baggy on the stripped wood floor. I walked through the reception and pushed open the studio doors. It smelled of men. Their sex, sweat and shit. More discarded clothing, condoms and drug paraphernalia littered the space, but it was empty. I felt a sense of relief and realised I was still worried about Sands, had half feared I would find him crucified on the sprung floor. I felt a movement behind me and turned, expecting to see Frank. A stranger stood in the doorway, a man I did not, and then suddenly did, recognise.

The leather queen was dressed in jeans and a black reefer jacket. He looked bemused. 'What are you doing here?' The door opened again, and Frank entered. He was dressed in his own clothes, his feet safely booted. The leather queen glanced him up and down. 'Thought you'd done a runner.'

Frank took something from his pocket and passed it to him. 'That's the lot.'

The man looked at it and nodded. 'Okay, you're off the hook.' He patted Frank on the head. 'Fuckitty-bye, till next time.'

Frank met my eyes. I saw that he hated me for witnessing this fresh humiliation. Somewhere in the building there was a vibration, a noise too distant to identify. All three of us looked towards the door of the gym, suddenly united in apprehension.

The leather queen whispered, 'What the fuck was that?'

I stepped cautiously into the reception area and out to the landing beyond. Frank and the leather queen followed me. The noise was still vague, but I thought I could hear a rumble of male voices somewhere on one of the floors below.

'I think the cleaner called the police.'

The leather queen muttered, 'Fucking bitch.' He punched Frank on the shoulder. 'And yous are a pair of bitches for letting her see you.'

The voices sounded again. The words were indistinct, but

they were definitely male and there was more than one of them.

Scientists have identified three different reactions to danger: fight, flight or freeze. The leather queen stood stock still, Frank pulled back his shoulders and barrelled out his chest. I grabbed him by the shoulder. 'Come on.' I made a dash for the fire escape. This time I was the faster one. I heard two sets of footsteps clattering behind me and knew that the leather queen was following too.

Frank hissed, 'They'll be waiting by the exit.'

I glanced back over my shoulder. 'Depends how many of them there are. If we're lucky, they'll have sent one patrol car. We'll be gone before they reach the fifth floor.'

The leather queen was breathing heavily. He gasped, 'There was an Old Firm match. Busy night for the popo. That's why we chose it.'

The football fans should be safe in bed or locked up in the cells by now, but I did not bother to correct him. Football and violence have long been good friends on the west coast of Scotland. Ripples from the game might still be making themselves felt in homes across the city.

We reached the lower landing and stopped. The corner of the stairwell concealed the exit door from view. I turned and looked at Frank and the leather queen. Neither of them volunteered to check if the police were waiting on us.

'Fuck it.' I stuck my head around the stairwell. A CCTV camera winked at me. Whoever had disabled the other surveillance cameras had overlooked this one. The exit door was made of solid wood. A sign above the escape bar informed me, This Door Is Alarmed. I whispered, 'You and me both,' and turned to the two men. 'I'm going for it. You can do what you want.'

Frank was still carrying a carrier bag that presumably contained the clothes I had lent him. He stepped forward. 'Okay, let's do it.'

The leather queen hung back, waiting to see how things worked out. I told Frank to cover his face and wrapped my scarf around my mouth and nose. We crept to the door. I nodded to him. 'Ready?' He nodded back. 'Go for it, boss.'

It was the first time Frank had called me boss. Perhaps it should have given me a warm, fuzzy feeling, but my heart was beating too fast at the prospect of what might be waiting outside. An echo of male voices travelled down the stairwell from one of the landings above and the leather queen shifted himself. 'Fucking do it.'

I counted to three, banged the bar down, and threw myself at the door. It opened with a racket of sirens and then we were out into the dark and the wet of a back lane. The lights of a main thoroughfare glimmered to our right. I kept my scarf around my face and ran towards them, not bothering to see if the other two were behind me, or if the police were in pursuit.

Glasgow city centre is peppered with networks of CCTV cameras, alert as snipers. I took my cap from my pocket shoved it on my head and walked purposefully, keeping to the edges of buildings, scarf wrapped around my face, collar up as if to protect me from the cold. I caught sight of Frank walking on the other side of the street, still clutching his carrier bag. We ignored each other, but I knew that he had marked me too. We were like actors in some old horror film. A man and his shadow, creeping through the dark.

Twenty-Nine

I DOUBLED ROUND the block, my hand cradling the car key in my pocket, cursing myself for parking opposite the offices. Saturday night had long since shifted into Sunday morning. I glanced at my watch. It was just after six-thirty. A couple of smokers loitered outside a 24-hour call centre. A refuse lorry rumbled past, jaws open, breathing out decay. I pulled my scarf high over the bridge of my nose and turned the corner into the street where I had parked the Skoda.

A policeman was peering into the car, jotting down something in his notebook. I retreated, unseen. Frank was watching me from the shadow of a shop doorway. I crossed the road to join him.

'Fancy some breakfast?'

'What's up?'

'The police are interested in my car.'

'Shit.'

I put my head down and kept walking. Frank trudged

beside me, silent except for the rustling sound of the carrier bag swinging at his side. A queue of taxi cabs waited at the rank opposite Central Station. A middle-aged man in a Celtic strip, a casualty of the Old Firm game, slumped bemused by the station's entrance, cradling a can of Fürstenberg he had done well to find at that time in the morning. A down-on-his-luck jakie approached the man, who growled and then held out his beer. They hunched by the entrance together, watching the early morning travellers, like a sentimental portrait of old comrades fallen low.

Frank and I walked towards the buttress of the Grand Central Hotel. I loved the old building. It had been built around the time Oscar Wilde met Lord Alfred Douglas and had opened its doors to enchantment and disgrace. When men and women obeyed strict dress codes, except for when they did not. When Vesta Tilley invited audiences to 'come, come, come, and be one of the midnight sons'. When trains were cutting-edge and guests travelled in first-class carriages, trailed by their servants in third.

The hotel had gone through some tough times in its hundred-plus years. I had had more than a few tours of its upper floors, back in the 1990s when it was falling into decay. There had been other interlopers amongst the attic floors. Stories circulated of disgruntled ghosts and rooms where walls ran red with blood. I did not believe the tales, but I had seen strange markings and crawled through a low-ceilinged attic room whose walls were neatly studded with razorblades. The Grand Central had been restored to luxury, but word was the upper storeys remained untouched, awaiting renovation – the razorblades still sharp, ghosts still walking.

A couple of coaches were angled outside the hotel

entrance. Their drivers loitered on the pavement, smoking. They watched us as we passed. No one would guess that Frank's clothes had spent the night bundled in a bin bag. His charcoal suit and white shirt hung smooth beneath his unrumpled raincoat. He had slicked his wet hair back from his face, like Bryan Ferry before the cardigans set in. Even his dark overnight growth of stubble looked sculpted. The hotel doorman gave me a dubious look and a stern nod that was more warning than welcome. He smiled at Frank and bid him a respectful 'good morning, sir'.

Danny Bain was holding forth to an audience of elderly American tourists, pointing out the staircase that TV cowboy Roy Rogers – and his horse Trigger – had climbed when they visited Glasgow back in the 1950s. Danny's anecdotes were polished like well-rubbed charms and guaranteed, he claimed, to squeeze a tip from the tightest tourist. Danny tilted his head. His spiky white hair caught the light of the chandelier. He looked like a man you would trust with your kids, but perhaps not your wallet. He raised a hand and gestured towards Gordon Street.

'There were hunners of weans packed into the streets yonder, waiting for Roy and the cuddy. Roy shot off a few bullets out the window of his room then gave them the full Billy Graham. Like Sunday School with guns, my da said . . .' The Americans looked perplexed but smiled politely. Danny caught my eye and winked. Frank and I took a seat in the foyer while Danny told them how Trigger had signed the guest book himself. 'When they played the Edinburgh Empire, Roy's hand slipped and he shot poor Trigger in the arse, but that's Edinburgh for you . . .'

Danny's eyes twinkled and the Americans laughed.

I stretched out my legs and pulled my cap low. In the

chair next to me, Frank was dozing off. His breath became regular. I closed my eyes.

I could hear Danny reassuring the Americans that Trigger had survived. 'A true professional, that horse. The show must go on . . .'

A gentle hand on my shoulder jolted me awake. The lobby had emptied of tourists. Danny's cheeky-chappy face was close to mine. He was wearing a touch of mascara, a dab of blusher. Close up, the make-up gave his face the look of a ventriloquist's painted dummy.

'You after a room, Mr Rilke?' Danny's voice relaxed into the camp he used amongst friends. He gave Frank a swift up-and-down approving glance. 'That's a coach tour of Yanks away to Dublin, so there's plenty going if you're not too fussy about clean sheets. They were all of an age, so I doubt there would have been much sweating, except we gave them haggis and bagpipes for dinner so I can't guarantee the linen will be lily-white.'

I rubbed my face. The thought of a hotel bed, even an unmade one with slept-on sheets, was appealing but I shook my head. 'Any chance of a coffee and a fry-up for me and my friend Frank?'

Danny said, 'Like that, is it?'

I had no idea what Danny meant by that. I doubted he did either. It was part of an ongoing performance, a combination of 1930s Weimar, Danny La Rue and Old Mother Reilly, honed by black-and-white movies and an eventful life. Danny had been an actor when I first met him, but it had not worked out and he had drifted into bar work and from there to hotels.

I said, 'We've been up most of the night.'

'I thought yous looked knackered. Burning the candle at

both ends, are you? Gives a lovely light, right enough.' Danny flashed his dentures. 'Come on. I'll get you and Miss Frankie signed in to the breakfast room.'

We hauled ourselves out of our armchairs. My knees creaked. 'Cheers, Danny.'

'Nae worries, Mr Rilke. You got something for me?'

'Maybe.' Danny maintained a keen interest in music-hall memorabilia, specifically old-time drag acts. I took out my phone and showed him a photo I had taken of a publicity poster for the Britannia Panopticon on Argyle Street. 'Looking at the font, I'd guess it dates from the early 1890s. A bit chipped round the edges, but otherwise it's in remarkable condition for its age.'

Danny chirped, 'A bit like you and me, love.'

'I'd say we're both doing okay.' I put an arm around Danny, hoping he had not noticed Frank wincing at his display of camp. 'You want to lay down a bid?'

'For the poster?'

'One-twenty should do it.'

'Go on then.' He winked at me. 'I've got a space in the back bedroom needs filling.'

Some other day, I might have capped the double entendre with one of my own, but Frank was an inhibiting presence. I gave Danny's shoulder a flirty squeeze instead. He ushered us to a table and told one of the waiters to take special care of us.

Frank ordered a coffee and poached eggs with spinach on toast, hollandaise on the side. I asked for a strong cup of Tetley and the full Scottish. Frank smoothed the linen napkin over his lap. His lips were pursed, as if he was doing a Donald Trump impersonation. I had an urge to ask him what right he had to judge Danny, who had taken more than a few beatings in his time for the right to be who he was. But I was tired, and I knew Frank well enough by now to know he would turn a blank face on me.

The food arrived. I spattered mine with brown sauce. Frank poured a restrained swirl of hollandaise onto his plate and picked at his spinach.

The waiter appeared with pots of tea and coffee and filled our cups. I added a spoonful of sugar to mine and stirred.

Frank raised his cup to his lips. 'What's Rose got against me?'

'She thinks you're a lazy arsehole and she's not wrong.' I loaded a piece of black pudding with baked beans and brown sauce and conveyed it to my mouth. 'And that's before she knows you're working for Jamie Mitchell on the side.'

Frank gave me a sulky look. 'I'm not working for him.'

I shrugged as if it made no odds to me. 'You know Jim Anderson's interested in Mitchell?'

'Rose's boyfriend?'

I buttered a slice of toast. 'He's got it in for Mitchell and anyone associated with him.'

Frank pushed the spinach around his plate. 'Any specific reason?'

I dabbed my toast in baked bean sauce and took a bite. 'It probably comes under the heading, None of My Business.'

Frank turned to look at the half-empty dining hall, the staff tending to tables on the other side of the room, then fixed his eyes on me. 'What do you want?'

I went for the straightforward answer. 'I want to find out why my mate Jojo, and another gay man who was fond of a party, ended up dead in doorways, within a mile of each other.'

Frank looked me straight in the eye, cool as Lance

Armstrong denying he ever swallowed a Pro Plus. 'I don't know anything about any dead guys.'

I broke the yolk of my fried egg with a slice of black pudding. Yellow viscous goo slid towards the baked beans. The plate was beginning to resemble one of those anonymous abstracts that grace airport hotel rooms.

'You're involved with the parties Jojo frequented.' I wiped my mouth with my napkin. 'Normally I wouldn't give a stuff, but Jojo was one of Bowery's loyal customers and a friend of mine.'

The longer Jojo was dead, the closer I was becoming to him.

Frank shook his head. 'I told you, it's nothing to do with me.'

I washed my egg down with some hot, milky tea. 'I saw you passing something to Victor Mature back at the gym.'

His face creased into an incredulous smile. 'Who?'

'Legendary Hollywood beefcake. Learn your history, Frank.'

He folded his napkin into a neat triangle that made me think he had waited tables in his time and got to his feet. 'Thanks for breakfast.'

I drank another mouthful of tea. 'If I were you, I'd sit down and listen.'

Frank looked like he was about to tell me to fuck off, but he thought better of it and sat down again. A waiter wafted over and asked if he could get us anything else. Something about the way I told him we were done made the waiter glance from Frank to me and back. He cleared our dishes away, swift and efficient, as if crockery was in short supply and there was a fight in the offing.

I waited until he was out of earshot. 'My guess is you're

selling drugs on the side for whoever organises these X-rated get-togethers. I'm also guessing that somewhere down the line that person is Jamie Mitchell who, by coincidence, was trying to throw his weight around at the sale the other day. It's all beginning to feel too close to home, so if you don't want me to start dropping strong hints about you to Rose's best boy, Police Inspector Anderson, I suggest you tell me what's going on.'

Across the other side of the room, Danny Bain was ushering a young couple who looked like honeymooners to a table. He flourished menus at them and said something that made the woman laugh and the man blush.

Frank spoke softly. 'You think Jamie Mitchell had something to do with these guys turning up dead?'

'I didn't say that.'

'But you think he's involved?'

'I think he's connected to the parties and the parties are connected to the deaths. I don't know what pie you've got your finger in, but you'd better be careful you don't end up an accessory to murder.'

'Don't you think you're laying it on a bit thick?'

'Depends what you mean by thick. Two men have died.'

Frank gave a *so what* shrug, but he looked away as he gave it. He signalled for another cup of coffee and waited until the waiter had filled his cup and drifted away. 'I need you to promise to keep me out of things.'

'I'll do my best.'

'Best isn't good enough. I need you to guarantee my name won't get back to Jamie Mitchell, or the police.'

'No one will hear your name from me.'

Frank took a sip of his coffee and made a face as if it had been too hot or too bitter, or maybe both. He glanced around the room, checking no one was close enough to overhear our conversation. 'Mitchell doesn't run the parties, but he does kind of franchise them.'

I sipped my tea. 'What do you mean?'

'Other people set them up, different people, people who owe Mitchell.'

'Drug debts?'

'Yes, but it's more complicated than that. Mitchell engineers debts. It's partly a business model, partly a kink. He spins a line of credit and then uses it to reel people in. Once they owe him, money isn't all he wants.'

'What else does he want?'

'The usual things. Power. Control. A chance to make more money. The opportunity to humiliate them.'

I set the cup on its saucer. The tea was cold, a scum about to form. 'He's not the only drug dealer in town. Why not go elsewhere for your kicks?'

'Once you're in, you can't get out.'

'People are scared of him?'

'It's not just fear, it's the parties.'

'Fear I get. Mitchell's got the psycho edge. But I don't get the parties. What's wrong with Grindr if you want to get your end away?'

Frank grimaced. 'They're addictive, like breathing's addictive.'

It does not matter what the kink is; everyone suspects their own one is irresistible if people were only to try it. I took out my tobacco tin and started to put together a roll-up. 'How much do you owe Mitchell?'

Frank set his hands on the table. He stared at them. 'Who says I owe him?'

'Why else would you be dealing for him?'

'What makes you think . . .?'

I looked at my watch. 'We don't have time for this. I saw you passing your takings to that leather queen. You wanted your clothes and the rest of your gear, sure. But you were desperate to make sure you got the money to him.'

Frank's eyes met mine. 'It doesn't matter how much I owe. Jamie Mitchell doesn't want paid off. I told you, it's not just the money. He likes the power my being in debt gives him.'

I remembered the photography commission Mitchell had given Sands: *Looking in from the Inside*. I had thought it was a means to get at me, but perhaps it was an opportunity to establish another unpayable debt. Even if he escaped the chemsex lure, the boy would still begin his career with Mitchell's shadow hanging over him.

'What's his endgame?'

Frank shrugged. 'Like I said, the usual things: power, money, control. He likes to humiliate people. It's not just the parties. He's into pubs and clubs, whatever gives. Did you hear about the illegal raves that popped up along the west coast during lockdown?'

I remembered reports in the media. Hundreds of music lovers and dance fans starved of their festival fix had congregated in country parks and by remote lochsides to get out of it to beats blasted from loudspeakers. Some gatherings had been so large that even when the police arrived they had been unable to break them up safely and had had to wait until the raves petered out. Hospitals had complained of having to mop up the casualties of drug and alcohol overdoses, fights and falls.

'I read about them. Those raves were on a different scale to last night. The logistics of getting all that tech into the middle of nowhere is mind-blowing, never mind keeping the venue quiet while sharing it with hundreds of kids. You're saying Jamie Mitchell was responsible? He's gone up in my estimation.'

Frank made a face. 'Other people took care of the difficult stuff. The tech, the transport, the big reveal about where it was happening. He provided the drugs and the muscle. You could say he allowed the raves to happen, then once he allowed them, he insisted they continue. There's a couple of kids in jail right now who thought they'd host a fun party or two and then found out they were working for a boss they didn't know they had, until it was too late.'

It did not bode well for Sands. 'Why bother with G parties when you can have a rave with a thousand folk or filter stuff through legal venues?'

'You'd have to ask him that. My guess is they're easy money. They're smaller, less visible than the raves. Even Mitchell must know that you can only make a nuisance of yourself for so long before the big guns come out. Plus, with the sex parties, someone else takes the risk. He supplies the drugs, he gets paid, but he's pretty much invisible. The guy who hosted last night used to go out with the owner of the chiropractor's studio. He made out that holding the party there was revenge for being dumped, but you could tell he didn't really want to do it. Mitchell knew about the premises and forced him into it.'

'Sounds like a sadistic bastard. Closeted?'

Frank shrugged. 'Who knows? He gives the impression of being disgusted but . . .' There was no need to say anything else. We had all met gays who acted like warped mirrors, reflecting internalised homophobia onto the world. 'I thought about going back to Newcastle, but it's too close. I'm going to get a wad together and head for Spain.'

I nodded. 'I can see you changing your name to Franco and managing a bar in Sitges.'

It was the first time I had seen Frank smile. 'Franco isn't the most popular name in Catalonia.' We laughed. Frank asked, 'So why does Mitchell have it in for you?'

I shook my head. 'I was hoping you'd tell me. I didn't let him buy a painting he wanted, but it's more than that. Rose's relationship with Anderson isn't a secret. Maybe he knows I'm interested in Jojo's death and suspects I could make things difficult for him.'

Frank said, 'You know he was up at the Forrest house before the big sale?'

'Mitchell?'

'He visited them before he came to the viewing.'

I remembered the black BMW parked outside the farmhouse. The way Forrest had been comatose in his chair when Rose and I visited, the evening before the sale. I was beginning to wonder what the Forrests were growing in their polytunnels.

'Ever see either of the Forrests at one of the G parties?'

Frank shook his head. 'But it's not like I attend every party going.'

'Glasgow's a small city.'

'Too small for comfort, but there's more than one party in town – or out of town, come to that.'

Our table was cleared, our coffee and tea drunk. I saw Danny looking at us from across the room. He caught my eye and gave a questioning tilt of the head. I nodded and he sashayed to our table.

'Enjoy your breakfast, did you, gents?'

I got to my feet and shook Danny by the hand. 'Best breakfast in town. Give our compliments to the chef.'

Danny grinned. 'Ach, his heid's big enough already.' He squeezed my arm. 'Mind and put that bid in for me, Rilke. That poster you showed me would look a treat on my wall.' He looked at Frank. 'Well, Miss Frankie, how did you like your breakfast?'

Frank nodded, serious as a banker with cancer. 'It hit the spot.'

Danny stuck his tongue in his cheek, as if the porter had just made an outrageous pronouncement. 'We aim to please. Come back and see me some time, as the late, great Mae West didn't ever say.' He jerked his head in my direction. 'And don't feel you have to bring the walking dead with you next time. You'll always find a warm welcome chez Danny.'

A parking ticket was trapped beneath the Skoda's windscreen wiper. I peeled it free and passed it to Frank. 'Your shout.'

He gave me one of his sullen looks, but he slipped it into his pocket without a word and passed me the carrier bag. 'Here's your gear.'

Another man might have thanked me for rescuing him. But thank-yous were not Frank's style. I tossed the bag onto the back seat. 'You okay to take care of the van?'

Frank nodded. 'As long as no one breathalyses me, or whatever it is they do for G.'

I said, 'That's part of the problem. No one tests for it. I reckon that's one of the reasons Jojo and Anthony's deaths were dismissed as misadventure.'

'Accidents happen. What makes you think their deaths weren't just bad luck?'

'My gut.' I handed Frank the keys to the van and told him where I had parked it a long, long night ago. 'Don't forget to pick up Abomi tomorrow morning. I'll see you at Ballantyne House for the clear-out.'

Frank looked at the keys and then at me. 'I'll be glad when this job is over. You know what I keep thinking about?'

I shook my head. 'Payday?'

He did not bother to smile. 'I keep thinking of that Jack Russell trapped in the trunk. Whoever did that was a proper bastard.'

There was no arguing with that. I got into the car and rolled down the windows, hoping a blast of fresh air would help chase the dead fish smell from the interior. I steered the car out of its parking space and drove in the direction of home, wondering why Frank had been more shocked by the dead dog than Jojo's death or the sudden appearance of Phan, running as if his life depended on it.

My phone buzzed. I glanced at the screen and saw Les's name flashing on the display. I was not in the mood for another bollocking. I killed the call and drove on, towards bed.

Thirty

MOST OF THE crew were already at Ballantyne House by the time I arrived on Monday morning. The rooms were being disassembled, like a stage set at the end of a show. Soon there would be no trace of Auntie Pat the concert pianist or the rest of the Forrest ancestors. A presence of two hundred years would be erased, except for names in the parish register and whatever gravestones they had planted in the local cemetery.

I worked through the sales lists with Hannah and Lucy, making sure that our records of who had bought what and at what price tallied, then we checked who was yet to collect their purchases. I put a cross next to the names of habitual recalcitrants and set the girls to phoning and reminding them of the storage fee for late collection.

Frank and Abomi arrived around the same time that the removal vans and carriers started turning up. Frank gave me a business-like nod. Except for the fact that he had taken to calling me boss, no one would guess that anything out of the ordinary had passed between us.

The driveway was too narrow to accommodate more than one Luton at a time. I told one of the casuals to stand at the top gate and direct waiting traffic into the field where the Micra had come to grief. The ground was crisscrossed with tyre tracks from the day of the sale. A passer-by might easily miss the wild course the car had ploughed. I knew it was there and could still see the lunatic twist and dent where the car had raced across the field and lost its fight to stay upright.

It was a dull day, but the rain stayed at bay. Clumps of snowdrops nodded in the tall grass of Ballantyne's overgrown garden. It was possible to believe that spring would eventually come. I exchanged pleasantries and gossip with various regulars and antique dealers, aware all the time of the farmhouse on the hill above. The clouds shifted on the wind. A hint of sun graced us for a moment. The polytunnels gleamed on their terraces. I remembered what Frank had said about no one noticing a brick in a wall and wondered again what the cousins were growing there.

Specialist movers arrived for the Bösendorfer Baby Grand. Our team stopped to watch as they manoeuvred it into the back of their lorry. Hannah and Lucy snapped photos for Bowery's website. Abomi's eyes were wide. He whispered, 'Imagine if they drop it,' and the girls giggled.

My phone buzzed in my pocket. I saw Les's name on the screen and pressed reject. It was the third time he had called me, but I was busy and in no mood for a monologue on the Aberdeen drug scene. The movers strapped the piano into place. Our team gave a small cheer and a couple of the men took a bow.

Hannah whispered, 'They can tickle my ivories any day.'

Frank pursed his lips. I resisted an urge to tell him to stop being a prude.

'Okay, everyone, that was a masterclass in piano wrangling.' I raised a hand in the air, like a conductor giving the orchestra their cue to stop tuning up and get down to business. 'Break's over. Sooner we get out of here, sooner we get to the pub.' I caught Frank just as he was about to follow the team into the house. 'Mind keeping an eye on things for a bit? I've got to go up the hill and make sure the cousins are happy with the way the sale went.'

Frank looked uncertain but he nodded. 'Sure, boss. Want me to go with you?'

'That's sweet of you, but I'm a big boy.'

The old Frank would have taken umbrage, but new, improved Frank stood his ground. 'You know what I mean. What if Jamie Mitchell's up there?'

'Why would he be?'

The Luton loaded with the Bösendorfer swung onto the road and headed in the direction of Glasgow. A waiting removal van turned into the drive and bumped slowly towards the house. Frank followed its progress with his eyes. 'I don't know. He was there a couple of days ago.'

The van parked in front of us. A carrier emerged and handed a chit to Frank. 'Can you show me where this gear is, mate? I've been waiting in that field for half an hour.' His tone said that he had not enjoyed the break.

'No worries.' Frank took the chit. 'I'll be two secs.' He turned to me. 'Can the Forrests not come down here?'

I gave him the same smile I shone on the punters from the auction podium. Full-on charm and hard as nails. 'Professional courtesy, Frank.'

The carrier shifted impatiently. 'That's what I'm talking about. I've six more loads to pick up and it's already after ten. A bit of professional fucking courtesy would go a long way.'

I nodded to Frank. 'Sort this gentleman out, please. I'll phone you if there's a problem.'

I had parked the Skoda at the side of Ballantyne House. It was hemmed in by the removal van so I decided to walk. A gate at the back of the kitchen garden led onto the field that bordered the farmhouse and stretched uphill towards the polytunnels. I went through it and began the climb towards the house. The field had been used for cattle at some point. Cowpats littered the uneven ground and I had to step carefully to avoid them. I was aware of the incongruous figure I cut, picking my way through the grass in my auction suit and handmade brogues, occasionally losing my footing. I imagined Hannah and Lucy watching me from one of the windows of Ballantyne House, giggling at my awkward progress.

The pub landlady had told me that the land had once been used by the MOD. I spotted the flat-topped roofs of decommissioned military buildings on the perimeter, concrete and mysterious. The cowpats were a sign that the site had long been cleared of any landmines, but it was possible for stray mines to be overlooked and unsuspecting walkers to be suddenly scattered across the landscape in dogfood chunks. I grinned, imagining Hannah and Lucy's surprise if I were to explode. I wondered what Rose's reaction would be. How much money she would put behind the bar to pay for drinks at my wake. An explosion would save on the price of a coffin. There would be no need of a new suit to dress my corpse. No corpse. I started to hum a song under my breath.

Once a lonely caterpillar sat and cried,
To a sympathetic beetle by his side.
I've got nobody to hug,
I'm such an ugly bug . . .

Come on, let's crawl,
Gotta crawl, gotta crawl,
To the Ugly Bug Ball,
To the Ball, to the Ball,
And a happy time we'll have there
One and all at the Ugly Bug Ball.

I had embraced my inner freak a long time ago. Rose and Les had embraced theirs too. Frank still had a way to go. Sands loved the idea of freakdom. The boy had been born into a world of protected characteristics and equal rights legislation. The idea of a life on the edge fascinated him. Perhaps that was what drew Sands to Jamie Mitchell's parties. The secrecy of the Ugly Bug Balls harked back to when queerness was against social decency.

I could remember the days when a look in the wrong direction would earn you a kicking or even cost you your life. My stock of nostalgia was small, but my sexuality had been formed back then, and, whatever app I used, I had never quite managed to disentangle sex and danger. That was the trouble with a life on the edge. It could be hard to know where the edge was, until you tumbled into freefall.

I made a mental note to introduce Sands to Danny Bain. The hotel manager's love of classic queer culture would chime with the boy's sensibility and Danny would get a kick from Sands' old-fashioned attraction to decadence. Maybe it would be a detour from the underworld, though I doubted it.

Crows set off a chorus of harsh screams in the trees that divided the field from the road beyond. They were carnivores who would peck a lamb's eyes from its head while it was still alive. I slipped on another cowpat and almost fell. I would be glad to get back to Glasgow. Another bank of trees waited, dark and gloomy beyond the fields. I wondered if they were the site of John Forrest's failed woodland burial business and how many people he had planted there. What happened when that venture had failed? Did the already buried remain, doing their bit for the mulch, or were they relocated somewhere more successful? Somewhere with a café?

The polytunnels loomed. Close up, they looked sturdier than I had realised from a distance, like plastic Nissen huts, robustly made to withstand the Scottish weather. I reached the lowest terrace and looked up towards the farmhouse. The lights were off. I wondered if the Forrests were out, my journey wasted.

I climbed towards the second terrace and then the third. I had expected to encounter workers, but the only movement was the slight shimmer of the tunnels' polyethylene surface responding to the wind. I called, 'Hello, anyone about?' so that if I was caught no one could accuse me of snooping, and pulled open one of the flaps that acted as a doorway.

It was warm and damp inside, like a greenhouse. There was a smell of rot that reminded me of the dead dog and made me clamp a hand to my nose and mouth. I had anticipated lush greenery, but the plants arranged on the slatted wooden benches that stretched the length of the tunnel were brown and decaying. Another scheme had failed John Forrest. It occurred to me how hungry the landlady at the Black Bull would be for news of this fresh business collapse and I found myself smiling as I left the tunnel to continue my climb.

I had reached the next level of tunnels when I heard a shout and turned in the direction I had travelled.

'Hey!' Alec was standing in the doorway of the empty polytunnel I had peeked inside. He barked, 'What do you want?'

He looked like he would happily bury me amongst the unsuccessful dead, beneath the trees beyond. I summoned a bright, business-like smile. 'Just a courtesy call.'

Alec was dressed in a navy overall. He had a bucket in his hand, which he set down on the terrace. 'What's wrong with driving up to the front door like a decent Christian?'

The phrase 'decent Christian' made me smile for real.

'My car was blocked in and I fancied stretching my legs.'

The walls of the tunnel bent in the wind that was now sweeping across the hillside. The open doorway slapped to and fro. A muffled thud-thud-thud sounded somewhere distant, like a subterranean mechanism.

Alec picked up his bucket and pointed towards the farmhouse. 'John deals with the business stuff. He's up at the house.'

It was no concern of mine, but I added, 'With your aunt?'

Alec held my gaze and the knowledge of her absence passed between us. He said, 'John will sort you out. He's the clever lad. I do the grunt work.'

Forrest picked up his bucket. He went back inside the polytunnel and closed the flap behind him, but I was aware of his dark figure standing on the other side of the semi-translucent entrance, waiting for me to leave. I picked up my feet and continued the climb, humming my song to myself.

Oh, they danced until their legs were nearly lame,
Every little crawling creature you could name.
Everyone was glad,
What a time they had,
They were so happy they came!

There were all sorts of ugly bugs in the world. There was the dancing kind and the ones who waited to prey. Alec did not look like much of a dancer.

I wondered where he had been when I glanced into the tunnel. I would have sworn it was empty. I turned to look at the tunnels again and saw they were equipped with flaps at both ends, so workers could step from one to the other. I left him there amongst the dead plants and headed for the farmhouse.

Thirty-One

MY PHONE BUZZED just as I opened the farmyard gate. I took it from my pocket, expecting to see Les's name on the display, but it was Anderson. The thought that something might have happened to Rose flashed unwelcome into my mind and I answered.

Anderson used his policeman voice. 'What were you up to in the city centre in the early hours of Sunday morning?'

I bit back a curse. 'I was home, sleeping the sleep of the just.'

'Bollocks. You're on CCTV exiting an office building that was used for an illegal gathering.'

A traffic light beeped in the background of wherever Anderson was. There was the sound of a revving motorbike and a rumble of car engines. I hoped his phoning me from outdoors, rather than from behind his desk at the police station, was a sign that he was willing to keep things unofficial.

I attempted a tone of injured innocence. 'That's impossible.'

'Don't insult my intelligence, Rilke. I've known you since you were eleven years old. You covered your face, but it was you. The same skinny body and Catweazle clothes. Same stupid run that lost us the school relay in 1980.'

Somewhere nearby, a magpie started its machine-gun rattle and a blackbird let out an emergency call.

'There are plenty of blokes who look like me.'

'If that's the case, you won't mind me setting up an identification parade. You and five guys picked at random off the street.'

'What's this about, Anderson?'

'A respectable premises was used as a knocking shop last night. I've seen teenage Facebook parties that made less mess. The proprietor is blaming an ex-boyfriend, but he's got zero proof. All the CCTV cameras were out of commission, except for one that some sloppy bastard forgot about at the rear fire exit. Three men were recorded running away from the premises in the early hours of the morning, after setting off the burglar alarm. One of them was you.'

'I've no idea why you'd think—'

'I have a credible eyewitness who saw two of the men enter the premises. She has agreed to identify them for us. What do you predict she'd say if I showed her your photo?'

The cleaner had got a good look at me and Frank. I lowered my voice. 'I had nothing to do with the party. I just went there the next morning to help a friend get his clothes back.'

Anderson said, 'Have you any idea how pathetic that sounds?'

'I guess I'm too old for you to chalk it up to a youthful indiscretion?'

'I'm too old to cover up your stupid escapades. I used to have some sympathy, back in the day. Guys like you were denied equal rights, discriminated against, blah, blah, blah. But these days, no one gives a fuck if you're animal, vegetable or fucking mineral. You can get married and take an equal share in the sum of human misery. What the fuck are you doing skulking around office premises in the middle of the night? Why can't you behave like a decent fucking normal citizen?'

There was something heartfelt in Anderson's rant that made me want to laugh but I felt a surge of anger too. 'When did Police Scotland become the Morality Police?' A light went on in the front room of the farmhouse. A curtain moved in the window and I saw John, white and ghostly on the other side of the glass. I raised a hand in greeting, and he raised his in return, like a man saying hello to his past. His face was grave. I hoped he was not going to tell me he was unhappy at what the sale had raised. I said, 'I've got to go. The client's waiting. What are you going to do, Anders? Should I pack an overnight case?'

'Strictly speaking, I should report my suspicions to the investigating officer, but as things go, I only saw the CCTV clip by chance, over someone else's shoulder. No one needs to know I viewed it, or that I can identify one of the culprits. But if someone else brings your name up, you're on your own.'

I breathed a sigh of relief. 'Thanks, Jim. That's one I owe you.'

'Yes, it is. And I'm going to collect.'

I felt the stone-in-the-stomach sensation that denotes a sinking heart. 'What do you want?'

'Talk me up to Rose.'

I tried to put some sincerity into my voice. 'No talking-up required – you're her number one squeeze.'

Anderson sounded offended. 'I'd prefer to be her only squeeze.'

'That's what I meant. You're her top squeeze. Her only squeeze.'

'Just put a good word in, Rilke. Tell her it's time she settled down.'

The inspector had been asking Rose to marry him at roughly eighteen-month intervals over the last five years. I said I would do my best, but it was an empty promise. Anderson should have known that there was no point in trying to persuade Rose to do anything she did not want to.

If I had not visited the farmhouse before, I might have thought that the place had been burgled. The kitchen was the same mess, the air stale and flyblown, the draining board stacked with unwashed dishes, but now document boxes were piled around the room and papers littered the floor, as if someone had carried out a frantic search. John showed no sign of embarrassment at the state of the place. He unburdened a couple of kitchen chairs of dirty laundry and made space at the table for the sales documents I had brought along. I went through the purchase lists with him, pointing out items that had sold beyond their estimate price, skipping those that had failed to achieve what we had hoped.

John's charm was dimmed. He punched the sales figures into a pocket calculator, muttering the numbers under his breath. He smelt faintly of last night's, or maybe that morning's, whisky. I wondered again what Jamie Mitchell had been up to at the farmhouse and if his visit had anything to do with John's fractured demeanour.

Forrest lost his place, swore and returned to the top of the sales list. Eventually he nodded and set the calculator aside. 'All seems to be in order.'

I gathered my documents, got to my feet, and shook his hand. 'It's been a real pleasure, Mr Forrest, a privilege to handle goods of such a high calibre. I'm very grateful to the late Mr Nugent for putting us in touch.'

His face was blank. 'Mr Who?'

'Joseph Nugent, Jojo to his friends. He was the original conduit between yourself and us.'

John pushed his boyish flop of fringe away from his face. A line furrowed his forehead. 'Jojo's dead?'

I was clutching the documents to my body like a shield. I set them on the table. 'Sorry, I assumed you knew.'

He blinked. 'What happened?'

'I heard he was found dead in the street. A sad turn of events.'

A not-quite-full whisky bottle stood amidst the chaos on the table, less than an arm's reach from John. He unscrewed the cap and poured himself a good measure. The creases on his face deepened as he raised it to his lips and drank. He tilted the bottle towards me in invitation.

'What do you mean "found in the street"? Someone attacked him?'

The bottle trembled in the air, the whisky an unquiet sea with no shore. I was tempted to accept the offer, but held up a hand in polite refusal.

'No, thanks. I've a long day to go yet.' I could have mentioned the doorstep beneath the fire escape where Jojo's body had been found and my suspicions that he had been abandoned there. But there was nothing to be gained by associating Bowery Auctions with drugs and sordid parties. 'I'm not sure what killed Mr Nugent. He had the kind of schedule that would have challenged a much younger man. Maybe his heart gave out.'

John blinked again. He echoed, 'His heart,' and took another sip of his drink. His Adam's apple rose and fell, the creases on his face tightened. 'Glasgow's a dangerous place. You're certain no one attacked him?'

Rain spattered the window.

'I don't know enough to be certain. It could have been that way, I suppose, but I didn't hear any mention of a beating.'

'When I was younger there was a phrase, *life is long*. It's a crock of shit. Life's short. You don't realise how short until you get to our age. You've got to grab it while you can.'

John Forrest had more than a few years on me, but it was not the moment to correct him.

'I don't know enough to be sure. Someone said Jojo had been at a party. I don't want to speak ill of the dead, but Jojo was gregarious. He liked a good time. Maybe he overdid things.' I glanced at my watch. 'You've been through a rough patch. I hope this sale's the start of a better period for you and your cousin.'

John gave me a sharp look. 'What do you mean, "a rough patch"?'

My fingers wanted the comfort of a cigarette. I resisted the urge to reach for my tobacco tin. 'Your aunt entering a care home and the car crash on the corner next to Ballantyne House. That must have been a shock.'

He flapped a hand in dismissal. There was a wet gleam to his eyes. 'My aunt's departure is sad. But the crash . . . Auntie Pat used to call that kind of accident natural selection. Stupid boys drive too fast.' He looked at his glass. 'And old men drink too much.' Forgetting that I had turned down his offer of a drink, he raised it in a toast. 'To Joseph Nugent. And to stupid boys.'

I raised my right hand in an awkward, empty-fisted salute. 'To Joseph Nugent and stupid boys.' I wondered if he knew how appropriate the coupling in his strange toast was. 'How did you and Jojo meet?'

He drained his glass. The nip seemed to revive him. He started bundling papers into the boxes again, as if time was running out. 'Why do you ask?'

'Just making conversation. Jojo was a mutual friend.'

He gave a bark of laughter. 'That's how we met. Through mutual friends.' He paused in his task and his eyes met mine. 'You know that Michael and Simmy, the boys who died in the crash, worked for Alec?'

'I think someone mentioned it.'

He did not bother to ask who had been discussing his business. 'Before they came to us, they used to do odd jobs for a pawnbroker Jojo did business with. I think Jojo was a kind of mentor to them. He dropped by and we got talking. I know he would have liked to have got his hands on some of Auntie Pat's prizes, but he didn't have the capital and I wasn't interested in selling things off piecemeal. He recommended Bowery. Said you'd be conscientious but faster and less hassle than some of the bigger firms. I was dubious at first, but I looked you up and you checked out. I'm assuming you gave him a commission?'

I nodded. 'It's standard practice.'

His face darkened. 'You're certain it was his heart?'

'Not certain, no.'

He returned to his packing. 'I can't wait to be shot of this bloody country.'

Abomi had mentioned that one of the dead boys came from his neighbourhood. He had said nothing about him being an occasional employee of his uncle Razzle, but there were only so many pawnbrokers in town, and Ray Diamond was the only one who operated in the district the boys had come from. The thought made me uneasy.

I was giving the papers John had signed a final scan to check they were in order when my phone rang. Les's name shone

from the screen. It was the fourth time he had called me. I
flashed John an apologetic smile and walked to the window.

'Excuse me, I need to take this call.'

Les sounded out of breath. 'What the fuck was that message
you left on my phone about? I told you I was up in Aberdeen
with the sheep shaggers and the oiled men. Anyway, you're
persona non grata. I don't want to know about your social life.
Surprised you've got one, right enough.' He laughed, and I
guessed he was high. 'Bet you were with that wee wank Sandy.
Is that what you were trying to do? Show off your new boyfriend?'

It felt strange being in the Forrests' kitchen with Les's
voice rasping in my ear. I pulled back the curtain and looked
across the farmyard towards the hill that led down to the
main house. 'Is that what you wanted to tell me?'

Les ignored my question. 'Where the fuck have you been
anyway? I've rung you half a dozen times.'

The rain was growing stronger. I wondered if I should
phone Frank and get him to give me a lift back.

'I've been busy. I'm busy right now, as it happens. Winding
up the sale at Ballantyne House.'

'Anywhere near Ballantyne Farm?'

I whispered, 'Connected – they're one and the same.'

'You up there at the moment?'

'Yep.'

'I'd shift on out of it if I were you. It's one of Jamie
Mitchell's places.'

My stomach descended for the second time that day. 'What
makes you so sure?'

'I got speaking to a boy up here. He knew I was in a jam,
but not who with. It's not the kind of info you shout about
– unlike your love life apparently. I was trying to get the
name of a new wholesale connection – any connection – on

the west coast out of him. He suggested Jamie Mitchell. That was about as much use to me as a fart in a spacesuit, but he told me he'd heard some wee foot soldiers had been selling stuff out the back of the van, from a place called Ballantyne Farm. A bit dodgy, as it was one of Mitchell's concerns, but worth a try if you're hard-up and willing to risk your eyeballs being replaced with your bollocks which, surprise, surprise, I wasn't. Then I realised Ballantyne Farm rang a bell and thought you'd like to know your arse is in the lion's den.'

'I think that operation might have crashed and burned a while ago.' Had Mitchell poached the dead boys from Razzle's stable and brought them to work at Ballantyne? My hands trembled but I kept my voice smooth and professional. 'Okay, thanks, Les. I'll certainly bear that in mind.'

Les became suddenly serious. 'Christ, you're with them right now, aren't you? Is he there? Mitchell?'

'Not yet.'

'Well, get going before he fee-fi-fo-fums it over there and kebabs your head.'

'I appreciate the advice.'

'I mean it, Rilke. He's a mad gadge.'

John was tossing the contents of one of the document boxes into a bin bag.

I said, 'I'm going to put your suggestion into play immediately.'

Les snapped, 'See that you do and remember you owe me for fucking up my livelihood.'

The wind caught the rain, sending it in needle battalions against the windowpane. Alec was walking towards the house looking like Death on a mission, a hat pulled low over his face.

I said, 'What about Mr D? He might be able to offer you some assistance.'

Les was back to sounding bitter. 'Ray Diamond? I burnt my bridges there, stupid bastard that I am. Mitchell was giving out good deals when he arrived on the scene. I took him up on them. Ray heard and booted me out of the fold.'

'I saw him the other day. He was mellow.'

'Yeah, well, you're on Mitchell's hit list, which puts you on the side of God and the angels, as far as Ray Diamond's concerned. Thanks to you I'm out in the fucking cold.' Les's voice tightened. 'Listen, just shift yourself. If Mitchell gets his hands on you, there'll be nothing left for me to stick the boot into when I get back to Glasgow, and I'm looking forward to giving you a kicking.'

My tone was formal and final. 'I'll look forward to that too, with interest. Thanks for getting in touch.'

I hung up and stowed my phone. A blast of cold air swept into the already cold room as Alec walked through the door. He glanced at me, went silently to the sink, filled the kettle and set it on the stove.

'I want your guys out of my mother's house and off our land by the end of today. That was the deal.'

An incoming text buzzed my phone. It was from Frank. *Mitchell's BMW on its way.*

I nodded. 'Don't worry. We're on schedule.'

Gravel crunched beneath car tyres at the front of the house. John went to the front window and peeked out from behind the curtains. 'It's Mitchell.'

I folded the sales documents into my pocket. 'I'll leave you in peace.'

I stepped smartly through the French windows and out into the backyard. Part of me wanted to confront Jamie Mitchell about the art commission he had used to snare Sands. The wiser part remembered the boys who had stolen from him and then crashed and died on the Ballantyne Road. I reached the ridge at the end of the farmyard and glanced back at the house. The curtain I had drawn had not quite fallen into place. Jamie Mitchell had his back towards me. He was dressed in a long raincoat. Alec was out of sight, but I could make out John's face, a scrap of white in the dim room. He was talking quickly, gesturing with his hands, as if trying to explain something.

My phone buzzed again. Another text from Frank: *Boss?*

I stabbed back, *b there in 10*. I nipped through the gate and onto the steps that would lead me to the field that sloped down to Ballantyne House. The rain was getting heavier. I cursed myself again for venturing out without a raincoat or an umbrella. I had reached the third terrace when the downpour intensified into a torrent with the power to batter through cloth and flesh and soak to the bone. Ballantyne House had vanished behind a curtain of fog and rain. My leather soles lost purchase in the wet grass. I slid on my arse, jarring my hip bone and soaking my trousers. I fell twice more, slick as an upturned bug, before I regained my leverage in the mud and got to my feet. Rain battered down on me all the while. I half jogged, half skidded into the closest polytunnel and stood there shivering, waiting for the storm to ease.

It was the same tunnel Alec had caught me peeking into earlier. Inside, it was warm and dry. Had it not been for the foul smell and rotting plants, my soggy trousers and bruised hip, it might have been pleasant to shelter there, listening to the sound of the rain drumming against the plastic. The storm showed no sign of abating. I cleared some of the plants from one of the slatted benches, dusted its surface with a handkerchief and boosted myself onto it. The bench was high. My feet dangled an inch above the dirt floor. The thudding that I had noticed earlier sounded faintly somewhere beneath me. Thunder rumbled in the distance.

I took out my phone and texted Frank: *Sheltering in polytunnel 3*. I sat quietly for a moment, letting the events of the last few days run through my mind. I had a feeling that a wrong move might tip me towards some disaster, the way the wet mud had slid the ground from beneath my feet. I did not know enough to recognise a good move from a bad one.

I texted Sands: *How's the commission going?* The boy must have had his phone in his hand because a series of photos immediately slotted into my inbox.

The New York pretensions of the chiropractor's studio had been stripped away by the slide of Sands' digital shutter. The mirrored wall, designed to give an impression of space, merely doubled the bedlam. The men's naked and half-naked bodies were frozen like an all-inclusive dance troupe indifferent to body shapes. I recognised the stranger who knew me with the familiar rose tattoo above his heart, the fat bank manager who had joked about raping Frank, the smug leather queen.

The best of the images were tense with contradiction. The men in them were as close to their animal selves as sentient beings could be. Alive in moments that acknowledged no past and no future, no consequences. The men might come to regret their escapades, hold them as sacred memories or forget them entirely. They would grow older (if they were lucky) and die, but Sands' images had potential to endure. It was easy to imagine the photographs hanging large-scale on cool white walls, stared at by elegantly dressed gallery-goers. The smell of sex and sweat and amyl nitrate would be replaced by the scent of cooled air and superiority. Raucous laughter, groaning voices and the slap of flesh on flesh would be erased, the gallery silent except for the hum of air conditioners, the clink of wine glasses and whispered conversation. An eddy of unease trembled in my stomach. I scrolled on, looking for myself.

Sands had captured me in the act of hoisting Frank onto my shoulders. My white shirt shone electric against the melee; my hair was sweat-slicked against my head. Frank's head had fallen over my chest, his face concealed by dark floppy hair. The raincoat I had shoved on him more or less covered his nakedness, but it was clear that his was a good-looking body. A viewer would not be able to say if I was saving or abducting Frank. My face strained with the effort of lifting him, the cords of my neck stuck out, my mouth as grimly set as one of Goya's beasts. It was horrible and rather good. The kind of image that might find its way onto the cover of an exhibition catalogue and posters pasted around city metros.

I was staring at it when my auction phone started to ring. *Bobby Burns* flashed on the screen. I accepted the call and forced a dash of bright into my voice. 'Shouldn't you and your lucky husband be on your Caribbean honeymoon?'

'We are. Listen to the sounds of Jamaica . . .'

There was a pause, presumably while Bobby held his phone out towards lapping waves or exotic birds flocking through exotic trees, but the Galloway rain drowned out the sounds on the other end of the line.

I squeezed my eyes shut, trying to block out the image of myself, hot and sweaty in the middle of the orgy. 'Sounds blissful. Makes it extra mysterious why you're wasting your time calling me instead of sooking back the cocktails.'

Bobby laughed. 'Don't worry. I've a rum punch sitting next to the sun lounger. Bob's desperate to know if we got our bid. I told him it would either be waiting for us when we got back or it wouldn't, but you know what he's like.'

Bobby McAndrew was serious and long-suffering, a patient man who I doubted was desperate for news, but it was not my place to say so.

I took the sales documents from my pocket. 'Hang on. I've got the list here.' I scanned the columns and found the painting the two Bobbys had bid for. 'You did well. You got it at just under your max.'

Hundreds of miles away beneath a Caribbean sun, Bobby said, 'Ach, that's fantastic.'

I promised to look after the picture until the two Bobbys returned from honeymoon and to waive the usual storage fee, as an extra wedding present.

Bobby said, 'You're a gentleman, Rilke.' He dropped his voice as if he was worried about being overheard, a true gossip's habit. 'I heard about Jojo. Sad news. A surprise, but not really a surprise, if you know what I mean.'

I jumped down from the bench and walked to the doorway of the tunnel. The rain was still bucketing down, Ballantyne House still hidden behind a chainmail of fog, but there was a vague brightening behind grey clouds that suggested the deluge might lighten soon.

'I guess he wasn't in the best shape.'

Bobby gulped on his rum punch. I imagined it, cool and fruity, garnished with a paper umbrella. How long since sunshine had touched my bare skin?

Bobby said, 'He was a disaster and getting worse. I had a soft spot for Jojo, you know that. The poor sod had more than a few bad breaks, but he didn't help himself. Bob went mad when he heard I'd invited him to the wedding. I knew he was on the slide, but he honestly wasn't that bad the last time I'd seen him. You did us a favour huckling him away from the reception when you did. Jojo had lost his boundaries.'

'He went down fast, that's for sure. I was surprised at the change in him. Any idea what pushed him over the edge?'

Bobby lowered his voice into a dramatic whisper. 'Between ourselves, he'd fallen in with a young guy. They were living together, him and Jojo. Well, I don't suppose they were *living together*, more sharing a dump with Jojo picking up the bills – for a change. I think maybe Jojo thought the kid was his boyfriend, but you just needed to take one look at this boy to know he was stringing Jojo along. Nice enough on the surface, polite, but a stone chancer.' There was a pause while Bobby sucked on his cocktail. 'You know the type: tell you what you want to know, keep you sweet and see what they can squeeze out of you. Me and Bob ran into them one night in the Polo Lounge – not my kind of a place, a meat market, but you know Bob, he likes to keep his eye on the scene, for which read, total lech. I kept my eye on Jojo's beau. He was one thing with Jojo, another with us. He flirted with my Bob, which of course Bob loved. He knew better than to try it on with me. Knew I'd tell him to get to fuck.'

Bobby's conviction that everyone was after his husband, a sixteen-stone conveyancing lawyer in his late fifties, made me smile. 'You're a one-man man. How did Jojo take it?'

'Ach, you know what Jojo was like. Nerves tuned tight as Sandra Dee's quim, but easygoing with it. Always looking for the next deal. He saw us, and dollar signs started flashing. Jojo wanted Bob and me to buy one of the young guy's paintings. Kept shoving his phone in my face, showing me photos of them.'

'Were you tempted?'

Bobby's voice took on an edge of shrewdness. 'You seen them?'

'Yes, gruesome but good.'

'Couldn't have put it better myself. A talented boy, for

sure, but not the kind of thing I'd want up on the wall. Christ, much as I loved him, I don't want to pass a picture of Jojo getting his jollies on the way to my boiled egg and soldiers in the morning.'

We laughed. I said, 'So you think Jojo was bumped off by a midlife crisis?'

Bobby took another gulp of his drink. His voice took on the pompous tone of a man about to give his opinion. 'I don't really approve of speculating on these things – after all, neither of us are medical men – but Jojo went downhill after he started keeping company with that boy. You've got to ask yourself why a good-looking lad in his twenties would want to hang around with an old soak like Jojo. What was in it for him? It wasn't even as if Jojo was minted.'

It was nothing I had not asked myself, but I had lost sight of the strangeness of Jojo and Sands' connection. 'I met the kid when I helped organise the funeral. He said he liked Jojo's stories.'

Bobby spluttered on his cocktail. 'Jojo was a laugh but he was hardly Armistead Maupin.'

The rain was starting to ease. I would be able to make my escape soon.

I said, 'You saw his paintings. The boy's obviously interested in the dark side of things, maybe Jojo was a safe entry into a world he found exotic.'

'Maybe, but my left ear itched when I was talking to him, and that's a sure sign that something's not quite right.' Bobby laughed. 'Bob's rolling his eyes at me, but you know what I'm saying. No harm to the boy, but he was out for what he could get. He calculated badly though – poor Jojo had sod all.'

We chitchatted back and forth a little more. I passed my regards on to Bobby McAndrew, held my phone outside the polytunnel so they could hear the rain and revel in their tropical weather, wished them both a happy honeymoon and hung up. Despite being a lecturer at the university, Bobby had always seemed down on youth, especially good-looking youth that might catch his husband's eye. He would not have taken to Sands had the boy been Michelangelo reincarnated.

I crumbled a leaf from one of the dead plants between my thumb and index finger and smelt the powdery residue. I was no expert, but I thought maybe it had been a tomato plant. Tomatoes were two quid a punnet tops. I wondered how many you had to sell to make a decent living.

I looked again at the photo of me dragging Frank onto my back. I had told the porter no one would care that he attended sex parties, but it turned out I was not so keen on having my presence there advertised.

Jojo had not minded. He had been proud to be at the centre of Sands' art. Was that what had lain at the heart of their unlikely friendship? A need to see and be seen? I put my phone away and tried to wipe the mud from my trousers. Once the photo of me and Frank was out in the digital ether it would be impossible to erase, but Sands was a problem that would have to wait.

I could hear the rain slackening. I glanced out of the polytunnel to assess how wet I would get on the walk back to Ballantyne.

All thoughts of Jojo and Sands vanished. My immediate problem wore a suit and a smart raincoat and was walking alongside Alec Forrest, down the terraces, to where I was sheltering. Jamie Mitchell lifted his head and stared across the hillside, towards Ballantyne House. His expression was hidden by the shadows thrown by the golf umbrella he was sheltering under, but the set of his body told me he was unhappy.

Thirty-Two

I RETREATED, SLIPPING through the plastic flaps at the far end, into the neighbouring polytunnel. The stench was less pronounced there, though the plants were as dead as the ones I had left behind. Jamie Mitchell and Alec Forrest had looked like a citified laird and his down-at-heel gamekeeper, walking the boundaries together before a shoot. I heard their voices as they approached and crouched low amongst the benches stocked with drooping plants, hoping the pair would pass me by. Their words were snatched away by the wind, but I detected an aggrieved tone in Mitchell's voice.

Despite Anderson's gibe about the school relay, I have always been quick on my pins. I debated making a run for it, exiting the tunnel, slipping and slithering down the hill to the safety of Ballantyne House. The chance of my skidding on cowshit and breaking my neck was somewhere around sixty–forty in my favour, but my fear of Mitchell was outweighed by the urge to know what he and Alec were up to. I saw their shadows enter adjacent polytunnel number three and turned my phone to silent.

Mitchell was angry. 'Your brother should be here.'

Alec was a stolid lump of misery. I had to hand it to him, whatever the conditions, he was consistent. 'He's my cousin, not my brother, and he's not well.'

'If he's well enough to take a share of the profit, he's well enough to cover our backs while we're down there.'

Alec said, 'You should have brought help if you wanted someone to cover your back.'

Mitchell was getting worked up. 'More people means more risk. Leaving the entrance uncovered means more risk. Letting stupid twats come and go – a big, bloody, pointless risk.' There was a sound of smashing plant pots. 'Fuck's sake. State of this place. No one's going to believe you're running a viable business if they see this.'

Alec's voice was calm. 'My mother took a turn for the worse. We've only just managed to get her sorted. It's put a lot of strain on my cousin, that and the other stuff.'

There was another crash. Mitchell snapped, 'How hard can it be to water a few plants?'

Alec stood his ground. 'Smashing the place up won't help. We don't have the right equipment to look convincing.'

'So, buy a fucking watering can and a bottle of Baby Bio.'

Mitchell was a world away from the quiet man who had collected the contraband from Jojo's flat. I wondered what had rattled his cage and if he had come alone, or if some heavy was waiting patiently in the black BMW, scrolling through his phone for new jujitsu moves.

I could not see Alec's silhouette from my position, crouched low in the neighbouring tunnel to his, but his voice became strained, as if he was grappling with something heavy.

'This set-up wouldn't fool anyone. It needs a full-scale irrigation system and a team of workers.'

Outside, the wind was rising; the polytunnels quivered.

Mitchell said, 'I sent you workers.'

Alec's voice wavered with exertion. 'You sent me a couple of Glasgow neds. Daft boys, more trouble than they were worth.'

There was the sound of metal against metal, something opening or giving way.

'What did you expect? Five Highers? A gardening degree?'

'I expected a bit of loyalty. They stole from us, killed my mother's dog and brought the police to our door.'

Mitchell's laugh sounded rusty. 'They won't be doing that again.'

'The other one might.'

'He'll say nothing.'

Alec's voice seemed to fade and expand, like a man talking down the wrong end of a megaphone. 'He already has. The police did a door-to-door search, asking if anyone knew where the fucker came from. We played schtum, but they'll be back.'

Mitchell said something, but his voice had taken on the same muffled echo as Alec's and I could not make out his words. There was a clatter of metal on metal again and then the hillside was quiet, except for the noise of the tunnels' walls buffeted by the wind and the cries of the crows in the roaring trees beyond.

I was cold, wet and tired. Somewhere in the city, there was a warm pub and a pint of IPA with my name on it. I crouched in my spot until I was sure the two men were not going to reappear and then edged cautiously back into polytunnel number three. It was empty. One of the benches and a section of rubber matting beneath it had been moved, revealing the tightly closed lid of a metal service hatch sunk into the ground. I squatted low and looked at it. The hatch had the solid, utilitarian look of UK armed forces design. The deep thud of some machine reached me. I knew the wiser course was to leave while the coast was clear but curiosity got the better of me. I grasped the hatch's handle and gently pulled it open an inch. It gave, and an unmistakable skunky, musky smell reached into the chilly polytunnel. Jamie Mitchell and Alec Forrest had established a cannabis farm in a bunker abandoned by the Ministry of Defence. They had not bothered, or were unable, to lock it from the inside. I was too nervous of the consequences of getting caught to open the hatch fully. I lowered the lid softly back into place.

This must have been where Phan had escaped from, where the boys who died in the crashed Micra had been journeying to and from. I thought briefly of putting something heavy on top of the hatch and trapping the two men in whatever bunker lay beneath my feet, but the idea of burying them alive, no matter how temporarily, made my flesh creep. I stepped quietly from the polytunnel. The winter dusk made my journey more difficult, but I was glad of its cover as I stumbled down the hill.

Thirty-Three

I SAT IN A chair in the butler's pantry, sipping a tot of the brandy I had secreted there. The sodden cuffs of my tweed trousers dripped onto the flagstone floor. Anderson's mobile phone was turned off. I called Partick Police Station and asked to speak to him. The person who answered put me on hold and then told me he was unavailable. I hung up without leaving a message.

The cousins had auctioned Mrs Forrest's effects and sold the family home. Their aunt was gone – to Chiang Mai or somewhere else – and the farmhouse had looked ransacked when I visited. They were liquidating their assets, getting ready to run. I wondered if Jamie Mitchell had twigged yet and what he would do about it when he did. I called Anderson again. An electronic voice told me his number was unavailable and I cut the call.

Ballantyne House echoed with the shouts of porters, the crash and scrape of packing cases and furniture being manoeuvred from dusty rooms and along hallways to waiting vans. In an hour or so we would be gone.

Rose was shouting instructions in the corridor beyond. I sprang to my feet, unlocked the door and stuck my head out. 'Got a moment?'

Rose was wearing an oversized shift dress, crystal earrings that might originally have graced a chandelier at Versailles and a pair of white running shoes. She raised an eyebrow. 'What the hell happened to you?'

I stepped into the corridor. 'I got caught in the rain.'

Rose stuck her hands in the front pockets of her dress. It ballooned out around her like a Pierrot costume. 'What's it raining? Cowshit?'

'Very funny.' I had fallen more than once on my way down the hill and my suit was a mess. 'Where's Anderson?'

Rose wrinkled her nose. 'Keeping the city streets safe for degenerates like you. I was going to suggest a drink when we got back but I'm not going anywhere with you dressed like that.'

Abomi appeared, heading into the house for another load. Rose caught him by the arm. 'Andy, could you fetch Mr Rilke one of the overalls I saw hanging in the kitchen, please? He seems to have got himself into a bit of a state.'

Abomi's eyes widened as he took in my soiled suit. He was nervous of Rose and rarely spoke in front of her, but he asked, 'Are you okay, Mr Rilke? Did someone bother you?'

I snapped, 'Has no one ever been caught in the rain before?' The boy's face flushed. I suppressed my irritation. 'I'm fine, thanks, son. Just lost my footing coming down the hill and got a bit muddy. It's turned me into a bad-tempered bastard.'

Abomi was about to say something else, but Rose gave him a look and he hurried in the direction of the cloakroom.

She waited until he was out of earshot. 'The poor boy only asked if you were okay. Did you see his face when he thought someone might have duffed you up? That lad would kill for you.'

I tipped back the last of my brandy. 'He'll grow out of it.'

The glow of a successful sale was still on Rose. She forgot about Abomi's hurt feelings and brought out the one hundred watts. 'Clients happy?'

'They're fine.'

Rose cocked her head. 'Just fine?'

'Ecstatic.'

Something in my expression must have beaconed trouble. Rose's smile faded. 'What's wrong?'

Rose Bowery can cut through bullshit like nitric acid through steel. There was no point in flimflamming her, but I tried. 'Nothing. Everything's hunky dory.'

Hannah and Lucy ran laughing into the corridor, carrying a box each. They saw us, slowed their pace and straightened their faces.

Hannah said, 'That's the ballroom cleared.'

I nodded. 'Good. Can you check the rest of the ground floor, please?'

'Yes, Mr Rilke.'

The girls walked on smartly, aware of something in the air between Rose and me. They turned the corner and started giggling again.

Rose kept her voice low. 'It's not just cowshit you smell of. Something's up. What did you want with Anderson?'

'Nothing I need bother you with.'

Rose's smile vanished. 'I swear, Rilke, I'll swing for you one day. You've got three seconds before I go up to that farmhouse and ask French and fucking Saunders what's going on.'

I unlocked the butler's pantry and drew her into the smell of beeswax and decaying leather. 'You're not going to like it. Remember Jamie Mitchell?'

'The dead pheasant?'

I was confused for a moment, then I remembered the ugly oil painting Mitchell had wanted to buy. 'That's the man.'

'What about him?'

I lowered my voice. 'He's involved with the Forrests. I'm pretty sure the polytunnels are cover for a cannabis farm. The Forrests are Mitchell's growers.' I paused, unsure of how much to tell her. 'The boys who died in the crash were involved somehow. Probably a bit of enforcement, a bit of selling and distribution.'

Rose shook her head. Her crystal earrings swayed. 'You're off your head. John is an old duffer, and Alec doesn't look like he's got the brains to run a lemonade stand. They must be getting a hefty sum for the house and we know they've made a killing on the contents. Why would they risk getting involved with drugs?'

I shrugged. 'Greed? They didn't have any money until they sold up and, according to John, the proceeds of the sale are going to pay for his aunt's upkeep.'

Rose wrinkled her forehead. 'No, you're talking mince. Anyway, this is Galloway. It's too bloody cold to grow anything except kale and potatoes. Anderson would laugh in your face.'

I decided not to tell her that Anderson was after Mitchell. 'I don't mean they're literally cultivating cannabis on the hillside. They're growing it in an abandoned MOD bunker beneath the polytunnels.'

'You've seen this with your own eyes?'

'Not exactly . . .'

Rose shook her head. 'You've got an inflated imagination. Remember when you read that book on the Masons? You saw Masonic conspiracies everywhere for weeks afterwards.'

It was an old argument, one I would not win, but I said, 'The Masons' reach is wider than you realise. Anyway, this isn't like that. I heard Alec and Mitchell arguing when I was sheltering from the rain. They didn't know I was there. The two of them went down into some old bunker. I lifted the hatch and sneaked a peek. It was too dark to see much, but it smelt fresher than anything Les ever managed to lay his hands on.'

Rose looked like she wanted to hit me. 'Fuck's sake, Rilke, are you serious?'

I nodded. 'Serious as taxes.'

Rose sank into one of the leather chairs. 'We should have pulled out when that woman came to the door screaming about Mrs Forrest going missing.'

I took the other seat. 'The pub landlady's sister? Rilla?'

A door slammed somewhere in the house. We both looked in the direction of the noise but neither of us moved. After a moment Rose said, 'I knew there was something up, but you convinced me—'

I interrupted her. 'You convinced yourself.'

Rose made a face. 'Maybe we convinced each other.'

I took the spare glass from the shelf, poured a measure of brandy and passed it to her. 'The money convinced us.'

Rose took the glass from me and drank. 'Being broke convinced us.' She closed her eyes and frowned, as if the brandy tasted bad. 'You don't think they . . .?'

'What?'

Something clattered in the hallway outside and one of the porters swore.

Rose lowered her voice. 'Rilla mentioned she used to look after Mrs Forrest. She wanted to see the old lady, made quite a fuss about it, but the cousins were adamant. They wouldn't let her. Why not?'

I shrugged. 'John said Rilla had taken advantage of his aunt's age and stolen from her.'

Rose nodded. 'It's possible. These things do happen but . . .'

'But what?'

'You don't think they did away with the old dear?'

The thought had crossed my mind, but I said, 'I don't think so. Whenever they talk about Patricia Forrest, I get the feeling they genuinely care for her.'

'That doesn't mean anything. I loved my dad, but I lost count of the times I walked away to stop myself from pushing him down the auction-house stairs.'

Joe Bowery had been a difficult man. There had been times when my foot had tingled with the urge to boot him into the beyond.

'Point is, you walked away. I don't think the cousins killed Mrs Forrest, but I'm not convinced she's in a care home in Thailand. Maybe they're trying to keep her whereabouts a secret from Mitchell, so he doesn't have any more leverage on them.'

Rose looked tired. She took off her earrings and slipped them into the pocket of her dress. 'Which brings us back to the drugs thing. How sure are you?'

There was a small, barred window high on the outside wall of the butler's pantry. I stared up at it and saw dark sky, no sign of a moon.

'Pretty sure. Ninety per cent. Ninety-five per cent.'

'And you were going to keep it from me?'

'I was going to tell Anderson.'

Rose got to her feet and delivered a jab to my upper arm that was hard enough to bruise. 'If you tell him, our sale will be fucked. The courts will grab the Forrests' assets and freeze them until they can decide whether the money's the product of illegal earnings. Our commission will probably be frozen with it. Bowery can't take that kind of hit just now.'

I stood up so I could talk to her eye to eye. 'I didn't go looking for problems.'

Rose stepped close enough for me to smell the cherry scent of her lipstick. 'Just because you found problems doesn't mean you need to engage with them. We do what we were going to do. Clear up and clear out. People like drugs. Christ, we like drugs. If it wasn't the Forrests and this Mitchell specimen supplying them, it would be someone else. When did you suddenly become Anderson's deputy? His job's law and order. Yours is selling antiques.'

I rubbed my arm where she had hit me. 'I don't need you to remind me what my job is. I know the score. Throw a blind eye, move quick and hope we're long gone before the shit hits the fan, but—'

Rose shoved me. 'But what?'

I took a step backwards. 'Remember Phan, the runaway who's still too scared to let on where he was being held?'

It dawned on Rose what I was trying to tell her. 'Oh shit. You mean . . .?'

'He won't have been the only one being held there. Mitchell and the Forrests have some kind of underground lab or cannabis farm. They'll have more unfortunates like

Phan down there, cultivating it for them. Christ only knows what conditions they're being kept in.'

Rose gave me a pleading look. 'The funds will clear in less than a fortnight.'

'Rose . . .'

She made a face and clenched her fists like a thwarted child. 'Fuck, fuck, fuck, fuck, fuck. Okay, I know.'

Someone opened the back door to the house. The through draught slammed the front door shut and blew open the door to the pantry. Abomi stood on the other side, a set of blue coveralls draped over his arm and a guilty expression on his face.

I got to my feet. 'Were you listening at the door?'

The boy shook his head, eyes wide. 'No, Mr Rilke. I just got here.'

Abomi called me Mr Rilke when he was worried that he had done something wrong, but my voice was stern, and he might still have been smarting from when I had shouted at him earlier. I looked the boy in the eye and softened my voice. 'Are you sure?'

Abomi moved his fingers over the breast pocket of his dust coat. 'Cross my heart and hope to die.'

I drew him into the room and shut the door. 'Swear on Rambo's life.'

He hesitated, then whispered, 'I swear on Rambo's life.'

I resolved to have a word with the boy before the end of the day, but it would have to do for now. I took the overalls from him. 'Okay, but don't hang around in doorways in future. It makes people nervous. Go and see what job Frank has for you.'

Abomi sped away like a schoolboy reprieved of six of the belt.

Rose shut the pantry door behind him. 'Do you think he heard anything?'

I was not sure. 'No. He's a good lad. I'd know if he had.'

Rose sat down. She unfastened her ponytail, ran her fingers through her hair, then secured it on top of her head in a loose bun. 'You know where this place is? The underground bunker or whatever it is?'

I nodded. 'There's a hatch in the floor of polytunnel number three. The pair of them went down it.'

Rose's eyes gleamed with the same conviction that had enabled her to keep Bowery Auctions afloat after her father's unexpected death, despite the volcano of debt he had left and a string of crises since.

'Okay. We go up there, let their slaveys out and carry on as if we know nothing about it. I've read about people trafficking. It's never out of the papers. I could get a bloody PhD in it. The traffickers threaten the victims' families. They'll be scared rigid and grateful to escape. It'll be a while before the police pin down what's been going on. In the meantime, our commission will be safe in the bank.'

I took another sip of brandy. 'Simpler to set Anderson on the case.'

Rose shook her head. 'Anders would play it by the book. We'd be stuffed.'

I rubbed my face with my hands. 'I don't know . . .'

'Do you have a better solution?'

'Telling Anderson?'

Rose leaned forward and looked me in the eye. 'How do you rate your employability prospects if Bowery goes down?'

We both knew they were zero, but I muttered, 'I'd probably pick something up.'

Rose snorted. 'Come off it, Rilke, your *Midnight Cowboy*

days are over.' She reached out and plucked the clean set of overalls Abomi had brought from my hands. 'I'll take these. This dress is way too expensive to get ruined.'

I tried to grab the overalls back, but Rose snatched them away from me. 'Your suit's a goner. The best drycleaners in the world couldn't bring it back to life.'

I said, 'I'll get Frank to come with me. He owes me.'

Rose kicked off her trainers and pulled her dress over her head – a flash of black lacy underwear. She pulled the navy overall on. 'I noticed you two were suddenly best buds.' She buttoned the overall up the front and transformed into a saucy Land Girl. 'As far as I'm concerned, Frank's still on probation. He's not been here long enough to be trusted. My auction house, my mission. You can come too, if you're up for it, but no one else. More people equals more risk.'

It was almost exactly what Mitchell had said, just before he and Alec had descended into the bunker. I took a last swig of brandy and set my glass down on a shelf. 'It's not as simple as that. They didn't leave the hatch open. It's a big metal thing.'

'How did they secure it?'

'A bolt and padlock. They lock it from the outside.'

Rose lifted her dress from the back of the chair and rustled through the material until she found her pocket. She took her phone from it and pressed quick dial.

'Frank, do you still have the bolt cutters you were using to get into the sheds at the back of the house?' She waited a moment while Frank confirmed that he did. 'Would you mind getting them for me, please, and leaving them on the kitchen table. I've mislaid a key for a padlock at home.' Frank said something and she replied. 'No, no worries. Nothing I can't handle myself. If I need any help, I'll ask Mr Rilke.'

She hung up and shoved her phone in the pocket of her overall. 'Problem solved. Soon as we're finished here, we nip over the hill, cut the locks on the hatch cover, open it up and skedaddle. We don't even have to go down into the bowels — just make sure the poor sods have an exit route. After that, it's up to them.'

Rose has a knack for making things sound simple. In that moment, secure amongst the smell of old polish and faded servitude, I thought her plan might actually work.

Thirty-Four

IT WAS AFTER nine o'clock by the time we dismissed the crew and locked up the empty house. I had been up and down the hill so many times I should have known it like the back of my hand, but the night was black as Jamie Mitchell's soul and I kept losing my footing. I was carrying the bolt cutters in a black rucksack on my back. Rose was ahead of me, her white trainers shining occasionally as she stepped surely through the mud. I had swapped my filthy suit and shirt for a navy overall, a twin of the one Rose was wearing. She laughed when she saw me in it and joked that we looked like a 1980s new wave band.

The farmhouse was a dark shape against the black sky. It sank behind the rise as we climbed. Rose waited for me to catch her up at the first terrace. The polytunnels' plastic walls slapped in the wind, making a noise that conjured images of unfurled sails on storm-tossed yachts. I could just about make out the shape of the tunnels and felt a sense of dread at the idea of stepping inside them.

Rose's voice trembled with excitement. 'How far?'

The wind caught my breath. 'Two more terraces.'

I pointed upwards, though I was not sure she could see me in the dark. Something screamed. An amorous fox, an owl on the kill or a rabbit about to breathe its last? I was too much of a city boy to know what. Rose giggled nervously. I started up the rise. A feeling was growing on me that I had used up all my chances. I considered taking my phone from my pocket and calling Anderson, dialling 999 if he did not answer. But Rose and I had been partners in crime for over half my life. Her recklessness called to some chivalrous part of me. I would not let her down. We would get it over with and be done with Ballantyne House.

The beam of a car's headlamps bent through the trees on the road beyond the fields, picking out the white polytunnels, luminous in the sudden light. We froze, but the car continued onwards, and the field was cast into darkness again.

'Remember the night we went to the farmhouse?' Rose sounded nervous.

'John was out for the count.'

'Do you remember what time it was when we got there?'

I thought back. 'Around nine-thirtyish.'

Rose said, 'Around the same time it is now. Alec came back from somewhere. He was carrying a bucket.'

'I remember. As if he had just been feeding livestock or something.' I realised what I had just said and stopped still. 'Do you think . . .?'

Rose turned to face me, her face pale against the night. 'I don't know. But if he's a man of regular habits, we should watch out. We don't want him rocking up to hand out the rations and finding us breaking and entering.'

We resumed our climb. I said, 'You keep lookout. I'll cut the padlocks.'

Rose's voice bristled. 'Why not the other way around?'

'You're the brains, I'm the brawn, remember?'

'You're not so brawny.'

'You're not so brainy either.'

It was an old joke between us. Neither of us laughed, but its familiarity was a comfort.

Polytunnel number three looked identical to the others. I pushed open the flaps and we stepped inside. I had forgotten to warn Rose about the smell. She covered her nose and mouth with her hands. 'Phew, this place honks.'

The bench laden with withered foliage was back in place, the plastic matting flat on the floor. Rose stood by the entrance, staring out into the darkness while I shifted them and uncovered the service hatch. I turned on my phone's torch, just long enough to illuminate two heavyweight padlocks holding sturdy bolts in place. I killed the light and took the bolt cutters from my backpack.

Rose whispered, 'How does it look?'

'Possible. Anything happening out there?'

'No, all's quiet on the Western Front.'

I trapped the hasp of the first padlock in the jaws of the bolt cutter. It was a hard job and I found myself wishing that Frank, with his youth and muscles, was here to help. Eventually there was the teeth-grinding sensation of metal cutting through metal and one side of the hasp gave way. I repeated the procedure on its other side. Perhaps I had gained a knack because the second cut was quicker.

Rose whispered, 'What's happening?'

'One down, one to go.'

I wondered how many people were trapped beneath our feet and if they could hear me breaking in. It would be frightening to be entombed down there, unsure of who or what was about to appear. I remembered tales of trolls and troglodytes and realised that I might be as frightened of the people being held prisoner below as they were of me. I paused and rocked back on my haunches, gathering my strength.

Rose hissed, 'I think there's something out there.'

I joined her at the front of the tunnel, and we stood there together, listening to the sound of the wind in the trees. Air gusted from all directions. I thought of Macbeth and the witches. He should have turned back at the start of the play and made the most of his lot. Not gone fucking about on stormy moors, looking for glory.

After a couple of minutes, Rose whispered, 'Sorry, false alarm.'

I returned to the hatch and started on the second padlock. It took a while, but eventually it gave way. All that remained was to pull back the bolts.

I said, 'Okay, that's them off. What do you want to do? Open them and scoot? Hope for the best?'

Rose abandoned her post and stood by my side, looking down at the hatch. 'I'm going down.'

I got to my feet. 'Hang on. You said we would open it and skedaddle. Make an exit route and let the poor guys work the rest out for themselves.'

Rose's voice held an unfamiliar, apologetic tone. 'Now that we're here, I need to see it through. We didn't do all this just so Alec could come by and lock them in again.'

I hissed, 'Was this your plan all along?'

Rose sounded pensive. 'I don't think so.'

'And what if he comes along and locks us in? Did that occur to you?'

'He can't. You've broken the padlocks. I'll be quick. In, out and gone.'

'Just leave the poor guys on the hillside?'

Rose shrugged. 'Depends how many of them there are. We've got the van. We could drop them in the city centre. Make an anonymous phone call. Get them some help.'

The simple plan was taking on complications I did not like. I glanced at my watch. It was 9.45 p.m. I stepped in front of the hatch, blocking it with my body. 'For fuck's sake, Rose. I should have known better than to listen to you. I'm phoning Anderson right now.'

I reached for the phone in my pocket. Rose grabbed my arm, her grip tight. Her body was slight against mine. It would have been a simple thing to shove her away, but I did not.

'Please, Rilke. You know what Anderson's like. Mr Upstanding Citizen. He'll "do the right thing", except it'll be the wrong thing for us. It'll mean the end of Bowery Auctions, the end of everything we do. No more big sales. We'll end up becoming runners, always one last deal away from the street. I couldn't stand that. Neither could you.'

I thought about Jojo, the miserable room stuffed with boxes of bric-a-brac where he had been living when he died. Then I thought about Phan, the bruises that had marked his body when Abomi and I had found him, running along the road, terrified.

'Oh, for fuck's sake.' I pushed her from me. 'Okay. You win, as usual.' I started to lift the lid of the hatch. 'But on condition you stay out here and keep watch. Brains and brawn, remember?'

I could tell from the way she hugged me that Rose was uncertain, but she whispered, 'You're not that brawny and I'm not that brainy.' And then she gave me a kiss.

Thirty-Five

I PULLED OPEN the hatch. Its hinges made a grating sound that seemed to split the night. I froze for a moment, listening hard. The slap of the polyethylene walls and the rush of the wind in the trees drowned out any other sounds. I took out my phone and shone its torch down into a vertical shaft. An old-fashioned light switch was set into the concrete wall next to a set of metal rungs that reminded me of the swimming baths of my youth. I clicked on the light, half hoping, half dreading that a cluster of anxious faces would appear below, but there was no sign of life.

Rose hissed, 'What can you see?'

'Nothing – a ladder, that's all.' I heaved myself over the top and found the first rung with my foot. 'If anything happens, screech like that owl or whatever it was earlier.'

Rose whispered, 'Before or after I shit myself?'

'Before, if you can manage it.'

She said, 'Be careful,' like a female patriot sending her man off to war.

I took the descent slowly, holding tight with my hands, my leather soles slick against the metal rungs. It felt like a long time before my feet touched solid concrete. There was another light switch. I pressed it, and a series of bare bulbs, secured behind metal grilles, flashed alive, revealing a narrow corridor with grey painted walls. An enamel sign that would fetch a good price at auction declared, No Unauthorised Personnel Permitted Beyond This Point. It was decorated with a black-and-yellow nuclear hazard symbol. I was inside a nuclear bomb shelter, part of the MOD complex that had been on the site for decades before the Forrest family had been invited to reclaim it.

The smell that had infected polytunnel 3 was more pungent below. The thud of machinery that had been a faint quiver above ground sent tremors through the atmosphere. I guessed it was some mechanism designed to recycle uncontaminated air, and wondered what would happen if it suddenly failed.

The lights stopped up ahead. The corridor beyond was cast in pure darkness of a depth I was unsure I had experienced before. I paused for a second, gathering myself, and called, 'Hello. Don't be afraid. I've come to help you. Phan sent me.'

I thought I heard something, a rush of atmosphere, a distant sound that might have been voices or simply the trees above caught in a gust of wind. I called again, 'Phan sent me. Don't be afraid. I'm here to help you.'

I reached another switch, another set of lights. I turned them on, and the rest of the corridor came alive: grey walls, concrete floor, official notices and a set of heavy metal doors secured by a deadbolt. A rush of anger and relief swept over me. I had risked myself for nothing. Without keys to the locked door, the only way to save anyone held down there was to do what I had always wanted to do and call the police. The door looked thick enough to block out all sounds, but I leaned against it and called, 'Don't worry. I'll be back with help. We'll get you out.'

I had started to retrace my steps when I heard a rumble of voices from the polytunnel above followed by the sound of several pairs of feet descending the metal ladder. I hit the light switch and flattened myself into the dark, spine rigid against the concrete wall, my breath shocked from my chest. I thought of Rose, and the sound of my heart pulsed in my head. I caught hold of my phone, ready to text her, but realised the signal would be dead. All I could do was hope she had managed to hide before Mitchell spotted her.

Ballantyne House had bristled with Stanley knives and other potential weapons as we packed the last of the goods away, but it had not occurred to me to slip one into my pocket. Even the bolt cutters, which would be good for staving heads in, were up above, beyond my reach.

The murmur of approaching voices drew closer. I could smell them now, a locker-room scent of sweat and sports gel. Jamie Mitchell had a reputation for taking joy in other people's pain and humiliation. It sounded like he had brought an audience with him. I scrabbled in my pockets for something that could act as a weapon. All I found was an end of string and my bundle of keys. I slotted the keys between my fingers and formed my hand into a fist. I closed my eyes, steadied my breathing. Mitchell would likely slice the skin from me, but I would do my best to get a few blows in first.

The intruders drew closer, and I realised that I recognised one of their voices. The light came on, bright and unforgiving, shrinking my pupils though I had only closed my eyes in the darkness for an instant.

Ray Diamond smiled gently. He had set aside his usual nondescript grey and beige outfits in favour of a black track-suit, black quilted jacket and black knitted cap.

'Hello, Rilke.' He held up a set of keys. 'Were you looking for these?'

I nodded. Two other men, both dressed in black, accompanied Ray. They were broad-shouldered with the solid silhouettes of heavyweight boxers. He did not bother to introduce us.

I did my best to peel myself from the wall. 'Where's Rose?'

Ray gave me a reassuring smile. 'Rose is fine. She'll be waiting in the van for you when we go up.' He showed me the keys again. 'Shall I do the honours?'

My legs felt strange. 'What are you doing here, Ray?'

He said, 'I don't want you to hold it against the lad – young Andy was doing his best. He thought you might be in a bit of bother, so he called me.'

'Is Andy with you?'

'No. I sent him home with Frank. Andy's sensitive. He's not suited to this kind of business. That's why his mum and me are happy he's working with you.' Ray held the keys in the air. 'Don't know about you, but this stink is getting to me. Shall we get this over with?'

I stepped to one side and he went to the locked door. The two men moved like shadows behind him.

I asked, 'Where did you get the keys from?'

Ray looked at me over his shoulder. 'Where do you think?'

The idea that he might somehow have been involved in the business from the start was growing in my mind, but I said, 'The Forrest cousins, or maybe Jamie Mitchell.'

Ray nodded. 'Right on both counts. I think the Forrest boys were glad to see me, actually. Jamie Mitchell had started having a go at them. Apparently not very happy to hear they were shipping out. I don't think Mr Mitchell's much of a believer in freedom of movement. Probably a Brexit voter.' He turned his attention to his shadows. 'Okay, lads. These guys in here have had a hard time. They're frightened, so don't be surprised if they attack first and ask questions later. If they're anything like the lad our Andy found, they'll be on their last legs, so no threat to big guys like you. Treat them with kindness. Our aim's to get them above ground in one piece.'

I said, 'Is this a mercy mission?'

Ray took a torch from his pocket. He grinned. 'Depends on who you ask. Jamie Mitchell might not think so. He was proper pissed off when we turned up at the farmhouse. Not what you'd call a happy camper.'

The men laughed softly. Their huge shoulders seemed to span the walls. The narrow corridor was the perfect space for an ambush. Advantage would go to whoever held the exit route. It was easy to imagine Mitchell storming us with a band of men, like pirates boarding a treasure ship.

I said, 'Where is he now?'

'Mitchell? Don't worry about him. He won't be bothering us.' Ray nodded at the door. 'Designed to resist a nuclear blast. Don't know about you, but I'd rather let my eyeballs melt than spend my final days down here.'

He turned the key and pushed open the door to reveal a chest-high forest of cannabis plants, dark green beneath banks of grow lights. I had expected the prisoners to be crowded around the entrance, eager to greet or to attack us, but there was no sight of anyone – just the plants, their leaves spread like welcoming hands.

After the tightness of the corridor, the space looked enormous, but I was aware of the low ceiling bearing a weight of concrete above our heads and felt claustrophobia threatening to close in on me. An open door waited at the other end of the miniature forest.

Ray put a hand on my shoulder. 'Let's see what we've got here, then.'

'I think I'd better go up and check on Rose.'

Ray gave my shoulder a squeeze. 'I told you, Rose is fine. Don't worry about her.'

He kept his hand on my shoulder as we walked through the plants, their leaves brushing against our clothes, the smell fresh in our nostrils. We went through a door at the far end into a space strung with what looked like washing lines. Harvested cannabis plants hung upside down on the plastic ropes, drying in neat rows. There was another door and another corridor beyond this room, and I got an impression of rooms beyond rooms. Ray was right: it would be better to let your eyeballs melt, your skin frazzle until you were nothing but a shadow on the pavement, than to live in this hellhole.

Ray said, 'Quite an operation.' He sounded impressed. 'Okay, boys. We want all this taken down and in the big van tonight. Think the squad can manage it?'

One of the men said, 'Shouldn't be a problem if they put their backs into it.'

I would have wanted a full inventory before I committed myself, but the man sounded relaxed.

Ray smiled. 'That's what I like to hear. Maybe we'll get the lads from down here to give a hand. Let's see what kind of state they're in first.' He took his mobile from his pocket and swiped through a few downloads until he found what he was looking for. He glanced at us – 'No laughing' – and raised his voice. '*Chung toi da den de giup bạn. Khong phai lo lang. Bạn an toan roi.*' Ray repeated the words, awkwardly stumbling over the consonants, but something of the sense of what he was trying to say must have translated itself to the men hiding inside the bunker because they crept tentatively into the room.

The men were dressed as Phan had been, in cut-off trousers and vests. They were emaciated, their skin pallid, as if they had been underground for a long time. None of them were bruised like Phan, but they moved slowly, as if their bones hurt. Their expressions were wary.

Ray repeated his mantra and one of the men replied in his own language. Ray squared his shoulders. 'Sorry, son. That's as far as my lingo goes.'

The man said, 'Police?'

'Not police – friends.' Ray turned to his shadows. 'These guys are going to be more hindrance than help. Let's get them up and into the first van.' He grinned at me. 'We've got a present for them. May as well give them it now as later.'

One of the men said, 'Think they'll want it?'

'Are you kidding? After what they've been through? Course they will.'

The Vietnamese man who had already spoken said something again. Ray shook his head and showed his dentures. He pointed upwards, to above ground, smiled and read his script from his phone. The Vietnamese conferred amongst themselves. There was a short dispute and then the man said, 'We go. Safe?'

Ray nodded. 'Yes, safe.'

'No police?'

Ray grinned. 'Not if I have anything to do with it.' He said more slowly, 'No police. You're free now.'

The Vietnamese men edged their way to the door, keeping close to one another. One of Ray's men led the way; the other followed the small group, almost herding them into the corridor.

Ray turned to me. His eyes were bluer than you would

expect in a man of his age. Ice-cold, calm as a cutting blade. 'What's your interest in all this?'

There was water in my bowels. 'Humanitarian. Fiscal. I savvied what was going on. I didn't want the poor sods on my conscience, but Bowery can't afford to lose the commission from the sale, which is what would have happened if the polis got involved. I reckoned the easiest thing was to let the guys out and let them take it from there.'

Ray nodded. 'Makes sense. Stupid. Reckless. But I get where you're coming from. Where does your mate Jojo fit in?'

My stomach executed another swoop. 'Jojo? He's dead.'

'I know that. But before he was dead, Jojo was palling about with a couple of wee poofs from round my way who were in with Jamie Mitchell.'

I guessed he meant the boys who had ended up wrapped around the tree in the joy-crashed Micra but I said, 'I wouldn't know anything about that.'

'Are you sure? Think carefully before you answer. These boys thought they were hard men. They stole from me. Lucky for them they were barbecued before I could get my hands on them.'

A bead of sweat slipped down my spine. I wondered if Ray knew that Sands and I had passed the G on to Mitchell in return for Jojo's funeral. 'What did they steal? Antiques?'

Ray stepped close enough for me to feel his breath on my face. 'Doesn't matter what it was, but I heard on the grapevine that Jojo might have palled about with them. You mentioned Jojo when you were round the other day. Seemed curious about him.'

'I was curious about the way he died. It was sudden. A friend of his went shortly after. It got me thinking.'

'Too much thinking can be bad for your health.' Ray

gazed into the distance. 'Jojo had a way of pissing people off. Far as I'm concerned, it's good riddance to bad rubbish.' His voice was low and serious. 'How come you got involved with this place? Seems like a bit of a coincidence.'

'Jojo gave us the tip about the house.'

Ray thought for a moment then nodded. 'That makes sense.' He sighed. 'Under normal circumstances, I'd take certain measures at this point, just to be careful.'

Ray paused, giving me an opportunity to speak. I pressed my lips tight shut, buttoning up the urge to plead my case. Eventually Ray nodded, as if I had passed some test. 'You've been good to our Andy. He'd be upset if something happened to you.'

I tried to keep the wobble out of my voice. 'I wouldn't be too happy either.'

Ray smiled. 'Your happiness doesn't really figure in this.'

He rubbed a hand over his face, as if he was trying to make his mind up about something. I pictured distant rooms of the bunker, where a man could scream as loud as his lungs would let him and no one would hear.

Ray said, 'I've always pegged you for a good listener, Rilke. Your type often are. So I reckon I only have to tell you this once. You weren't here tonight. You saw nothing. Know nothing. Okay?'

I nodded. 'I wasn't here. Rose will be good with that too.'

Ray said, 'I've already spoken to Rose. She's not such a good listener.'

I closed my eyes and said, 'I'll make sure she keeps schtum.'

Ray grinned. 'Don't worry. Joe Bowery brought her up to know the score.' He lowered his voice and whispered, 'Not a word, okay?'

I nodded and drew my fingers over my lips. 'Zipped.'

'Good, and don't worry about what happened to Jojo, or anyone else for that matter. Sometimes people get what they ask for.' Ray squeezed my shoulder, hard. I resisted the urge to pull away. He said, 'Let's get out of this place. It stinks worse than one of Rambo's farts.'

Two black Lutons were parked at the top of the terraces. The farmhouse was still in darkness. Ray and I caught up with the small procession of Vietnamese men. They were wearing sliders more suited to a summer's beach and their progress was slow.

I turned to him. 'What about the Forrest cousins?'

'Proof that age doesn't necessarily lead to wisdom. A pair of lazy fuckers looking for a quick buck. Didn't do their business research, got in too deep and ended up getting their fingers skelped. Don't worry about them. They'll be fine.'

'Rose and I have paperwork to conclude with them before we can put the sale to bed.'

'Conclude it. As far as they're concerned, you know nothing about all this. Keep it that way.'

'And Jamie Mitchell?'

Ray's teeth shone white in the dark. 'You really want to know?'

Rose was sitting in the front of the van, next to a large man in the driver's seat. She saw the straggle of Vietnamese men approaching and jumped out.

Ray said, 'Told you we'd sort it.'

Rose bit her bottom lip. 'What now?'

Ray gave her an avuncular smile. 'Don't look so worried. We're the good guys. We'll head back to Glasgow, drop them in the city centre. One of the lads knows a Vietnamese restaurant in town. We'll let them out there.' He put a hand on her shoulder. 'Wait in the van, Rose. It's cold out here and I've got a couple of things to go over with Mr Rilke.'

Rose looked uncertain. She touched my arm. 'Okay, Rilke?'

I nodded. 'Yeah. Ray's right. It's cold enough to freeze the tits off a brass monkey.'

I remembered Sands' attraction to the multi-armed Hindu goddess and wished I had given it to him while I had the chance.

Ray said, 'Bit crude.'

'An old joke of Joe Bowery's.'

Ray led the way. 'A good man but a foul mouth.'

The Vietnamese men were waiting by the back of the van with Ray's deputies. I saw fear in their eyes and knew it was mirrored in my own. Gangster movies flashed through my mind. Guns to the head on nights as dark as this, men digging their own graves, buried alive, shoved into car boots, strangled, slashed, suffocated, battered with shovels, doused in petrol and set alight.

Ray made a sweeping gesture with his hands, like God designing the world. 'Move the guys back a mo. I want Mr Rilke to get first peek.'

One of the men gently guided the Vietnamese away from the van. The other one rolled up the back of the vehicle. It was too dark to see what was inside.

Ray said, 'Who's got the big light?'

One of the men produced a torch and Ray said, 'Good lad. Get in and make sure to keep it in the interior. We don't want to attract unwanted attention.'

The man climbed up into the van and aimed the beam into a far corner. Jamie Mitchell was a huddled mess of blood and bruises, bound by polypropylene rope. I thought he might be dead, but then he raised his head, showing the horror his face had become and stared at me through eyes that were smaller and larger than they were designed to be.

A murmur came from the Vietnamese. I made a move to climb into the van.

Ray caught me by the elbow. 'Best leave him be.'

I wanted to beg Ray not to do whatever he was going to do, but self-preservation stopped me. I whispered, 'Can I ask him about Jojo?'

Ray said, 'I told you to forget about Jojo. What was he? An old flame or something?'

I shook my head. 'No, nothing like that. Just a friend.'

Ray sighed. 'If you must.' He nodded at the Vietnamese, who were talking in low and rapid tones amongst themselves. 'Make it quick. These guys are getting restless.'

I pulled the sleeves of the overall over my hands and climbed into the van, careful not to touch anything. Jamie Mitchell raised his head and moved his lips. I thought perhaps he was going to ask for my help but then he spat a gobby mass of blood and spit that landed just short of my boots.

I whispered, 'I'll put a word in with the big man, if you tell me what happened to Jojo.'

Mitchell closed his eyes. I thought he had passed out but then he opened them and looked up at me. 'The big man?' He spat again. I thought that was it, but then he whispered, 'I never met Jojo. Only time I saw him he was in a box, heading for the big fire.'

I whispered, 'Was it you that sent him there?'

Blood bubbled in Mitchell's throat. He whispered, 'Get to fuck.'

Ray called, 'Time's up.'

I jumped from the van. Ray nodded to his deputies. 'Okay, get them on board.' They started to herd the Vietnamese men into the back of the van where Mitchell sprawled, bound and bloodied. Ray turned to me. 'I'm a firm believer in natural justice. How about you, Rilke?'

His meaning dawned on me.

'I think these guys have suffered enough. Don't put something on their conscience they might not be equipped for.'

The men were climbing aboard the van, muttering to each other in words I could not decipher. One of Ray's men passed the torch to them and jumped to the ground. His companion shut the door and locked it.

Ray said, 'We'll have to agree to disagree on that one. I've given them a choice. We'll find out what they decide when we open the back of the van in Glasgow. You could call it a moral experiment. Who knows? One of them might turn out to be a doctor and have a go at patching up our pal there, or they might be more inclined to my way of thinking.'

I whispered, 'The way of the warrior is the resolute acceptance of death.'

Ray grinned. 'Exactly. I wouldn't waste any sleep on Mitchell. He knew the odds. Same as you and I do. The man made his choices.' He reached into his pocket, took out a set of car keys and handed them to me. They were mine. 'One of the lads brought your car up the road.' He grinned and called to the man who had shone the torch. 'First time you'd driven a Skoda, wasn't it?'

The man laughed. 'Surprisingly smooth ride, but never going to impress the ladies.'

Ray said, 'Mr Rilke doesn't have to worry about that.' He turned to me. 'The Forrests will want a quiet night. You can conclude your paperwork tomorrow. Best thing for now is to give Rose a lift back to Glasgow, have a glass of wine and an early night. It takes it out of you, all this.'

There were no lights on the road out of the village. I waited until we had put Ballantyne House well behind us and pulled into a layby.

Rose said, 'What are you doing?'

I took my phone from my pocket and dialled Anderson. This time he picked up. 'Where's the fire?'

'Ray Diamond has Jamie Mitchell in the back of a van headed for Glasgow.'

I had memorised the registration plate and I recited it now. Rose tried to grab my phone. I unfastened my seatbelt, jumped from the car and ran up the unlit embankment, the wind whipping around me. I heard the Skoda's passenger door slam and Rose's voice shouting my name.

I ignored her. 'Ray's had him beaten to a pulp. There's a bunch of guys in the back of the van with Mitchell, forced labour from Vietnam. I think they're going to finish him off. He won't make it out alive.'

Anderson said, 'Is Rose with you?'

'Yes, she's fine.'

'Are you sure?'

I could still hear Rose calling my name from the layby below. 'I told you, she's okay.'

Anderson said, 'We didn't have this call. Forget what you just told me and make sure you get her home in one piece.'

He hung up, and I was left alone in the wind and the dark. I stood there for a moment, Rose's voice catching on the gale. I swore, threw my phone on the ground and swore some more. Then I got down on my hands and knees. It took me a while to find the phone. I shoved it in the pocket of my overall and walked slowly, down the embankment, towards the car.

Thirty-Six

I DID NOT EXPECT to get any rest that night, but I slept the sleep of the drugged and the dead. I woke to the sound of someone battering on the front door. My muscles were stiff after a day of steep hills and sodden clothes. I dragged my dressing gown on, shambled down the hallway and looked through the spyhole. Les was waiting on the other side, a stupid grin plastered across his face. I unlocked the door and let it swing wide. He swaggered into the hallway, shutting the door behind him. He did a Northern Soul style spin on one foot and came to a halt, with his hands above his head.

'Will the Real Slim Shady please stand up?'

I turned my back on him and went into the kitchen, my bare feet cold against the floorboards. The clock above the cooker read 10 a.m. I filled the kettle and clicked it on. Les followed me into the room. He was unshaven and dressed in black. No sparkles or make-up, though there was a nod towards Western cool in his cowboy boots and pearl button shirt. He looked like a weathered, down-at-heel busker who had been on the road for a while and got accustomed to sleeping in his clothes.

'What do you want, Les?'

'Tea . . . no, make that a coffee.' He boosted himself onto one of the kitchen cabinets. 'Got any hot chocolate? A Weetabix wouldn't go amiss either. I'm straight off the Aberdeen bus. Fucking famished. Could eat a scabby horse.'

I had not been asking what he wanted to drink but I made us each a black coffee, rooted in the cupboard and found a packet of Rich Tea biscuits I could not remember buying. I split the plastic wrapper with a knife and offered them to Les. He took three and slid them into his mouth at once. His lips jutted out. He choked and reached for his mug. The coffee was still boiling, and he spluttered as he tried to wash the biscuits down.

'Christ, what are you trying to do to me, Rilke? You're worse than that poisoning bastard Putin.'

He picked up the packet of biscuits and his mug, carried them through to the sitting room and sank into the couch. I followed and took the easy chair. My phone was on the coffee table. I lifted it and swiped through the *Evening Times*, looking for news of skinned-alive gangsters and a squad of scantily dressed Vietnamese men, drenched in someone else's blood.

Les put his feet up on the coffee table and started to roll a joint. He cast his eyes around the room, taking in the piles of books that had outgrown my bookcases, the paintings stacked against the wall.

'Ever thought about Marie Kondo-ing this place? It's a slog, but you get into it after a while.'

I repeated, 'What do you want, Les?'

He offered me the joint. 'I was just passing. Thought I'd pop in.'

I lit up and took a long drag. My head swam. I passed it back to him. 'Cut the bullshit.'

Les took the joint and inhaled. Smoke curled from his nostrils. 'Ray sent me round to check on you. I'm back in the fold.'

I rubbed a splatter of mud from my bare calf. I was filthy, the smell of the bunker still on me. 'You can tell Ray I'm living a blameless life, keeping my nose out of other people's business.'

Les snorted. 'Oh aye. That'll be a first.' He offered me the joint again.

I shook my head. 'I've got to get going.'

'Ray said to remind you, careless talk costs lives.'

'You one of his Goon Squad now?'

Les stuffed another Rich Tea in his mouth and talked through the crumbs. 'He asked me to pass it on, so I'm passing it on. I reckoned it might be useful advice, what with your habit of sticking your neb where it's not wanted.' He picked up the packet of biscuits and looked at it. 'What's with the old lady biscuits? Never heard of Tunnock's?'

There was nothing in the *Evening Times* about Mitchell or the escaped Vietnamese. I checked my messages. Three missed calls from Frank from the night before. The two Bobbys had sent me a photo of a beach edged with palm trees. The sand was white, the sea the same blue as the sky. There was nothing from Rose or Anderson, no new missive from Sands. I considered going back to bed and letting things take their course without me.

'How come you're back in the fold?'

Les shrugged. 'I served my time.'

I leaned forward. 'You gave him Mitchell, didn't you?'

Les sucked on the joint, hiding his expression behind a sliver of smoke. I thought he was going to deny it, but he said, 'You fucked me up, Rilke. You might not have meant to, but you did. I had to get back in somehow.'

I could have told him he had fucked himself up when he got involved with Mitchell, but I had fucked myself up too, when I accepted the favour of a funeral from him.

I said, 'I told you Mitchell was on his way to the farmhouse and you told Ray.'

Les's voice went up an octave, the way it used to when he thought a teacher was picking on him. 'I was showing willing.'

'You were setting a death sentence. And you put me right next to the chopping block.'

Les looked towards the window. It might have been raining, but the windows were dingy, and it was hard to tell. He took another pull at the joint in his hand, narrowing his eyes, and then stubbed it out on the ashtray that lay on the table between us. 'You can't blame me. I didn't know what Ray would do with the information. And I warned you first. I told you to get out. Anyway, I got the feeling that it was old news to him. All I did was prove my loyalty.'

If Les was right, Abomi must have got to his uncle before Les had, or maybe Ray had been aware of Mitchell and the Forrests' set-up for a while. He had known the boys who died in the crash were working for Mitchell; it would have been a simple thing to find out where. I picked another splatter of dried mud from my leg.

'Ray Diamond can't be the only game in town?'

Les rubbed a hand over the bristles on his chin and made a face. 'He is as far as I'm concerned. I'm getting too old to duck and dive. I need a nice stable connection and an easygoing client base. Guys like us, who like a smoke or an energy boost but know how to keep their noses clean.' The irony of what he had said dawned on him. 'Who usually know how to keep their noses clean.' He looked at me. 'Ray got him, then? Mitchell?'

'Not a pretty sight. One I could have lived without.'

Les had an enquiring mind but he did not ask me to go into details. 'Is that an end to it?'

'I don't know. Maybe.' I remembered the way Anderson had told me to forget I had phoned him. His voice had been flat, like the voice of a machine. 'The police don't give a fuck.'

Les snapped, 'What do the polis have to do with it? Don't start getting ideas about phoning fucking Anderson.' He looked at me and got to his feet. 'You didn't, did you?'

I lied. 'Of course I didn't. But if we know, they must know.'

Outside, a car alarm started to wail. Les perched on the edge of the couch. His mouth had a bitter twist. 'The polis don't give a fuck, as long as there isn't open fucking warfare.' His eyes met mine. 'Don't tell Anderson. If you find yourself coming over all funny in the conscience department, remember how Jamie Mitchell looked when you last saw him.' He sank back and took his tobacco tin from his pocket. 'Was it bad?'

I nodded. 'A fucking horror show.'

'Is he . . . you know . . . ?' Les drew a finger across his throat and made a squawking sound, like a duck being strangled.

'I don't know. Probably.'

'Fuck.' We sat in silence for a while then Les said, 'Ray did you a favour. Jamie Mitchell was an evil bastard. He'd taken against you.'

'I still don't know why.'

'You crossed him. The way Mitchell saw it, he did you a good turn, burying Jojo, and you didn't show any appreciation.'

'It wasn't really me he was doing the favour for. I'm sure Jojo was thankful.'

Les grinned. 'The Grateful Dead.'

I rolled my eyes at the bad pun. 'Think we'll ever find out what happened to Jojo?'

'Who cares? He's gone. Nothing you can do will bring him back.'

Les shut his eyes. After a while, he started snoring, gently at first, then with more gusto, the way I imagined an elderly rhinoceros might snore. I finished my coffee and then went for a shower. I washed, shaved, dressed and returned to the living room. Les was still asleep, his head thrown back, mouth gaping. He looked old. I laid my spare keys on the coffee table and went out, locking the door behind me.

It was drizzly outside, but somewhere something was burning. A smell of painted wood and melting plastic reached inside the car. I closed the driver's window and was hit by the lingering stench of old fish. A man in a suit darted across the traffic, too macho to cross at the pedestrian lights. I slowed to let him pass then put my foot down and joined the slip road onto the motorway. The memory of Mitchell's face, raw as steak mince, triggered a queasy sensation in my stomach.

I was not naïve. I knew corruption ran like a fault line through the force, but I had thought Anderson, the boy who had stood up to school bullies, was clean, and, though I was not clean myself, his hypocrisy was cutting.

The gate that led to the farmyard was chained and bolted. I parked the Skoda on the verge, blocking access and exits, and walked to the front of the house. It was in darkness. No one answered when I rapped at the door, but two cars were parked in the driveway, and my gut told me the cousins were home. The curtains were drawn at the back of the farmhouse, the French windows locked.

I banged on the window. 'Forrest, are you in there? Open the door or I'll smash it in.'

I found a rock amongst the overgrown flowerbeds, and was preparing to lob it through the glass when the curtains were pulled aside and John peered out. He looked pale but unscathed.

I let the rock fall onto the mud. 'I just want to talk to you.'

He opened the door and turned away without saying anything. I followed him as he limped into the living space, occasionally leaning on the furniture to take the weight off his leg. The limp was new. It looked painful.

An extra layer of chaos had been imposed on the room's usual confusion. A dining chair lay upended. The papers he had been sorting through when I last visited were scattered like wind-tossed rubbish. Broken crockery littered the floor, as if someone in a rage had swept piles of dishes from the kitchen worktops.

John indicated the mess. 'I'd offer you a cup of tea, but we're low on cups.' Close up, I saw that his face bore a nasty bruise, shaped like the sole of a man's boot. He said, 'What do you want?'

I looked towards the door that led to the hallway and the rooms above. 'Where's your cousin?'

'Upstairs, in bed.'

'Is he okay?'

'He'll live.' John had been trying to put things in order. A black bin bag slouched in the middle of the floor. He bent slowly and picked up a broken plate, the residue of a meal still smeared across it. He looked at it without revulsion. 'One way to save on the washing-up.' He straightened his back. 'Who are you with, Mr Rilke?'

'Bowery Auctions.'

'I know that, but a man can have two masters.' He dropped the plate into the bag. 'I thought you might be working for the police, but if that was the case, you'd probably have arrested us by now.' He picked up another segment of broken china, careful of the sharp edges, and bagged it. 'You're not with Jamie Mitchell, that much is clear, so that leaves his nemesis. Are you here to issue another warning?'

'I'm not with anyone. I'm my own man.'

He gave me a weary look. 'If that's true, it takes me back to my first question. What do you want?'

'I want to know what happened to your aunt.'

He shook his head in disbelief, but his brow puckered. 'I told you, she's in Chiang Mai.'

The door to the hallway opened. Alec had taken a beating. His face was swollen and purpling with bruises. He held himself awkwardly, as if his ribs were sore. One of his hands was bandaged. He looked a mess, but compared to Jamie Mitchell he was in Olympian condition. John was right. His cousin would live.

I looked at him. 'I was just enquiring after your mother. Where is she?'

The belligerence had not been beaten out of Alec. He went to the sink, ran the cold tap, bent his mouth beneath it and drank. He straightened up, water dripping from his beard. 'What's it to you?'

'I don't believe she's in a care home overseas. I want to see her.'

Alec and his cousin exchanged looks. Alec wiped his sleeve across his beard, then bent gingerly and lifted a black hoodie from the floor. It was creased and scuffed with dirt, but he used his undamaged hand to drag it over his head. 'My mother's my business.'

I looked from one to the other. 'If you can't prove her whereabouts, it'll be police business.'

Alec glared at me. He was injured, but he looked ready to go another round. 'Are you accusing me of mistreating my own mother?'

'No one's seen her for months. You dismissed her carer. She wasn't upstairs in her room when you said she was and I'm pretty certain flight schedules will show she didn't fly anywhere, anytime recently. So where is she?'

John gave the bin bag a kick. The broken dishes clinked. He winced as if the movement had pained his damaged leg. 'What are you after? Money?'

I shook my head. 'Fuck your money.'

John closed his eyes. The bruise on his face was the colour of damson jam. It made me think of the pulp of Jamie Mitchell's face again.

I took a deep breath. 'I'm not here to cause trouble. I just need to know that nothing bad has happened to her. Illegality I can cope with, cruelty I can't. Just let me see that she's fine and I'll be gone.'

John and his cousin exchanged another look. John said, 'Give us a minute.'

They went into the hallway together and closed the door. I heard the rise and fall of their voices, but not what was being said. I texted Rose: *At the Forrests' farmhouse*. I righted the dining room chair, sat on it and stared out into the drowned landscape beyond the cottage. I was still sitting there when the two men returned.

John entered the room first. 'Did you mean what you said? Illegality doesn't bother you?'

I got to my feet. 'I'm as reluctant to go to the police as you are.'

He leaned against the edge of the kitchen table. 'Okay, I'll take you through it. My aunt had her own ideas about how things should be run—'

I held up a hand. 'Talking isn't enough. I need to see her.'

He gave me his old, smooth grin. 'It's a little difficult—'

I interrupted. 'I saw what you did to the men you kept in that bunker. You treated them as if they were subhuman.'

He clasped his hands together, still determined to play the squire. 'It was Jamie Mitchell who brought them here. I didn't—'

I raised my voice. 'It doesn't matter what Mitchell did. You held them prisoner. You were responsible for their treatment—'

Alec interjected. 'I'll take you to her.'

John looked at him. 'Alec . . .'

Alec shrugged. 'You heard the man. He needs to see her.'

The pleading note in John's voice was close to a whine. 'We agreed: we've been given a second chance. We're not going to do anything that might blow it.'

Alec touched the nape of his cousin's neck with his good hand. 'Trust me. It'll be fine. I'll take him to her, explain everything and bring him back safe.'

John said, 'Solemn promise?'

Alec spat on the palm of his hand. 'Solemn as they get. You stay here. We'll be back in half an hour.'

Alec went to the gun cupboard, took out a shotgun and broke it open, over his arm. He took some bullets from a different cabinet and fed them into the barrel.

John whispered, 'Alec . . .'

I said, 'What are you doing?'

Alec grinned. 'Don't worry. This isn't for you. I'm having a battle with the crows. May as well bag a few if we're heading in their direction.'

John said, 'For Christ's sake, put that away and leave the fucking birds be.'

Alec's work boots were sitting by the door. He shoved his feet into them, stepped out into the courtyard and gestured with the shotgun. 'Come on.'

It occurred to me that I could refuse to go with him. I imagined what Rose would say if I told her I had gone to the woods with an armed man, but Alec gestured with the gun again and I followed him out into the afternoon smirr.

This time, instead of heading down towards the polytunnel terraces, Alec turned right and led the way towards the boundary of the farmyard. I walked, a pace behind him, to where a stile stood over the fence. Alec mounted it awkwardly and climbed down into a muddy scrub of field. He slipped on the last step. I caught him by the collar, nervous of the gun, still broken across his arm. He caught his breath, steadied himself and headed towards the trees.

This time, I had had the sense to put on walking boots. I followed him, my feet sure against the damp earth. It struck me that Ballantyne estate was larger than I had thought. My attention had been focused on the big house and the farmhouse where the cousins camped – it was hard to call what they did living. But estates like this had always had a stock of labourers' cottages, outbuildings, stables, follies and gatehouses. Some places made a tidy sum tarting them up into holiday lets. It dawned on me that the cousins had stashed Mrs Forrest in some cottage, safe from harm.

A flurry of crows flew from the trees as we approached, cawing warning cries into the quickening wind. Alec cocked his rifle, aimed upwards at the flutter of black wings and let off three quick shots. His aim was botched, and they flew away, their cries like mocking laughter. He broke the gun, reloaded and walked on. I took out my phone, texted my whereabouts to Rose again and followed him.

It was colder beneath the trees, damp-smelling and rotten. The crows followed our progress, calling to each other in the bare branches above. The track through the forest was overgrown and littered with dead branches, but I could tell that it had been cleared at some earlier point. There had even been an effort to decorate the pathway by edging it with the occasional boulder.

The beating Alec Forrest had taken was catching up with him. His breath was laboured, and he had started to limp. I remembered the way the Vietnamese men had hunched their shoulders as Ray's men ushered them into the van and the bloody mess that had once been Jamie Mitchell's face. I was glad that he was hurting.

'How did you get involved with Mitchell?'

Alec glanced at me. It was cold and damp beneath the trees, but his face was sheened in sweat. 'How much do you know?'

'I know you were growing cannabis for Mitchell in an old nuclear shelter and that you had a bunch of trafficked men down there, slaving for you. And I know Mitchell's likely dead by now.'

Alec looked away. 'We were careless. John came back from his travels broke. Got married and divorced. Got more broke. I'd been broke for a long time too. When he moved back here, we got to talking about how we could make some money. We egged each other on and temptation got the better of us.'

'There are easier ways to make money.'

He glanced at me. 'Not big money. Big money always involves a few risks.'

I kept pace with him, conscious of the gun. 'Seems to me you had big money at your fingertips.'

'You mean the house?'

'And its contents.'

A toppled tree blocked our path. I went first and steadied Alec as he struggled over. He made it to the other side and shook me free. 'None of it was liquid.'

'So why not do what you're doing now – liquidate?'

'You're forgetting Mum. She didn't want to sell up, even though the place was falling apart and too big for her by then. As far as she was concerned, the ancestral pile was the family legacy. No use explaining the family was just Johnny and me, and that as soon as we got the chance we were selling the lot and shooting the coop. Mum was determined. The big house was staying in the family, even if that meant us living like paupers while the place rotted away at the bottom of the hill.'

'According to the documents you showed us, you have power of attorney. She'd signed everything over to you and your cousin. You didn't need her permission to sell.'

Alec snapped, 'I wasn't the best of sons, but I sure as hell wasn't going to bully my mother into selling up.'

'What changed?'

He shook his head. 'Things. You'll see.'

A crow let off a warning signal. Alec looked towards the sound, but the bird was hidden amongst the foliage and he did not attempt a shot.

I asked, 'How did a good son like you get mixed up with cannabis farms and Jamie Mitchell?'

Alec's laugh resembled a snort. 'Twenty per cent greed, eighty per cent boredom. If the nuclear shelter hadn't been on our doorstep, maybe we wouldn't have bothered, but it was too good to resist. It was simple at first. John and me kept things small. We looked after the plants ourselves, but we needed a distributor. I heard about Mitchell through a friend of a friend. He seemed okay at first.'

'And then . . .'

Alec looked at me. 'I've got my faults. A bit lazy, always going to take a shortcut if I can, but I'm not evil. I didn't want to hold the guys down there.'

'But you did.'

Alec paused. 'Mitchell went from being our distributer to being our controller. He didn't give us any choice. There was no exit route. Any hint we were trying to break away, Mitchell would get us. We were as much victims as the Vietnamese.'

'Except they were buried alive, six foot under.'

'It's easy to judge. Not so easy when you're involved with a mad bastard like Mitchell. I did my best for those guys. I made sure they were fed and watered. The bunker was probably better than whatever shithole they were escaping from.'

Alec turned his back on me and walked on. I followed him, deeper into the woods. The undergrowth became thicker, the path more overgrown. It grew quieter, without the noise of the wind that had followed us until now.

'You treated those men worse than livestock. You're lucky Ray Diamond released them before anyone died.'

Alec's voice rose. 'I was the one who was in danger of dying. It's me Mitchell turned on when he realised we were planning to take the money and run. I don't know why Ray Diamond chose last night to do what he did, but if he hadn't come along, Mitchell would have killed me.'

'Your cousin could have called the police. A jail cell's better than a coffin.'

'John was comatose. I'm not sure Mitchell even knew he was there until he knocked the armchair over and John rolled onto the floor. Mitchell gave him a boot in the face. That was when Diamond and his heavies walked in. They did a number on Mitchell and then warned me, in ways I won't forget, to close up shop. Diamond took the keys to the bunker and told me to forget about it, which is what I am going to do. Soon as the money from the sale comes in, we're off. John's going back to Thailand, me' – Alec looked at the ground – 'I've not decided where I'm going. Somewhere with no extradition treaty, far away from all this shit.'

We had reached a small, man-made clearing. Alec lowered himself onto a tree stump. His outburst had sounded heartfelt, but it was himself and his cousin he felt sorry for. He had not asked about the Vietnamese men, whether Diamond enslaved them or set them free.

I looked at my watch. 'Point me in the direction of your mum's cottage and I'll keep walking.'

It was the first time I had seen the man smile. He nodded at a spot to my right where a small cairn stood. 'We're here. That's Mum's cottage.'

I took a step backwards.

Alec said, 'She drifted off in her sleep, the way I hope I go when the time comes. She'd always loved this place. John had managed to get it designated as a woodland burial site, so why not?'

'You buried her here, by yourselves?'

'We buried her with dignity. A twilight ceremony, just John and me.'

I had a ghastly vision of the two cousins creeping through the dark in the dead of night, carrying a makeshift coffin between them, quiet as grave robbers. 'Why would you do that?'

'She was our alibi. If Mitchell had known we'd come into money, he would have had every penny off us. We'd have had no chance of escape. We told him the money from the sale was going to take care of Mum in her final years. He didn't like it, but from where he was standing there were too many outside authorities for him to do anything without being caught.

'It was John who blew it. I told him we'd walk away, leave her death unregistered, leave the farmhouse as it was. No warning – just wait until we got our hands on the money from the sale, use our power of attorney to clean out the bank accounts and then vanish. We were going to tell whoever was interested – which was no one except Rilla – that we'd taken Mum with us. It was a solid plan, but John started packing up early. Mitchell saw the signs and went ballistic.'

I sat on a nearby tree stump and put my head in my hands. When I looked up, I saw a faint movement in the undergrowth, back in the direction we had come from. I thought it was a bird disturbing the branches and looked away, but when I looked again the movement was still there, focused and heading towards us. Alec had his back to whatever was approaching.

I whispered, 'What makes you think I won't shop you?'

Alec's grin vanished. 'You said it yourself. You'd lose the money from the sale, same as we would. Plus, if it gets out that you knew about the bunker and the farm, it won't just be the law you'll have to worry about. It will be Ray Diamond too. Mum's safe here. She's doing no one any harm, and neither are we. John and me will keep this strip of land. No one will be allowed to farm it or build on it. She'll rest in peace.'

Whoever was coming towards us was closer now. I braced myself, getting ready to run. The person came into focus, and I saw Anderson staring at me through the bushes, his face serious. He put a finger over his lips. Perhaps it was the glance I gave Anderson that gave the game away, or maybe Alec heard something. He turned, cocking his gun. Anderson broke cover, holding out his warrant card. Two uniformed officers were behind him. They froze when they saw Alec's gun, but Anderson held his ground.

'Unload the shotgun, drop it and step away.' Alec hesitated, and Anderson barked, 'Shotgun. Down. Now.'

Both men's faces were puce. Alec stared Anderson out. For a second, I thought he was going to ignore the order and fire, but then he broke the gun and slowly unloaded it. He dropped the cartridges, one by one, onto the ground, bent down and laid the gun on the forest floor.

'It was for the crows.' He nodded towards me. 'He'll tell you. The only thing I'm interested in shooting is birds. Otherwise, why would he come into the forest alone with me?'

Anderson came closer. 'I've long given up questioning the logic of Mr Rilke's actions.'

Alec listened quietly as one of the uniforms cuffed him and read him his rights. He only spoke to indicate that he understood he was under arrest and to ask how his cousin John was.

Anderson said, 'Your cousin doesn't have your stoicism. He's a wee bit upset, but I'm sure he'll be fine when he sees your smiling face.'

The inspector and I held back while the uniforms led Alec away. Anderson put a hand on my shoulder. His face was still red. 'You thought I was a bent bastard, didn't you?'

I restrained an urge to hug the police inspector. 'Not even for a second.'

'Rose did.'

'Rose is complex.'

Anderson was wearing climbing boots beneath his suit. He nodded at the cairn, frowning. 'What are we looking at?'

'His mother's grave.'

He made a face, but he sounded unfazed. 'Interesting bonus. Why was he showing you that?'

'I threatened to tell the police if he didn't take me to his mother. For some reason he thought I wouldn't be too upset by the idea of an unofficial burial.'

Anderson took out his phone. He gave instructions for someone to come and secure the site, then turned to me. 'We'd better stay until the forensic boys make it over. Natural causes? Or did they help the old lady on her way?'

'Who knows? They stood to get a lot of money from the sale of the house and its contents, and they'd got themselves into a bit of a jam.'

Anderson turned to face me. 'When did you find out about all this?'

'Am I under interrogation?'

'God forbid. Just two old pals chewing the fat. Come on, satisfy my natural curiosity.'

'I came up to the farmhouse yesterday, to check they were happy with the sale, and stumbled on Mitchell and Alec going into the bunker.'

Anderson nodded. 'Let's move away from the crime scene. I don't want to compromise it any further than it has been already.' We walked down the path in the direction of the house and stopped, still in sight of the cairn. 'That's better.' He pulled back his right fist and punched me on the jaw.

I hit the ground hard. I sat up and rubbed my face, too shocked to retaliate. 'What the hell was that for?'

'That's for not getting in touch with me as soon as you saw that fucking bunker. I should give you another one for getting Rose involved but I'm not sure I'd be able to stop at one. I had Mitchell in my sights. We were going to wrap him up and take him to trial, nice and neat. Now he's wrapped up in the morgue. And the Vietnamese guys you allege were part of the story are no place to be seen.'

I struggled to my feet. One of my teeth had ripped my gum and there was blood in my mouth. 'What about—'

Anderson interrupted me before I could say Ray Diamond's name out loud. 'So far, you and Rose are the only people who have mentioned a particular individual. Rose has indicated that she's unwilling to be an official witness. I'm imagining you might not fancy it either.'

I blotted the blood with my handkerchief. 'I phoned you when Mitchell was being driven away. I thought you could stop it. You hung up on me.'

'I put out a call for the number plate you gave me. It took us a while to find the van in question. It had been towed after it was illegally parked in the city centre. The exterior and cab were clean as a whistle. The interior was a different matter. It was covered in bits of Jamie Mitchell.' Anderson leaned in close. 'You and me go back a long way, but don't think I'm keeping a certain individual's involvement out of the story to help you. I'm doing it for Rose. If I ever find out that you have endangered her in any way again, you will find out what police corruption is. I'll have you banged up for the rest of your puff.'

I spat out blood and saliva.

The inspector gave me a shove that sent me reeling. I got to my feet and punched him in the ribs. The sound of footsteps quickened towards us and two policemen raced into the clearing.

Anderson put his hands up before they could get to us. 'Don't worry, boys. Mr Rilke's an old friend of the force. Just practising a few moves while we waited.' He put a hand to his ribs and gave me a gorilla grin, lips peeled back to reveal his teeth. 'Not bad for a big poof. Your right hook's improving.'

Thirty-Seven

Four Months Later

ROSE WAS WEARING a YSL dinner suit over a crisp white cotton shirt, unbuttoned low to reveal a black lacy bra. A pair of Ray-Bans peeped from the top pocket of her tux. Her lips were scarlet, her eyes smoky. The effect was high-class stripper, ready to terrify a room of businessmen. She was standing in front of a large painting of a small room, occupied by three people of indeterminate gender, their faces concealed by Covid masks.

Her eyebrows creased. 'Must have taken a lot of work.'

It was Rose-speak for not very good.

The Glue Factory was rammed. People were brushing past each other, patting backs, hugging and air kissing, as if recent prohibitions on touching had made them eager for flesh on flesh, breath on breath. I had felt the same sensation in the auction house earlier that morning and as I walked to Maryhill, where the degree show was being held. Sex was in the air.

I was wearing a new-to-me houndstooth Hugo Boss sports jacket that had come out of a house in Hyndland. I had paired it with a salmon-pink shirt and black suit trousers that bagged at the leg. The broker I am, the flashier my outfits.

I took a sip of warm white wine from the plastic cup in my hand and nodded at the picture. 'Reminds me of us, during lockdown.'

We had spent the last lockdown holed up in her flat, drinking too much, smoking like lums and bickering. My night-time walks had been filled with tempting shadows, but for once Rose and I had mostly stuck to the rules. Rose joked that we had saved each other from ourselves. I thought she had probably saved me.

Rose made a face. 'If that's us, who's the third body?'

'Anderson?'

She rolled her eyes and moved on to the next picture. Bowery Auctions' commission from the Ballantyne sale was still frozen, while lawyers worked on untangling the cousins' finances. Rose and I had taken a temporary cut in salary and Anderson had chipped in a tidy sum from his savings to help tide us over. Rose had been unhappy about accepting Anderson's offer, declaring she would rather marry the inspector than owe him money. Anderson had taken this as a cue to propose again and she had refused. They were currently on a break that I suspected was on the brink of being mended.

A group of students surged across the crowded room, jolting my wine from my glass. Rose slipped an arm through mine. 'Let's find your wee pal Sandy's work. That's what we're here for.'

I crushed my empty cup and dumped it in a handy bin. 'He's not my wee pal. And his name is Sands, not Sandy.'

Rose patted my arm. 'Okay, your protégé, or whatever he is.'

She made protégé sound like something indecent.

I had not seen Sands since the G party where he had photographed me with Frank. He still sent me the occasional picture via WhatsApp, but I associated the boy with bad luck and had resisted meeting up. It had not been a complete surprise to find an invite to Sands' degree show in my inbox, but it was a surprise to find myself there.

The heat of bodies crowded around the artworks was beginning to make my forehead spike with sweat. I took out my handkerchief and dabbed at my face. Rose and I made way for a couple of skinny girls in funky onesies and ugly trainers, their hair coiled in Bantu knots.

Rose's eyes followed them. 'You need to be thin to carry off those tracksuits.' She looked at me. 'You're very quiet. Worried you'll find yourself up on the wall?'

Sometimes it was as if she could read my mind. I looked away. 'Maybe.'

Rose grinned. 'Up on the wall naked?'

'Not quite.'

She arched her eyebrows. 'Not quite? Don't worry. I'll still love you, even if it's a *Man in Polyester Suit* situation.'

A copy of Mapplethorpe's photograph of his lover with his dick hanging out of the trousers of a synthetic suit had graced the wall above Rose's kitchen table until the evening Anderson had set down his knife and fork and refused to continue eating beneath its shadow. Rose had found it funny, then annoying, then funny again. Eventually she removed the photo. It had now hung above my couch for so long I barely registered it.

I consulted the guide we had been given at the entrance, and we negotiated our way through the scrum of people towards Sands' portion of the exhibition. The Glue Factory was dark. It smelt of brick dust and mildew. The earthy scent and Sands' proximity made me think about Jojo and the Ballantyne House adventure again.

Anderson had been as good as his word. He had kept Ray Diamond, Rose and me out of the picture. I figured at the trial solely as a witness to the discovery of Patricia Forrest's grave. The cousins, aware of Ray's long reach, had accepted sole responsibility for the cannabis factory. The Vietnamese men had been absorbed by the city without leaving a ripple. Jamie Mitchell's death remained unsolved. It was generally perceived as murky underworld mischief, intriguing but nothing that respectable people need worry about.

The weather had improved as we drifted from winter into spring and towards summer. No more unwise old men had been found dead on doorsteps. I had not forgotten Jojo though. I remembered him whenever I walked through the Merchant City and he was a bit player in my dreams. Quieter than he had been in life. Hanging around like a shy partygoer, waiting to be noticed.

Rose said, 'Why don't you ask Frank out for a drink?'

'We went for a drink last Saturday, after the sale.'

She sniffed. 'I don't mean an after-work pint. I mean, why don't you ask him on a date?'

Rose had been campaigning to get me and Frank together since she and Anderson had split.

I shook my head. 'You concentrate on your own love life and leave mine alone.'

'Neither of us have a love life – that's the problem.' Rose suddenly stopped. She squeezed my arm, tight enough to bruise. 'Look, there's Jojo.'

I followed her gaze and saw Jojo, six-foot-high, bollock

naked with a dick in both hands and a monkey-like grin on his face. The painting had gathered a crowd. It was bold and rude and joyous. A fuck-you to heteronormalists and moralists.

I whispered, 'Can you imagine Jojo's face if he could see that? He would have loved it.'

Rose nodded. 'Imagine what Anderson would say if I hung that in the kitchen.'

We burst out laughing. I felt weirdly jealous of Jojo, for being so free in his impiety. But there was no point in feeling jealous of the dead and the sensation quickly passed.

The rest of the paintings were smaller in scale. They gave the impression of being dashed off quickly. As if the artist had been sitting on the edge of the action, recording it in real time, though I knew Sands had been working hard on them for months. The evidence of the artist's hand, the sense that he had painted them as his subject went about his misadventures, added vitality to the images. The series was hung in chronological order. Rose and I followed Jojo from sale to bar to house party to drinking den and orgy. Rose took a deep breath at the picture which showed Jojo being beaten. She squeezed my hand when we reached the breakfast scene that followed, Jojo's bruised face as wet and meaty as his full Scottish.

She whispered, 'Jesus, poor Jojo.'

I did not answer her. I was staring at the picture of Jojo's death. Sands had painted Jojo slumped on the steps beneath the fire escape, his body slouched to the left. His head was thrown back, his mouth an open cavern. A discarded Starbucks cup lay on its side at his feet. Above him, on the fire escape, I saw the ulcer-mottled legs of Mary, the street woman I had talked to months before. The fire escape, the weeping ulcers, Mary hiding from the viewer: the scene was stark with details Sands could only have known if he had been there when Jojo died.

Rose squeezed my arm. 'There's Sandy.'

Sands had dyed his hair red. He was dressed in close-cut trousers and a cropped T-shirt that showed a slice of stomach. He stood in the middle of a group of fellow students, holding court, a star of the show.

I touched Rose's arm. 'I need a word with him on my own.'

The boy caught sight of me. He raised a hand in greeting.

'I'll be at the bar when you're through,' said Rose. 'I need a drink after all that.'

Sands broke away from his friends. The crush of people was growing stronger; the air in the Glue Factory was wet with sweat and condensation. It made me think again of the nuclear bunker.

Sands flung an arm around me. He grinned, and I realised he was half-drunk. 'I didn't think you'd come.'

'I wasn't sure I would.'

He waved a hand at the pictures. 'What do you think?'

I saw the two Bobbys amongst the crowd clustered around the boy's paintings. Bobby Burns was talking intently to his husband. I knew the sign. He was trying to persuade Bobby McAndrew that they had room on their walls for one of the pictures.

I said, 'You're an artist.'

Sands' grin grew wider. 'I know. Did you see the red dots? They're selling. Jojo's going places.'

Someone jostled us, white wine splashed across my jacket and I slipped out of the boy's grip. 'Any chance of going somewhere quieter?'

Sands shook his head. His hair was wet with sweat. A droplet of it hit me on the cheek. 'It's opening night of my degree show. I'm sticking around.'

I had not wanted to confront the boy in front of his friends. I leaned in and whispered, 'You were there, weren't you? When Jojo died?'

This time it was Sands who pulled away, his eyes wide and disbelieving. 'I told you, I paint from imagination. It's part of my process.'

He looked so sincere I almost believed him.

'Hmm. Jojo was a good storyteller, hot on description. He knew how to paint a scene. A good listener could pick up a lot from Jojo, but he's dead. That picture of him on the doorstep shows things you couldn't know . . . without being there.'

Sands shook his head. 'I read all the newspaper reports. I've got a good visual imagination, you know that.'

'The papers didn't mention which street Jojo died on, but somehow you knew the exact spot and you painted it brilliantly, right down to the poor woman hiding on the fire escape. She didn't make the *Evening Times* either. You saw her there and you couldn't resist including her.'

Sands took a step backwards. He chewed his lower lip. 'You're going to fuck up my graduation.'

He looked like he might make a run for it. I caught hold of his arm and gripped it tight. 'I can fuck up more than that, son. I can fuck up your life.'

People were shifting all around us. We stood still, like the centre of a storm. Sands' skin was white as clouds, white as seafoam.

'I didn't touch Jojo.'

'So what did you do? Stand by and enjoy the show while

he carried on for your benefit? Drag him into the lane when he was comatose and dump him there?'

He shook his head again, as if he could not believe what I was saying. 'We were friends, proper friends. I helped to bury him.'

'You thought Jojo was old and expendable. Fodder for your art.'

Sands hissed, 'I can get you thrown out.'

'Do it. I can go to the polis.'

'I'll tell them, same as I'm telling you, I didn't touch Jojo.'

'What about Mary, the homeless woman on the fire escape? She saw you.'

Sands' lower lip caught in his teeth again. 'I don't know who you're talking about.'

'Aye, you do. She saw your face. You must have thought it was too dark or that you managed to cover up with a scarf or that no one would believe the testimony of an old down-and-out, but put her evidence next to your painting and a jury might suspect you're not the sweet-faced boy you appear to be.'

'I'm not sweet-faced. And I'm not a liar.'

'Wrong on both counts. You're a fucking baby-faced liar. Jojo wasn't interested in your personality. He liked the way you looked. You'll be amazed what youth buys.'

Sands looked up at me, eyes wide. 'What do you really want?'

'I want you to tell me the truth about what happened.'

'Why?'

I kept my answer simple. 'Because I need to know.'

'Then what?'

'Then we'll see.'

Sands pushed his way through the crowd. I followed him,

into the blighted streets outside the factory. The sky was pale blue, creased with white contrails. High-rises sparkled in the distance like mica. A few students were congregated near the entrance, smoking and enjoying the buzz of their first big show. One of them waved and shouted at us to join them. Sands held up a hand and led me away from the building, up a set of concrete steps to the canal. It had been a warm day and sunlight still dappled the water. Someone was weatherproofing the roof of their narrow boat. Joggers were running along the towpath, competing with bicyclists and walkers for space. A few men were fishing from the bank.

Sands walked on until we reached the massive pylon that straddles the path and dominates the corner of that stretch of canal. He ducked under it and sank into the long grass beneath. His face was blank.

I lowered myself onto the grass beside him. I gestured upwards at the pylon's frame, looming silver and angular above us. 'These things are meant to be bad for the brain.'

Sands picked a strand of long grass and started chewing on it. 'Maybe that's what I like about it. The idea it might mess with my perceptions.'

It was as if the conversation in the Glue Factory had never happened and we were friends again.

I said, 'Tell me what happened.'

He looked at me, eyes screwed up against the brightness. 'No police?'

I could have said that there was no point in going to the police. That Jojo was dead and gone, and there was nothing to be gained by ruining Sands' life with courts and jail sentences. Or that I had no idea if the homeless woman was still on the scene, and if she was, whether she would even be believed by a jury. But I wanted to keep the pressure up. I looked him in the eye and said, 'Depends.'

Sands took the piece of grass from his mouth and rolled it between his fingers. His expression was drained of the joy of his exhibition. His voice was hoarse. 'I went to a party with Jojo.'

'What kind of a party?'

'What kind do you think? Old guys with beer bellies and tribal tattoos getting jiggy.'

'Each to their own.'

'I didn't go to join in. I went to take photos.'

'Aren't people usually required to give up their phones at these types of gigs?'

Sands shrugged. 'Jojo introduced me as a "curious young friend", a "watcher". I wasn't exactly waving my phone in the air, but after a while they were so busy getting down the guys didn't seem to notice me. It was pretty sordid, but that was part of the appeal, I suppose. Things were winding down when the doorbell rang. No one bothered to answer, but it kept going, so in the end I stashed my phone and went to the door. The moment I opened it I knew I'd made a mistake. There were three men there. Two big guys and another man who seemed to be in charge – kind of anonymous-looking. A guy that would usually fade into the background. They flashed warrant cards and said they were police. Of course, I found out later they weren't really police. I thought they were, but they weren't.'

I could picture Mitchell standing in the doorstep, cocksure, flanked by a pair of heavies.

Sands continued: 'There was a young guy with them. Skinny, out of his depth. He kind of apologised and then legged it. I took my cue from him, slipped past them, out into the street and away. As I scooted out the door, I heard one of the men telling Jojo he'd been keeping bad company. I thought it was about antiques or maybe money.'

Jojo had never been fussy about the company he kept but he had crossed a line when he got involved with Michael and Simmy, the boys he 'mentored'. They had been wild lads who had double-crossed Ray, ripped off Mitchell and come a cropper in the crash at Ballantyne farm.

I said, 'Was that the last time you saw Jojo?'

The boy closed his eyes. I got a sense that he was vacillating between stories, deciding which one to choose. Eventually he said, 'I saw him again, later that night. I'd left my camera at the flat when I bolted. I couldn't afford to lose it, so I waited a couple of hours and went back. Marcus was there.'

'Who?'

'Marcus, the guy running the party. You met him.'

My mind was blank and then I remembered the gym bunny in the leather harness. 'The leather queen?'

Sands gave a small smile. 'Is that what you call him? Yeah, I guess he is.' He threw the strand of grass away. 'He wasn't keen on letting me in, but I managed to persuade him. Everyone else was gone. Marcus said the men had put everyone except Jojo into one of the bedrooms. They'd taken their money and watches and warned them to be careful who they partied with in future. Marcus didn't know what they'd done to Jojo, but he was asleep in a chair when everyone else was allowed out. He was still asleep when I got there, snoring like a drain. Part of me thought it was funny, to be honest. Jojo sleeping while all this chaos played out around him. I tried to wake him, but he was dead to the world.' Sands winced at his own choice of words. 'In the end, Marcus said I could have my camera back if I helped him straighten the place up. It seemed like a good way to find out more about the scene. We tried to clear up, make sure there was nothing dodgy lying about, but then I noticed Jojo had stopped snoring. I thought he'd woken up, but it turned out he'd stopped everything. Stopped breathing. I tried to revive him, but it was too late. I was scared. Shitting my pants.'

'So you decided to dump Jojo's body?'

Sands shook his head. 'I got my phone out to call an ambulance, but Marcus told me to put it away. I didn't want to leave Jojo, but the best thing seemed to be to get out and call for help as soon as I was out of there.' He met my eyes and repeated, 'Jojo was dead. By this time, only me and Marcus were left. He grabbed me when I tried to leave.' Sands plucked at the grass. 'I've thought about it a lot. I think he wanted me to be complicit. It buys silence.'

I said, 'When the homeless woman told me she'd seen a man with bleached blond hair helping to carry Jojo down the back lane, I thought it was Anthony, but it was you?'

'It was me.'

'What happened to Anthony?'

'No idea. Jojo used to call guys like him pill-popping party boys past their prime. You saw how he was. Skinny as a Peperami. There's only so long you can live the way he did. I guess his time was up.'

Something about the way the boy dismissed Anthony's death so casually made me like him even less. 'You told me that Anthony and Jojo's deaths were connected.'

Sands kept his eyes trained on the ground. 'I was ashamed of dumping Jojo's body and worried someone might find out, especially after we discovered Jojo was hiding a big stash in our flat. I thought maybe if I said Jojo and Anthony were connected, it would shift attention away from me.'

'There was no attention on you.'

'I felt like I was walking about with a big "M" on my back, like that guy in the old German movie.'

Some other time, I might have told him that 'M' had been Peter Lorre's breakthrough role, but the boy was no longer someone I could banter with.

Sands looked across the canal to where the barge owner was still weatherproofing his boat. The man had stripped to the waist. His back was tanned, his brush strokes steady. 'Have you ever wondered what it would be like to become an outdoors guy and live a healthy life?'

I shook my head. 'Not really, but there's still time, if that's what you want to do.' We sat in silence that was not silence, listening to the thud of runners' feet against the path, the whir of cyclists' wheels, the sounds of people calling to each other. Someone stopped to talk to the man painting the barge and he set his brush aside. 'What happened next?'

Sands sighed. 'Marcus was as shit-scared as me. We dressed Jojo together. It was horrible. He was flopping about like a rag doll. While we were getting him dressed, we came up with a plan to leave him somewhere nearby, where he wouldn't wait too long to be found. We carried him down the stairs like he was dead drunk, with his arms around our shoulders.'

'Why didn't you just leg it?'

'I don't know. I was in shock, I think. Part of me was glad to be told what to do – and then there's the artist thing.'

'What "artist thing"?'

Sands met my eyes. 'An artist shouldn't run away from experience.'

'Is that what they teach you at Art School?'

The boy shrugged and looked away. I guessed that, despite

the way he had used Anthony's death as a smokescreen, mortality was not the abstract it had once been.

'We settled Jojo on the doorstep and said our goodbyes. I vowed I was through with the whole G thing, but then you and me found the stash in Jojo's room. I know it sounds stupid, but I wanted to make it up to him, and it turned out I wasn't through after all. It became more than research. I hooked up with Marcus for a while. We had a shared secret. It kind of took a hold of me.'

'And now?'

'I'm done. I've completed the series. I've been accepted to do a Masters in Chicago. I can leave it all behind, get away from all this, reinvent myself.'

'Take up healthy outdoor pursuits?'

'Maybe. Who knows?'

He did not have to tell me that any revelation of his involvement in Jojo's death would kill that opportunity.

I took a deep breath. 'Well, you don't have to worry about Mitchell coming out of the woodwork and putting pressure on you. He's dead.'

Sands nodded. 'I read about it, but I still have nightmares about the other man, the one who turned up at the party pretending to be a policeman. Jojo was straightening up when I legged it and comatose when I came back. Marcus thought maybe he'd fed Jojo his own merchandise to teach him a lesson.'

I stared at him. 'Mitchell wasn't the person who threatened Jojo at the party?'

Sands shook his head. 'What gave you that idea? This guy was older than Mitchell: balding, kind of beige clothes, glasses. He smiled to show you how dangerous he was, know what I mean? Marcus said it was better for me not to know his name.'

Jamie Mitchell and Ray Diamond looked nothing like each other, but they were both anonymous men, with features that were hard to pin down. The picture slotted into place. The drugs that the young joyriders had stolen from Ray and stashed with Jojo. The misplaced alliance that had made Les phone Mitchell, instead of Diamond, to collect the stash and arrange Jojo's funeral. The misassumption that had led me to blame Mitchell for Jojo's death. The desire for stability in the city's underworld that made Anderson turn a blind eye. The fear that would keep me from telling anyone what I had learned.

I got to my feet. 'Congratulations on the exhibition.'

Sands looked up at me. 'Is that it?'

I nodded. 'Jojo would have been raging at being dumped in the gutter but he'd have loved your paintings. I'm guessing he'd consider your debt cleared.'

Sands got to his feet and shook my hand. He looked older than when we had first met, but there was a lightness in his expression that had not been there before. 'I won't forget Jojo. I mean it. He taught me a lot about how to live.'

'And how not to die.'

Sands repeated, 'And how not to die.'

We turned back to the canal and descended the steps that led to the industrial park below. Some students were spray-painting a gapsite wall with Basquiat-inspired graffiti while others were tearing across the concrete on skateboards. I wondered if it felt dangerous to them.

Sands shook my hand again, beneath the painted lips of the Glue Factory sign. 'I'm heading to Chicago at the end of the month.'

I battened down an urge to tell him to be careful. 'Good luck.'

He smiled. 'Thanks. I'll need it.'

Someone shouted that they were going to take a group photo and for Sands to hurry up. The boy gave me a last tentative smile and jogged across the tarmac to join his friends. I took out my tobacco tin and put a roll-up together.

Rose stepped from the gallery space. 'Where have you been?'

'Sorry. I needed a word with Sands.'

Rose glanced in her compact mirror, made a face at what she saw, took out a lipstick and touched up her lips before sliding her Ray-Bans from her top pocket and putting them on. 'I'd stay away from him if I were you. Did you see his pictures? I mean, they're good, but, Jesus, they're creepy. That boy's fucked-up.'

I slipped an arm around her shoulder. 'You always were a good judge of character. Where do you fancy going for a proper drink?'

A cab drew up. Rose put her lipstick away, glanced at her phone and checked the car's registration.

'Sorry, Rilke. You're too late. Anders phoned. He's waiting for me in Brett.' She waved at the driver then turned her smile on me. 'Your pal Les is here, looking like he won the Lottery and spent the lot in Catherine's of Partick. He's *very* pleased with himself. Even apologised to me for being a wanker.'

The driver hooted. Rose blew me a kiss. She ran to the cab and got in. The driver laughed at some joke she made, and they drove away, in the direction of the West End.

Half an hour ago, I had been immersed in the atmosphere of youth and sexual promise. Now, I felt complicit in Jojo's death. I remembered what Sands had said about an artist's obligation not to run away from experience and I wondered if he had told me the whole truth. Had the boy been over-whelmed, a curious witness? Or had he helped Jojo to just one more hit? Perhaps one of the other partygoers had grown fond of seeing the light die in another man's eyes.

I put a match to my roll-up and turned to go.

A voice like caustic soda ripped through the peace. 'Rilke!!!'

Les was wrapped, tight as an enchilada, in a black sequined gown that might once have belonged to Liberace's mother. He had an arm clamped around a redhead in tartan bondage trousers and a military cap that made me think of the deter-mined old woman who had tried to force her father's Nazi gear on me.

I waved at him and walked away in the direction of the city, but despite being a professional waster, Les has a lot of stamina. His high heels clattered as he ran after me.

'Rilke!' He grabbed me by the arm. 'Jonti and me are going to a party.'

I shook him off. 'Some other time, Les.'

He kept pace with me. 'That's what you always say, but you have a good time when you get there. There'll be lots of talent. Young talent. Arty talent. You like that.'

I put my arm around Les and kissed him. 'None of them would give me a second look, not with you there. Go on. Enjoy yourself.'

Les touched his cheek. He smiled. 'Ach, you're an anti-social bastard, but you know what? You're right.'

I left him there and walked down the hill, towards the city centre. My phone rang. Frank's name flashed on the screen. I ignored the call and kept on walking. It was getting late. The night was coming in, but there were hours to fill before the dark.

Afterword

IT IS TWENTY years since I wrote *The Cutting Room*, the book which first introduced Rilke and his merry band of pranksters. The landscape for LGBTQ+ people was different back then. I wrote the novel in a white-hot rage, during the Keep the Clause Campaign. The campaign objected to the repeal of Section 28 also known as Clause 2A which made it an offence for schools and local authorities to 'promote homosexuality'. The clause contributed towards intensifying an already hostile environment for LGBTQ+ people.

The campaign was enthusiastically endorsed by Brian Souter, now Sir Brian Souter, who financed a referendum of every household in Scotland, soliciting support for the maintenance of the clause. The campaign fell back on old tropes equating LGBTQ+ people with paedophilia and sexual incontinence. Most days I passed a huge billboard that shouted PROTECT OUR CHILDREN, KEEP THE CLAUSE.

Mr Souter owned the bus company Stagecoach and it was

often difficult to travel without putting more money into his pocket. I frequently raged as I travelled the motorways of Scotland from the uncomfortable depths of his tartan seats. That anger seeded *The Cutting Room*, a book that changed my life.

Twenty years on and other things have changed. We have, as Rilke notes, equal marriage, increased visibility, access to hate laws, improved awareness of queer and trans rights, more nuanced identity politics. There is a general consensus that violence and prejudice against LGBTQ+ people is wrong. Many schools embrace TIE (Time for Inclusive Education). Many more people can be open about their sexuality. Gays on TV are not just for laughs as they were when I was growing up – *Shut that door! Are you being served?*

Queer might even be desirable. My cat Minnie's packet of Dreamies is emblazoned with a rainbow in support of LGBT History Month. A phenomenon she is indifferent to. More than once I have spotted a rainbow flag flying and started forward with renewed energy, assuming it signals a gay bar, only to discover it is a queer-washed building society or estate agency signalling its grooviness. People in committed relationships with a member of the opposite sex, some with children and a mortgage, regularly tell me that they identify as queer. Like Rilke I have been judged too much myself to start judging others, though being imperfect, I sometimes raise an eyebrow.

Outrages still occur. Just the other week a couple were badly beaten by a group of youths in Edinburgh while some bystanders laughed and shouted the same old slurs. Various churches still refuse to recognise equal marriage. Acceptance is also not international and LGBTQ+ people are still murdered, tortured, forced to flee their homelands or to live straight lives, keeping their queerness under the radar.

There is no place for complacency. But the Glasgow I inhabit is largely better, in terms of sexuality, than it was twenty years ago. It cheers me up, because if this can change, then other prejudices can be smashed too. Here's to equality. Here's to not forgetting. Here's to keeping alert. Here's to righteous anger that prompts creativity and change!

As ever I have a lot of people to thank. My editor Francis Bickmore who has always been a big Rilke supporter and who encouraged me to return to his world. The Saltire Society and Scottish readers who voted *The Cutting Room* the 'Most Inspiring Saltire First Book Award Winner', to mark thirty years since the First Book Award was established. Colleagues at Canongate Books who got firmly behind this sequel. Alison Rae whose copyediting skills are interplanetary and who saved me from embarrassing myself on several occasions. My agent Sam Copeland whose literary knowhow and firm common sense is a compass through choppy literary seas. My dad John, who has been unfaltering in his belief in my genius. My mum Ena, who is still with us, and still guiding me – sorry for the swears, Mum. My sister Karen who is constant in her faith in me. My lockdown bubble buddies, Paul Sheehan and John Jenkins who this book is dedicated to. David and Cathy Fehilly for keeping the fun times going. Clare Connelly and Laughlin Bell for being consistently up for risk and change. The team at Woodlands Community Garden who help make our community green and inclusive. All this would be nothing without the love and support of my wonderful partner in crime, the writer Zoë Strachan who is always my first reader and most consoling critic.

Louise Welsh in conversation with Paula Hawkins

PH: There are some things that locate this novel very much in the here and now – it takes place in the wake of the pandemic. You also talk about somebody Marie Kondo-ing their flat. But I think one of the things I loved, and I'm sure *Cutting Room* fans will all love, is that sense of going back to a place that you know from before, seeing it afresh and seeing all those things that have changed; what has changed and what has remained the same. I wondered how hard that was for you, to sit there and think which places are the same, what streets are different, what sort of areas are 'hip' now that weren't then or where is everyone going. Was that a thing you could do easily?

LW: As you know, writing is never easy. There are always moments of slog and hitting a wall but that aspect of place did come easily because it's a place I know. I've lived in the city of Glasgow for a long time so those changes are a part of my consciousness. One of the delights of being a little bit older is that you know the place better and you know the history of the place. You see the street you are walking along but you also see the history of the street. Sometimes you remember what was there before; what's missing, what's better. *The Second Cut* explores Rilke's consciousness, not mine, but I could feed that knowledge of the city into it. I have to look at it through Rilke's vision. Rilke and Rose both work in an auction house. They know the texture of things, they know the provenance of things. Other characters I have written don't necessarily know the fabric of objects but Rilke and Rose know. They know their history, and that's just a delight.

PH: Because you're known for this, for evoking sense of place so brilliantly but it's a very distinctive Glasgow. It's not just any Glasgow, this is Rilke's Glasgow that you take us through, isn't it?

LW: It is his Glasgow. As writers, part of our job is also to get into the back room, isn't it? You're meant to get into the back room of everywhere in your city, whether that's the back room of the corner shop or the back room of the city chambers. The book relies on Rilke's vision — what is he interested in and where does he want to go, and the rhythm of his voice and, of course, the quest that he's on.

PH: Rilke's such a fascinating character and not at all a traditional crime protagonist. He's not a hero, nor does he aspire to heroism. I think you've said this before, that in older times he might have been more suited to being the villain or the victim as he's that sort of man.

LW: Crime fiction is a fascinating and exciting genre. It has parameters and conventions that we can choose to go with or go against. Historically, when you spotted the queer person, or spotted the person who's not from around here or the person with the limp, you have spotted the villain. But as other writers have shown us – including Val McDermid, who is in the audience tonight – it does not have to be that way. The prejudice within the crime genre also presents us with an opportunity. In Val's Lindsay Gordon series, we have a queer heroine at the centre of the book. Genre invites us to turn things around. We can have Rilke, a gay man who has, as Philip Marlowe has, his own moral code. It's a classic trope – his code may not be everybody's code but, really, he's a decent guy. When the pandemic comes along, Rilke doesn't think, 'Oh, you know what? I could start making some money out of dodgy PPE.' He just tries to do the best that he can. We suspect he might have broken lockdown a few times, but he's not held a party in the auction house [laughter].

PH: Yeah, he's not amoral. He says at one point, 'Illegality I can cope with, cruelty I can't.'

LW: I think that's a key difference. The crime novel, the noir novel, the detective novel – all are multi-genre. In some novels there might be a police procedural aspect. Think about the Martin Beck novels – we want to solve the crime from the police's perspective. With Rilke, he's interested in a different type of justice. I suppose he's interested in the Chester Himes' kind of thinking: 'Okay, well, we might not be sticking to the law but we're sticking to the natural justice.'

PH: We're not going to give away the plot, but Rilke in this novel is clearing a house in Galloway (which he's very rude about, by the way). He suspects there are unsavoury things going on: car accidents, deaths of both man and beast, all sorts of things. There is a suspicion of abuses being perpetrated by respectable folk. This is something that I often find in your work – there's something about the veneer of respectability that wealth confers and you like to sort of poke at that and expose the hypocrisy of that, don't you?

LW: Rilke in previous times would have been somebody that people would judge because of his sexuality. I'm influenced by Robert Louis Stevenson's distrust of what lies behind the respectable doors of people who judge others. In the first book Rilke quotes this proverb, 'if you're rich, you're either a thief or the son of a thief'. There's a thread of anti-capitalism in this book. When you go past these big houses and see wealthy, respectable institutions and the people that run them, sometimes you think 'where did the money come from', you know. And do we think less of people for not having economic wealth? Questions that perhaps we don't ask often enough. So yeah, I guess the rich are an easy target, aren't they?

PH: Because you are asking about where the money comes from, aren't you? And not just the money they might have now but where the family's wealth comes from. You're drawing parallels between what might be going on now and between colonialism or empire.

LW: These things are very joined up, if you think of them holistically and I suppose we're thinking a lot more now about the North Atlantic slave trade profits from that really iniquitous, organised, legal trade of people, as well as goods, you know, that it's a very short time away. On May Day, I often post a short film of Paul Robeson leading a May Day parade through Glasgow. He was the son of enslaved people and there are people in the city who still remember shaking hands with him. That is how close we are to that particular, completely immoral trade. We know that when [slavery] had ceased, the people who owned enslaved people were compensated hugely and that we still have people in our government who benefited from that and who are not at all inclined to give the money back. They regret it very much, just not enough. They're not going to give it back and I guess that might come across as rather smug because of course we are part of this society and benefit in all sorts of ways. Rilke is a man who's lived in this city for a long time and knows his history; he knows that there's blood in the mortar and when he looks at the buildings, he sees where they came from, too.

PH: Absolutely. I want to talk to you a bit about trouble and the sense of embracing chaos because it seemed to me that there was a celebration or at least a respect for people who take risks. I think Rilke, you say, 'has never cared too much for caution' and there's a lovely line about 'the imp of the perverse' which has ruled his life, but he isn't the only one. You've got this whole cast of characters – Jojo, Sands, Rose – who don't like to live on the safe side.

LW: It's not in their nature to play it safe. They're compelled to take that extra step and to push things too far. Do you ever think, 'I wonder what would happen if I did this? What happens if I press that button?' They're inclined to press the button and find out! They embody energy and fun and understand that this is one life. And I guess that can make you cautious as it has me during the pandemic. I stuck to the rules, I stuck to lockdown and all of these things. Then there are moments when you just think, 'Ah, you know what? I'm just gonna step off now, step off the ledge.' What did the Deacon Brodie say when he stepped off the gallows? 'Ah, what is it but a step in the dark?' I often think of that [laughter]. There's also that economic imperative, too; they must make some money and that's inclined to make them a bit reckless sometimes.

PH: I wondered if you could talk a bit about generational conflict because I felt there was quite a lot of that going on in this book. There's a glorious confrontation between Les, who's more of Rilke's generation, and two gender non-binary kids that he meets at a protest and it's all about the way people speak and the way they identify – they're on the same side really, but there are generations rubbing up against each other. There is a sense of people getting on a bit. You've said Rilke hasn't aged that much but he is feeling his age.

LW: Yeah, he is feeling his age and he gets turned down at one point by somebody and there's a guy in a taxi who makes an advance which Rilke doesn't take him up on and the taxi driver says, 'pretty soon, no one's going to want to fuck you' [laughter]. I guess Rilke and Les are not up on the nuances of identity. We say 'identity politics', but it's not necessarily politics: it's just identity and new, more nuanced identities. And Rilke and Les are not up on this. I don't think they're particularly interested, actually. They don't know the language. They're blokes that have taken their beatings, given some beatings back because of their sexuality. Les is irked by these young people that have this whole new language and code. It just irks him a wee bit but they talk about how they identify and he says, 'Well, I identify as a tranny,' and they say, 'Well you should love yourself more,' and he's like, 'I love myself fine.' It's acknowledging that idea of a different language. It's a moment of comedy and satire.

PH: I think you were very good at poking fun at both sides . . .

LW: I don't like to think of things as being sides. I think sometimes we look at the internet and we get an idea that things are bizarrely binary and they're not at all binary. There's more discussion and exchange of opinions than one would think from the media. So I suppose it's a little bit of fun but I hope that the younger and older folk all come out okay. And the youngsters are pretty cute, they're pretty savvy, and the older guys are just trying to catch up – oh, maybe they're not trying to catch up [laughter].

PH: I realise we're talking a lot about issues because I do feel your books are quite political, without you being on a soapbox, but it feels like you have your finger on the pulse. But that aside, there is quite an intricate – well, many – intricate plots going on in this novel, aren't there? And I was wondering from a crime writer's perspective how much of that you know in advance: how much you plotted out, where it came from, why these particular parts. That's a lot of questions in one but are you one of those people who kind of knows from the beginning or did you just sort of feel your way around it?

LW: Maybe a little bit of both. There are several plots going on here. Jojo, who we met briefly at the beginning, is very quickly dispatched, and the police aren't particularly interested. He's an older drug user who drinks too much, it's a very cold night and he is found dead on a doorstep. The police are like 'fine, nothing to see here'. Rilke thinks there might be more going on. And then there's also the old mansion plot – there are several plots that hopefully come together. There's something about the rhythm and logic of multiple plots, how you connect them and how you connect your cast.

PH: And you're one of those writers that doesn't necessarily tie everything up into neat little bows – you leave quite a lot of space, don't you, for the for the reader to wonder . . .

LW: Everybody's asked me 'who killed the dog'. I thought it was obvious [laughter]. But we already know, this life isn't neat.

PH: Absolutely, and they're the sorts of books I think that you want to go back and read again just to make sure that 'Were you right? Was I right? Was he right?' You want to go back and investigate a little bit further. You have been called a 'literary crime writer' – I was wondering if that was a label that you liked or whether you thought of yourself as just literally a fiction writer or just a crime writer or none of the above.

LW: I love being called a crime writer. I mean, really, you're just happy if people aren't calling you rude things most of the time [laughter]. But sometimes people will say, 'Oh, you know, the crime writer thing.' These are the books that I read as a child, the books that you found not on the shelf but in the carousel at Bobbie's Bookshop. The books with the great covers, the books that when you took them out, the librarian would say to your parents, 'Are they allowed to have this book' [laughter]. That's what you want: a lurid cover.

PH: The ones where there were bullet holes and you could open the cover and then there was something else under-neath . . .

LW: Then there was a naked lady hidden behind [laughter]. The picture where there's a gun and a rose and a half-drunk glass of whisky with lipstick on it – all of those things. Also, perhaps crime writers might sell more books than literary writers [laughter].

PH: But you have written a lot of different genres. You've written historical fiction, *Tamburlaine Must Die*; dystopian, speculative with the Plague trilogy; *Naming the Bones* felt very gothic, didn't it? *The Girl on the Stairs* was more psycholog-ical, and I was wondering if there was one that you sort of felt most at home in or indeed whether you want to try something completely different?

LW: I love the gothic. Gothic and crime go well together. Both genres deal with the elemental. They come from the guts as well as the heart and engage with essential fears.

When you talk about the origins of the crime novel we must go back to folk tales. The first stories ever told about justice, about fear. Marrying the genres is rather easy to do. But yeah, I do like the gothic, I like the dark corners – there's an awful lot of rain in my books. It rains all the time [laughter]. The sun comes out towards the end.

PH: We'll go back to Rilke – where did Rilke come from originally? Is he just purely imagination?

LW: I worked for a long time as a second-hand bookseller. I went to a lot of auction houses, I went to a lot of markets, I went to a lot of jumble sales, I went to house clearances. It was a fantastic experience. I got to meet a lot of people. Rilke came from those shelves and auction houses, those second-hand objects – but in the end I think Rilke is his own voice.

Louise Welsh in conversation with Paula Hawkins, from event at The Portobello Bookshop, Thursday 3 February 2022.